The Rules

Kerry Barnes

ONE PLACE. MANY STORIES

HQ
An imprint of HarperCollins*Publishers* Ltd
1 London Bridge Street
London SE1 9GF

This paperback edition 2020

1

First published in Great Britain by
HQ, an imprint of HarperCollins*Publishers* Ltd 2019

Copyright © Kerry Barnes 2019

Kerry Barnes asserts the moral right to be
identified as the author of this work.
A catalogue record for this book is
available from the British Library.

ISBN: 978-0-00-833648-6

MIX
Paper from
responsible sources
FSC www.fsc.org **FSC™ C007454**

This book is produced from independently certified FSC™ paper
to ensure responsible forest management.

For more information visit: www.harpercollins.co.uk/green

This book is set in 10.7/15.5 pt. Sabon

Printed and bound in Great Britain by
CPI Group (UK) Ltd, Croydon, CR0 4YY

To my Uncle Peter, a kind and loving family man.
My cousin Sean Gable, who told me he was proud of me.

CHAPTER ONE

Detective Lowry hurried down the corridor to the end room of the burns unit. Panting furiously, he impatiently moved aside the two police officers who were on guard duty. He stopped in his tracks as he entered the sterile-looking room. The silence sent his senses alive. He wanted to gasp but quickly put his hand to his mouth. He peered closely at what looked like clingfilm over the girl's face and shuddered at the horrific sight. *Was she once pretty?* he wondered. It was so hard to tell. Her face looked like a mask of melted pizza. While one eye was entirely covered with wadding, the other was peeping out through the mangled mess. He jumped when he saw she was awake and looking his way. She must have known that he was staring with morbid curiosity. But, sadly, it would be something she would have to get used to. Her face would never look the same again.

Breathless, he stepped closer. A sheen of sweat covered his brow, his mouth became dry, and his hands trembled. He'd seen many injuries in his thirty years on the force, but this was the worst one ever.

'Sonya, I'm Detective Lowry. Are you okay to talk? I mean… '

Sonya Richards could barely move her lips with the swelling, but she'd been given a seriously massive number of painkillers to numb the pain. Only a small part of her face could feel intense throbbing. The rest was almost completely burned down to the bone, killing all the nerves.

'Yes,' she murmured.

It was hard to take his eyes away from her face, but he had a job to do. Pulling up a chair, he sat close to her bed. His pot belly hung over his suit trousers, and his wheezing increased; he needed to cough to clear his throat.

'Can you tell me who did this to you?'

She closed her eye and tried to swallow. The acid had not only managed to rip the insides of her mouth but also the larynx. 'Is my husband dead?' she croaked, her voice barely audible.

Lowry fidgeted in his seat. The raw flesh around her swollen mouth crinkled, and he winced, almost feeling her pain. 'Um, have the doctors spoken with you about... er... ?'

'No, they said you would talk to me.' Her voice was a gruff whisper.

He guessed she already knew the answer.

'I'm sorry. Yes, he died at the scene.'

She nodded, still with her eye closed. 'Do you think it was quick?'

'Um, yes, it was. Do you know who did this?'

'He was selling that drug.' She paused to take a breath. 'You know the one. Flakka, it's called. He changed after that, you know. I never really knew him anymore.'

Lowry took out his pocketbook and began scribbling notes, allowing her time to get her words together; he could sense she was struggling. 'Did he know the man who did this? Was he a dealer? Or perhaps a user?'

She shook her head again. 'All I know is he's called the Governor. He's an evil man.'

'The Governor? What does he look like?'

'He's a big man, a huge man… but he had a balaclava on his face, and so did the others, including the girl.' She stopped and took a laboured gasp for air.

Lowry held his pen poised. 'The girl?'

'Yes, the girl. She was the one who did this.' She slowly lifted her arm and pointed to her face.

'Do you remember anything about this girl? Can you recall her age, her name, anything at all?' He knew he was pushing her, but he had to get answers, in case she didn't make it.

The drugs were obviously taking control as she began to talk more slowly. 'No. You see as well as the balaclava, she wore a Mickey Mouse mask, and it was very dark. But I remember two things. She had long dark hair and she was young. She laughed at me, like a kid would, and then the men put a bag or a sack over my husband's head. He didn't stand a chance, they were so big… They were *so* big… so cruel… Why me?' Her words were now slow and drawn-out. The drugs were taking hold.

Lowry stopped writing. The poor woman was asleep. He sat and stared at her and then studied his notes. This attack shocked him more than anything, and it wasn't the first case. The whole world was going mad. *Had the Devil come down to earth?* he wondered.

***

3

Rebecca Mullins stared at her brother's white face. 'For God's sake, Conrad, you need to keep this quiet. Father has pushed me forward for this opening, and I cannot let him or my husband down. It's what you've all been working towards. How the hell will it look if these latest events are splashed all over the news?'

'And Brooke? What about *her*? She needs help!' said Conrad in a low voice, as his eyes looked up to the ceiling of his sister's kitchen, knowing his sweet niece was suffering somewhere upstairs.

Rebecca gave a dramatic sigh. 'Oh, for goodness' sake, I am more than capable of looking after my daughter. She does *not* need a therapist or a bloody counsellor, she needs me... and' – she paused as her eyes fell to the floor – 'we don't need any dirt dug up at this stage, do we?'

Conrad shook his head in disbelief. 'Are those your words or Father's? Honestly, Rebecca, is the idea of becoming a senior minister so important?'

Rebecca glared with fire in her eyes. 'Ask Father *that* question.'

'I don't need to. I already know why you're so cold and desperate in your quest for success. You have to prove to Father that you're the person he wishes you to be. Making a few mistakes as a young woman doesn't mean you have to do everything he demands to stay in his favour, you know.'

With a dismissive hand gesture, she closed the conversation and led her brother to the door.

***

Three Months Later, HM Prison Maidstone

Mike Regan had a huge grin on his face as he watched his son pot the black ball.

'I think, my boy, when we get outta this shit pit, I'll 'ave ta buy you a full-size table. If Ronnie O'Sullivan can make a living, then maybe you can too.'

Ricky chuckled. His face was beaming; he had just cleaned up, leaving his father with two yellow balls on the table.

Ricky placed his cue on the green baize. 'Talking of which, Dad, will I be living with you then when we get out?'

Mike, at six foot seven, with shoulders that touched a standard doorframe, placed a meaty arm around his son's shoulders. 'Eleven years. I thought you were… er… well, you know. Now I've got you back, you ain't going outta my sight.' He ruffled Ricky's floppy, wayward hair and stared into his childlike grey eyes that were laced with thick black lashes.

Their conversation was halted when Officer Patton came noisily marching towards them.

'Fuck, I've only been 'ere three weeks. Surely I ain't getting put on report already,' mumbled Mike, under his breath.

Patton, a slim man in his late thirties, stopped the other side of the pool table, where he looked up at Mike. 'Regan, you have a visit.'

Mike frowned and looked at his watch. 'Er… Gov, I haven't booked a visit and it's only ten o'clock. Are you sure you got that right?'

Patton nodded, and his eyes shot a sideways glance at Ricky. 'They're police officials. They want to ask you a few questions.'

Mike sighed and ran his hands through his hair. 'Oh, fuck me. What's going on now?'

Patton edged himself around the table and leaned closer to Mike. 'I don't think it's about having you arrested. I could be wrong, but I think they just want to have a conversation with you.'

Mike screwed his face up. 'Since when do the Filth just want a conversation? Look, d'ya think I need my lawyer?'

Patton shook his head. 'No, I didn't get the impression it was that sort of meeting... Listen, I wouldn't normally tell you this, but a word in your shell-like.' He edged even closer, so no one could hear. 'It's the Police Commissioner accompanied by a detective, and neither are dressed in uniform. You didn't hear that from me, okay?'

With a deep frown etched on his face, Mike chewed the inside of his mouth. 'All right. Are they here now?'

Patton smiled. 'Yeah. Follow me.'

'Hang on... My son. I don't want to leave him on his own.'

Patton knew the score. Ricky came to the prison under the name of Richard Menaces. But when Mike arrived from Wormwood Scrubs, Ricky soon found the massive monster of a man was his father. Mike had believed his arch-enemy had killed Ricky, but the truth was his wife had run off with his son and pretended to Ricky that Mike was dead.

'Ritz's in the gym. You can join him, Ricky.'

A broad smile that showed Ricky's dimples adorned his face. He loved Willie Ritz, who was one of his father's best mates, and was happy enough to do a few workouts with him on the punchbag. He wanted to build up his skinny frame and be more like his father, who was probably the most prominent man in the prison.

Patton escorted Mike along the corridors and through

reception before heading to a room at the back. It was similar to a police interview room. As Patton opened the door and stepped aside, Mike walked in. There, behind a long table, were two men, who quickly rose to their feet. Right away, Mike knew he wasn't there to be arrested. No police official would have stood up in respect if that had been the case.

'Please take a seat, Mr Regan,' said the bigger of the two men. 'I am Detective Simon Lowry, and this is Police Commissioner Conrad Stoneham.'

Mike politely nodded while sussing each man out in turn.

Lowry was dark-haired with pale skin and sores in the dip of his chin. His large hands also had very dry skin. Mike assumed the thickset man suffered from eczema. His other distinguishing features were his hooded eyes and the round belly that was prominent in the tight blue suit, which had seen better days. The collar on his pale blue shirt was at least two sizes too small and was pinched by a navy blue tie that appeared to strangle him. Mike guessed the detective was in his late fifties. The Commissioner, however, was much smarter-looking altogether. Dressed in a beige jacket, white shirt, and dark trousers, he could just as easily have stepped off a yacht. His silver hair didn't match his dark eyebrows and wide-open green eyes. It was hard to assess his age, but he was probably in his late forties.

Lowry looked at Stoneham to start the conversation, but his boss was still eyeing over Mike and hoping he'd made the correct decision in coming to see him.

Mike was huge and unusually very self-controlled. His grey eyes were intense, and they revealed a lot about him. He was a no-nonsense, straight-up kind of person. There was no point in beating about the bush with Mike.

'Mr Regan, I have a proposition for you. You have a parole hearing in a year's time, and it is possible that you may be out in eighteen months, but your prison records suggest you may not get parole. The amount of time spent in solitary confinement doesn't look good for you.'

He paused and waited for Mike to respond, but he was left feeling uncomfortable by Mike's cold stare and tight-lipped expression.

'So, would I be right in thinking you would like to see the back of this place sooner rather than later?'

Mike remained silent, much to the annoyance of Lowry, who felt he needed to jump in. 'Well?'

'Well what? You're assuming a lot, gentlemen, and I'm still none the wiser as to your visit.'

Stoneham clasped his hands together and leaned forward. 'This conversation is highly confidential, so whatever you decide to do after our discussion has to stay strictly between the three of us.'

Mike smirked. 'Oh, come on. Seriously? I'm in prison, so I owe you guys nothing. Therefore, don't ask anything of me, unless I'm going to benefit from it myself!'

His words were firm and left Lowry with a positive view that Mike was the man for the job.

Stoneham nodded. 'South-East London's knife crime rate has hit an all-time high. We have a serious problem on our hands, and the fact of the matter is… ' he sighed, 'the gangs are growing bigger by the day. Harsher punishments to make examples of these characters aren't a deterrent. The truth is, these kids, if you can call them that, are out of control.'

Mike's face remained impassive. 'So, what's all of this got

to do with me? Unless, of course, you think I can make a great therapist, in which case I charge by the hour. I just don't get why you're 'ere.'

Stoneham gave a short, uncertain laugh. It was a trait of his when he was at a loss what to say. It was quite clear Regan wasn't going to make things easy for him, and he certainly wasn't buying what he'd come to tell him.

'Let me answer that. I know you see me as the enemy—'

'I never said that,' Mike interjected. 'Don't tell me what I think, feel, or believe. You, Mr Stoneham, can only tell me what you factually know. Please don't assume you know anything about me.'

Stoneham had done extensive research on Regan. He'd read every statement, every file, and he knew right this minute that all the previous quashed convictions were because this man was smart and premeditated. Even the rise of his eyebrow was done with thought. He also guessed that Regan would coldly torture information out of his enemies without even flinching. What he needed to be sure of was that Regan had a moral compass and an appreciation of the rules to keep the streets safe to walk on.

'No, quite right. It's probably a habit of mine, being in the police force since I left school.'

Stoneham knew he needed to come off his perch, lower his own guard, and be honest with the man, for Regan to trust him.

'I know one thing about you, Mr Regan, and that is this. You've never been arrested for anything other than a few heists, and, of course, the murder of Scottie Harman, but I also understand you believed he had kidnapped your son.'

Stoneham watched Mike's chest rhythmically move up and down as he breathed evenly.

'I may have done the same if I had believed that he had kidnapped my daughter.'

Mike sniggered. 'Come on. Don't fuck with me. You're the Filth, and I'm not. In your tiny mind, you would want whoever kidnapped your daughter, God forbid, dead. But would you do it yourself? Nah, not in a million fucking years. Why? Because the law runs through your veins and you would believe that your boys in blue would have the power to catch the person who did your family wrong. Me, all I have is my own blood running through my veins. You don't believe in an eye for an eye, but I fucking do.'

'And so, it appears, does your mother!' exclaimed Stoneham, with a sharp tongue. He stared straight into Mike's eyes and looked for just a hint of anxiety, but, again, there was nothing.

'We have a good enough reason to suspect she was responsible for Tracey Harman's murder.' He hoped that would stir some emotion and he could then barter Regan's mother's liberty.

'If you suspected my muvver, you'd have had her down the nick, but, as far as I'm aware, she's at home pruning her roses. Now, I suggest you get to the point or fuck off.'

Stoneham could see that there was no point in trying to use emotional blackmail with Regan. 'I need you and your men back on the outside working for me, and before you laugh it off, take note. Last week in Bromley, we had two knifings. One was an old lady, who was attacked as she stepped off the bus, and the other was a twelve-year-old kid, who was similarly attacked on his way home from school. Seventeen pensioners were held at knifepoint – robbed and battered in their own homes. Luckily, none were killed. And a baby in a pram was snatched and held with a knife to his throat, all for eleven pounds fifty. These are just a few examples of what I've come to talk to you about, and, believe me, they are off the top of my head. Crimes like these are soaring.'

Stoneham clocked Mike's lips turn down at the corners. He thought he may have hit a nerve, so he paused and waited.

'And this meeting between us is your idea, is it?'

Lowry coughed and wiped his brow; the room was stifling.

Stoneham turned to Lowry. 'Could you wait outside? I think Mr Regan may feel more comfortable with just myself present... and before you question my safety... ' – he turned to Mike – 'I think I am pretty safe. Do we agree, Mr Regan?'

Mike held up his huge hands and sighed. 'Of course you are. I'm not a fucking caged bear, ya know!'

Lowry looked somewhat miffed by his boss's request.

'And, Lowry, ask one of the officers to bring us some coffee, please.' He watched as the detective begrudgingly rose from his chair and left the room.

'Right, yes, you surmised correctly. The initiative isn't mine, and I won't pretend otherwise because you're a clever sod, and I won't waste your time or mine.'

Mike suddenly smiled. 'Good. I was wondering when the fuck you'd get to the point.'

'Mr Regan, I need you on the outside. This gang contains real low-life, total scum. Muggings, shoplifting, and even the odd bit of drug dealing is pretty normal on a day-to-day basis, but what's going on now is a whole new ballgame. I've got kids, and I mean kiddies, on a new drug called Flakka; old ladies are being murdered for their pensions, and gang rapes of young girls are prevalent as well.'

For a moment, Mike seemed unfazed. 'I want to know who initiated this meeting.'

Stoneham was quickly gauging the influence of the man. 'The local MP, Rebecca Mullins.'

Mike laughed. 'So, then, some toff has asked you to clean up the streets by using me as a vigilante?'

Feeling uncomfortable with those words, the Commissioner swallowed hard. Whichever way he dressed this up, the plain fact was that Regan would clearly spot bullshit a mile off. He knew he would have to speak Regan's language for him to get anywhere. 'Yes!'

Mike raised his brow and smirked. He hadn't expected *that* reply. 'So why would I put myself on the line for you or this Mullins bird?'

Stoneham knew he was getting somewhere at last. 'Your freedom for starters. We will turn a blind eye to your own business in exchange for cleaning up the streets.'

As Mike chewed the inside of his mouth, he calculated the risks and whether he could even contemplate working for the Filth.

Stoneham read his mind. 'I know it goes against the grain, I get that, but I also believe that you and I are on the same page when it comes to these sorts of crimes. Old-school gangsters have a moral code I believe. It's thou shall not hurt women, children, and pensioners. Am I right?'

Mike laughed louder this time. 'Jesus, you've been watching that film *The Krays*.'

'No, actually, Mr Regan, I listened to my father. He was a detective in South-East London, and he learned the code from the likes of your father, Arthur Regan. So, like you, I'm also not what you assume.'

'Fair play, Mr Stoneham.'

Mike's shoulders visibly relaxed, and Stoneham could almost see the sternness in his eyes melt away.

'I don't want an answer now. Please think about it before you make a decision. But the deal is this. You, your son, and your firm – and, yes, of course, I know your associates are tight, as I've done my homework – will be released within a week. Your businesses will not be watched, the deaths of all the Harmans will be placed in the solved case file, and all I want in return is for my streets to be cleaned up. I would prefer the scare tactic and not more bloodshed, but we will cross that bridge when necessary. I will give you everything I have on these gangs and the rest is up to you. Now, I will be back next week for an answer, and, as I said, please would you keep this confidential? I mean, between us and your firm.'

Mike nodded. 'Of course. I can see your problem, and I'll keep schtum, so don't worry on that score.'

Stoneham sat back, surprised that Regan was not playing games. He really was a straight-up person.

Lowry opened the door, holding two hot coffees on a tray. He watched in amazement as the Commissioner and Regan rose to their feet.

'Sorry, Lowry. Our meeting is over.'

***

Brooke Mullins pulled the bed cover over her head as soon as she heard her mother entering the room.

'Come on, sweet pea, you have to eat something. Hettie has made a wonderful chocolate cake with sprinkles on it.'

Just the shrill tone of her mother's sickly, over-the-top voice grated on Brooke. At nineteen, she was annoyed with life in general, but the last three weeks had been sheer purgatory. The normal emotional teenager–parent issues had been well and truly put to one side. They were replaced by feelings of devastating anger, humiliation, and – worse than anything – pure fear.

In one fluid movement, she threw the pink daisy-print duvet off her head and sat upright. Her hair was sticking out in all directions, and her once fresh cherry blossom-coloured cheeks were now a wishy-washy grey colour and covered in a layer of grease.

Rebecca tried to stroke her daughter's arm but was instantly shrugged off.

'Sweetheart, I know what you've been through is so difficult, but you need to eat and… ' she sniffed the air, 'take a shower. Come on. Please get out of this bed. You will feel so much better.'

Like a deranged young woman, with brown rings under her eyes and the intense hate casting doom, Brooke spat at her mother, 'Don't you ever tell me that I will feel better. You have *no* idea what I've been through. And don't you dare try to tell me it will be okay, because, Mother, it won't. Now, leave me alone!'

Rebecca backed away. Of course, she didn't know how her daughter felt, or what on earth was going through her mind. She felt her tears well up and her heart was heavy. 'I know, darling, I know, but I am just trying to help. I will leave you alone then.'

Brooke heard the door close, and she pulled the duvet back over her head. Her mother and father were the last people she wanted to console her now. They'd never shown any real interest in her or her sisters. She and her siblings were more like a by-product or an accessory. Talking to her mother was like conversing with her former headmistress – cold, stiff, and stilted.

She didn't care if she needed a bath, and she certainly didn't need to fill herself with food – that would only result in vomiting it back up. The windows had to be kept locked, no matter how hot it was, and her door closed. The light was permanently on and a kitchen knife lay under her pillow. She trusted no one and probably never would, *ever again*. She hated herself and the world around her. Things would never be the same, ever. The vision of those wide-eyed men clawing at her like they were devouring a hog roast would be with her for the rest of her life. She couldn't cry anymore; the tears had dried up, and now she was angry, but also terrified. Her dreams were gone, and she felt her life was over.

Rebecca crept down the stairs, her eyes filling up once more, recalling the moment the police had brought Brooke home. It wasn't so much the ripped clothes and exposed breast covered by a police blanket, or even the claw marks down her face: it was the dead look in her once bright, shiny eyes that would forever haunt her. Her daughter hadn't stood a chance. The little bookworm, with her oversized glasses perched on her button nose and her sweetness as she gracefully wandered about, almost on tiptoes, seemed to be a distant memory. A well-liked, clear-headed teenager, who had so many dreams for the future. She worked hard at uni and still ensured she had time to have fun with her friends.

As Rebecca entered the kitchen, she found Kendall, her daughter from her previous marriage, perched on a stool devouring Nutella on toast. Dressed in black leggings and a T-shirt with a derogatory logo on the front, Kendall ignored her mother and swayed to the music streaming through her Beats by Dre headphones.

'Kendall, do you think you could try to get Brooke at least to eat *something*? I am so worried about her. The poor little thing, she won't listen to me… '

Rebecca watched as her daughter continued to stuff her face and sway her head. Suddenly, Rebecca slammed her hands down on the table, which made Kendall jump.

'Take those headphones off!'

Slowly, Kendall did as she was told, but with a sneering, disapproving look. 'What now, Mother?'

'I said, would you talk to Brooke? She won't come out of her room, and I am so worried. She won't eat, she is so… Look, please try to talk to her. Would you?'

'For fuck's sake, she's *your* kid, it's *your* job. Anyway, I think she needs professional help, or she will carry on like this and just end up milking it.'

No sooner were those words out of her mouth than Rebecca snatched her daughter's arm and pulled her awkwardly to face her. 'How dare you say such a cruel thing! That poor girl was raped by three lads! Jesus. And you have the audacity to say she will milk it? You, Kendall Mullins, should be totally ashamed of yourself.'

Kendall shrugged her mother off. Her younger sister was no concern of hers. 'Well, for your information, Mother, I am not ashamed of myself. And all the bloody time you and Alastair fuss over her, but deny her proper help as well, she's never going to get her fucking shit together, is she?'

Rebecca looked at her daughter long and hard and shook her head. Her once charming child was now a rebellious twenty-year-old with a lousy attitude. 'Your language, Kendall, is absolutely disgusting and it's hurtful to hear, I have to say. And calling your father Alastair is so disrespectful, and after all he has done for you…'

Instantly, Kendall hopped down from the kitchen stool, and squarely stood in her mother's face, in defiance. 'What he's done for me? *Hello!* He's a creep! I never asked to be taken away from my father and dumped into your so-called happy family, did I? I was fine where I was. Just because you felt guilty about leaving me behind and—'

Bam. Rebecca slapped Kendall's face, and then she immediately regretted it. 'I am sorry. Look, I didn't mean…'

Kendall didn't even hold her cheek, although it bloody well stung; instead, she glared back with a glacial expression. If looks could kill… 'Fuck off, Mother. You're so pathetic, weak, and fucking stupid. Seriously, take a look at yourself. On the surface, the perfect wife and mother. Then strip back the facade.'

Rebecca wanted nothing more than to shut Kendall up, but she'd already gone too far with the slap.

'Running around like everything is wonderful, when, really, you know fuck all about what your husband is up to. Then there's Brooke going out of her mind, and Poppy… well, do you even *know* anything about the jumped-up secret squirrel? The truth be told, Mother, I am probably the most normal person in this shambles of a family. And just a warning: don't you ever hit me again, or, next time, I'll forget you're my mother.'

Pushing past her mother, she reached the door and looked back. 'Oh, and by the way, I am going to be moving in with my father next week. I am twenty, and I'm sick of you telling me I can't go anywhere until I pay you back the university fees.

I don't want to be a lawyer, I just want to be a hairdresser. I'm done with you telling me I owe you. You'll get all the money back from my tips.'

Rebecca gasped. 'What? No, you mustn't. I mean, look, please, Kendall, don't do that, you will—'

'Ruin my future and blot your social standing? Yes, I know, Mother, and does this fucking face look like it's bothered? No! Fuck you and fuck your career as well. That's all you care about. God forbid, I should be a hairdresser! Well, I'm not going into law, and I don't give a shit about your precious career either.'

Standing in shock, Rebecca jolted as the front door slammed shut. Kendall was right, though. No matter how much she pretended that her eldest daughter was a rebellious, spiteful young woman, she also knew that every word coming out of the girl's mouth was the sodding truth. Pushing Kendall into a professional career in law – demanding she take a post in chambers – had obviously run its course, and there was no way she could stop her leaving now. The family was falling apart, and, even worse, she was powerless to stop it.

***

Willie Ritz was holding the punchbag while Ricky was tearing into it. His T-shirt and hairline were dripping in sweat.

'Cor, son, you can hammer this all right,' said Willie, using all his strength to hold the punchbag still.

As they swapped positions and Willie began throwing punches, Ricky noticed how the scar that ran down the man's face reddened. He was right when he said the quack had basically made a pig's ear of it. Still, as much as Willie was frighteningly ugly, he was, as far as Ricky was concerned, kind on the inside.

Ricky was just strong enough to hold the bag, but as soon as his father walked into the gym, he let go.

Willie held his hands up. 'No way I'm gonna be holding the bag for that fucker.' He pointed to Mike, who, in turn, laughed.

'Listen, Willie, can you meet me in me cell with Staffie and Lou? We need to talk.'

'Er… and me, Dad?'

Mike gave Ricky a full cheek-lifting smile. 'Goes without saying, my boy.'

'What's up, Mikey? Everything okay?'

Mike surveyed who was in the room and then looked back at Willie. 'Yeah, of course.'

Willie knew then that it was serious. Between the lads, they understood every wink, nod, and expression – it was like an unspoken code. Growing up together from babies, they were as close as brothers.

***

An hour later, they were gathered inside Mike and Ricky's cell. Ted Stafford and Lou Baker sat on Ricky's bed, while Willie and Ricky sat on Mike's. Mike shut the door and remained standing as if he was about to give a lecture. They all waited for the announcement.

'So, I had a visit from the Police Commissioner, no fucking less.'

Willie licked his fag paper and raised his brow. 'Oh yeah? What the 'ell's that all about, then?'

'Well, lads, he wants our help—'

Lou jumped in. 'Since when do we 'elp the Filth?' It was unusual for Lou to interrupt; he was usually the quieter one, who generally chose his words carefully. He was the man who could pull off acting like royalty, if need be.

'My thoughts exactly, Lou, but here's the thing. They have been overrun with crimes that not even the likes of us would condone, and it's rife out there. The police haven't got the manpower they used to have. It's to do with politics and cuts or something like that, so there ain't enough of the Ol' Bill to bring these gangs to their knees.'

Staffie, who was Mike's closest friend, scratched his bald head. 'I dunno, I don't get it, Mike. What's it got to do with us, anyway?'

'Listen up. We'll be released early, all of us, in return for throwing our weight around and looking like we're helping them, when, really, we ain't. I don't know the exact details. The Commissioner will be back to visit me in a few days to discuss it a bit further. But, whatever, I ain't said yeah to it. You know me. No fucking way would I help the Filth. But what if we agree to their deal, and then, once we're out, we treat it like a game to our advantage? What d'ya say if we rough up a few scallies that we would anyway, and, in the meantime, we use their blind eye to make a fucking mint?'

Willie puffed on the end of his roll-up, and then he let out a smoke ring. 'We ain't grasses, and we ain't the Ol' Bill.'

Mike nodded in agreement. He'd expected this reaction. It was who they were. Grassing to the Filth was a no-no in their line of work. 'Yep, mate, you're right, but these little firms have not only been mugging pensioners but they're into killing kids as well. A twelve-year-old boy was murdered on his way home from school. And, oh yeah, they've been gang-raping young girls.'

Staffie sat up straight. 'Shit! Fucking bastards.'

'Yep. So, they may be villains, but, really, they ain't like us, or like the real Faces in London. If these two-bit gangs think they can muscle in on my manor, then they'll get a shock, and whatever happens, we won't get nicked. See what I'm saying? We won't be helping the law, we'll be helping ourselves to take back our turf and run the little shites out of town. Let's face it, we would do that anyway. I've been away a long time, and I wanna get back out there and take back what's mine, as ya know.'

'If we were to agree, how far will they let us go? And what's really in it for us? I mean, what about our own business? Are they gonna turn a blind eye, or, after they get what they want, will we find ourselves back in the slammer?' asked Lou.

Mike shrugged his shoulders. 'The finer details, I don't know, but, before I get another visit, I need to know what you guys want. Let's face it, we could make a lot of money out of this. Think about it. We ain't being informants, are we? And besides, we won't be working for the Filth, 'cos if we're clever enough about it, they'll be working for us. They'll give us tip-offs, and if I push 'em, they could give us information that'd work in our favour.'

Willie chuckled. 'Sounds like a fucking plan, mate.'

Staffie's face was loaded with disapproval. 'I don't know about this. It ain't what we're about, is it? And what do we really have that'll guarantee we'll stay outta jail?'

'Fuck off, Staffie, you're always unsure these bleedin' days,' spat Willie.

'No, Willie, Staffie has as much say as any of us.'

Staffie's narrowed eyes widened. 'Are you sure you're gonna be one step ahead of the law?'

Mike grinned. 'Haven't I always been – well, in the past, before I was banged up?'

Staffie chewed his top lip and sighed. 'S'pose so.'

Mike grinned. 'If we're all in agreement, I'll need to work out how to guarantee our continued liberty.'

Ricky watched the dynamics and how the men looked up to his father, hanging on his every word. He felt proud, but, also, he wanted to be a part of the firm and not just 'Mikey's son'. Although he and his dad had been apart for twelve years, it didn't matter. He wanted to be by his side, no matter what that looked like.

'Can I say something?'

Mike's stern face lit up when he looked at his son. 'Of course you can, my boy.'

Ricky nervously looked at the other men. 'Um, your lawyer. Couldn't he have a contract drawn up, or, better still, be present as a witness when the judge signs your release papers?'

Willie patted Ricky on the back. 'Good idea, Ricky. See, up there for thinking, down there for dancing.'

Mike nodded, encouraging his son. 'Yep, he may well be the brains of the outfit,' he laughed, as he looked over at Willie.

Staffie jumped in. 'And the fucking brawn. Ya should've seen him bash the fuck outta Tit and Tat.'

All four men laughed while Ricky blushed.

CHAPTER TWO

With Tatum and her son in prison, Jackie had to get off her arse and make her own money. She'd syphoned off a very healthy amount from Mike before she'd done a runner. The house near Ely was the first to be flogged off. Cash was king as far as she was concerned and what was the point in keeping the place on? She'd dwindled the proceeds away to the point that now she was nearly skint. And the regular poke she'd received from Tatum for using her son on the burglaries had now gone. Having pissed off half the site with her temper tantrums, she was down to no friends, with just herself and a bottle of Grey Goose for company. But even that had recently been replaced with a cheaper bottle of vodka.

She looked out of the window and watched as Cora, Tatum's wife, stood gossiping with two other women. Holding bags of knocked-off T-shirts, Cora was now confident enough to have the women running around for her. It was once Jackie's job: she had the contacts and the suppliers and could make a few bob. However, one supplier got a bit cheeky, so Jackie slapped her. Word spread what a bitch Jackie could be, and hence, slowly but surely, the suppliers and the runners backed away.

Cora turned her head to look right through Jackie's window,

allowing Jackie to see the smirk that slithered across Cora's face.

Firmly under Tatum's thumb, Cora had led a somewhat oppressed life. Even though they'd had six kids together, Tatum still had the energy to look elsewhere for sex, and he didn't have to look very far. He and Jackie had compatible sexual appetites, and so whenever he could – which was often – he would find an excuse to see her and they would fuck 'til the cows came home.

Selling her arse to Tatum had been a good money earner for Jackie, but that all stopped too when he went inside.

Jackie had to admit that after a few trips to the beauticians and a few high-end shops, where she could purchase some decent clobber, Cora did look pretty good. In fact, the woman scrubbed up better than she did. And because Cora's kids were older now and mostly off her hands, giving Cora more time for herself, she had the means to have a life *she* wanted. It was an everyday insult to see Cora flashing the cash while she had zilch.

Slamming the glass tumbler down on the table, Jackie walked away from the window and stormed into her bedroom. Furious, she looked around. Her once brand-new caravan was, at one time, the best on the site. She'd bought it when she'd moved to Ireland, and it was still the best model when half the site, herself included, moved over to Essex.

But everything was changing around her, and Jackie felt angry and jealous. Not only were the younger travellers buying top-of-the-range caravans and four-by-fours, but even Cora – the bitch – was swanning around in a brand-new Land Rover, courtesy of her own business.

Jackie looked at her wardrobes and gritted her teeth. Two doors were leaning against the frame. She couldn't exactly remember how that had happened, but she knew she'd probably pulled them off their hinges when she'd overdone it with the drink. Rifling through her now old-fashioned gear, her frustration increased.

It was time she sorted herself out – got out of her pyjamas, dyed her roots, and put on a bit of slap. She could always turn a pound into a tenner. With her looks and her cheek, it used to be a doddle, but that wasn't the case now. She wasn't getting any younger, and Botox was expensive. She'd already sold most of her jewellery and designer rig-outs.

After pulling every last item of clothing from the wardrobes and throwing them onto the bed, she stepped back and gazed, wondering if among them there was something decent enough to go out in. She noticed a wine-red-coloured velour tracksuit, one that she'd never worn before. With her hair dyed black and curled, she could probably pull it off.

An hour later, she was showered, dressed, and had added the finishing touch of hairspray. As she opened the drawer in which she kept her tobacco, she noticed she was down to her last packet but then clocked the small drugs parcel. She'd forgotten all about that.

When Tatum had arrived at Maidstone Prison, he'd called her and set up a meeting for her with a man named Leon Khouri. He gave her the parcel to take into the prison, but the handover had never taken place. Her son Ricky had been expected to take the drugs on the visit, but he'd flatly refused, and she'd been left shitting herself. Luckily, she'd managed to get away from the visiting room with the parcel still concealed in her oversized hair bun.

Her mind went into overdrive: *there was always money in drugs*, she thought.

***

Before leaving her caravan, she had called Leon in the hope that he would see her. To her surprise, he'd agreed. Heading over to South-East London, Jackie pondered what she would say when she met the man. She was aware that he was seriously dangerous because Tatum had already given her the heads-up when she'd picked up the parcel. His deep, intense glare had been concerning enough. Compared to her husband, Mike, though, he was probably only small fry, but she'd escaped that relationship twelve years ago and hoped that Mike had given up looking for her and Ricky. Little did she know that Ricky had met up with his father in prison.

The sun beaming down turned her car into an oven. Dressed in the velour tracksuit more suited to colder weather, Jackie was sweating buckets. She peered into the rear-view mirror and cursed; her eyeliner was embedded into the wrinkles around her eyes and her drawn-on eyebrows had smudged. Her hair had lost its lustre and gained a frizzy halo. As she looked away from the mirror and straight ahead, she suddenly had to slam on the brakes. A tall, slim woman, wearing a flowy dress, stepped onto the zebra crossing. Jackie gritted her teeth. She'd once looked like her, but the last twelve years had left her tired, and although she hated to admit it, she was looking old. Without the money to get her lip fillers and Botox, she was bordering on ugly.

Once the woman had crossed the road, Jackie set off again.

Turning into the long, overgrown drive that eventually widened into a dusty track, Jackie could smell the dryness in the air. A few chickens ran out in front of her, making her slam on the brakes again. At that moment, she felt nervous. This place was miles away from anywhere, and no one knew where she was going or would even care for that matter. She hesitated. It would be sensible just to turn around and head back. But behind her was another car, a large black BMW, and so she continued along the drive.

The farmhouse looked like an unsuspecting old cottage, with rambling roses and a wishing well by the front door – a typical pensioner's palace. Then, as she parked the car, she noticed more vehicles behind the cottage. Her heart began to beat even faster. There was no way she could go back because the Beemer had blocked her in. She would have to hold her head up and not show she was nervous. Her whole body shook anyway, from all the drinking, but clutching her fake Chanel bag, she managed to steady her hands.

Jackie didn't need to knock at the door because the man who had followed her in his car placed a thick, muscly arm over her shoulder and pushed the door open.

She turned enough to nod politely and was met with a cold stare. She didn't recognize the tall, heavily built man and wondered if he was a business associate of Leon's or someone higher up the chain. He certainly wasn't a copper. The tattoo on his neck and across his chunky knuckles confirmed that little notion.

Stepping inside, she was surprised at the layout. What was probably once the main living room was now an office with just a few essentials. However, the room kept its rustic charm, with exposed oak floorboards and a beamed ceiling. To the right was a large wooden desk and directly in front of her were two brown velvet sofas. The random mismatch of dining-room chairs and a coffee table with magazines on it reminded her of a dentist's waiting room.

The previous meeting had been brief. All she'd done was to knock at the door and give her name and take the parcel. At the time, she just assumed it was the dealer's house. She hadn't realized that the cottage held any special significance. Judging by the hard-faced men in the room, though, she had clearly been mistaken.

Sitting behind the desk was Leon. He appeared to stiffen and looked uneasy when the tattooed man came in. 'Everything kosher, Steph?' he asked nervously.

The tattooed man snatched a briefcase from one of the seated men, gave a menacing sneer in Leon's direction, and marched out the door. The tension suddenly lifted, and the men, who were gathered and poring over a large map of South-East London, went back to circling areas on it, using black felt-tip pens. Jackie didn't know whether to say hello or ignore them and walk over to Leon. She suddenly remembered her make-up had run in the heat; she'd been distracted by the car behind, causing her to forget about the state of her appearance. Now, she was feeling uncomfortable and could have kicked herself.

Leon looked up and waved his hand for two of the men to leave. He grinned and leaned back in his chair.

'Hello again, Jackie.'

She took two steps forward and nodded. 'Hi,' she said, feeling very awkward.

'So, Jackie, what can I do for you?' His sly grin widened. He was mocking her, and she knew it.

With her back now to the ominous men, a surge of gumption shot through her veins. 'It's more about what I can do for you.'

Leon raised an eyebrow and lost his grin. She noticed how his deep-set eyes were close together. They were dark, like his hair. His skin was olive. *Maybe he's Italian or an Arab*, she thought, yet he spoke like a Londoner.

'Is that so, Jackie? Only I didn't come knocking at your door, you came knocking at mine.'

She smiled and hoped he was joking, but his eyes narrowed again. 'So, what is it then that you can do for me?'

'I know people and—'

He laughed. 'We all know people, darling.'

'Yeah, but I know people that I can sell to.'

No sooner had she got the words out of her mouth than Leon lunged across the desk and snatched her hair, pulling it an inch from his face. 'Bad fucking move, tramp!'

She almost tasted the whiskey on his breath, but it was mixed with the taste of her own fear. Wide-eyed and petrified, Jackie didn't move.

Leon let her go and looked over at the men sitting on the sofa. 'Leave us, gentlemen, please.'

He didn't have to ask twice; they swiftly headed for the door, leaving him glaring at Jackie.

'Who the fuck do you think you are, coming onto my premises and announcing to everyone in the room that you can sell stuff? You don't even know who those fucking men are, do ya? Who the hell do you take me for? I ain't no small-time fucking street dealer. I gave you a parcel for an associate of mine, and now you're presenting yourself like you're some kinda gangster! The only thing you could sell, Jackie, is ya fucking fanny, a score at most. Now, get outta my house and never fucking come back!'

Shaking all over, Jackie was on the point of leaving, but she'd driven all this way, and she needed money. 'Look, Leon, I'm sorry about that. I stupidly assumed... well, never mind. I just thought I could work for you. I'm a grown woman. The Filth won't sniff around me, if ya know what I mean.'

Leon stretched his neck and rubbed his bristles. 'So, then, you want to sell drugs?'

Jackie thought he was a bit blunt, but at the end of the day, he was right. Swallowing hard, she nodded. 'I don't take drugs myself and I've got no criminal record. I keep meself to meself, but I reckon—'

Leon interrupted. 'You don't take drugs? Really?' His eyes regarded her ragged appearance.

She shook her head. 'I've never touched hard gear.'

Slowly, and still keeping his eyes on her, he opened a drawer to the right of him and pulled out a packet. She watched as he pushed it under her nose. 'Go on, then, open it and try some!'

'Er... what? No, seriously, I don't take drugs.'

A heavy sigh left Leon's mouth. 'Well, you're no fucking good to me, then.'

'I don't understand.' She tilted her head to the side. 'I'm clean. I wouldn't be taking the drugs meself, ya see. I just wanna make some money.'

'You cannot sell that shit without telling the punters what it's like, 'cos they will ask ya. In fact, the first words that will come outta their mouths will be "Is it good shit?" and you can't fucking answer that, unless you've tried it yaself.'

'But—'

Leon raised his hands. 'No buts, darling. Either you wanna sell my gear, or you don't. Now, try it, or fuck off!'

Jackie tried to suss out if it was some kind of test or if he really meant it. 'Nah, it's all right. I'll leave it 'cos I don't take shit.'

'Bye-bye!' He waved his hand, leaving Jackie flummoxed.

'Hang on. Are ya serious? Ya really want me to try it?'

Leon shook his head. 'For fuck's sake, listen, will ya? I never joke, and I don't have time for this bullshit, so go on, girl, fuck off!'

'All right!' she said, as she snatched the small packet. Carefully, she unwrapped it and stared at the white powder, and then, with wide eyes, she looked at him, hoping he would say he was joking.

Leon took a ten-pound note from a pen drawer, rolled it up, and passed it to her. His eyes were still firmly fixed on hers. 'Snort it!'

She had smoked skunk before but had never touched powder. Her legs were like mushy peas, and her heart raced. Her mind went back to Tatum when he snorted cocaine. It didn't turn him into a zombie. He just became more alert and a real chatterbox and, oh yes, very horny.

She shoved the rolled-up note up her nose and reluctantly sniffed some of the powder.

'All of it, ya silly tart!'

She did as he said and immediately felt a burning in her nostrils followed by a heavenly feeling that slowly eased its way around her body. The anxious state left her, and she was on a high. The sensation was a thousand times better than any amount of Grey Goose could offer. Within a few minutes, her legs felt heavy, and she had the need to sit down, the room becoming blurred as a warm fuzziness engulfed her. As her head touched the arm of the sofa, she was floating on clouds in a world far away from her current miserable existence.

Leon got up from his chair and strolled over to Jackie. He stared at her gaping mouth, and then, slowly, his eyes descended to her breasts. He grinned to himself, thinking they must be fake; no one her age had tits that pert. He could easily help himself, but then he wondered if he could even be bothered.

The bang as the door pushed open pulled him out of his thoughts. Standing there, at six foot five, with a face like thunder and eyes like saucers, stood the Governor.

'Are you some kind of cunt?' he bellowed, gripping a heavy-looking metal bar.

Leon stepped back in shock, his mind working overtime, trying to think why the Governor was in his cottage, and, more worryingly, why he was holding a weapon. The Governor only ever made phone calls. He worked from his car; no one ever really got to meet him face-to-face. Yet the firm knew that if you crossed him you would be dead within two days. There was no bartering or begging. The man was ruthless and took no prisoners. His punishments went far beyond what any rational person would dish out.

Leon locked eyes with him and felt his bowels move. Those grey eyes that stared back were the Devil's – he was convinced of it. And there was no way he would argue with him because death would knock at his door – that was a dead cert. 'What's up, mate?' he asked, as his hands began to shake and his legs felt heavy.

'Mate? I ain't your mate. You fucking call me the Governor.' The Governor's face was tightened by his bottom jaw protruding. He shot a glance over at Jackie, who was slumped on the sofa. 'What's up? You prick. How the fucking hell does some random slapper' – he pointed to Jackie – 'know where you work from, and, more to the fucking point, how does she know you supply drugs?'

'She's as safe as houses, Governor, I swear. She took some gear into the nick for Dez.' The confidence in him plummeted as his voice cracked in panic. 'Look, Governor, I wouldn't take stupid chances, I swear to ya. She's straight up.' Leon could only guess that one of the men had grassed him up for having a tart turn up. Probably Stephan.

The Governor looked over at Jackie again and turned his head as if he recognized her. 'Straight up, yeah? Look at the fucking state of the skanky bitch.'

'Nah, she ain't like that. I made her sample the gear.'

The Governor shook his head in disgust. 'Where's my money? You were supposed to fetch it to the drop-off point.'

Leon hurried over to the desk and opened the bottom drawer and pulled out a white cotton bag, 'It's all there.'

With a quick movement, the Governor grabbed the corner of the bag and tipped out the notes. 'I want you to fucking count them in front of me. Now!'

Leon gathered up the money and began counting it. Each hundred bundle was carefully separated and put into piles until it totalled a thousand. Then, he placed every one in the bag. 'Fifteen grand.'

'Right, tomorrow, I want the next *fifty* grand dropped off at the Swan and Mitre, at noon. Not a fucking minute later. And if I *ever* have to come here in person again, I swear to God, you won't have a fucking hand to count out the money.'

'Look, I was gonna drop it off today. I swear to ya.'

With his fingers turning and tapping the metal bar, the Governor's anger reached a pitch. 'You're a fucking idiot. Those drop-off points are timed, you mug. When I say a place and a time, then you get your skinny fucking arse there on the dot. Do I make myself clear?'

Leon nodded furiously. 'No worries, Governor. It'll be there, no question.'

'It'd better be. Oh, and one more thing. The Daylight Inn is getting a bit hot. You make sure that drippy bog attendant has a lookout, even if it means it's you. That's a good earner, and I don't want it fucked up, or... well, I don't need to tell you, do I?'

With that, the Governor snatched the bag and left.

As soon as he was out of sight, Leon let out a large lungful of air; small beads of sweat gathered on his brow, and he felt his heart beating wildly. He thought for a moment about jacking it all in, but the money was too good; besides, fixing cars at ten pounds an hour was a distant memory.

Jackie stirred, and his annoyance caused him to kick her leg harder than was necessary to wake her up. 'Get up!'

Her eyes flicked open, and a huge smile spread across her face, showing the chipped and blackened back teeth.

'Come on! Get up and get out!'

Jackie's euphoria was slowly descending. For a moment, she wanted to be back in that place of comfort where nothing else mattered. Getting to her feet, her eyes were heavy, and her muscles felt relaxed. 'Wow, that's good shit.' She laughed, totally unaware of the scowl on Leon's face.

'Yeah, and ya fat gob nearly got me killed!'

Jackie, still detached from the real world, waved her hand. 'Aw, don't be like that, babe. I'll tell ya what. You sort me out with that stuff and I'll make you a fortune.' She giggled like a child. 'And, of course, meself.'

Leon nodded, not in the least interested. Ensuring he could come up with the fifty grand and in time for the drop-off tomorrow weighed heavily on his mind. He robotically walked back to his desk and retrieved ten packets of the powder. ''Ere, take this lot, and by Friday, I want five hundred quid on my desk. If ya fuck up, I know where ya live, and trust me, woman, you won't have a caravan left. Got it?'

Jackie looked down at the carefully wrapped parcels. 'That's cheap for cocaine, ain't it?'

With a caustic tone, Leon snapped, 'You thick prat, it ain't cocaine.'

Oblivious to his evident annoyance, Jackie looked up with her silly grin. 'What is it, then?'

'Flakka.'

'What's that? Some kinda heroin?'

He gave her a dismissive blink and let out a jaded sigh. 'No, it's a new drug… Never mind. Five hundred quid on my desk by Friday, and if you do well, then I'll up the amount.'

'How much do I sell it for?' she asked naively.

'Whatever the fuck you like. Now fuck off!'

By the time Jackie reached home, narrowly missing three parked cars and an old dear crossing the pedestrian lights, she was still high. The soft pillows on her bed were so inviting that she lay spreadeagled and soaked up the fuzzy, warm comfortable feeling. With serenity carved on her face, she drifted back into that other heavenly world, far removed from reality.

Three hours later, she was wide awake and feeling like shit – worse, in fact, than a significant hangover. Her body ached as if she'd been in a fight and her head was a mess. She struggled to fight off her inner demons, the two voices battling each other – one telling her to pull herself together and the other pressuring her to give in. Through blurry eyes, she stared at the packets on the bedside cabinet, knowing that she had to sell the gear or face the consequences. Her addictive personality had her by the throat, and she had to bite her nails to stop herself from touching any of it. It was as though the powder was calling her.

She jumped up from the bed to distract her weak thoughts but almost fell over. The dizziness knocked her sideways. As she steadied herself, waves of the sweats engulfed her body and violent hot rushes made her feel sick. A second later, in contrast, she started to shiver, and her mind begged for relief in the form of euphoria – the escape to another dimension. With a bathrobe around her shoulders, she rushed from the bedroom to escape the calling packet. Switching the small electric fire on, she huddled up to keep warm. Yet, outside, it was sweltering. The hot and freezing cold changes in her body temperature were making her desperate to have another line of the new drug. When her eyes shot towards the bedroom door and then back at the red glow from the fire, she saw herself in the mirror on the wall. What with a runny nose, her nails that were bitten down to the quick, and her sallow skin, she knew that she was probably now on the path to becoming a fully fledged junkie. But it was no use; it was impossible to rid her mind of that craving.

Another wave of sickness caused her to jump to her feet, and instead of rushing to the bathroom, she headed back to the bedroom. Nervously fingering the parcel, she told herself that just one small line would hopefully perk her up. Or was it that other voice that constantly nagged: *Go on, Jackie, it won't hurt*? Without another thought, she rolled up her last tenner and snorted the flaky white powder.

She found herself back in the land of Disney.

CHAPTER THREE

Kendall tossed her rucksack over her bare shoulder and trundled off towards the station. It was approaching ten o'clock and the next train to Orpington was in three minutes. If she wasn't outside the station in half an hour, her father wouldn't wait; he'd made that crystal clear.

A surge of commuters barged past her, leaving little room to swerve in and out to make the train. The whistle blew, and just as the doors began to close, Kendall managed to slip sideways and squeeze in. Her exposed arms and neck were coated in a sheen of sweat. Removing her rucksack, she flopped onto the only empty seat. With her head down, she plugged her earphones in and took a few deep breaths.

The packed carriage sent her into a panic attack. She hated closed spaces, yet she detested people more, especially strangers. Her music stopped: the battery on her phone had just died. Reluctantly, removing the plugs from her ears, she heard two women whispering to each other. It was clear from the way they were glancing her way that she was the focus of their attention. 'Yeah, she's probably one of those Goth people,' one said. 'Ya know, all into the Devil.'

Kendall looked up, and her eyes narrowed. Two chubby

women were standing, while holding onto the bar above to maintain their balance. One of them, wearing a lemon cotton dress, was exposing a hairy armpit. The sweat stains darkened the fabric and it turned Kendall's stomach. She was about to retaliate with a smart comment, but she didn't want to draw attention to herself. Instead, she offered an enchanting smile and hid her petulance like an invisible veil. Both the women reddened and looked away in embarrassment.

Kendall inwardly sighed. Why did people assume she was a Goth or was even into devil worshipping? She couldn't help that she was naturally pale or the fact that her hair was overly dark. Black was her favourite colour, and she felt most comfortable wearing it. The black boots she wore improved her high instep and the faded dark grey T-shirt with the skull and crossbones was just to piss her mother off; other than that, she wasn't a Goth at all. She could have slipped on a floral dress and some pretty kitten heels and had her hair in a neat plait, but why should she? Rebecca had her little dolly in the form of her younger sister, Brooke. One doll-like girl was quite enough in the family.

A sudden thought had Kendall gently feeling her cheek. The slap from her mother had actually hurt quite a bit, and she hadn't checked to see if it had caused any swelling. She didn't think it had, but, in some ways, she wished it had. At least when she met her father, she could show him, in the hope that he would feel guilty.

Her father was a no-nonsense man with a tough exterior. She admired him even though she wasn't sure if she actually liked him. Perhaps it was because they were so much alike, and the complete opposite of her mother. She mused over the idea of her parents ever being together again, let alone getting married.

They really were like chalk and cheese. Her mother, with her particular ways, bordering on OCD and ensuring everything was perfect, even down to the way she spoke, really grated on Kendall. She would cringe and almost squint her eyes when her mother made the most ridiculous demands like 'Make sure you greet my guests politely.' Then there was the other one: 'Sit up like a lady.' She wondered if at any age her mother would consider her a woman. Yet Rebecca spoke to everyone as if they *were* children. Her campaigners, her housekeeper, her personal assistant, yes – but not Alastair. Never him – he was the vocal one, the head of the family who dished out the orders when Rebecca wasn't around. *How ironic was that?* she thought. Would her constituency supporters and those who voted for her still have faith in her, their local MP, if they could really see how feeble she was under Alastair's watchful eye?

The little respect she did have for her mother went out of the window the day she had arrived to take her out of her father's care. She'd heard the whispers and the undertones. Rebecca's career was flying, and there must be no dirty laundry aired, no matter what.

The train came to a stop, and the bleeping as the doors opened brought Kendall out of her thoughts. She joined the queue of departing passengers. In flinging her rucksack over her shoulder, she deliberately managed to catch the woman with the sweaty armpits in the face.

'Careful, young lady!' she hissed, to which Kendall turned and smiled – devilishly.

Opposite the taxi rank and through the hordes of people, Kendall could just make out a black BMW. She hurried over with a genuine smile; it was the first one in a long time.

The blacked-out window slowly opened and there with mirrored sunglasses and a dazzling smile was her father. 'Quick, Kenny!'

She had no sooner sat on the cool leather seat than he pulled away. 'Ease up, Dad, will you? I haven't even shut the bleeding door!'

'Shut ya whining and buckle up. I can't get pulled over by the Ol' Bill.'

Kendall threw her rucksack behind her and put her seatbelt on.

'Right, I just need to pop in the pub. It's not far from here. I'll only be two minutes, and then we can have a chat.'

Kendall felt her heart sink. Typical. Why could he never drop everything just once for *her*? She wondered who was best at being indifferent to her. Was it her mother or her father? She noticed him look her way and shake his head in disapproval. She wasn't sure if that look of disdain was because of what she looked like or whether he was into telepathy. He had an uncanny ability of getting inside her mind.

'What?' she snapped as she sensed her father's dismay.

'How old are you now? What? Twenty-one?' The smoky edge to his voice, implying he was annoyed, left an uncomfortable feeling in the pit of her stomach. She hated the tension when he was moody. And he had a knack of being unpredictable with his temperament.

'Twenty, but shouldn't you know that? I thought you were there at the birth?'

'Oi, don't get fucking lippy!' he growled. 'What's with the fucking rebel T-shirt and studs in ya ears? Are you some kinda biker, or are you still acting like a kid? What's that fucking Meat Loaf bollocks spread across ya chest?'

Kendall laughed. 'Aw, this little number? I only wear it just to get right up Mother's nose.'

She sensed his mood lift.

'Still got her big bugle stuck in the air or up her arse, has she?'

'She slapped me one today.' Her voice was a mere whisper.

'No doubt you deserved it, Kendall. Anyway, what was it for?'

'I told her Alastair was a creep!'

With a sudden raucous laugh, her father started to cough, tears now filling his eyes, as he tried to clear his throat. 'Fuck me. I would've loved to 'ave been a fly on the wall. I can just see her snooty face, like a bulldog chewing a wasp, eh?'

'Well, yeah, something like that. She wasn't a happy bunny, that's for sure.'

Ten minutes into their drive, they turned into a residential side street and arrived outside a small pub that nestled in between a row of two-up two-down houses.

'Wait here!' he demanded, as he leaped from the car that was still ticking over and carelessly parked in the middle of the road.

The street was narrow. Kendall looked behind her, hoping that no other vehicle wanted to pass, as there was no room. Left alone, she idly popped open the glove compartment and pulled out three CDs and looked at the covers: Madness, The Specials, and Bad Manners. She smiled to herself. The titles spoke volumes about her dad's taste in music and perhaps his warped sense of humour. As she opened the Madness case to play one of the titles, she found to her shock and horror that there was no disc; instead, she was looking at transparent bags of white powder. The hairs on the back of her neck stood on end. Quickly, she opened the Bad Manners case; again, she found a similar quantity of what she could only guess were drugs. Her eyes shot back to the pub door. She shoved the CD cases back into the glove compartment and slammed the lid shut; yet it sprung open. It took three attempts before it would shut properly, and by this time, her heart was almost beating outside her chest. *Christ, my dad's a dealer*, she said to herself.

Her inquisitive nature pushed her to look down in the footwell of the driver's side, and there, just like in the gangster films, she saw a metal cosh. The centre console was another temptation, and her hands trembled; if she opened the lid, would she find a gun too? Just as she was about to go for it, she was distracted by the pub door opening. And there, taking up the doorframe, stood her father. Suddenly, she was seeing him in a different light. As if she was a gangster herself, she, like her father, scanned the surroundings. Was anyone watching?

He hurried over, opened the door, and threw a white cotton bag onto the back seat and pulled away. Kendall, still in gangster style, looked behind her at the building from which her father had just left. There, standing half in and half out of the doorway, scribbling something on a piece of paper, was a man almost the same size as her father.

'Dad, a bloke back there is taking down your number plate, I think.'

Without a word, he looked in the rear-view mirror and came to a halt. Ramming the gear into reverse, he put his foot down and tore all the way back. He didn't even close the door behind him after he'd jumped out, and before she knew it, he had pushed his way through some customers entering the pub. Within no time at all, he was dragging the man out and onto the pavement.

Kendall watched in horror as her father had the man in

a headlock, clearly intending to smash the granny out of him. A mist of blood sprayed the wall. Her father didn't stop, even after the man was out cold on the pavement; he continued to kick him deliberately and methodically. It sent Kendall's blood cold, just watching her dad acting so mercilessly in full view of any residents who might be watching what was going on.

Kendall shook from head to toe; never in her life had she seen such a violent fight. No. Wrong. It wasn't a fight. The guy had stood no chance whatsoever. Unsure whether to get out and run or just stay put, her indecision was halted when two other men came hurtling along the road, both of them wielding metal tools. Her father didn't see them behind him. Kendall knew she would have to act quickly or watch her father being beaten to death. Making a spur-of-the-moment decision, she opened the centre console compartment, thinking that maybe there was a gun. What she would have done with it though was another matter. Her eyes tried to focus on a metal canister. She snatched it, popped the lid, and jumped from the car, hoping that the pepper spray was as effective as it was claimed to be.

One of the men who was tooled up managed to whack her father on the back, but just as the other one went to follow suit, she appeared like a whippet on speed and used all her strength to push down on the nozzle of the can and spray it directly into the two guys' faces. Her father, who had been knocked to the side by the heavy blow, turned to see his daughter. In her Goth outfit and brandishing his can of pepper spray, she looked wild and fearsome as she went for his attackers in a rage. Suddenly, with their hands over their eyes, they backed off, coughing and spluttering. Doubled over, they gasped for breath as saliva ran from their mouths and snot poured from their nostrils.

He pulled her arm down and removed the can. She stumbled back in total shock and looked at the devastation. The two men were almost choking to death, and the man on the ground was bloodied and lifeless. Her father dragged her away. 'Get in the car!'

Numbed by the event, she hurriedly did as he told her. He wasted no time in pulling away. Once again, Kendall looked behind her and this time there were a few customers peering out from inside the pub. She guessed they had stayed there while the fight ensued; it was none of their business. She knew then her father was a very dangerous man. Controlling her breathing, she wanted to appear unfazed; really, though, the experience had left her traumatized. She could have laughed out loud with hysteria, but, again, her veil of silence was her best form of protection. Like her, her father said nothing; instead, he drove like a bat out of hell until, finally, they were on a main road, heading for God knows where.

She wasn't going to be the one who broke the silence. This was a world so far removed from her own, but, strangely, as the shock wore off, she felt an inner excitement. Her father, a hard-core gangster; it was laughable until she realized that what she'd seen had been anything but a laugh. In fact, if the truth be known, it had been terrifying. But she'd been an essential part of that. If she hadn't been there for her father, he could have been seriously hurt or worse. She may have just saved her father's life, so she wondered how he would regard her now. Surely, he would have some respect for her, wouldn't he? She really wasn't sure what to think.

'You've been searching through my motor, haven't you?' he asked her coldly.

She hadn't expected *that*! 'Lucky I fucking did, 'cos I think I saved your life.'

A laugh escaped from his mouth and he said with an evil grin, 'It would take more than those pair of mugs to kill me. I've pushed bigger cunts than that out of the way to get to a fight.'

Those words chilled her bones. She knew then he was capable of far worse, and her illusion of being his hero was immediately shot down, but she wanted some acknowledgement – at least a verbal pat on the back – for her timely rescue act. Yet the look on her father's face told her she had as much chance as a snowball in hell.

'But—'

'Next time, do as you're told. Any more sauce, and you can get out and walk home!'

'But I'm not a kid,' she replied, now hurt by what she saw as a patronizing remark.

'You are when you're in my company. Got it?'

'Where are we going?' she asked, deciding to change the subject.

He flashed her a quick smile, and then he sighed. He could see just from his daughter's expression that his words had hurt her. And the fact was she'd pulled off a fucking blinder back there at the pub. He was amazed by her quick thinking and courage to confront men who were seriously dangerous. But he wasn't going to tell her that and let her think she was invincible.

'Listen up, Kendall. I know you wanna move in with me, and I want nothing more than to get back at ya mother for what she did to us, but the plain fact is that ya can't.'

She turned her face away, staring out of the side window,

his words whirling around inside her head. He was so cold. Did he not realize what he'd just said? Her idea was that he would have her move in with him just to piss her mother off, as in some type of emotional revenge. It was a solid plan and she honestly thought he would go for it. She would have in his position. *What the hell has happened to my dad*? she thought. Well, if he was that stand-offish and callous, then why should she worry about worming her way into his affections. She blinked away the start of tears and cleared her throat. 'So, Dad, you're a drug dealer, I take it?'

He cast a speculative glare, stubbornly ignoring her, and pulled into a McDonald's drive-thru on the A20. Once he'd put the handbrake on, he turned his whole body to face her. With an unreadable expression, he hissed, 'You may think because you're my kid, that you fucking know me. Well, ya can get that notion right out of ya head! Ya know fuck all, and, ya know what, Kendall? That's just how I like it.'

Her breath locked in her throat. Glancing over at him, his eyes were empty. There was not a trace of compassion on his face, nothing at all. She swallowed hard, now believing that every flash of a smile he'd shot her wasn't a warm expression of endearment but a fake and almost sarcastic gesture. At that precise moment, she learned he wasn't who she thought he was. Maybe the years of separation had conjured up a dreamlike portrait of this wonderful loving father, a father who was left out in the cold, his child ripped away from him. But, obviously, she'd been living in a fantasy world, dreaming of her *ideal* father, not the one who was sitting next to her with that curled lip and an expression that told her she was a nobody in his life.

Hurt and angry, she wasn't going to let it go. 'I get it, Dad, you are into something dangerous, and you don't want me to know or be a part of your life so that I don't get caught up in it, or, worse, hurt.'

His face lit up and flushed red, as a laugh left his mouth. 'Jesus, fucking shit! You really are fucking clueless, ain't ya?' He shook his head and laughed again. 'I'm gonna take you back to the station.'

Now fuming that her father had the gall to laugh in her face, she spat back, 'Spineless!'

'You fucking what?' he growled.

'You heard, Dad. You're fucking spineless. You should have fought to keep me, and now I'm old enough to leave home and live with you, you really haven't got the guts to fight her, have you?'

Suddenly, she saw a threat in his gaze and her heart beat wildly. 'Do you know what? You're actually right. I haven't got a clue. Just take me back to the station, you get on with your drug peddling, and I'll find my own fucking way in life, without you and my stupid twat of a mother.'

Suddenly, the tables had turned. *Jesus, I hadn't expected that rebuke*, he thought. His face fell as he blew out a deep sigh.

'Okay, listen. My life ain't all about that. My business is my fucking business that you have no clue about, so get the notion of drugs and dealing outta ya head. It ain't what you think, but, see, herein is where the problem lies. You see a small picture and blow it up into a full-length feature film, and that, Kenny, I can't fucking 'ave… But I'll tell ya what I'll do. I have a flat above the hairdresser's in Petts Wood. You can have it with my blessing. You're twenty, I know, even though that mother of yours has demanded you stay under her roof until you pay back all you owe, so it's time you grew up. Next week, I'll meet you at the Daylight Inn and I'll give you the keys. Have ya got a job lined up?'

Wow! She hadn't seen *that* coming. In wide-eyed excitement, her thoughts rapidly processed the idea of having her own pad. But then she felt her elation plummet. She didn't have a job because her mother had put a stop to that. Shoving job applications right under her nose every five minutes, demanding she put herself forward for positions at legal firms, had driven her mad; she really had no interest in any of them.

'I can work for you. Dad, you can trust me.'

He laughed again. 'Kenny, I trust no one, and I mean no one. Let's be honest, you may be my kid, but I don't even know you. And, for all I know, she could have you clocking my every fucking move – the sly bitch.'

'But why would she do that, Dad? I mean, she's got her life with Alastair and the girls, a big house, and the poxy career of her dreams.'

Kendall clocked the tightness in his face melt away, as his green eyes clouded over, and his heavy brows dropped.

'You really have led quite a sheltered life… ' He paused. 'Maybe it was for the best.'

A sudden urgency to know what he meant urged her to push for an explanation. 'Come on, Dad, give me some clue as to what you mean? I at least deserve that. For fuck's sake, I didn't *ask* to be born into this family, or *any* fucking family.'

The serious tone in her voice made him sit up like a soldier. 'Your mother hasn't worked hard for her career, ya know, she was forced into it. Yeah, she loves the status, but, in truth, she's just a face behind a puppetmaster.'

Kendall chewed the inside of her mouth in contemplation. 'Who's the puppetmaster, then?'

A stubborn silence lingered a few moments before he huffed. 'Look, Kendall, forget I said that. Yeah, ya mother has a good career. That aside, as much as you find her a toffee-nosed irritant, she's still ya mother. You can have the flat… But I need to get going, so I'll drop you off back at the station.'

***

It had been a month since Mike had been reunited with his son, and as he awoke before the buzzer sounded, he looked across at him sleeping. He had done the same thing every morning. Eleven years of believing Ricky was dead had left him with a constant feeling of worry. He watched his son's soft-skinned face and floppy hair glow from the sun shining in through the small toughened glass window. His heart skipped a beat with excitement that beside him was his boy, his reason for living.

As much as his son put a loving smile on his face, in the back of his mind, there were thoughts of revenge that ate away at him. Dez Weller. He was the monster who had burned nearly every one of his photos of Ricky when Mike believed he was dead. And within hours of his arrival at Maidstone Prison, he'd found this bastard with a knife at his son's throat. That was resolved, but then he discovered that Weller wanted Ricky as his bitch. Revenge for the latter abomination should have been a given but it wasn't safe enough. He now had too much to lose; his liberty was paramount to ensure he'd be on the outside with his family, where he could protect them.

The last twelve years had been a whirlwind of frustration. Not being able to help his girlfriend Zara Ezra when she'd seemingly disappeared off the planet, and powerless to do anything to find his son, were not the normal kinds of challenges of life for anyone, and he rightly felt that he'd had more than his fair share.

Ricky stirred, and his eyes fluttered open. 'Morning, Dad.'

Mike was sitting upright in just his boxer shorts. At forty-five years old, he was as solid as any younger man in his twenties. He smiled. 'Did ya sleep well?'

Ricky nodded. 'Yeah. Actually, I've slept like a baby ever since we shared a cell.'

Mike laughed. 'I thought as much. Cor, you can't half snore.'

'You can talk,' said Ricky, jokingly. 'I'm gonna have a shower and then see what job they've assigned for me. I bet it's mopping floors again.'

Ricky quickly pushed the sheet away and sat up straight. His fringe bounced, covering his eyes.

Mike watched him, remembering the six-year-old with his messy hair. Really, he was still the same. 'Wait for me, Ricky... '

'Dad, honestly, I'll be fine. Dez gives me a wide berth now, and his mates don't even look me way. As for Tatum and Tyrone, I ain't seen much of 'em.'

Mike stood up and reached for his tracksuit bottoms neatly folded at the end of the metal bedstead. 'I ain't taking any chances, though.'

'Listen, Dad, I get it, right? But when I first arrived 'ere, I didn't know anyone, and I was scared. When I lived with me muvver, she let Tatum and Tyrone do what they liked to me. I had no one to go running to. So, I accepted what life had in store. I couldn't argue or fight back because the minute I did, I would've had Tatum's three sons on me back. And Muvver always sided with Tatum. When Dez started bullying me, I was back in the same situation. I had no one to back me up, except Willie, but now I've got you. Having my family back means I can stick up for myself because I have protection. I can be who I want to be now.'

Mike could feel the lump in his throat. Ricky hadn't gone into too much detail of what his life had been like. Mike believed that his son was saving him from further heartache. The thought of his boy feeling alone was enough to cripple him. And now he was worried because inside prison the rules were not the same. The sly dig with a shiv could end anyone's life, not least his son's. The likes of Dez wouldn't go a single round in the boxing ring: he would be too underhanded. Just the sideways glance from the Yardie's shifty eyes made Mike nervous – not for himself, but for his son.

'I'm going for a shower anyway.'

Ricky's smile reached his eyes and deepened his dimple. 'Okay, Dad. I'll see ya there.'

Just as Mike stepped outside the cell, Lou appeared with a smile that showed his back teeth. 'I've just been down to reception to collect me mail, and it looks like ya nan's gone overboard again.' He looked over at Ricky. 'You've got a whack of gear down there. They're all fancy labels an' all.'

Slowly getting up from his bed, Ricky frowned. 'What, more clothes? Jeez, me nan's right spoiling me, eh?'

Mike popped back inside the cell and laughed. 'You wait until you get out of 'ere. She'll have you up Oxford Street kitting you out in whatever the hell ya like and… ' He paused and gave a cheeky grin. 'Pops will be taking you shopping too, but not for clothes.'

Ricky's eyes widened; he was so excited, but he never predicted what his father would say next.

'The new BMW model's out soon, and he thinks it has ya name written all over it.'

Like an electric shock, Ricky jolted. 'What?' His skin suddenly became covered in goose bumps. 'No way. Oh my God! A BMW? That's way too much.'

Lou shook his head. 'I bet that's just the start as well, trust me. Ricky, your grandparents will want to give you the world and quite rightly so. You've twelve years of catching up to do, mate. Me, I'd soak it up and savour every bit of it.'

Ricky's eyes returned to look at his father. 'But that's such a lot. A new car. Wow! I never thought. Well, what I mean is… I can't believe my life could go from nothing to now this.'

'Well, get bloody used to it, Son. You'll never go without again. So, start thinking about which motor you'd really like, and when we get out, you can go on one of those intensive driving courses and get ya licence. You can cruise around in a nice set of wheels, a pair of Ray-Bans, and all the designer clothes ya can wear.'

Ricky lowered his gaze. 'Dad, I'm not really into all that designer gear. I'd be happy with clothes that actually fitted, and, to be honest, I'd feel better if I could work for my money.' He looked up and grinned. 'Let me on the firm, Dad… Well, I ain't gonna be a lawyer, am I?'

Lou shuffled uncomfortably. This was really a private conversation and one best left for Mike. 'Look, I'll catch ya later.'

Mike sat back down on the bed. 'Listen to me, sunshine. I've enough money for us to live more than comfortably, and there's no need for you to go down the same road as me. It's hard, ruthless, and extremely dangerous. Look at the boys and me. We had a target on our back for years.' He paused for a moment and sighed. 'No doubt there'll be another firm wanting to muscle in. It's always gonna be dog eat dog in our world, and I don't want that for you.'

With a stern face, Ricky replied, 'I understand that, Dad. Really, I do. But what if it's what *I* want? I'm eighteen now. Don't I get a say in this?'

'Sorry, Son, if I sounded a bit controlling, but, surely, you can see I'm looking out for ya, can't ya?'

Ricky's face relaxed. 'I know, Dad. Sorry. The thing is, I'm a crook, not by my choice, but by my own muvver's selfishness, so I don't know much else. I don't want to be a thief robbing innocent people's houses, though. I hated it, every bloody single second of it, but I hate the authorities too. I mean, where were they when I was growing up? 'Cos they sure as hell never looked out for me.'

Mike felt his son's pain again and this time he gave him a hug. 'All right, let me think about it. I'm sure we can find you something to do that won't put your liberty at risk and also make ya a bit of money. You've probably got a sharp eye and could show us oldies a thing or two.'

'All I did with Tatum's lot was watch and listen. I didn't spend any time talking. The funny thing is when you can't speak, people assume that you're deaf as well.'

'Well, let's get out of this dump first and get back to normality and then make a decision. In the meantime, ya deserve a nice car, so start thinking about which one ya fancy. No ifs or buts.'

Ricky's face glowed, and he chuckled. 'Righto, chief.'

With a towel over his shoulder, Mike winked and was gone, leaving Ricky to get ready and daydream about driving a car.

After a few moments, Ricky was pulled from his fantasy by the dark, daunting face of Dez, peering into the cell. He immediately jumped to his feet. A week ago, he would have been shaking all over, terrified of the man, but not today. 'What the fuck do you want?' he brazenly hollered.

Dez looked sheepish. It was an expression that probably most of the inmates hadn't been privy to. 'Look, no beef, bro, yeah?'

'Fuck off. No beef? Bro? I ain't ya bro. You're only here because ya know me ol' man wants to fuck you up.'

The cold, cocky words leaving Ricky's mouth left Dez totally shocked. It was more than a stark contrast to the timid boy who'd only arrived a few weeks ago. Dez's eyes were on stalks, and for a moment, he was rattled. 'All right, Ricky, I was just being straight up and apologizing for upsetting you, that's all.'

Ricky stepped forward with a new-found stance, square shoulders, and with his head up. 'Upsetting me? You held a knife to me throat. You wanted to use me as a woman. You're fucking disgusting. Now go and shove your apologies up your arse, or me ol' man will do it for ya.'

Dez daringly looked Ricky up and down. 'So that's it, is it? A threat using ya ol' man's name? A real man wouldn't threaten me with someone else.'

Just as Dez was about to turn and walk away, Ricky spat, 'No, a real man would rip you a new arsehole, but I would rip your head off!'

With an anger emerging, Dez gripped the doorframe and glowered at Ricky. As much as he was afraid of Mike, he wasn't going to let a kid talk to him like that, not after seeing the boy as a pathetic mute, cowering in shame. The idea that overnight this kid had grown a pair of balls, and was now acting so arrogantly, didn't sit well with him. 'You fucking wait, ya little shit. I'll have ya, mark my words, I will!'

'Come on, then!' screamed Ricky, who had gone from mellow to mental in less than a second. By inflating his chest and protruding his jaw, his face changed, demonstrating an intense fury that penetrated through his eyes.

It made Dez jump.

'Don't make fucking threats, you bastard. Come on!' Ricky now hopped from foot to foot, holding up his fists.

Only used to a blade, Dez was taken aback. He'd heard how Ricky had poleaxed Tatum and Tyrone and wondered if he'd seriously underestimated the kid.

Unexpectedly, as Dez stood in the doorway, a colossal fist cracked him on the side of the head and knocked him clean off his feet. There was no wobble or unsteadiness, Dez lay on the deck, out cold.

Mike shook his head. 'I forgot me toothbrush. Lucky I did, eh?' He then looked at his son's expression. 'What happened, Ricky? For fuck's sake, you weren't gonna fight him, were ya?'

Ricky was still standing in a fighting stance, his face tight and angry.

'Ricky?'

'Yeah, Dad. I was gonna have it out with him. I ain't scared anymore, like I said.'

CHAPTER FOUR

Ex-Detective Superintendent Magnus Stoneham sat back on the modern, low-backed armchair with his fingers rhythmically tapping the end of the armrests. For a man in his early seventies, his demeanour mirrored that of Conrad, his youngest son, who sat opposite. Although Magnus was now grey, and he had thinner features and tighter lips than Conrad, the men were easily identifiable as father and son in many other ways.

'So, how did the meeting go? I suspect if Mike Regan is anything like his father, then it began like pulling teeth.'

Leaning against a window in the oak-panelled study of the eighteenth-century country manor, Conrad smirked. 'Yes, that's exactly how it was. However, Father, you were right. He does have a sense of morals.' He tutted. 'It's madness when you actually think about it. Mike Regan, a bank robber, an arms dealer, and someone serving time for torturing and murdering another man. Regan's a piece of scum, isn't he?'

Magnus laughed. 'Yes, well, no doubt you are right. This idea of using a sense of morals among the immoral—'

'Hold on,' interrupted Conrad. 'I wouldn't say Regan is immoral. Lawbreaking, yes, but immoral, I'm not so convinced about that.'

'No, quite, but the point is, we need to ensure this idea of yours and your sister's doesn't have serious repercussions.'

Pushing himself away from the window, Conrad walked over to his father's drinks cabinet and poured two glasses of Redbreast Irish Whiskey.

Magnus tutted once more. 'Not too much. That's saved for special occasions.'

Yes, when you invite the Gentlemen's Club over, thought Conrad. 'How are the bridge nights going?'

Magnus raised his brow, knowingly. 'Yes, fine. Anyway, what plans do you have in place for this clean-up operation, and, more to the point, have you had a chance to speak to your sister?'

Conrad handed his father the glass and sat opposite, settling himself in the luxurious Chesterfield leather armchair. 'Well, that's the issue. I have asked Regan if he would consider the idea, but, in all honesty, I feel like I will end up in a situation where I will probably have egg on my face. I can't instil any rules in the man and his firm when their moral compass is so different from the average man in the street. Take retribution, for example. They believe in an eye for an eye. Well, that might be any person's *natural* reaction, but would we resolve our problems in that way? No, of course not. We would expect our law enforcement and justice agencies to deal with those.'

Magnus slowly nodded and pursed his lips. 'I see, um… Yes, well, the fact is, if Regan felt he was being controlled, then the actual project would fail. He has access to every known crook in South-East London and Kent. The man is very well respected within his fraternity. He will have these gangs pulled out from their hiding holes and either they will be brutalized, or, if he is amenable, he will hand over the garbage to the law. However, with regard to the latter, I very much doubt that will happen. And about your sister. You haven't told me if you have spoken with her. Have you?'

After taking a generous gulp of his whiskey, Conrad shook his head. 'No, I feel sick to my stomach. That poor girl, Brooke, having gone through such a despicable assault, I just don't know what to say to her. Me, Rebecca's brother – the bloody commissioner – can't even keep the streets clean.'

'You are not God, Conrad. Besides, Brooke has a soft spot for you. Don't delay the visit. Also, you need to discuss every-thing with Rebecca, to keep her in the loop. She cannot afford to lose the next election, and I won't have her looking weak. We have got her this far. With a little more support, she will be on the front bench before we know it. She could be a good contender for the next prime minister.'

'Yes, I know, but, as it stands at present, the crime rate is increasing so fast, and there is no money in the pot for more police officers on the streets. Three detectives who are trying to get the head honcho of these drug-fuelled gangs are due to retire shortly, and the way they look, I think they will be victims of a heart attack before they do retire. The work is sloppy and slow, and I am beginning to feel as though the gangs are making a mockery of us.'

'Well, Son, you have answered your own doubt. You need the likes of Mike Regan on board because without the budget and with the lack of staff, this hideous gang situation will soon turn Kent into the Bronx. Rebecca will lose her career and that, Son, we cannot let happen. I came from nothing, but

I've worked damned hard to have you in your position and Rebecca in hers. Don't let me down.'

***

Zara was sitting in the Regans' large and well-appointed lounge, flipping through the pages of a wedding gown brochure. A tear trickled down her nose. The long-sleeved gowns were beautiful and the women modelling them looked stunning, but how would she look with only one hand?

Gloria, Mike's mother, watched her future daughter-in-law's sad expression and guessed the reason. Hurrying over to put Zara's mind at rest, Gloria put the brochure away.

'Listen to me. Stop torturing yourself. You, my babe, will look stunning in anything you choose to wear. The only less than perfect thing about you at the moment is your downtrodden smile. Now then, there's nothing we can do about your hand, but we can concentrate on everything else. The first thing you need to do is get your confidence back. There's no point in hiding away from the world. Didn't Davey Lanigan want to meet up with you?'

Zara smiled up at Gloria with admiration, and for a moment, she felt like a kid. Gloria was so much in control of herself and those within her orbit. With her hair fashionably styled and her clothes sharp and tasteful, Zara had never seen her without make-up or a piece of jewellery around her neck. Then, she looked down at her own attire and wondered why she was still dressed like she had been for most of her time in that basement cell. There was no need to do so now.

'Ya know what, Gloria, you're right. I'm going to get my

hair styled. And it's been so long since I wore anything new and fashionable. Fancy shopping?'

Gloria was ecstatic. Firstly, she'd hoped that Zara would get herself together, and secondly, she never needed an excuse to shop. 'Arthur, where are the credit cards?' she shouted, with a hint of excitement.

Everything seemed daunting at first, and Zara couldn't explain how she felt. Having spent five years kept as a prisoner with no daylight and only a television for company, the world seemed almost alien to her now. Yet, she also knew that come what may, she would have to pull herself together. She was Izzy Ezra's daughter and now the head of his estate and the business. Although the Lanigans had taken over, thinking she was dead, the proceeds of all profits had still been split fifty-fifty and her half placed in an offshore bank account, in the unlikely event she was found alive.

Mentally, she had to retrain her mind; she wasn't a captive anymore, she was a businesswoman, with one fuck-off firm behind her. She only hoped that she still had the balls to take back control.

***

Wandering around the department store, Gloria held up a pretty blue Ted Baker dress with long sleeves and a gold trim. 'Zara, this would look stunning on you.'

Zara laughed. 'But who would take me seriously?' She held up a black blazer and dark jeans. 'Now then, look at these! These are what I need to fit the part.'

Gloria jovially rolled her eyes. 'Aah well, let's see if they have this gorgeous blue number in my size then.'

As Zara headed for the changing rooms, Gloria watched the slim, graceful woman and wondered if Zara was really ready to carry on with her firm. She was older, damaged, and probably not geared up just yet. Most women Gloria's age would never have understood why Zara would want to go back to her business when she was already worth a small fortune and could comfortably retire. With properties here, there and everywhere, she could live the high life and never lift a finger. However, Gloria understood *entirely* why Zara was committed in this way because her own husband and his pals used to run South-East London many moons ago. Then Arthur's two sons took over. While they too became very wealthy, it wasn't all about the money. A life of crime was in their blood – it never went away.

Another thought crossed Gloria's mind – her son Mike and Zara's relationship. Of course, they both loved each other, but they were at the top of their firms, with equal standing. Would the relationship work? She wasn't sure; in reality, family, business, and friendships still had a pecking order. She couldn't see either of them relinquishing their role as leader. Realizing that her musing was getting herself agitated, she sighed and found the floral dress she'd spotted on entering the store. It was in a size 12. Perhaps this would look ideal for the mother of the groom.

***

The shopping trip had exhausted Zara. If she was honest with herself, the outing had been a bit of an eye-opener because it told her that she was still very weak. Her sudden pale complexion and tired eyes sent Gloria into mummy mode. As soon as they returned home, she cooked Zara a chunky meat pie, determined to get her strength up.

The hearty meal was gratefully received, and as they placed their cutlery down and leaned back on their chairs, they could hardly move.

Arthur winked at Zara. 'It's such a pleasure to have you with us. At last, I get to have proper home-cooked meals.'

Gloria gave an exaggerated tut and whacked Arthur with her tea towel. 'You ain't done too bad by my cooking. You're still alive, ain't ya?'

The teasing came to a sudden halt when the phone rang.

Gloria, as always, got there first, hoping it was Mike. 'Hello?'

'Good evening, Mrs Regan. Could I speak with Zara? It's Davey Lanigan.'

Gloria beckoned Zara over. Holding her hand over the receiver, she whispered, 'It's Davey Lanigan, Zara. Remember you're still recovering, babe.'

Zara smiled and answered. 'Davey?'

'Zara, I called just to say how delighted I am that you're…' He paused. 'Er, well, that you're alive.' He hadn't thought over his words before he made the call. The news that Zara was found alive was a relief, but on hearing that she'd been brutally disfigured, it had sickened him.

'Thank you, Davey, thank you for everything. I know you did your best to find me and keep the business running in my absence.'

The silence seemed to linger, and Zara wondered if he was about to make a statement.

'The business is, er… fine. I can carry on, and we can talk about the future once you're well.'

She could tell he was holding something back. 'What's going on, Davey? Please tell me, or I won't get back on my feet if I'm worrying.'

'I didn't call to talk about work.'

'No, I know you didn't, but tell me anyway. What's going on?'

'Okay', he replied, 'but not on the phone. How are you fixed for tomorrow lunchtime? I think it's better discussed away from the public. Would it be convenient to come over to Mike's parents' home?'

Zara looked over at the dining-room table where Arthur and Gloria were sipping the last of their wine. 'Would it be okay if Davey Lanigan comes here tomorrow? Say, lunchtime?'

Arthur smiled and nodded his head. 'Of course.'

Unexpectedly, Eric appeared. They hadn't heard him come in through the back door, too intent on trying to listen to Zara's conversation. It wasn't for any reason other than to make sure she was okay.

Once she'd completed the call, she turned around, and as she sat down, she was surprised to see Eric seated at the table.

It wasn't so much that he was there, it was his appearance. His hair was cut short similar to Mike's, and instead of his T-shirt and jeans, he wore a fresh white button-down shirt and black trousers. She had to blink because for a moment she thought it was Mike.

Even Gloria was surprised and had to remark, 'So, off out with anyone special, Son?'

'No! Christ, can't a man wear a decent shirt without some-one suggesting there's a date involved?' Instantly, he realized how harsh and childish he sounded.

But the tension wasn't lost on Gloria. She arched her brow, and then her eyes flicked to Zara. Zara looked equally troubled but for a different reason.

'Are you okay, love?' asked Gloria, somewhat concerned.

'I feel bad. This isn't right. I should be back at my own home, not have people come to your house to discuss—'

Arthur waved his hand to interrupt her. 'Now, no talking nonsense. You need our support.' He looked at Gloria. 'Besides, Old Mother Hen here would be lost. And it's what our Mike wants, so, my babe, you treat this place like your own, and when you're completely better, if you want to go back to… that house, then, that's up to you.'

Gloria almost screeched. 'What?… Go back there after what the poor girl's just been through? I won't be surprised if she wants to burn the bloody place down.'

With her mind back to when she was held against her will, Zara smiled. 'You'd think it would be the last place I'd ever go, but the truth is, if it wasn't for Ismail's pathetic attempt to keep me alive in my father's basement, then the Segals would probably have finished me off. My dad would turn in his grave if he knew that the suite he built would end up holding me a prisoner. But the rooms were styled and designed by him, so, weirdly, I felt at home. When I do go back, though, I'll have the metal door removed and keep the basement as guest rooms.'

She looked up to find both Gloria and Arthur with their mouths open.

She chuckled. 'Don't worry. I wouldn't ask *you* to stay there.'

Gloria knew then that Zara was no ordinary woman; she was hard and had taken on more than most people could handle, but she would still face her demons.

Zara, though, miraculously didn't see these as demons, merely challenges.

Eric placed his hand on her back and gently rubbed it. 'If you need to go back there for anything, I'll go with you.'

Gloria clocked the look on her son's face. She didn't like it one little bit.

***

Rebecca sat at the kitchen island with her head in her hands, the tea towel covering her sodden cheeks. At forty-three years old, she should have been in her prime, but she wasn't. The signs were all there: a thickened waist, grey hair, and crow's feet around her once bright and, some would say, come-to-bed eyes. She wasn't even sure if her husband knew what she looked like under her elastic-waisted trousers and iron-free blouse. All the intimacy that had once been between them had diminished over the last two years. His business – so he said – was growing, and his excuse for staying away was that he had to strike while the iron was hot. *It must be bloody molten lava by now*, she thought.

The stress of it all pushed Rebecca to consider resigning, but as soon as she mentioned those words, Alastair and her father went off like a Catherine wheel, spitting, hissing, and spinning in circles. Her eyes looked to the cupboard under the sink, the place where she thought every housewife hid her booze. Her husband certainly wouldn't look there; he didn't even know where the kitchen sink was.

Just as she bent down and opened the cupboard, a crashing sound made her jump. Spinning round, she almost lost her balance. There, giving her an unwelcome sneer, stood Kendall. The noise was from her daughter flinging her rucksack onto the worktop. Like her sisters, Kendall had not an ounce of respect for her.

Usually, she would have offered her daughter a drink or something to eat, but not this evening, though; she was sick to the back teeth of pussyfooting around Kendall. So, instead, she sneered back and tutted.

'So, tell me, Mother, who exactly is your puppetmaster?'

Rebecca tilted her head to the side with a questioning expression. Silently, she wondered why she'd ever bothered to take Kendall away from her father. She should have left her there. There was not a smidgen of her own genes in the girl – not in looks, attitude, not even in interests. If she didn't look so much like her real father, Rebecca would have sworn she'd been swapped at birth.

'Kendall, I have no idea what you're talking about, and, to be quite frank, I really don't care!'

She turned away from her daughter and searched for the bottle of Bombay Sapphire. Pulling a tumbler from the top shelf, she poured a generous helping and took two large gulps. So uptight and angry, she didn't bother to add the tonic; instead, she swallowed more of the bitter, clear liquid and smarted as it ripped the back of her throat. After taking a deep breath, she looked up at her daughter, who appeared to be stunned. Well, she would be; she'd never seen her mother do that before – she'd thought her too straight-laced to knock back neat gin.

'What's up, Mother? Did you find Alastair with another woman?' she scoffed.

Rebecca stared at her daughter's ridiculing eyes and was

hit by overwhelming anger that shot up from her feet to the top of her head. Instantly, she threw the glass tumbler at the wall, and then, with both hands, she wiped the centre island clear, sending the vase, the condiments, and Kendall's rucksack flying to the floor.

Still incensed, she smashed both her fists on the worktop and glared with fire in her eyes at her daughter. 'Now, you fucking listen to me. You're a spiteful, evil bitch, and if you weren't my daughter, I would give you what-for. So, fuck off, away from me.' She paused, sucking a deep breath as she stared at the horror-stricken look on Kendall's face; yet she didn't feel in the least bit sorry or guilty for those harsh words.

'I wish I'd never applied for custody. I wish I'd never brought you back into my home to give you a better life. In fact, I wish you'd never been *born*, you ungrateful, nasty girl. Now, before I do something I really do regret, fuck off, go back to your bastard of a father, and leave me alone!'

Kendall stood frozen to the spot. Never in her life had she seen her mother act that way. The overly polite and sickly sweet manner had been replaced by a raging lunatic, but Kendall wasn't going to stand there and take that. 'My dad, the bastard, yeah? Weren't *you* the one who couldn't keep your knickers on? Weren't *you* the one who fucked off with Alastair and left Dad and me on our own? I think the truth is, Mother, you're the bastard – or the puppet.'

She knew the minute the words left her mouth she was going to get it from her mother, so she turned to rush out of the door before something was thrown her way. However, she wasn't fast enough and was ripped back by her T-shirt and pushed against the wall. With a tight grip around her throat, Kendall's eyes nearly popped out of her head and her heart felt like it was beating outside her chest. Her mother was a millimetre away from her face and foaming at the mouth. This wasn't her mother, surely? This was a demon who had taken over her mother's body. Then, to her horror, her mother pulled her fist back ready to launch a punch. Kendall stared into her mother's eyes, searching for any sign of the rage leaving. To her relief, her mother dropped her arm and pushed her away.

With legs like jelly and her body trembling, Kendall scurried away. As soon as she was out of reach, she shouted back, 'Don't worry, I'm moving out next weekend. My father has a flat for me, so you can go and fuck yourself.'

Heading to her bedroom, only too pleased to have had the last word, Kendall didn't hear her mother sobbing. As soon as Kendall reached the end of the hallway, the front door opened and in walked Alastair, looking very chuffed. Dressed in a grey suit and with a golden tan, Kendall had to admit he wasn't bad looking. She could see why her mother was attracted to him. A well-built man, with ripped muscles and piercing eyes, he wouldn't seem out of place at a prefight weigh-in. However, the way he looked at her still made her want to cringe.

'Hello, Kendall, how's Brooke?' he said, not noticing the sheer spite on her face. He took off his jacket, placed it on a hanger, and rolled up his sleeves. Kendall didn't reply but went up the stairs, leaving him to see for himself the carnage in the kitchen. Once she reached the landing, she strained her ears to listen, wondering if her mother would revert to the sweet housewife fussing over her husband like it was the 1950s.

'What's the bloody matter now, Rebecca?' Alastair's voice

was less than compassionate, which sent Rebecca into a further downward spiral.

'Where have you been?' she snapped.

'Where the hell do you think? I've been to work, Rebecca. Now, will you pull yourself together and stop badgering me. I'd have thought you had more pressing issues to be concentrating on, like the upcoming election. Oh yes, and not forgetting, you have our daughter up there suffering.'

Kendall crept back down the staircase and waited midway, listening.

'Brooke won't even look at me, and damn the bloody election. In fact, Alastair, I might resign. I've had enough.'

'What!' he bellowed, his tone now deep and masterful. 'Don't be so bloody ridiculous, woman. We've come this far, and now you want to bail out? Well, all I can say is, Rebecca, you aren't the woman I thought you were. I thought I'd married someone with guts, drive, and determination, not some pathetic crybaby who wants to give up at the first hurdle!'

There was silence and Kendall could only picture her mother's crumpled expression. She got that very wrong.

'We, Alastair? *We*? Who is the we? Because as I recall, it's me who happens to be the member of parliament. I hold that seat, not you, and this isn't the *first* hurdle. I've been working my bloody arse off to get to where I am.'

Alastair's voice instantly mellowed. 'Sorry, love. Look, it was just a turn of phrase. I *am* proud of you, and what you've achieved. You're such an amazing MP. It's tough, I grant you, but it'll get easier. The voters love you and no doubt they'll vote you in again and then you can relax. How about after the election we take a short holiday, just me and you, eh?'

Her stepfather, the ace manipulator, Kendall thought. She pictured the scene and recognized her father's skill at managing the situation to his own personal advantage. She could just imagine her mother falling into Alastair's arms and wiping her eyes. *She is so pathetic*, she thought. *Why, Mother, can't you see through him?*

'Forget it, Alastair. I am fed up with everything. Our marriage is a mess because either you're working or I am. We never spend time together, and as for my job, I hate it. I am sick of it. The crime rate in my constituency is climbing daily, and I'm damn sure my voters will view it as me being incompetent. Why should I have to go through all this stress? I've enough money saved not to work ever again.'

'I know, my darling, it's hard. I'll tell you what. I'll take a week off and help you as much as I can. I don't like to see you like this. What do you say?'

Kendall cringed, wishing her mother would flatly refuse his offer. *Stand your ground, Mother*, she willed.

'Well, you've no need to do that, Alastair.'

Kendall sensed her mother was taking back control.

'I want to, Rebecca.'

'No, I mean, I have help. I have Father and Conrad and they have a plan to—'

Alastair interrupted before his wife had a chance to finish. 'You what! You never said. How? I mean, what do they propose to do?'

The sudden panic in Alastair's voice made Kendall stay put. Surely, her mother would have recognized that worried tone?

'Conrad has a plan to clean up the streets and get to the bottom of this gang problem.'

'What? How? I thought he didn't have the budget for that?' Alastair asked, now quite agitated.

'He doesn't have the budget, so I guess he has another plan. Anyway, I'm bushed. I'm going to have a shower.'

Finally, Kendall was about to creep back up the stairs, before her mother caught her earwigging, when she realized her parents hadn't finished talking.

'Wait a minute. What's going on, Rebecca? Your brother is the chief of police. If he doesn't have the budget, then what does he propose to do? We need to know because… well, what if he makes a mess of things? Christ, Rebecca, if he does, then you'll be the one with egg on your face, not him. You need to find out what his intentions are, and then we can decide whether or not to let him get involved.'

'I'm pretty sure he has a good plan because he's been discussing it with our father!'

Kendall sensed her mother's tone was now tainted with annoyance. She waited to see who was next to serve, thoroughly enjoying this game of tennis.

'Your father? Jesus, it gets worse. What the hell does your father know about politics? Seriously, Rebecca, you should be discussing this with me, your bloody husband, not running to your daddy like a child!'

'Alastair, I am not discussing it anymore. I'm going to take a shower and then I'm off to bed. I've had quite enough rows for one day.'

Kendall quickly snuck away to her room. *This is getting interesting*, she thought. Maybe she should have studied politics or puppet mastery.

CHAPTER FIVE

Mike looked behind him to find four eager faces. 'Before we get outside, just remember, not a word to anyone, even family. We got released early because of overcrowding and cutbacks.'

Staffie frowned. 'D'ya think they'll buy it?'

Mike nodded. 'Come on, Staff, they'll be only too pleased we're out to bother about questioning it. Not a word though, 'cos who would understand it, and we don't want to lose respect, now do we?'

The others nodded in agreement. It was a good point and they certainly didn't want to lose face.

The last secure door slid open. He winked as if to say, 'This is it, lads.' There, waiting to greet them, stood Arthur, Mike's father, and Teddy Stafford, Staffie's father. Embraces were exchanged, and, excitedly, they hurried to the cars. Mike stopped for a moment and looked up at the clear blue sky and sighed. He was free – for almost twelve years he'd been locked up, and now he could breathe and learn to live again. Ricky was by Arthur's side, held close with Arthur's arm around his shoulders. Mike looked on, fondly. He knew that Ricky would be fussed over for months or even years to come.

Ted opened the door for Staffie, Willie, and Lou to climb in, while Mike and Ricky travelled home with Arthur.

For Ricky, it was a dream come true. He'd been sentenced to a year in the nick, believing he would come out only to face his mother and their tiny caravan – a way of life that he detested. To be sitting next to his grandfather in the front seat of a new car and driving off to his real family's home, after serving only a few weeks, felt overwhelming and left him with a permanent grin.

As Arthur pulled away, Mike looked back at the dark, miserable building and tears began to well up. All those years of sitting in solitary confinement, believing his son and Zara were dead, tormented with all the what-ifs, the whys, and the where-fores, and now to be free and to have his loved ones back once more, he wondered if he should actually start going to church because God had undoubtedly answered his prayers.

Mike knew the outside world would have changed in twelve years and if he had served out his full sentence, he suspected it would have been a slow process to acclimatize to the life of Civvy Street. Having missed out on so many changes, the first one he noticed was the billboards advertising new technology and the number of pedestrians with their faces glued to a phone or wearing, as he saw it, oversized headphones. And while his mind was on those, looking at the interior of his father's car, it seemed as though he'd entered the space age. The technology was incredible, and he gazed in wonderment at the huge dashboard with sat nav, hi-fi, and telephone, all integrated and shown on just one screen. He clocked the way people dressed – these new skinny jeans – on men – and it made him shake his head. What the fuck did they look like? He saw some young women walking down a street and noticed that their hairstyles were different too, now every shade of the rainbow.

Ricky took less interest in his surroundings. He'd only been inside a short while, so to him the outside was nothing new. His eyes were on his grandad and being driven in his latest Jaguar, with the smell of expensive aftershave pervading the interior. And having his family around him was all he cared about.

Once they arrived at the house, Ricky's eyes were wide with excitement. The memories of his grandparents' home came flooding back, along with that distant recollection of the day his mother had bundled him into the car and taken off.

They pulled onto the long gravel drive. As they approached the six-bedroom property, huge yellow ribbons were tied to the concrete pillars. This and his father's home were where his fondest memories had been made. And he wouldn't let the past with his mother override them. He now had the future to look forward to. He beamed when he spotted Gloria at the door, with Zara and Eric behind her. His grandmother was waving and hopping up and down like someone demented. It was just like the day she faced him in prison for the first time in twelve years, when she went bananas and screamed with excitement.

Mike left his plastic bag inside the car, a stark reminder of prison. As he stepped out and took a deep breath, Zara hurried over and threw herself at him. He lifted her up and spun her around, noticing how light she was. As he heard the crunching sound of the gravel from the other car drawing up, he smiled. They were all together: the whole family, his mates, their parents, and Zara.

'Come on, let's get inside!' ushered Gloria, who was in her element. She'd planned a homecoming party with food to feed an army and drink to fill a pub. Everyone trickled out of the French doors into the garden where a hired barbecue was on the go. The outside summerhouse was decorated like a Hawaiian cocktail bar with waiters shaking piña coladas.

As expected, Ricky was being hugged, kissed, and complimented. Zara was clinging to Mike as if her life depended on it, and then the fun and banter began.

As the drinks flowed and the laughter was at its peak, Zara's mobile phone rang. Staring down at the flashing number, she frowned; there beside Davey Lanigan's name were four missed calls. She hurried away from the party and walked into the lounge where it was quiet, only to hear the landline ringing. Picking up the receiver, she listened to a strong Irish accent. 'Zara, is that you?'

Detecting the panic in the tone, she replied, 'Yes.'

'It's me, Shamus. Davey's been trying to call you. I'm sorry, I know it's Mr Regan's homecoming, but we've a serious situation going on. Neil's at the hospital. He's been knifed in the chest… ' His words faltered for a moment, but not quickly enough to give Zara a chance to comprehend the situation. The next bit of news came as a bombshell. 'He may not pull through.'

Zara had to sit down – the information had knocked her sideways. She had a lot of feelings for Neil; he had worked alongside her for five years before she was brutally attacked and held in her father's basement. Taking a deep breath to stop the crack in her voice, she asked, 'Who attacked him?' Her mind was back to the darkest place – a war with the Harmans and the Segals.

'We don't know who they are. They were just two black

guys, Yardies, we think. They've robbed him and beaten him and then the feckers plunged him. Jesus, he's in a bad way, Zara.'

Just as she was about to ask more questions, her mobile phone rang again. It was Davey.

'Er... Shamus, it's your uncle on the other phone. I'll call you back.'

With that, the phone went dead, and she quickly took the call from Davey. 'Oh my God, Davey, I'm so sorry. Where is Neil? What shall I do?' Her words came out so fast, she had to stop for air.

'Zara, we may need Mike's help here. I want those bastards shot. This minute, my hands are tied. All my men are back in Ireland. We had some issues back there, so I pulled them out of London. It was supposed to be a temporary thing, but, now... Oh, feck me... Oh, I have to go. The doctors are calling me.'

Zara gasped as she replaced the receiver, her mind now on Neil, fervently wishing him to live. He was like a little brother to her. Not a brother like Ismail, a rat of the first order, but the brother she wished she had.

As she was about to call Shamus back, Eric appeared, holding her drink. 'Hey, are you okay, Zara? It's a bit overwhelming, eh? All the family and... '

She waved her hand distractedly. 'No, it's not that, er... Could you get Mike for me please, Eric?'

He turned his head to the side. 'Zara? What's happened?'

Near to tears, she replied, 'Sorry, Eric, I haven't got time. Could you fetch Mike for me?'

Ignoring her request, he walked over to her and crouched

down. 'Talk to me, Zara. What's going on? I can sort it out. Mike's a bit pissed. Let's not burden him for the moment.'

Almost the spitting image of Mike, Eric didn't have that same open smile.

'Neil has been knifed.'

'Fuck, no! Where did it happen?'

Zara frowned. 'I, er... I don't know where, but Shamus thinks... Oh, hang on. I need to call Shamus back.'

As she pressed the Return Call key on the landline, she slowly turned to see Eric still there and mouthed the words 'Get Mike'.

'Shamus, where was Neil when he got knifed?'

'Zara, from what I can gather, Neil was attacked just outside one of the restaurants. We need to meet up. I feel like a sitting duck. Another one of our places was turned over last night. It's the second one in a week.'

'Why didn't someone tell me?' she asked, firmly.

'Uncle Davey wanted to talk to you about it, but Mike was coming home, and you were poorly, so... Anyway, the fact is, some fecking gang smashed the fecking lights out of the owner of the Pomodorra, took all the gear and the money, and threatened to kill his grandson. The Belle restaurant was also done over, and it was the same gang, judging by the description.'

'Okay, Shamus. Tomorrow, can we meet first thing?'

There was a pause. 'Er... yeah, sure... if Neil is okay. I mean, if he pulls through.'

'Yes, look, sorry, of course. Let's cross one bridge at a time, eh?'

As she replaced the receiver, she gave Eric a puzzled look. 'Why didn't you get Mike?'

Eric dropped his shoulders and sighed. 'Listen, Mike's just got out of the nick. He's catching up with old mates. I thought it best to keep him in good form. Any problems, Zara, let me help. Mikey's had enough to worry about to last him a lifetime.'

Zara looked down at her wrist and felt Eric had a point. Mike should be allowed time to enjoy life and not jump right back into another war, one that really wasn't his business. She nodded and smiled. 'I guess you're right. Anyway, I wouldn't want to pull him away from his family.'

Eric chuckled. 'Yeah, not when Jennifer's strutting her stuff in that short skirt of hers.' Without a second thought as to what he'd just said, his voice turned serious. 'So, what did Shamus say? I mean, do they know who stabbed him?'

The thought of Mike flirting with another woman hovered at the back of her mind. She looked at her wrist again and suddenly felt lost. What was she thinking? Maybe Mike's proposal of marriage came because he was in a dark place and seeing her again after all those years of believing she was dead, it may have pushed him to act irrationally? She'd seen Teddy's niece arrive and was taken aback when she swanned in, with the shortest of skirts and a low-cut top. She was probably in her late thirties but had the figure of a younger woman. Zara couldn't compete with someone who looked like that. She suddenly came out of her daze. 'Sorry, Eric, I was just in shock. Shamus reckons it's the Yardies who have done over two of my businesses. Anyway, you're right. I won't worry Mike with it.'

Eric leaned forward and rubbed her shoulder. 'You ain't on your own, Zara. I'll help. I can drive you to a meeting tomorrow, if you'd like me to.'

Unexpectedly, Zara's eyes filled up and two large tears

cascaded down her cheeks. She hastily brushed them away and tried to push herself out of the chair.

Eric quickly assisted, by sliding his arm under hers. 'Hey, Zara, what's the matter, babe?'

His gentle words almost had her blubbering. 'Oh, I'm so worried about Neil. I don't know what I'd do if anything happened to him.' As soon as she said that, she felt his grip tighten.

'I didn't know you and Neil were so close.'

'Yes, very close, actually. We worked together for five years. He was always popping in to see I was okay. The Lanigans were good to me, you know.' Her mind preoccupied, the severe look on his face escaped her, but she sensed his prickly tone.

'How good were they, Zara?'

Not realizing there was a dark undercurrent to his voice, however, she just smiled sweetly and replied, 'Like family, really. It was such a bonus when you have no one.'

She excused herself to use the cloakroom. Once behind the closed door, she allowed the tears to fall for many reasons. With Neil now fighting for his life and that niggling doubt that she couldn't compete with a younger woman, a multitude of emotions swept through her mind. But the worst of them was that she didn't feel a complete woman. She sat on the toilet seat and tried desperately hard not to allow herself to sob. She had to pull herself together; this was a homecoming for Mike, Ricky, and the boys, and, more than that, she had to hold her head up and show she was still a woman in control. Her weakness and vulnerability must not show through. She had to demonstrate she was the same person who could lead a firm – her firm.

After splashing some water on her face, she left and walked

back into the garden. The lights had come on. She spotted Mike with his back to her; he was engaged in conversation with Jennifer, the leggy blonde, and Eric was with them.

As Eric clocked her standing there, he quickly nudged Mike. Right away, Zara felt as though Eric was giving Mike the heads-up that she was watching. Instead of joining their company, she turned around and looked for Gloria. Everyone seemed to be in high spirits and chitchatting. For Zara, it was a stark reminder that apart from Mike's family, she had no one. *Pull yourself together, Zara*, she thought.

Pouring herself a drink, she felt a presence behind her and hoped it was Mike, but, as she craned her neck, it was Eric. 'Are you okay, babe?' he whispered.

She nodded and glanced back at Mike, to find him heading her way.

'There she is, the love of my life. Where were you, darling? No one knew where you were.'

She looked at Eric, who, surprisingly, winked. She wondered if he was trying to tell her something.

'Oh, I was in the cloakroom. So, are you having fun, Mikey?'

With a pint in his hand and his cheeks glowing red, he nodded. 'Aah, this means so much, here with my family, my mates. Let's get this party going.' He spun round and shouted to Ricky to turn the music up. Zara knew then he was pissed, and she suddenly felt drained. Mike was getting warmed up, and she was ready for bed. It was yet another reminder that she was less than the woman she was before.

Ricky was in his element. Gloria was showing him off to everyone, and he felt a different person. For the first time in his life, he felt he had control, with no one stopping him from doing anything. He drank, he ate, and he could play any song he wanted to. The hugs and kisses were endless. All the guests had something complimentary to say, but the one thing that lifted his shoulders and made him proud were the words, 'You, Ricky, are your father's double, a chip off the old block.'

He knew the best song to play: it was 'Happy' by Pharrell Williams. That would get everyone in the spirit. As soon as the song came on, Mike threw his hands in the air and began dancing. Ricky was in stitches because it seemed so funny to see his father, the giant, the dangerous badass man, skipping and turning with two left feet and not giving a shit what people thought.

Staffie and Willie were equally inexpert; with pints in their hands, they bopped around, singing the words at the top of their voices. Mike waved Zara over to join them.

Zara felt awkward and was on the point of walking away, but Mike laughed. 'Come on, Zara, show us how it's done.' But his playful mood suddenly plummeted as he went to grab her left hand and realized that it was no longer there. Her humiliation was written all over her face, and she couldn't hold back how she felt by laughing it off. Instead, she started to walk away, but as she turned, there, in front of her, was Jennifer, swinging her hips and waving her arms. Zara skirted around her, holding back the tears.

Once she was in the safety of the empty kitchen, she took a deep breath; it was all too much. She should pack her things and return to her father's home. Seeing a packet of cigarettes on the worktop, she tipped one out, placed it in her mouth, and lit the end. The first drag was soothing and let her muscles relax; the second one started to ease her mind. Taking a glance out of the window, she saw Jennifer grab Mike's hands and dance, showing off her body by exaggerating her sexy moves. He was looking around, no doubt wondering where she'd gone, but as Zara continued to watch, it was apparent that Mike's concern was short-lived; he was swigging back a fresh pint that was placed in his hand. If she went home tonight, she would look like a jealous girlfriend with the strops. She took one last drag on her cigarette and stubbed it out. Deciding to head for her room, she filled a glass with cold water, irritated by how long and awkward it was with her disability, and then, with the sob trapped in her throat, she went upstairs for solitude.

Within a minute, there was a knock at the door, followed by a deep voice. 'Can I come in?'

She assumed it was Mike and sat up straight on the bed. 'Yeah.'

But as the door opened, there, taking up the doorway, was Eric. 'Hey, babe, what's the matter? Are you okay?'

His sympathetic eyes almost caused the trapped sob to leave. She breathed in through her nose to clear the emotion. 'Yeah, I'm fine. I feel a little under the weather, and, obviously, I'm concerned about Neil. I just thought that rather than dampen the mood, I'd take myself off to bed. If Mike asks where I am, would you just say I'm asleep? That I drank too much or something?'

He eased his way into the room and sat beside her. 'Listen, Zara, Mike dancing with Jennifer is nothing. Serving a big lump means catching up, and once he has it out of his system, he'll be back to the old Mikey you know. Just give him time.'

Zara stiffened. She wasn't the type of woman to live like that – a husband getting his oats just because he'd missed out for twelve years. It wasn't as if she'd had it easy herself. She'd been locked up too. 'Well, maybe I should move out and give him time for, as you say, "catching up".'

Eric stroked her hair. 'You and Mikey will be fine. He's just pissed and enjoying himself.'

She would have removed Eric's hand, but her self-esteem and attempt at being in control were slowly ebbing away, so she let him continue. 'I'm going to move back home. Eric, would you drive me tomorrow? I can't… ' She broke off as the tears fell and the sob escaped. In between broken words, she cried, 'I am useless, now, I can't do this… Mike deserves a real woman… and my business. Jesus, how can I run that?'

She wiped her face and cleared her throat. 'I'm going to sell up everything and let the Lanigans take over completely. My dad was wrong. I just don't have it in me.'

As Eric pulled her close, she allowed his arms to wrap around her.

'Now, now,' he whispered, 'I'll go with you tomorrow to meet Shamus, and we'll take it from there. Your father wasn't wrong, Zara. You are a strong woman, with a good head on your shoulders. You've been through a big ordeal, and you ain't alone, babe. I'm here. I'll help. Besides, Mike has his own business to take care of. He doesn't really need me.'

Registering what he'd said, Zara, pulled away. 'What? You mean you're not back on their firm?' Her eyes narrowed in confusion.

He shook his head. 'No. Mike has Staffie, Lou, and Willie. Apparently, they've some other business they need to take care of. That's why they were released early, but I guess you knew that. Mike must tell you everything.'

A dark thought ripped through her mind. Mike hadn't told her why he was released early. In fact, he'd not discussed it with her at all. And she'd been too intent on making wedding plans and getting herself better even to ask. What was puzzling her though was why he hadn't mentioned anything to her, when, clearly, Eric was better informed.

'Er… do you know what this business is?'

He gave her another compassionate look. 'Nope. See, that's how I know he doesn't want me working with him in the firm or he would have said. Still, that don't matter. I'm just thrilled that he's out now and that you are too.'

How strange, she thought. *Mike would have told his family, surely, and herself, come to that, wouldn't he?* 'Are you sure you haven't any idea what this business is about?'

Eric smiled. He really didn't know himself; he'd only over-heard snippets from a conversation between Staffie and Willie while they were drunk at the homecoming. They had quickly shut up shop when they saw him hovering around. 'Well, all I know is he was asked to do something, in return for his liberty. He didn't elaborate, so I left it at that… Now, then, don't you worry about Mike. Let's just sort out your affairs. Like I said, I'll help you, babe. You get some rest, and tomorrow, I'll drive you to your meeting.'

He kissed the top of her head and made a move to leave the room.

'Er… Eric, have you got a cigarette?'

Eric sat back down on the bed and looked directly into Zara's desolate eyes.

'Babe, don't smoke. You don't need to.'

Their gaze locked for a few seconds, and as Eric slowly

blinked, he gently stroked her cheek. She felt the soft touch and unexpectedly craved more. She leaned into his hand, keeping it against her face, and closed her eyes. She could feel Eric's warm breath caress her skin and his lips softly brush over hers. Whether it was the familiar aftershave, or, in that moment, experiencing a sense of being wanted, it didn't matter. He pulled her closer, and his kiss that was harder, and more meaningful, suddenly snapped her out of the embrace. Subtly, she pulled away. 'I'm sorry, Eric, it's been a long day. I feel so tired.'

He didn't force the connection but simply stroked her hair once more. 'Of course, darling, you get some sleep,' he replied, with such an empathetic look that it almost brought her to tears again.

Once he was gone, Zara felt as though she was experiencing a terrible dream, her mind now back on Mike. She was getting bad vibes but needed to trust her instincts. What was her relationship with Mike? Had she imagined this tight bond between them? Christ, what if she'd got him all wrong? For a moment, she almost wished Eric was back beside her on the bed. He'd made her feel special and she'd missed that so much.

***

Zara was woken by the vibration of her phone squashed against her chest. She'd fallen asleep fully clothed, and the phone was still in her top pocket. Through blurry eyes, she noticed the missed calls from Shamus. She suddenly bolted upright, her hand shaking. *Oh my God! Neil!* she thought. With a gruff, croaky voice, she said, 'How is he, Shamus?'

There was a pause. 'He's pulled through, Zara. He's

gonna make it. I need to meet you this morning. Is nine o'clock okay?'

She glanced across at the bedside clock: it showed 6.45 a.m. *Christ, have I been asleep that long?* she thought. She cleared her throat. 'Yes, of course. You know where my father's house is. Meet me there.'

Shamus paused. 'Your father's?'

'Yes, Shamus, I know what you're thinking, but it's still my house and I'm not worried. In fact, I'll feel right at home there.'

Dragging herself away from the soft duvet, she got to her feet and crept to the bathroom. Her reflection in the mirror was a stark reminder that she was ageing fast, her hair lank and her eyes puffy. Her mind went back to the vision of Jennifer in that fitted red skirt and legs up to her armpits and then that fleeting moment with Eric. Taking a deep breath, she decided she wasn't going to cry again. The thought of jacking it all in was instantly pushed from her mind. She wasn't going to let her father down or Neil for that matter. Suddenly gripped by a gut-wrenching feeling, she hurried back to her room and the empty bed. Where was Mike, and, more to the point, who was Mike with?

Hesitantly, Zara crept down the stairs, not wanting to wake anyone up. As she reached the door to the lounge, she held her breath, afraid of what she might see. She sighed and shook her head. 'Pull yourself together. This is ridiculous, Zara,' she muttered to herself.

Yet when she pushed open the door, she gasped and shook from head to toe. Her eyes couldn't look away, too intent on absorbing the sight. A scream wanted to leave her mouth, but she fought to hold it back. There, on one sofa, was Mike, wearing nothing but his trousers. On another sofa was Jennifer, with her skintight skirt up over her arse and just her thong showing. Her hair was a mess, and her lipstick was smeared across her face.

Zara's world had just caved in but her instincts hours before had been proved correct. All her hopes and dreams were pouring bit by bit into a vast sinkhole. Their relationship was over before it had even begun. Mike's proposal must have been an irrational spur-of-the-moment promise – now just a throwaway comment. As if losing her hand wasn't bad enough, losing her man was worse. Feeling like a peeping Tom, she scurried away back to her room. After throwing a few things into a bag, she left, quietly closing the door behind her. Once she was on the street, she pulled out her smartphone from her bag and used the Uber app to call for a taxi to take her home.

The drive back to the sizeable gloomy house was spent with her teeth chattering in shock, her one true love having dismissed her at the sight of a pretty woman. Perhaps she'd never really known Mike at all. It was apparent he didn't feel the same way about her. All she wanted was to be in his arms and make up for all the time apart; and yet it was clear he was happy to flirt and obviously sleep with a tart right under her fucking nose.

The driver put the radio on and out blared 'Happy' by Pharrell Williams.

What? Is this a joke? 'Turn that fucking shit off, please, and if I want music while I'm paying for my ride, then I'll fucking ask for it.'

The driver was taken aback by the steely tone of the frail-looking woman's voice. Instantly, he turned the music off. 'I'm sorry, love. It was just force of habit.'

Zara didn't respond. Instead, she stared gloomily out of the window and planned her future.

Her angry mood stayed with her as she stepped out of the car. She waited until the driver was out of sight before she pulled the keys from her bag. She paused and looked up at the vast, almost devilish-looking mansion. The paint on the woodwork was peeling, the gardens – once stunning – were overgrown, and the windows certainly needed a good clean. Izzy would be turning in his grave. He had loved this house – it had been his pride and joy – and he'd had it designed to his demanding specification.

She felt that a new chapter was about to begin in her life. Once she pushed the big oak door open, she gingerly entered the hall. Inside, it was filled with antiques, which were not her choice. The red drapes always made her feel like she was living in some historic time warp, the Tudor era. Yet everything was to Izzy's taste. Assuming she would feel afraid, even just a little nervous, she was pleasantly surprised that although the house was tired and dusty, she felt at home. Perhaps it was the memories of how her father held her in such high esteem. Engaging her in all aspects of the business, he had gently and expertly prepared her for the takeover.

Closing the door behind her, she walked towards the back of the house, to the door that led down to the basement, where she'd been held a captive for five years. She had to brave it out and revisit her prison; yet, this time there were no captors, there was no sly, sneaky brother tormenting her, or the evil eyes of the Segals watching her as she pretended to be a brain-damaged, broken woman.

Surprisingly, as she faced the barred metal door, she felt

herself free at last of the mental shackles. Still holding her bag, she peered inside and looked at the boxes of antidepressants and knew that in order to take control of her life, she needed to ditch them.

Once she'd stared for a while at what was her home for so long, she turned and marched back up the stairs and into her father's office. She sighed heavily and plonked her bag on the desk. Guy Segal and his son Benjamin, with the help of Ismail, would have looked for every fucking file, trying to get their hands on her businesses. But they obviously didn't know her father that well. For although Ismail had been surreptitiously nosing into their father's affairs, there were still some things he'd never been able to understand, like the offshore accounts, the details of which were carefully concealed in several flash drives hidden under a floorboard. She pulled away the rug and removed the board, and there, to her delight and relief, were all the devices. Bingo! Now she could have the computer up and running and get back on track. As she lowered herself onto her dad's high-backed mahogany chair, she felt an overwhelming sense of power. She may only have one hand, but it was her brain that was really her best asset.

By eight o'clock that morning, she was up and running. The accounts, all showing vast amounts of money, were feeding her confidence. She would take back her businesses, and she would hold her head up and become the woman she once was, even if Mikey wasn't by her side.

Bang on nine o'clock, there was a heavy knocking at the front door. She glanced at the monitor to see who was there, but it was a blank screen. The CCTV cameras were either disarmed or Ismail had really let the beautiful house go to rack and ruin. She rose from her chair and headed along the parquet floor to the entrance. 'Who is it?' she called out, relieved to hear Shamus reply.

He hadn't changed much, still very muscular and with wide piercing blue eyes like his cousin Neil.

However, Shamus was shocked to see how thin, gaunt, and sickly Zara appeared. It was such a vast contrast to when they'd last worked together.

She looked over his shoulder. 'Did you come alone, Shamus?'

He nodded and stepped inside. 'There's only me in London. Davey's at St Thomas' Hospital with Neil, and the men are back in Ireland.'

She ushered him in and closed the door.

'So, start from the beginning. What's going on?'

He followed her into the office and gazed around. It was as though he'd walked into a vampire movie set, with the tall brass candlesticks and heavy curtains, along with the oversized gilt-edged paintings. The layer of dust everywhere added to the ambience. 'Er… I think you need to get a cleaner in.'

She smiled. 'Or hire it out for Halloween, perhaps?'

Shamus nervously chuckled, yet he still felt spooked. Then his eyes fell to her scarred wrist. Eerie thoughts whirled through his head all at once. The story of her having her hand cut off and then being kept a prisoner down in the basement of this creepy mansion plagued his mind.

That was until she said, 'Right, as I said, start from the beginning. Ignore the décor. Get your mind back on the issues at hand.'

Shamus felt his face flush and wondered if she was telepathic. Her frail state belied who she really was, and Shamus wasn't deluded by any means. Behind those hypnotic eyes was the Iron Lady of Gangland Britain. Even her voice had an edge that commanded attention.

'In the last six months, the cocaine leaving the restaurants has dropped by fifty per cent. The Colombians have upped their price because we aren't selling enough. The city slickers are still buying it, but the scallies who make up fifty per cent of the business have backed off. Apparently, they're into a new drug. It's cheaper and gives them a better hit.'

Zara listened, paying careful attention to every word that left Shamus's mouth. 'So, this new drug. Why don't we find our own supplier?'

Shamus sat back on his chair and slowly shook his head. 'I don't know about you, Zara, but there are some things we just don't get involved in. Like heroin for instance. And this new drug is worse. It's so addictive and although the hit apparently is euphoric, it also sends the kiddies mental.'

'Kiddies!' she gasped.

He gave her a stern nod. 'Yeah, it's cheap, really cheap, and the teenagers are buying it with their pocket money. Once they're hooked, they're fecked.'

She swallowed hard and sighed. 'So, if this drug is being sold and obviously the supplier is making a mint, why are they threatening my restaurants?'

Shamus clasped his hands together and bit his lip. 'I don't think it's about the drugs. I believe it's a takeover. It's just odd that one minute we had everything running smoothly, and then the next, it was as if ants were running all over everything.'

Zara frowned. 'Ants?'

'Yeah, yer know, how they all descend and take away bit

by bit whatever's on offer, but you just don't see them unless there's a mass. It's similar to that.'

'Give me examples.'

'We've had an issue with our gun imports. Since Willie, Lou, and Staffie got banged up, the gun trade has been reduced to nothing. But Staffie was kind enough to give us their arms contact so that we could carry on with the business.'

Zara nodded for him to continue.

'Well, currently, our supplier has gone quiet. We've no way of contacting him as the phone lines are dead. And I've got an update on what I told you yesterday. Now, three more of your restaurants are vacant. They fecking literally shut down overnight. No fecker knows where the managers went. I walked into Satiro's place and it was abandoned. The tables were laid, the kitchen was clean, and even the food was prepped, ready for customers, and yet there was no one in sight. And Nico and his sons left, with no warning as well. They just upped and went. Even that moody bugger Gino has gone. Luckily, the restaurants were locked with a closed sign on the door, or you wouldn't have a business standing. The looters would have been in.'

'Okay, right, so they haven't destroyed the business. They, whoever they are, have just run my dealers out of town. That's not a problem I'm concerned about for now. However, what I am livid over is that they have hurt Neil, and that I won't take lightly, so I want—'

Shamus raised his hand. 'Wait, that's not all, Zara. Raymondo gave away all the codes to the arcades. Every one of them was robbed in one night. They smashed the feck out of the machines, took all the money, and no one, and I mean no one, has a fecking clue who's behind it, except we know it's some black guys.'

'You what? Raymondo? Why did he do that?'

Shamus lowered his head. ''Cos one of the fecking bastards held a fecking knife to his baby's throat. Some cunt dragged his baby from her pram and held a fecking six-inch blade to her neck.'

'Jesus wept,' shrieked Zara, her eyes on stalks. 'Scumbags, fucking scumbags.' She could feel her anger rising, and her need for answers overruled her patience. 'What else, Shamus?'

'We've had trouble back in Ireland too. It seems more than a coincidence, but that's just my opinion. We have a set-up, counterfeits, yer know. Well, the two sites got burned down. Our pub, when I say our pub, I mean our meeting ground – Uncle Davey's office, as he calls it – that too was burned down. So, in short, we've been attacked on all sides. Yet this gang or gangs or whoever the feck they are, are going in really heavy, and they are recklessly disrespectful. Jesus Christ, who the feck rips a baby from her pram, eh?' He rubbed his stubbly chin.

Zara was taking it all in, her mind processing the ramifications of the reckless takeover. 'And you seriously have no fucking clue who's behind it?'

Shamus shook his head. 'Only that they're black, maybe Yardies. Yet, rough as feck they may be, I don't think they've the brain power to run a racket like yours. Sorry, I mean ours. Someone else is backing them, and for the life of us, we don't know who. We thought since Mikey's out of prison, he could do some digging. He still knows anyone who's anyone. Surely he would have a clue?'

Zara inhaled a deep lungful of air. 'No, leave Mike out of it. He's got his own business to deal with. I'm gonna sort this.'

Shamus raised his eyebrow as he looked over at the tiny woman. What the hell could she do, really? He didn't argue but nodded. 'I've got to get back to the hospital. Davey will need a break. He's been up all night.'

Zara was staring off into space. Then she jumped out of her thoughts. 'Shall I come?'

The offer was kind, but Shamus knew it would only bring further worry. Davey and Neil hadn't seen the state of Zara. It would just add to their concerns.

CHAPTER SIX

Mike slowly opened his eyes and blinked furiously at the light. His head was pounding as if it had been clamped in a vice. Knowing if he moved his stomach, he was likely to empty its contents, he decided to stay where he was.

As he lay there staring up at the ceiling, he tried to recollect last night's events. The flowing beers had wrecked him. After twelve years with no alcohol, he'd lost track of how many pints he'd consumed. In fact, he couldn't remember what happened after about four beers. He recalled worrying about Zara and then Eric telling him she'd gone to bed, but that was about it. Slowly, he took two deep breaths and eased himself into an upright position, holding his throbbing temples. Light-headed and feeling nauseous, he knew he would have to make his way to the kitchen and swallow a couple of tablets. His mouth was like the bottom of a parrot's cage. That mental picture did him no favours and made him almost gag.

Seconds later, he jumped up and bolted to the cloakroom, where he threw up a bucket-load of London Pride. Hanging on to the bowl, he gasped for breath. 'Never again,' he said aloud.

After he washed his face and cleaned out his mouth, he returned to the lounge and almost stopped dead in his tracks.

There, lying on another sofa, was the party girl – Jennifer – barely dressed, her hair covering her face. His mind went back to the events of yesterday evening and his heart sank. Zara. Where was she? He suddenly panicked and hurried up the stairs. Once he reached the top, he swooned. The hangover was still harsh, even though he'd thrown up a year's worth of drink and food. He paused and slowly opened the bedroom door, but tension gripped his shoulders. Empty. He dashed into the bathroom: ditto. She'd gone. Every possible thought shot through his mind. Zara must have seen him here with Jennifer, half-naked on the sofa. She would then have deduced that he'd shagged the woman, especially since he'd been drunk and after the abstinence of any sex for twelve years and counting. But no way would he do that, not to Zara.

Shaking with worry and reeling from his hangover, he returned to the lounge and roughly shook Jennifer. 'Oi, wake up.'

She stirred, farted, and breathed stale breath into his face.

'Oh, Jesus, give me strength.' He shook her again. 'Listen. Get your arse up and off this fucking sofa, will ya!'

Jennifer opened her eyes, and on seeing Mike's face, she tried to pass off a sexy, seductive look, yet her false eyelashes had stuck to her cheeks, and her hair was like a net over her face. 'Morning, Mikey,' she replied, her voice croaky.

'Get up and get out!'

He wouldn't usually talk to a woman like that, but if she was the reason that his Zara wasn't in the house, then he would snatch her by the hair and physically remove her. 'Fuck me, what the hell are you doing crashed out in the lounge anyway?'

He paced the floor, running his hands through his hair in frustration.

Jennifer stood up, tugged her skirt over her hips, straightened her hair, and sighed. 'Blimey, don't I even get a cup of coffee?'

'No, ya fucking don't!' he hollered. 'Why are you even here?'

She looked Mike up and down. 'What the fuck, Mikey. You used to be fun. Eric invited me. Bloody hell, we're practically family, ya know.'

Rifling through her bag, she pulled out a packet of cigarettes and lit one up.

Mike was irritated. 'Put that fucker out. Have some respect. This is my mother's house. Now, before I raise the fucking roof, I wanna know what the fuck you're doing 'ere, and, for the record, you ain't family. You're Teddy's niece by his sister who fucked off to Manchester, so what are ya doing 'ere?'

With her hands on her hips, Jennifer was about to launch a mouthful in reply, when Gloria, wrapped in her satin dressing gown, bowled into the room. 'My flippin' head. Whose idea was it to drink a bottle of champagne? That's it. Never again.' She stopped and tilted her head to the side. Seeing her son standing there with no top on and Jennifer still in her clothes from the night before, Gloria looked suspiciously at Mike. 'Er, where's Eric?' she snapped.

Jennifer gave her a dismissive hand gesture. 'Upstairs, I guess. I dunno. I crashed down 'ere, with ol' misery guts.'

'You what!' Gloria shouted. 'Where's Zara? Mikey?'

Jennifer didn't wait to get into a row. She snatched her bag and was out of the house, leaving Gloria with a face that could strip paint. 'What the hell's going on, Mikey? Please, tell me you didn't… ?'

Mike shook his head, certain he'd not got his leg over with Jennifer. 'Not a chance. I fucking never would. Ya know that,

Mum. But how the hell did she get left alone with me? Why is she even 'ere? Now Zara's gone. For fuck's sake, Mum. If she came in and saw me and that tart, well... '

'That Jennifer came with Eric. I thought he was seeing her?'

Mike sat back heavily on the sofa, with his head in his hands. 'Zara's gone,' he repeated, bitterly.

While Gloria headed to the kitchen to make the coffee, Mike reached for his new iPhone. He stared at the screen and wondered for a moment how to use the newfangled device. After playing around, he managed to get Zara's number up and pressed the call button. He wouldn't know what to say if the reason for her leaving was because of the tart on the sofa. The call went over to voicemail, so he tried again. This time, her phone didn't even ring, it went straight to divert. He knew then she was ignoring him. In a split second, he hurled the device across the room, just missing Gloria, who was holding a tray of coffee and biscuits.

'She's not answering me. That bloody Jennifer! What the fuck was all that about? Why didn't someone get her a cab home?'

Gloria placed the tray on the coffee table and settled herself in the armchair opposite. 'I thought she was Eric's girlfriend. She was sitting with Eric when I went to bed.'

'So where's Eric now?'

Gloria sipped her coffee and winced. 'Shit, that's vile. Er, I dunno, Son. He ain't in his room. Look, don't panic about Zara. Eric may have taken her back to the house to pick up a few bits and pieces.'

'What, now? Why would Eric do that? Why wouldn't she ask me?'

Feeling nauseous herself, Gloria placed the cup of coffee down and tried to nibble on a biscuit. 'Because, Mikey, you were probably out for the count. Blimey, you weren't half knocking 'em back, dancing and singing. Still, did you have a good time?'

'Mum! Listen! Zara's not answering her phone, and now she's switched the bleedin' thing off.'

'Stop worrying. Zara ain't bloody buggered off for good. You're getting paranoid. Now, drink your coffee and clear your mind.'

Mikey knew his mother was talking sense, and yet he regretted last night. So much so, he felt an empty feeling in the pit of his stomach. He should have left the party early and spent the first night at home in bed with Zara, making up for lost time. And there was so much they hadn't talked about: planning their wedding, for example, or even going over the past and preparing for the future.

He could kick himself right now; all this time he'd waited for his girl, and now he'd royally fucked up – on the first bloody night as well. His anger then turned to Zara. How stupid was she? She should've known he wouldn't be interested in anyone else. Acting like a kid running off, she should've fronted him out, like any grown woman would have.

Just as he was about to retrieve his phone and call his brother, Eric appeared – as if from nowhere – looking like he'd just stepped out of a fashion magazine. Fresh, tidy, and smart. Mr Cool. Mike had to blink. For a moment, he didn't even recognize him. 'Eric, where's Zara?'

Mike clocked the cocky smirk but wondered if he was seeing things. 'Eric?'

As if he was about to make an important announcement, Eric took a deep breath, fiddled with his cufflinks, and sighed. He'd been waiting for this moment for so long, it had nearly killed him. Big, powerful Mike. The man himself. Self-assured and always having his own way whenever *he* wanted it. *Well, sod you, big brother.*

'Well, now you're sober, I need to tell you that last night Neil got stabbed and I do believe Zara has gone to have a meeting with the Lanigans this morning.' Eric was a little frustrated himself, finding Zara had already left when he'd woken early this morning to get himself ready to escort her.

'What the fuck! Why didn't you tell me before?'

Again, Eric smirked; it was a new feature that Mike hadn't seen before. 'Like I said, Mikey. You were drunk, and so I thought it best to talk to you this morning.'

For a moment, Mike felt entirely out of control. Eric should have woken him.

'Is Neil dead, then?'

Eric shook his head. 'No, I called the hospital this morning. He's out of the woods but it was touch and go.'

'Well, thank Gawd for that!' piped up Gloria.

'Where's she meeting the Lanigans?' asked Mike.

Eric shrugged his shoulders. 'I don't know. I thought she would've told you. I guess she decided to go it alone.'

Mike couldn't work out whether Eric's tone was sarcastic or genuine; either way, his brother was different. Having been apart for so long, he now wondered if he actually knew his brother at all. 'So, where've you been?'

'Just making a few calls and sorting out a little bit o' business.'

Mike stood up and glared, not liking the sound of it. 'What business?'

'A bit o' knocked-off gear.'

Looking Eric over, and noticing the smart suit, he cast a questioning look. 'What, dressed like a fucking nightclub owner?'

'Does it matter? The fucking world didn't stand still while you were away, ya know. I was still earning a crust. What, d'ya think I was sitting twiddling me thumbs and waiting for you to tell me what to do?'

'Obviously fucking not! Ya never even wrote me a poxy letter!' bellowed Mike.

Gloria watched the tension between her two sons mounting and decided to nip it in the bud. 'Lads, listen. Our Ricky will be up in a minute. I don't want any bickering. Besides, it's not like you two. I thought you were both in the same firm?' She shot Eric a glare. And then she looked back at her eldest boy. Maybe he hadn't got over Eric abandoning him when he went to prison after all. She couldn't really blame Mike; she'd held it against Eric herself for fucking off to Spain when Mike needed him the most.

'Sorry, Eric. Listen, mate, I'm still edgy. Prison does that to ya.'

Eric nodded in acknowledgement, but he didn't offer his own apology. As far as Mike was concerned, it was like old times except his brother seemed to have gained an attitude. All the bollocks on the prison visit from Eric, pleading that he was really sorry and begging forgiveness, it all seemed so fake. Mike wondered if his brother had been taking acting lessons.

Storming from the room, Mike headed for the bedroom.

After a quick shower and a strong coffee to wake him up, he hoped that he would see things in a clearer light. Staying at his parents for the night had been a wrong move. He should have gone home with Zara and Ricky and eased back into life. *Damn it!* Well, if she wanted to be stubborn, he would trump her in that department.

The hot water jets hit his head like a thousand sharp needles, but they instantly relaxed his muscles and helped to soothe his worrying mind. First up, he needed to be clear-headed, ditch his own stubbornness, and track down his girl – in the hope she hadn't jumped to any wild conclusions. 'Shit!' he said aloud. He should've been more sensitive. After all, Zara was not herself just yet; she was quiet and seemed a little lost among the party guests. He should've known it would have been all too much for her.

Once he'd got dressed and hurried back to the lounge, he retrieved his phone; luckily, it was still intact. Zara's phone was still switched off. All he could do was send her a voicemail message. Having done that, he put his phone in his pocket. Now impatience and agitation set in again as he screamed to no one, 'For fuck's sake, what's she doing?'

Gloria returned again with a tray of fresh coffee and some more McVitie's digestive biscuits. 'Mikey, stop fretting. She'll be back. She's probably gone to meet the Lanigans or even headed up to the hospital. That poor lad. His father must have been worried to death.'

Mike listened as his mother rambled on, and then he frowned. 'I'm gonna let her get on with it, the silly woman. She should've known me better. Where's Eric gone now?'

'Son, your brother is a law unto himself. He tells us nothing.'

'What?' Mike sensed the sadness in her tone. 'But we've no secrets. We never have had.'

Gloria took her coffee and sat back down, crossed her legs, and sighed. 'Mikey, he ain't like you. He never has been. The truth is, when you ran the firm, he followed you around, but, left to his own devices, he's a bit of a dark horse; sort of detached, if ya know what I mean.'

'Devious?'

Gloria raised her brows. 'Oh, I wouldn't go that far, but let's just say he's not as open as you. The truth be known, you two were so close in age, we probably treated you as if you were one person. You were the voice for both of you. Eric seemed to stand by your side, you did the talking, and he just nodded in agreement. You led the firm, and with your ideas, you grew the business, and you were always the one who was on the front line. Even as a little lad, you would place Eric behind you, protecting him, in a way. You might not have realized it, but you did.' She stared off into space as if reliving a moment. 'You were always an open lad. Whether we liked what you did or said, or not, you never hid anything. You've always been a straight-up, no-holds-barred person and so honest.'

Mike listened and knew somewhere in his mother's words there was a 'but'. 'Mum, tell me, what did Eric do while I was away?'

She stared up at her son and chewed her lip. 'Mikey, I don't have a favourite. I love you both the same. But, I have to say, when Eric disappeared to Spain or wherever, I disliked him. I couldn't get my head around the fact that he left you inside to rot. Your father felt the same. He was so disappointed with Eric. You know, it made him sick. But the fact of the matter is, we've still no idea what his life is about, even though he's been back a while, and we've lost interest in his business affairs anyway.'

Turning the phone over in his hand, he looked at his mother, and a cold expression clouded him. 'Well, Eric seems to be doing okay for himself, so perhaps it's best that he stays away from the firm. I mean, when he did come to visit me, he almost pleaded to be back in with us. I dunno, that was a month ago. Perhaps he's changed his mind.'

Gloria slowly nodded, in acknowledgement. 'Mikey, the lads have been so good, they've well and truly had your back. My advice is to stick with them, babe.'

It seemed so natural to talk to his mother about issues he would otherwise have discussed with his father.

'I love you, Mum. I'm sorry for all the pain I've put you through. I just want you to know, I appreciate everything.'

Gloria tilted her head to the side, surprised at her son's remark. He wasn't the type to be soppy, and yet his kind heart made him the man he was.

Unlike Eric.

***

As Shamus left, he looked back at the imposing grand house and shuddered. He hadn't wanted to look at Zara's wrist, yet his eyes had been drawn, and a sick feeling coiled around him. It wasn't because what he'd seen was gruesome but for the fact that he'd been sitting with her in the house that had actually been her prison while she nursed a terrible wound.

His mind was electric as he walked to his car. Never in his

life had he met a woman more determined. His uncle was right when he'd told him not to be fooled by her dainty looks: she was smart and dangerous. He realized that for himself because there was no way he would sit in a house that would project so many horrific memories and act like it was nothing. With her obvious disability, frail and almost pitiful, she still managed to draw him in, hanging on her every word. It was surreal, and he couldn't get her off his mind.

***

Still racked with so many emotions, Zara tried to put her thoughts into perspective; maybe she'd got Mike wrong. The womanly thing to do would be to front him out over it, and if his proposal was a mistake, then she would walk away. She had a business to run, and first things first, she needed to get this place, which was full of dust and memories, cleaned up. As much as the red drapes reminded her of her father, they definitely needed to be replaced. The paintwork required a good touch-up, and the overgrown garden called for a gardener. As she wandered from room to room, wondering what her brother had sold or changed, she became aware of how much life had been extinguished from the place. Since her father's death, she concluded that he'd been the heart of the building and now it had simply stopped beating. Determined to make this her home once more, she would employ a team of cleaners, gardeners, and designers, and install a new security system. She returned to her father's office and smiled. 'Izzy, I miss you, but watch me. I will be the woman you wanted me to be.' She often referred to her father as Izzy, but only because he'd wanted it that way. Yet it had never detracted from the fact that he'd been a doting father.

The sudden banging at the door pulled her from her thoughts. She hurried to the window to see if she recognized the car. It was Eric. She sighed; she'd so hoped for Mike to be standing there.

As soon as she opened the door, the sweet smell of aftershave hit her; it was the same as Mike's. She was surprised to see Eric dressed immaculately, suited and booted, with his face glowing. Once he smiled, she noticed how white his teeth were, and his eyes, much like Mike's, edged in thick black lashes, slowly blinked and almost lured her in.

'I came because I was worried. Are you okay, babe?'

Zara was still taking in the sight. Eric was only ten months younger than Mike, yet today he looked ten years younger. The vision of her fiancé popped back into her head, sprawled across that sofa, baring his chest, and that awful Jennifer, with her arse on show. 'Sorry, Eric. Come in.'

As he followed her into the study, he observed the state of the place. The last time he'd been actually inside this monstrosity of a house was the evening he went with his father to rescue her. Of course, so much was happening then that he hadn't noticed the dated décor.

'Does Mike know where I am?' She got straight to the point.

'Yes, I said you had a meeting. Oh, sorry, I hope you don't mind?'

Zara took her seat and gave a tired, resigned look. 'No, of course not.' But she felt gutted all the same.

'Did you have your meeting?' he asked, in an even tone, not wanting her to think he was prying into her affairs.

She nodded. 'Yeah, it seems that someone has a grudge. My arcades, my restaurants, they're all being targeted, and so far, no one knows who the culprits are.'

'Let the Lanigans handle it. You need to get well. Look at you, babe. I bet you haven't even eaten this morning, have ya?'

'I'm fine, Eric.'

He stood up and held out his hand. 'Come on, Zara, I'm taking you out for breakfast, and I won't take no for an answer.'

She was about to take his hand but realized she had her bag on the floor. Awkwardly, she pulled away and reached for the handle. Instead of allowing her to feel self-conscious, he took the bag and slid his arm around her shoulders. 'Right. Full English or salmon and poached eggs? I know the perfect place to eat.'

His upbeat tone lightened Zara's mood. She was hungry and feeling a tad light-headed.

Helping her into the car, she gritted her teeth. 'This is so bloody frustrating, you know. I hate not being able to drive!'

Eric patted her shoulder and hurried to the driver's seat. 'There's nothing to stop you driving,' he replied, once he'd pulled away.

'Er, in case you've forgotten, I only have one hand.'

Eric quipped, 'Yep, babe, you do. And two legs and a set of teeth.'

'But I can't grip the wheel with my gnashers.' She chuckled for the first time.

'There are these gadgets that you add to your own car, to make it easier.'

Surprised by Eric's remark, she asked, 'How do you know that?'

He patted her knee and grinned. 'Because I went and checked that out at the garage. I guessed you'd want to be in a position whereby your… Well, what I'm trying to say is that you obviously don't want to be restricted. Ya know what I mean. So, if you're looking to get a new car, my mate can sort all that out for you. I'll give him the heads-up when you're ready.'

Zara looked at his side profile and smiled. He really was looking out for her best interests and so maybe the decision to leave Gloria's had been a bit hasty; they were such a kind and caring family.

'Thanks, Eric. That's really good of you. Can I ask you something?'

Eric smiled. 'Anything. Fire away.'

'I saw Mike in the lounge and that Jennifer was there. Er… ' She struggled for the words to ask if he thought Mike was shagging the tart.

'Yeah, I know… ' He sighed heavily. 'She's a bit of a slapper at times. She's a good girl but sex-mad, I think.'

He didn't need to say any more. Her heart sank to the pit of her stomach. She fought to stop the tears in her eyes welling up again. 'Do you think they… ?'

'What? Listen, Zara. Mike loves you, you're his fiancée, his real bird, but Mike is a man that spent twelve years inside.'

'So, what you're saying is he would take it if it was handed to him on a plate then?'

'No, oh, I dunno. But you remember one thing. Mike loves you, and so if he did what you were just asking, he would've done it without any feelings. So, just you rest that niggling doubt of yours, and if I were you, I'd just leave it. Don't push him away, Zara. Jackie had a real jealous streak, and it ruined their relationship. He hated her in the end… Er, not that I'm suggesting you're anything like her, of course.'

Zara was now staring out of the side window, Eric's words preying on her emotions and especially her own self-worth as a woman. She was so hurt that her whole body trembled, and she found herself too choked up to speak.

Just as they pulled up in Petts Wood Square, opposite the Daylight Inn, Zara wiped her eyes and took a deep breath. *What the hell was she doing here?* But it would look churlish to tell him to turn around and take her home. It was considerate of Eric to offer her some kindness, but sooner rather than later, she would have to get a grip and not let her feelings get in the way of her life. Forever a gentleman, Eric opened the passenger door and stepped aside as she clambered out.

'Thanks, Eric,' she said in a deflated tone.

'Well, hello,' came a deep voice from behind them.

Eric almost froze to the spot. Zara turned to see who owned that gravel voice. He was a well-built man, dressed in a dark suit with black, brooding eyes. He had to be at least the same size as Eric, and he was big.

Eric looked pale, and his confident expression vanished in a split second.

'Hi, mate. All right?' He tried to sound firm, but Zara noticed he seemed on edge.

'Yeah, good as gold. So, what are you doing in this neck of the woods?'

Zara raised her brow. That was an odd question, as Eric lived in Kent and this was his manor.

'Just having a bit of breakfast. Yaself?'

The dark-eyed man gave him a cocky grin and then flicked

his eyes to Zara. 'I'm meeting someone special. So, who's this lovely lady?'

Zara sensed the undertone in the man's voice, and so she didn't even attempt to introduce herself. Eric jumped in before she could, anyway. 'This is a friend of mine, a school friend. Anyway, nice to see ya.'

Before the man had a chance to say another word, Eric ushered Zara away.

Once they were seated in the bistro, Eric stared out of the window, and as Zara followed his eyeline, she noticed the dark-eyed man glance back, laugh, and shake his head.

'Who the hell was that, Eric?'

With the blood now drained from his face, Eric mumbled under his breath, 'No one.'

Burying his head in the menu, Zara could only imagine he was gathering his thoughts because whoever that man was, it had Eric shitting hot bricks. She looked back out of the window to see him talking to a young woman with jet-black dyed hair and an oversized rucksack on her shoulder. She certainly looked too young to be a girlfriend. He was probably a pimp and Eric may have been a regular customer. Of course, Eric would have been mortified if the man had mentioned that.

She looked at the menu, and straightaway, she asked for a sweet tea and poached eggs on toast. She figured that way she could ease Eric's embarrassment, as he could go up to the counter and not have to face her. He did exactly that.

***

Kendall was thrilled when she saw her father. He had stuck to his word and met her outside the pub. She wouldn't have been surprised, though, if he'd found some excuse to call the arrangement off. He was certainly a difficult man to predict.

'I wondered if you were saying I could have the flat, just to shut me up?'

'Yeah, you got that right, but I said you can have it, so 'ere ya go. These are the keys. That one' – he pointed to the larger key – 'lets you through the downstairs door, and the other key opens your own front door.'

Taking the small bunch, she looked up at him and smiled. 'Are you gonna show me around, then?'

'Nope, I ain't got time,' he said coldly. 'You wanted the flat, it's all yours, but I bet within a week you'll be back home with Mummy, wanting your clothes washed and your dinners cooked.' Without a hug or a goodbye, he walked away.

'Dad, wait up! Don't you want to spend any time with me, not even have a cup of tea in my new pad?'

With a mocking grin, he turned briefly, shaking his head. 'Nope. I've got a shitload to do, so you check out the place.' He laughed. 'Be lucky, girl.'

As he strode away, Kendall felt a sudden need for attention. She hated feeling so dismissed by her father.

'I know who Mother's puppetmaster is!'

Stopping dead in his tracks, he paused and spun round and walked back to her. 'You what?' He looked annoyed, and for a moment, Kendall wished she'd just let him continue on. 'It's Alastair. But I think the tables are turning because she told him that Uncle Conrad and Grandad were going to help her to win the election.'

With eyes like saucers, he glared. 'Why the fuck are you telling me this?'

'Er... I dunno, really. It's just you said she was a puppet, and I kinda wondered what you meant. Well, listening to those two arguing, I guessed he must be pulling her strings.'

'Well, if you like listening and spreading shit, do yaself a favour and get a job in that hairdressers.' He pointed to the shop below her flat. 'You can gossip all day and get fucking paid for it. Now then, I don't wanna hear no more about ya mother, Alastair, or that grandfather of yours. Got it?'

Kendall as per usual was like a dog with a bone when she had a mind to be. 'What is it with you and them, huh? 'Cos it seems that your hatred goes deeper than Mother cheating on you.'

With his face flushed an angry red, he spat, 'I never said I hate any of them. I just don't want to fucking talk about them, and you, Kendall, need to stop trying to dig for information, 'cos I can tell you categorically there is none, and your shit-stirring will do you no fucking favours. Now, grow up. Ya got ya flat, so now learn to be a woman instead of a silly kid. Christ, I don't need this shit!' With that, he marched away, running his hands through his hair as if he was in pain.

Kendall decided to leave it there. She would show him, her mother, and anyone else who was interested, that she could live on her own and make something of herself, instead of being the MP's daughter. In fact, she wanted to live the opposite of her mother's way of life. *Fuck the rules, fuck the law, and fuck the lot of them*, she thought.

She waited until her father was out of sight and then made her way to the back of the shops. Apart from the large industrial bins, the back entrance was pretty tidy. Sliding the key into the main door, her heart beat fast in anticipation. This was it: this was her new life. She only hoped the flat was decent and presentable. The stairwell to her own dwelling was clean, so everything was looking very promising. So far, so good. Then she reached the top of the stairs and looked down at the number on the key; it was thirty-four. To the left was thirty-two and to her right was her new home – number thirty-four. The lock was stiff at first, and she had to jiggle the key about a bit until she felt it unlock.

Holding her breath, she pushed the door open. To her surprise, the small hallway was like new. It was fitted with an unstained beige carpet and unblemished cream walls. She hurried through, straight into the sitting room. It wasn't particularly big, but it was large enough. A basic black leather sofa, a small flame-effect electric fire, a dated TV, and a small cabinet were the total contents of the room. The net curtains were plain but sufficient – not that anyone could see in unless they had a ladder. Next, she ventured into the kitchen, which consisted of just a plain, cheap white set of drawer cabinets, with an oven and a fridge. The bedroom was much the same in that it contained the bare essentials: a double bed, a cabinet, and a wardrobe.

She smiled to herself; with a few personal belongings, she would feel right at home. She sat down on the sofa and gazed at every inch of the room. It was perfect.

***

Zara pushed her food around the plate. 'Are you busy today, Eric?'

The colour had returned to his cheeks. 'I told you, babe. I'm here if you need me.'

'Could you take me to the hospital? I want to see Neil.'

Eric placed his knife and fork down. 'Yeah, no worries, but wasn't he just a business associate, really? I mean, if you're their boss… '

Zara shot Eric a look that he'd never seen before.

'I told you, Eric, the Lanigans are like family to me.'

'Are you sure they weren't just muscling in on your business, taking it over piece by piece, while you were… well, ya know, missing?'

At that moment, Zara realized that Eric actually knew very little about her now. It stood to reason: she'd been away in Ireland for five years secretly running the businesses with the Lanigans, and then she was kidnapped by the Segals and held captive for another five. And in all that time, Mike was in prison himself, without so much as a letter from Eric.

'I've no idea why you would think that, Eric, but you couldn't be further from the truth.'

Eric felt as though he'd been well and truly put in his place. He'd thought that placing doubt in her mind may work when it came to matters of the heart, but he now realized that it wouldn't when it came to her business affairs. He made a mental note not to underestimate her.

'Oh, and while we're on the subject of the Lanigans, please do tell me why you take issue with them because you have now made two snide comments.'

Eric stiffened and suddenly felt uncomfortable with the way in which Zara remained poker-faced, awaiting an answer. 'No, I've no problem with them, it's just you're gonna be a Regan soon, ya know, part of the family, and, well, I like to have a good understanding of the men behind the firm that we'll be getting into bed—'

Without allowing Eric to finish, Zara spat, 'Since when did me marrying Mike have anything to do with my business affairs?'

He sensed he'd pushed the wrong buttons and realized that once again he'd let his mouth run away with him. As much as he tried to be like Mike, he knew that he couldn't match the man's cunning tongue. 'Sorry, Zara. I'm not trying to interfere, I'm simply looking out for you.'

Zara's brow felt heavy. She wiped her mouth with the napkin and stood to leave. 'Thanks for breakfast. I'll see you later.'

Dumbfounded, Eric stared as Zara left the restaurant. *Fuck, what just happened?*

Slapping a fifty-pound note on the table, he hurried after her. 'Hey, Zara!' He grabbed her arm to turn her to face him, only to feel a sharp tug as she pulled it away.

'If you don't mind, I would prefer to be alone. I think I've made a mistake. You may have been the man who found me, but I don't really know you – or Mike for that matter.' She was about to march off, but he grabbed her again.

Seeing the angry look on her face, Eric released his grip on her arm. 'Sorry, babe. You have to believe me. I never meant to upset you. The Lanigans probably are decent and kosher. I'm worried for ya, that's all. You're not 100 per cent yourself, so I guess I felt the need somehow to look out for ya.'

She stared into his face, with not even a hint of a smile. 'I'm fine, really, and more than capable of jumping on a train. So, if you would excuse me.'

Eric knew he was losing the battle. 'Zara, please. Mike would kill me if he knew I'd let you get on a train when I have a perfectly good car sitting there.'

'Right now, I couldn't care what Mike thinks. He, like you, obviously doesn't know me very well. I ain't the type of woman who sits back and takes shit, and if he thinks because he's been banged up for twelve years that that gives him the right to fuck any young bit of skirt when he's supposed to be engaged to me, then he and you are very much fucking mistaken.'

Gotcha! Eric knew then his little plan had worked; now all he had to do was to reel her in for himself. 'All right, I'm sorry. I guess you're right, but you can't blame me for getting you wrong, eh? Look at you. A stunning woman who's been through the wringer and comes out the other end – most women would have rolled over and died. And there you are, as strong as an ox, and me, the dickhead, pandering to you. Listen, I'll drive you to the hospital, and if you want me to wait, I will, or I'll leave you to get a cab back.' He held his hands up as a sign of defeat.

Zara looked him up and down and wondered if he was being genuine or was patronizing her again. A wave of tiredness made her mind up for her. She nodded. 'Okay, then.'

The drive was spent in silence as Zara contemplated what Eric had been telling her about Mike. He hadn't denied Mike had slept with that tart; surely, he would have told her straightaway, wouldn't he? Her rational thought of confronting Mike over the issue disappeared. The hurt, if she allowed it, would consume her. Then a niggling thought popped into her head; it was a notion that she didn't want to believe, but was Eric deliberately trying to sabotage her relationship with Mike, or did Eric have genuine feelings for her? Maybe that kiss was just a momentary weakness. She shuddered at the thought that she'd led Eric on and now felt guilty for being so disloyal to Mike. She had to push the troubling thoughts aside and get her mind back on track, starting with who the fuck stabbed Neil and who had the audacity to ruin her businesses.

Eric parked in the underground car park at St Thomas' Hospital and opened the door once more for Zara to get out. She thanked him and was about to head inside the building when he stopped her.

'Hey, Zara. Listen. Two heads are better than one. I'll come with you if Neil can share as many details as he can remember. Maybe I can do some digging?'

Zara shook her head in annoyance. 'This is hardly the place, is it? I'm only visiting because I care about him. This isn't a boardroom set-up, you know.'

Eric stopped dead; her cold, flat words were now pissing him off. 'Okay, Zara. I'll wait in the car.'

Without bothering to reply, she marched ahead, wondering if she'd been too sharp for no real reason other than his affections for her.

After asking at reception for the Lambeth Wing, she followed the route and stepped inside the lift. As she looked at the map on the wall, a heavily built round-faced doctor, holding a file under his arm, joined her and asked if she needed the prosthetics department. For a moment, she was stunned.

'Pardon?' she said politely.

He looked at her wrist. 'Prosthetics?'

'Oh no. Sorry, I'm visiting a friend.'

'Oh, I'm very sorry, I thought… Well, look, I can see you don't wear a prosthetic. Is there any reason?'

'Well, no, I mean, can I… er… is it possible to have… ?' She held up her arm and instantly saw the shock on the doctor's face.

He stared for a moment and then gave her a sympathetic smile. 'I'm Doctor Hussain. I work on the fourth floor. Come and see me. I'm sure I can help you.'

He took another look at her scars. 'Please do come. I really think I can make a difference.'

'Thank you. I will do.'

With that, he exited the lift, leaving Zara with ideas of a prosthetic hand. Maybe that wouldn't be so bad.

***

Davey Lanigan looked exhausted, old, and haggard. Zara almost gasped when she saw him slumped in the chair half-asleep. The last time she'd seen him, he was a picture of health with a mop of black hair. Now he was grey and half the size. Startled by a presence in the room, he nevertheless smiled in relief when he saw who the visitor was. He rose from his chair. 'Zara!' his voice cracked.

Unexpectedly, Zara fell into his arms and hugged him tightly. Who would have thought it? Ten years ago, she'd nearly killed him by bludgeoning him with a rock. Yet she very quickly learned that he was the most faithful and trustworthy man she'd ever met. For five years, their businesses thrived, and they'd split the profits with not even a squabble. Even after she'd gone missing for all that time, he'd still put her share of the profits in one of her offshore accounts.

So much was said in that embrace, though none of it spoken.

As he held her away to get a proper look, she smiled and then her expression changed as she peered over at Neil lying in the bed, wired up to monitors. Surprisingly, Neil looked good, although he was very pale. He always was a handsome man; a few streaks of grey were apparent in places, showing his age, yet his body was still ripped with muscles.

'How is he?' she uttered through tears.

'He's okay. He gave us a fright, but the doctor reckons he'll make a full recovery. And you, Zara? How are you faring?'

She smiled and then chuckled. 'Well, I guess a lot better than you. Jesus, Davey, you look washed out. Why don't you book a room in a hotel? Get some sleep. I'll stay with Neil.'

He shook his head. 'I'm fine. Anyway, Tania's on her way. She's in a right state.'

Zara's memory of Tania, Davey's wife, was of a fiery redhead who probably had more mouth and trousers than any woman on the planet. 'Well, when we find the cunts who did this to Neil, we could always let her loose to do what she does best – vent her spleen.'

Davey laughed for the first time since he'd received the news that his son had been stabbed. 'Jesus, she is nuts, that woman. Even to this day, I still sleep with one eye open.'

That brief moment of humour was quickly brought to a halt as they both looked over at Neil's prone state. Zara pulled up another chair and sat opposite Davey. 'Maybe this isn't the right time to broach the subject, but I'll not rest until I have the bastards strung up. Shamus tells me that my arcades and my restaurants have been raped. Tell me, Antonio's? Is that still okay?'

Davey shrugged his shoulders. 'Up until last night it was, but who knows? All my men are back in Ireland now. Mind you, Zara, I've asked for six of them to come over to London. I want the filthy bastards caught.'

Zara nodded in acknowledgement. 'Can you call Antonio and tell him to close the restaurant and leave a sign that says due to staff sickness the restaurant will only be open on this coming Saturday? I don't understand why they are targeting our businesses. But one thing's for sure. We need to be a step ahead of the game. Let's keep this to ourselves. This firm will no doubt rear their ugly heads, and I, at least, will fucking blow the cunts away.'

Davey didn't argue; he pulled out his phone and spoke to Antonio to make the arrangements. Antonio didn't question him; he'd heard about the other restaurants and was a nervous wreck. In fact, he'd already booked flights back to Italy when he'd been made aware of the trouble.

Zara leaned forward and gently kissed Neil's forehead. As she sat back down, his eyes slowly blinked and then opened. Like his father's, Neil's eyes were a piercing blue. He blinked again, and as he focused, a generous smile spread across his face.

'Hello, handsome. How are ya doing?' She spoke with a gentle calmness to her voice, which masked her inner concern for him.

Still very weak, he nodded. He held her gaze, and then, as if he'd just remembered something, he frowned and looked at her wrist. His eyes were suddenly wide and alert. He didn't have to say anything: the expression of empathy was embedded on his face.

'Hey, it's okay, I'm still me. Well, older, and less handy, if you'll pardon the pun.' She laughed, to lighten the mood. 'I'm gonna get the bastards, Neil. I'm gonna rip their fucking hearts out.'

Neil looked at his father, who nodded in agreement.

Slowly, but surely, Neil came around enough to sit up and speak; they'd so much to catch up on that the time flew by.

***

Having waited patiently for an hour, Eric was getting frustrated. But he couldn't show his annoyance, not after putting his foot in it. Climbing out of the car, he straightened his suit and made his way to the reception area, where he was directed to the Lambeth Wing. Zara wouldn't mind if he made an appearance, surely? After all, he surmised, the Regans weren't enemies of the Lanigans. Confident that he would be welcomed, he walked towards the private room along from the ward.

As soon as he stood in the doorway, he saw Zara sitting on Neil's bed and kissing the man's cheek. The sight of her embracing Neil turned his stomach and fixed him to the spot. He continued to watch as she stood up and hugged who he could only assume was Davey. As much as Mike and himself had done business with the Lanigan family many moons ago, only Mike had met the man while serving time.

As Zara spotted him there, she instantly uncurled her arms from Davey and stared in Eric's direction. Davey turned to see the tall and smartly dressed man hovering.

Entering the room, Eric stuck out his hand to shake Davey's. 'Hi, I'm Eric Regan, Mike's brother.' It rankled, him saying

'Mike's brother'. He always felt second best. And it really made his blood boil that not only was he always seen as inferior to him, but everyone would sit up and take notice if he mentioned Mike's name.

Davey smiled and responded to the gesture. 'Good to meet you, and it gives me the chance to thank you personally for saving our Zara.'

Eric forced a smile. The words 'our Zara' had so many connotations. Did he mean her as a business partner or family? Either way, it established their bond, and it pissed Eric off.

He looked over at Zara, who didn't appear best pleased with his presence. 'Er, I thought it would be rude of me not to pop my head in and say hello.'

Davey patted Eric's arm. 'Well, it's nice to meet you. Zara was just saying goodbye, so your timing was perfect.'

Was Davey being sarcastic or genuine? It was hard to tell, thought Eric.

'Eric, I'll meet you by the car. Give me ten minutes. I've just remembered I need to talk about some business.'

'I can wait.' He smiled at Davey, but the older man's body language was a clear indication that he wasn't wanted. He'd been somewhat fooled by his elderly appearance, thinking that he could muscle his way in.

'Sorry, Eric, I think it's best you leave us now. Our business is private. I hope you understand,' responded Davey.

The cold, frank words hit Eric like a knife to the throat; straightaway, he thought about Mike and gritted his teeth. Davey Lanigan wouldn't have said that to *him*. With another fake smile, Eric nodded and walked away, fuming.

'I get the impression, Zara, you haven't yet joined forces with the Regans?'

She gave a heavy sigh. 'To be perfectly honest, I'm not sure what the best way forward is. Still, the one thing I do have is my business.' She smiled. 'With you, that's a constant and dead cert in my life, right now. As for the future with Mike, I'm not so sure. Hey-ho, life's a bitch, but I intend on being the biggest of them all.'

Davey hugged her again. 'You're never a bitch. Maybe you're one hard cow, yeah, but bitch – not a chance.'

Just as Zara was about to reply, a strident Irish voice could be heard down the corridor. 'Stick your fecking visiting hours up yer arse. I've travelled all fecking day to see my son, and for your fecking information, I'm paying two thousand pounds a day, so don't you tell me, Miss Hoity-Fecking-Toity, that I can't see my son!'

Davey laughed. 'Now, that there *is* a bitch.'

Zara laughed as she watched the short red-haired woman stomping along the corridor with the nurse, looking very flushed, hot on her heels. As soon as Tania reached her son's room, her angry expression melted. She hugged Zara. 'I fecking knew you weren't dead. It would take more than a few Jewish amateurs to take you out!' Her voice and manner of speaking were so hard and blunt that Zara had to laugh. Tania was always the same – swearing, hooting, and hollering – but underneath all that fierceness, she was a woman of reason and compassion.

As soon as she was in the room, she flung her arms around Neil. All Zara could hear was, 'Mum, you're squashing me.'

Davey turned to her, and in a mild manner, he whispered, 'We need to meet tomorrow.'

'I'll be at my house. You have the address. It's my father's place.'

He nodded and kissed her one last time before she left.

***

As soon as she opened the car door, Eric greeted her with a stony face. She wasn't even going to bother asking what was wrong. After ten minutes of congested London traffic, listening to a talk show on LBC, Eric broke his frustrated silence. 'I'm sorry if I've upset you. It's the last thing I wanted to do. I only want to help you, Zara.'

Zara was jolted out of her thoughts of vengeance. 'Yes, no worries. It's fine.' However, it wasn't really okay; she was sick to the back teeth of hearing those words: 'I only want to help'.

He sensed her distraction, and chewed his lip, thinking of the right words to say without sounding too nosey. 'Do they reckon Neil will make a full recovery?'

'Yes. Apparently, he's as strong as an ox.'

'Do they have any idea who did it?' asked Eric, in his most caring tone, hoping to keep up the conversation.

'No, but… well, no, they don't know.'

He knew she was deliberately keeping something from him and it spurred on his vexation.

'Does he have any enemies?'

Zara rolled her eyes. 'In our line of work, of course we have enemies.'

'We?' He'd done it again, allowing the words to leave his mouth before giving much thought to what he was saying.

Zara was now the one who was irritated. She turned to

face him. 'Eric, I don't know what your problem is, but let me lay the facts on the table. My business is *not* a two-bit set-up. I'm worth a fucking fortune, and I've managed to hang on to it with the full support of the Lanigans. I understand that marrying Mike would make me a part of your family, but that is a very separate issue. My business with the Lanigans is my business, end of story!'

'But wasn't Mike supposed to be part of your firm?'

Shaking her head in exasperation, she went on, 'Fuck me, Eric, that was twelve years ago. Mike went to prison, so what do you think? Did you think we just carried on where we left off? You, Eric, fucked off and got on with your life, and me, I had no choice but to do the same. Mike and I do have some business dealings like gun imports, but that's as far as it goes. So, as much as I appreciate your concern, please don't try to get involved in my own firm.'

Annoyed, Eric retaliated. 'What firm? All the Lanigans' men are in Ireland!'

A sudden hot feeling crept up her back, leaving her head with a tingling sensation. Her heart rate rocketed, and her hand shook. She had to answer quickly before he realized he'd said something he shouldn't have. She didn't want him to know she'd picked up on it.

'Yeah, but I've other men I can call on, so don't concern yaself. Look, Eric, can you stop the car? I feel sick.'

As soon as he pulled over, Zara snatched her bag and hurried out. Before she closed the door, she said, 'I need some fresh air. I'll get a taxi later.'

A car hooted from behind and urged Eric to pull away. Zara didn't look back; she stormed on ahead, hoping to weave her way into the council estate so that he couldn't follow her. As soon as she was out of sight, she caught her breath and went over his words and tried to rationalize how he could have known the Lanigans' men were back in Ireland. Leaning against the wall, she suddenly felt vulnerable. Who could she trust? Did Eric have anything to do with Neil's stabbing? Surely to God, not. After a few gasps for air, she calmed her panic. Maybe Eric had overheard her on the phone, or, more likely, he'd been earwigging in the hospital.

Crouching down to rifle through her bag with her one hand, she cursed. Everything was twice as hard. Clutching her phone, she left her bag on the path and scrolled down for the name of a taxi company. She could have walked to her father's former jewellery business. It was another one she needed to look over to see whether Ismail had cleared it out. She just hoped the shop wasn't left in a state. That would break her heart. Her father had used the shop as a front. Behind it was his office, where he did most of his business dealings. Suddenly, she felt her eyes fill up. 'Dad, if you're up there, I could do with your help.' It had become a pet saying of hers, ever since the moment she'd been locked up.

'Hi. Yes, could you send a taxi to the Old Kent Road, the BP garage?'

She knew many of the drivers didn't like to enter the estate, but the garage was relatively close by.

Once the taxi firm ended the call, she stared at her phone: there were more than twenty missed calls from Mike and four text messages. As she scrolled through, reading the excuses and pleas from Mike to call him back, she didn't notice two men appear from one of the run-down maisonettes.

They were roughly in their twenties, with baggy jeans trailing below their pants. Lennon, the bigger of the two, a known Face in the area, gazed at her oversized Louis Vuitton bag, and then his eyes checked her out. Right away, he could see the pound signs adding up. Designer sunglasses, expensive clothes, and the latest phone in her hand, she was a walking gold mine. He stopped and nudged his sidekick Germaine. 'I want that bag and phone,' he slyly whispered.

Germaine was ready to do anything to prove he was part of Lennon's gang. He hadn't been formally initiated but stealing the bag in broad daylight would be a good start. High on drugs and feeling brave, he eagerly agreed.

Still reading Mike's text messages, Zara didn't sense the man approaching until he was almost on top of her.

Germaine didn't have a well-thought-out plan, he just went all-in, like a bull in a china shop. Aggressively, he pinned her to the wall and tried to snatch the phone from her hand.

However, with no time to think, Zara went into fight mode, and with one swift movement, she kneed him hard between the legs. As he doubled over, she twisted her body to the side, and with all her might, she kicked the side of his head. The impact had him toppled over, but in fear for her safety, she had to finish him off. With her leg now pulled back, she kicked him so hard in the face, his nose almost caved in, and he was out cold.

Suddenly, her senses were on high alert.

Out of the corner of her eye, she detected a hand reaching down to claim her bag. Fired up and ready for a battle, Zara spun around and came face-to-face with the person she suspected was her assailant's accomplice. Although he was big, he wasn't tall; his eyes met hers and a cocky smirk formed along his face. It was a look that made her blood run cold – the same expression Benjamin Segal had, the day he watched her hand being severed from her wrist. This time, she wouldn't wait to process the dynamics. A surge of pure hatred and fury shot through her. With adrenaline pumping around her body, she pulled her head back and viciously cracked him hard across the bridge of his nose.

Lennon faltered, stunned by the power of the skinny woman. His brain just couldn't comprehend how the tables had turned. He had never lost a fight in his life, and he sure as hell wasn't going to lose one to a woman. His eyes focused, and just as he was about to pull a knife from his back pocket, she pulled her head back and headbutted him again. Dazed and senseless, he struggled to keep both feet on the floor. The crack was like a metal bat, and as much as he wanted to rip her head from her shoulders, he just couldn't seem to find the strength.

As Zara now shook from head to toe, she knew that all the time this evil-looking fucker was still standing, she was at risk. It was at that point she saw the knife in his hand, and her blood ran cold. In sheer terror, she dropped her phone, and although she couldn't take up her Shotokan stance with two hands, she could still use the one she had, and she did. A single open-handed strike to his throat was enough to paralyse him. Instantly, she saw the knife leave his grip, and his eyes bulged in disbelief. He couldn't breathe as she'd crushed his windpipe. Still afraid, she struck him again, and this time, he fell like a toppling tin soldier. He desperately gasped for breath, but it was no use – his lips were turning purple and then blue. He was choking to death.

Trembling, Zara picked up her phone, dropped it into her

bag, and ran towards the petrol station. Her mind was trying to process what had just happened. By the time she was inside, she felt safe. Her fast breathing slowly settled. All at once, as if time had stood still, something changed inside her.

For five years, she'd been brainwashed to feel weak and insignificant, with no way out, and the time spent as a prisoner had naturally affected her. Her confidence had been shattered because she'd become vulnerable and untrusting towards nearly everyone she knew. Right now, she felt, only the Lanigans were on her side.

So, although that fight with the two men may have initially shat the life out of her, she knew from this point onward she still had it in her. Her father had made sure she could fight. She'd mastered martial arts, winning medals and trophies from a young age. She suddenly thought about her father, as she often did, and this time, instead of asking for his help, she thanked him. All those times she'd prayed for him. It wasn't that she believed in God per se, but she still felt that there was a connection between them both, and she fervently believed that this was one of those moments when, somehow, he was there for her and willing her on to use the skills he'd taught her. Today, he'd answered her prayers, and she'd mustered the strength inside to let rip.

The cab pulled into the garage, and as Zara stepped inside, she could hear the ambulances and police cars in the distance. A satisfied smile adorned her face. They just shouldn't have fucked with her. Never.

CHAPTER SEVEN

Ricky tilted his head to the side as he looked at his father's sad expression. 'Are you sure you don't mind me going with Pops to the sales room?'

Mike was miles away, worrying over Zara. He waved his hand, gesturing it was okay. 'No, of course, Son. You go. I'm gonna make me way back home. I'll need to air and dust the place. It's been so long, I may need to get the decorators in.'

Gloria suddenly piped up, 'No, you won't need to lift a finger. We've kept it shipshape and Bristol fashion, and Staffie's been looking after the pool.'

Once Ricky and Arthur had left, Mike looked at his mother. 'I can't believe that skank fell asleep on the sofa next to me. I mean, what the fuck did that look like, and why the hell didn't Eric take her home? It's really pissing me off.'

Gloria sighed. 'Stop fretting, Mike. Zara will be back. She's not stupid. She knows you weren't up to no good.'

With a heavy heart, Mike shook his head. 'No, Mum. Five years ago, it would've been water off a duck's back. She would've fronted me there and then and fucked the tart off, but she's so affected. I can tell it'll only take one little upset and she'll crumble.'

'Leave her be for a while. Give her time. She'll come back. And just to let you know, we may be the fairer sex, but we can handle far more than you think. Inside her slim frame is a fighting spirit.'

Before Mike could continue the conversation, his phone rang. Instantly, he answered it. 'Zara, where the fuck are you? What's the matter?' His voice aired a pitch of desperation.

'Mike, listen to me. I need to be alone. I've some business to see to and I just need time.'

'No, Zara, please. What you saw, well… it wasn't—'

'Mike,' Zara instantly interrupted, 'I really don't care. I've more pressing issues. Please don't worry about me. I'm fine. But I just can't be around you right now!' With that, she cut the connection, leaving Mike with his mouth wide open in amazement.

'What'd she say?' asked Gloria, anxiously awaiting the details.

'She doesn't want me right now… I guess I fucked up.'

'Mikey, you've both been through so much and it's not easy, and even harder for her. Maybe she needs to find herself before she takes back up with you again. Leave her alone for a while.'

***

Zara stopped the cab just outside her father's place on the Old Kent Road. It was left vacant, as she expected. Her brother had taken the lot. Luckily, the actual shop hadn't been vandalized. Her throat tightened as she wandered around to the back of the building to the entrance of her father's old office. She choked on a tear as she stared at the stinking old rubbish heap in the open porch. She knew that behind the mess was the metal door that at one time had always been guarded by Quasi. Yet what greeted her today was silence. As she moved the rubbish away to reveal the steel door, her heart was in her mouth. She knew that once inside she would visualize her father sitting there with his eyeglass, examining some knocked-off piece of jewellery. Taking a deep breath, she placed her bag on the floor and reached inside for the large bundle of keys. Once she'd released the three locks, she pushed the door open and stared.

The sight just reinforced how greedy and heartless her brother really was. Her father's favourite Persian rug lay perfectly in place, and the large oak desk and rows of cabinets filled with books were still there intact. However, the contents of the drawers were on the floor, and the antique ornaments were gone. Everything of value had been taken. Only her father's much loved and practically worthless items were left behind.

A tear trickled down her face as she could almost hear him talking about how money makes the world go round, but how power and fear can stop it. She slowly wandered around the room, fingering the desk, the books, and the back of Izzy's chair, and then she stopped and stared at the rug. All those years, she never knew that it was her brother who was behind the leaked information. She could never have guessed it was Ismail who was hell-bent on setting her up. However, did he know every hiding place, every secret? *She* did because Izzy had made it his life's mission to prepare her to take over.

Crouching down, she gripped the corner and pulled the carpet back. A chuckle escaped her mouth. Surely Ismail would have checked this hidey-hole? Her giggle turned into a full-on laugh. *Jesus, Ismail, you fool, you really didn't have it in you, did you? You only saw what was under your nose.*

She sat back on her haunches. This was the reason her father had chosen her to take over, as Ismail lacked the skills and the mental and physical resources to run the family businesses. Under the rug was a hidden door that opened to reveal a large metal box. It held everything that was of any value: there were names, addresses, phone numbers, codes, bank accounts, and so much more. She tugged at the small handle and smiled.

Rifling through the paperwork, she found the small leather-bound ledger. 'There you are, my little beauty,' said Zara, as she kissed the cover, with a huge smile on her face. After carefully placing everything back inside the box, she returned the rug to how it was. She could have left her father's office exactly how she wanted it, but years of mentoring from her teacher and father made her put everything back in its original place. Shuddering, she thought of the times her brother must have been secretly listening by the door. But he couldn't hurt her now – he was in prison, on remand, along with the Segals.

Izzy had told her about the book and the numbers inside. 'The man called the Machine is someone who you must respect and only ever call if you have no other choice. Mike Regan is the man you want by your side, Zara, but one day, when I'm gone, and if you need more than the Regans, then you call the Machine. He's a lone wolf and invaluable.'

Outside, the traffic on the main road was almost at a stand-still, and Zara felt anxious. The thought of that man struggling for air swirled around in her head and raised her heartbeat. She took a few deep breaths before she made her next move. There, from a sideroad, pulling away from the kerb, a taxi was approaching. Suddenly his 'For Hire' sign came on, so she frantically waved him down. He wound down his window. 'Hop in, love!'

Relieved she didn't have to stand on the main road feeling exposed, she hurried over to the vehicle and got in. 'Head towards Kent, please. I'll direct you from there.'

She got herself settled and contemplated her next move. She opened the page of the notebook and stared at the phone number pencilled in. What if he'd retired? He was obviously much older. And what if he'd changed his number?

The streets were now crawling with police. Zara had no idea that she was the person of interest. The taxi driver pulled his partition screen ajar, leaned back, and said, 'I just heard that two gang members, part of that nasty Hadlow gang, were beaten up. One of them was killed.'

Zara was still staring at the notebook. Distractedly, she looked over to the driver, slightly flustered. 'Er. . . sorry, what did you say?'

'The police are everywhere, looking for a woman who's apparently killed that Lennon bloke. He won't be missed. He was a nasty bastard, part of a gang. I, for one, am glad. That gang business is getting out of hand... Anyway, sorry, love. You probably ain't from around these parts, eh?'

Zara's ears pricked up. 'Well, yes and no. My father had a few businesses around here. That jeweller's back there was one. So, what's this gang all about, then?'

The middle-aged, grey-haired driver was happy to chat for England, and Zara was equally glad to listen.

'I live just up the road, and in all my bleedin' life I've never had to worry about stepping out of me own flaming house.

Sure enough, back in the day, we had a few thugs, but not like these. They are wild now. There's no respect for no one or nuffin. Drugs cause it. I tell ya, I've been more busy cabbing in the last year than ever. All the old dears won't walk to the shops no more. The people are too afraid to walk the streets. It ain't right. The police don't do enough as far as I'm concerned. Me, I'd flaming gather all those thugs up and put 'em on a boat and sink the bleedin' thing.'

'Why do you think the drug situation has got worse?'

'Well, it's that new drug. It makes 'em wild, I'll tell ya. Once these kids get hooked on that shit, they'll do anything to get money to keep up their habit. Christ, I never believed in drugs meself, but compared to this new shit out there, I'd even legalize cocaine right now.'

Intrigued by the man's proffered information, Zara pressed for more. 'What's this drug called then? I've not heard about it.'

The driver looked in his rear-view mirror and smiled. 'Sweetheart, you probably don't mix in those circles. It's called Flakka, but they reckon it's mixed with something that turns the most decent of kids into demons. It's pure evil, poxy stuff. Whoever's making it and selling it to the kids needs to be shot. That Lennon bloke was one of the dealers, and if what I've heard is right, I'm glad he's dead… ' He paused and glanced in his mirror again. 'Sorry, love. Did you say your father owned that jeweller's back there?'

Zara nodded and wondered if she'd said too much. If Lennon was the man who attacked her, then the other guy may well be able to give the police a description. A woman with one hand would stand out like a sore thumb. She pulled her sleeve down to hide her wrist.

'See, now, love, this shit wouldn't be going on if your old man was alive, Gawd rest him. Now that there was a proper geezer. He was a decent fella. Er, didn't he own the Pomodorra over near Denmark Hill?'

Zara had to play it cool and not appear too eager, but this man may just know more about the black guy who stabbed Neil. 'Yeah, he did, but apparently the Italians were threatened, and they've taken off. I bet it was the same gang you're talking about.'

'Oh yeah, love, no doubt about it. See, now, if ya father was still around, no two-bit punk would even get their head through the door. He'd 'ave… Oh, listen to me. Sorry, babe. I've no need to tell you. Who owns all the restaurants now? I heard it was an Irish lot?'

Zara smiled. 'Yeah, the Lanigans do now. They bought my father out before he died. So, why are you so sure it's this Hadlow gang then?' she asked, changing the subject.

The driver was quiet for a few moments, and then he pointed across the street to a fried chicken shop. 'See that there? My old mate owned that. Now, I ain't saying he was as straight as a die, but that Lennon and his mob terrorized my pal, made him a nervous wreck, so he just handed over the business and buggered off down to Margate. And I know they don't just serve chicken wings. They're dealing that Flakka shit.'

The conversation stopped as both the driver and Zara were contemplating the situation. She yawned so widely, she almost broke her jaw and leaned back against the comfort of the cushioned seat.

The driver glanced in the mirror; the woman seemed miles away. At that moment, a text came through on his phone.

The Old Bill are looking for a woman with one hand missing. At first, he thought it was the start of a joke until he realized that it must be Izzy Ezra's daughter who had awkwardly got into the back. He looked again and traced her sleeve down to nothing. Yes, she was the daughter of a well-respected villain. He was in no doubt now that she killed the gang member, especially if she was anything like her father.

Just up ahead, there was a police stop-and-search. Victor watched as the police checked every car. He couldn't turn around and go back now.

'Listen, love, the police are searching up the road from us. Do yaself a favour. Cover yaself with that bag of yours and pretend you're asleep.'

His tone was not as jovial as before. He was stern. Without thinking for herself, she did as she was told and closed her eyes. But although she looked asleep, she was far from relaxed. She heard the officer as he leaned into the taxi driver's window. 'Where have you just come from?'

'King's College Hospital, mate. Me punter's just had an op, so she can't drive.'

'Okay, on ya way.'

As soon as they were hammering along to the end of the Old Kent Road, Zara sat up straight. 'What was that all about?'

'Me name's Victor. Your father sorted my boy out many moons ago, and I never did get to return the favour. I've just got a text. The Filth are looking for a woman who fits your description. Me, I don't care either way if ya did kill that bastard, but, nevertheless, I want to get you home safe and sound.'

'Look, thanks, Victor. I ain't gonna blag an excuse. I did fucking kill him. He tried to mug me, and he had a knife.'

Victor's eyes widened. 'Well, he's dead, and I'm glad it wasn't the other way around. Anyway, I'll give you me card, and if you ever need me, you just call, babe.'

Zara knew then she was as safe as houses if Victor was paying back a debt. Not only that, he had so much respect for her father that he was prepared to break the law to help her. For the rest of the journey, Zara bled him dry of everything he knew about this Hadlow gang and the drug, Flakka, safe in the knowledge that the man was more than happy to help her. Again, she thought about her father; he would always tell her that respect meant more than money, and today, she knew he was right.

'Being a taxi driver, I guess it means you get to hear a lot of what goes on around the streets?'

'It's almost like you take an oath of silence, once you get behind the wheel. Punters chat away to each other as if you're deaf, like they know you won't repeat anything... ' He laughed. 'I even got to know the ins and outs of a robbery two days before it took place. I never said nuffin, o' course.'

The openness of the man, comfortable in her company, made her warm to him. 'Victor, can I ask a favour? I will pay you well.'

Victor raised his thick bushy eyebrows. 'What's that then, darling?'

'This gang. Can you keep your ears open? I wanna know what they're up to.'

As Victor drove along the long winding drive up to her house, he was silent, contemplating. Not receiving a response, Zara didn't ask again. She wondered if she'd overstepped the mark.

He jumped out and opened the door for her. 'Can I ask you a question?'

Zara nodded. 'Of course, Victor.'

'This Irish firm, the Lanigans. Are they working for you?'

Zara looked into his eyes, searching for a sign that he was entirely trustworthy. What peered back was a genuine expression.

'Yes, Victor, they're working with me. They always have. They don't own the businesses, I do, but we work together, and I'm not about to sit back and allow a bunch of druggies to take down my father's good name.'

Victor relaxed his shoulders and a soft expression almost made his face melt. 'Well, darling, I'll be honest with you. Your father wasn't just an acquaintance, he was a close pal of mine. I worked for him for twenty years, but I got shot in the leg and wasn't much use after that, so I bought a taxi, learned the Knowledge, and retired. So, will I keep an ear out? Damn right, I will. And I'll do more than that, if you want. I thought the world of your old man. He did sort my son out and I never did get the chance to pay him back.'

Zara noticed his eyes staring off to nothing. 'Come in, if you have time. Why don't you share a coffee with me?'

Victor watched her unlock the front door and followed her inside. He gazed around and shook his head. 'Well, it ain't changed a bleedin' bit.' Then he turned to Zara. 'But, as much as your old man loved his antiques and period houses, he wouldn't want you to live like this, dust an' all.'

Lowering her gaze, she sighed heavily. 'You really did know my father well, didn't you? It's a shame I never met you before.'

Victor smiled. 'You did, when you were a nipper. But, you

know, your father kept me away from most people. His secret pal, he called me. I do miss the ol' fella. Aah well, life moves on, I suppose.'

'I think since you knew my dad so well, I feel the need to tell you what's been going on.'

Over coffee they sat in the office and chatted for an hour. Zara filled him in on what had happened after her father died. About how she was locked away in the basement of this huge mansion by her own brother – and the details of how she'd lost her hand and where she was now regarding the business, and particularly the recent events concerning her restaurants and the attack on Neil.

She leaned back on her father's chair and tilted her head to the side. 'It feels so good to go over the past. I miss my dad and listening to you talk about what you both got up to fills me with meaning. I'll carry on and fight to get back what was his.'

'Ya know, darling, listening to you reminds me so much of the old fella. He was right to have you take over. Now, I'm not a young and fit lad anymore but I ain't past it either, so if you need me, girl, I'm 'ere, by your side. Besides, I'm getting a bit bored ferrying people about.'

'Right, then. I'm gonna put you on my books, starting today. Give me your bank details. The first job is a trip to Margate. Can you find out everything about this gang from your mate who owns that fried chicken shop?'

Victor's eyes lit up. 'Yep, Gov.' He winked. 'Just a word though, sweetheart. You trusted me a little too soon. I'd be careful who you trust.'

Zara laughed. 'Oh, Victor, believe me, I'm not silly. The reason I trust you is because I know my father must have been friends with you since only his closest buddies ever came to the house.'

Just as Victor was about to depart, a loud knock at the door caused him to look at her sharply. 'Are you expecting anyone?'

'No, and I need to get the CCTV up and running again. I can't see beyond that bloody oak door.'

She headed down the passageway with Victor hard on her heels.

'Who is it?' she demanded, in her firmest voice.

'Eric!'

'It's okay, Victor. It's Eric, my fiancé's brother… ' She almost choked on the word 'fiancé'.

Victor nodded. 'I'll be gone, then. I'll call tomorrow and take a look at those cameras for you.' With that, he kissed her cheek. 'I'm so glad I got to meet you. Must 'ave been fate.'

Pulling the door open, Zara noticed that Eric's eyes instantly shifted to Victor and then back to her.

Ignoring his questioning glance, she said goodbye to Victor and waited for him to reach his taxi before she turned to face Eric.

'What are you doing here?'

He looked a touch uncomfortable because, in truth, he didn't have a reason. 'I just wanted to be sure you got back okay. You said you felt sick. Are you all right?'

She nodded, but she was distracted by Victor. When he'd left, he had a concerned look on his face.

Then her phone rang, which she'd left in the office. 'Excuse me,' she said to Eric, as she hurried back along the passageway. Luckily, she managed to reach the phone in time before it rang off. 'Hi, is everything all right?'

'Yes, Neil's having his ears chewed off by his mother, so I thought I'd slip away. I was hoping I could hold a meeting at yours. The men are on their way. They should get to London around nine o'clock tonight,' replied Davey.

'Yeah, of course. You have my father's address. Just come over.'

No sooner had she finished the call than Eric was behind her. 'Are you having guests over?'

Zara frowned, reluctant to elaborate. His comments in the car had her nerves rattled as it was, and right now, she didn't feel comfortable with him in the house. 'Yeah, it's a friend of mine. Look, Eric, I can understand that you may feel the need to check up on me... for your brother, but I am perfectly fine, and to be blunt, I think your fussing is almost undermining me. I want time alone, so if you don't mind?' She gestured to the hallway.

He didn't move but looked her up and down. 'I didn't come to find out if you were okay for Mike. I wanted to make sure for myself.'

Feeling self-conscious, she recoiled. 'Eric, I think it's best you go.'

Unexpectedly, he ran his hands down her cheek. 'I care about you, Zara. I always have done. I know you love my brother, but—'

The strange ambience caused Zara to make a sharp interruption. 'Enough, Eric. I really don't want to hear it. Mike is your brother... my... Well, anyway, I want you to leave.'

'Wake up, Zara. Mike may be my brother, but I do know him for what he is. Look at the party. It was me looking out for you while Mike was showing off. I know you've doubts about him or you wouldn't have let me... '

Zara took a deep intake of breath. 'That was because... Oh, it doesn't matter now, it was just a mistake. I'm sorry.' Her eyes looked to the floor in shame.

He gently placed a hand under her chin and lifted it. 'Hey, come on, Zara, it's okay. I probably took advantage. Anyway, I'm sorry, love.'

Those sweet words, the gentleness in his voice, and the slow blink, sent her feelings into a spin again. Somewhere in her subconscious, she had the urge for attention. She was still a woman with needs.

Eric sensed her guard was down. He cupped her face like before. 'You're beautiful, d'ya know that?'

No, she didn't know it, but to hear those words somehow sucked her into a vacuum, ripping away her barriers.

She didn't pull away, and for a moment, she wanted more, just to hold that feeling of being special, loved, and adored.

He leaned forward to kiss her lips, but the second they touched, she jerked away and glared, surprised at herself for being so weak. A surge of anger followed. Frustrated with her lack of self-control and Eric's ability to play on her emotions, she snapped at him.

'Stop it, Eric. This is wrong... ' She paused and stiffened. 'Mike may have been having fun, but it doesn't make him bad. Right now, I couldn't give a fucking shit. I want to be left alone, so whether you're here on Mike's behalf or your own, take note. I'm more than capable of looking out for myself. So, now, please, leave me in peace.'

She barged past him and stood to hold the door open.

Red-faced and frustrated, Eric left and stomped off like a spoiled child towards his car.

Zara then slammed the door closed, folded her arms, and held herself, as she took a deep breath. What was he thinking, and, more worryingly, what the hell was that all about? Gripping the phone in her hand, she contemplated calling Mike. But then the vision of that woman lying half-naked in the same room as him focused her mind. Shocked by her own emotional state and the image of *that* woman, she shook her head and lit up a cigarette.

***

By nightfall, Zara was exhausted, and her eyelids were heavy; yet she had to stay awake and prepare herself for the meeting. She needed to clear her head of emotional crap, so that she could focus on her priorities and act in control; she couldn't have Davey's men seeing her as weak, like Eric obviously did.

After spending a few minutes freshening up, she waited, going over in her mind everything she'd learned from Victor.

Just before nine o'clock, she heard a diesel car pull up outside the door. She cursed with frustration, not being able to see who it was. But to her astonishment, the knock was followed by a recognizable voice.

'Zara, sweetheart, it's me, Victor.'

Usually, her hackles would have been raised at being called 'sweetheart', but somehow it seemed comforting coming from him, the stranger she'd met in a taxi. How bizarre that was.

She opened the door, looked around, and ushered him in. 'That was quick, Victor.'

His expression looked flustered and yet serious. 'Are you alone, love?'

She nodded. 'Why, Victor? What's up?'

He gulped, and his large Adam's apple bobbed up and down. 'I didn't go to Margate.'

She tilted her head to the side, questioningly.

'That fella Eric, or whoever he's called, I thought I'd seen him before, but I wasn't 100 per cent. Me ol' mince pies ain't what they used to be, but there was something about the way he held himself. Anyway, I guess after this morning, and you saying you'd put me on your books, I got all excited. I know I'm a silly old fucker, but, anyway, I parked up while he was at your place and then I followed him into London. I'm known for using me ol' watch and chain, ya see.'

Zara listened, her heart thumping as if she was facing a herd of elephants charging across the savanna towards her.

'You do own Antonio's, yeah?'

She nodded, urging him to go on.

'Well, that Eric bloke pulled up outside and stared through the window. He looked around him like he was up to no good, and then, I thought he was reading the opening times. Anyway, once he drove off, I got out and had a look myself. I know Antonio. He always has the restaurant open, but it's locked up now and there's a note inside the door that says it's closed due to staff sickness, but it will be open this coming Saturday. Now, if this Eric fancied a bit of Italian, there are plenty of good restaurants in Kent. So, why did he drive all the way back over to London?'

Her face paled, and Victor could see she was shaken up.

'What is it, love?'

Her mind was off somewhere to a dark place. She sighed, making a sound through her mouth. 'My dad always said, "Fuck your friends but keep your enemies closer."'

Victor grinned. 'Yep, ol' Izzy had some great sayings. That was one of his favourites. Ya know, love, Izzy's riddles always made sense.'

'Eric either has information about my business or something so much worse. I'm beginning to get worrying vibes coming off him. I think he's the person trying to destroy me. But why? Why would he do that? I've never done anything to harm him except… ' She bit her lip to stop it from quivering.

'I get it, love. What a man can't have, he'll destroy. It was another one of your dad's phrases.'

She looked up, with her face slowly crumbling. 'After what I've been through, how cruel could he be? Surely to God, he wouldn't do that to me, would he?'

'Jealousy is a compelling and destructive emotion, love.'

Misty-eyed, she chuckled. 'That was another one of Izzy's sayings, wasn't it?'

'No, that's one of me own.' Unexpectedly, he placed his arm around her shoulders. 'If it's any consolation, you've got me to help ya. I know they're just words, but you can trust me. Izzy would be watching me, and I know he mates with the Devil.'

The meaty arm resting gently on her shoulders was like a comfort blanket, and she knew that he meant every word.

'Victor, I've a meeting in about ten minutes with the Lanigan firm.'

'Oh, okay, sweetheart. I'll leave you in peace, then. I just thought you should know, that's all.'

'No, please would you stay? I think you may be able to help us. When I say the Lanigan firm, they're my men too. Some of them, however, I have yet to meet myself.'

Victor winked. 'You bet ya. I'll be straight up with ya. I need to earn me money.'

'Do you not have a wife you go home to?'

A pang of sadness swept across his face. He paused before he could speak. Clearing the choke in his throat, he replied, 'She died, two years ago. She was my little duchess, a real little love, she was. Married to her for thirty years, good 'uns an' all… ' He swallowed hard. 'She was mugged and left beaten in the street. By the time the ambulance had got to her, she was unconscious. I sat by her bed until she passed away. The fucking saddest day of my life, that was.'

'Oh no, I'm so, so sorry.'

Watching his face, she saw the sadness turn to anger, and she knew he was a man determined to seek retribution.

'So now ya know, Zara, why I'm more than happy to help you. Ya see, that fucking gang killed her.'

Zara's hand flew to her mouth, in horror.

'I don't have the backing to hunt them down, Zara. But if you're gonna take them out of the picture, 'cos I'm surmising that you ain't gonna back down and allow those scumbags to take what's yours, then I'm with ya, all the way. But I know those gangs and all this drug business ain't organized by the likes of that Lennon arsehole. This is being carefully orchestrated by someone with a lot of clout, not a load of skanky kids trying to score a few quid to get their fix.'

Zara gestured for him to go into the dining room. 'Take a seat, Victor. D'ya fancy a brandy?'

He smiled. 'Any of your Izzy's finest going?'

Everything Victor was saying was ringing true. He really must have been a good friend of her father's because, as a rule, the most expensive brandy was consumed at the house and only with close friends.

Searching through the drinks cabinet, she was surprised to find that Ismail hadn't touched the brandy. Then she wondered whether he actually knew a good label if he saw one. *She* knew, though, because her father had once taught her. She poured two generous measures and they sipped their drinks in silence for a few moments, each with their own thoughts.

'Only the best, Victor. Cheers.'

As they took their drinks through to the study, Zara thought about the man her father called the Machine and her concern regarding Eric. 'Er… would you excuse me a second, I just need to make a phone call.' She politely got up and headed back to the office. Pulling the notebook from her bag, she dialled the number, half expecting it to be out of use.

To her surprise, it not only rang, but, more shockingly, it was ringing in the study. Startled, she rushed back to see Victor clocking the number on his phone. Instantly, she ended the call and watched as Victor's lips turned down, and he slid the phone back into his pocket. Surely, this kindly-spoken, gentle giant couldn't be this dangerous, almost psychopathic, man that even her own father respected?

As he looked up, clearly unaware that she had called him, she pressed redial on her phone and it rang again.

A sudden cheeky grin slithered across his face. How could he have gone from a man who could have dressed as Santa Claus and got away with it, to be a Bram Stoker character? *Jesus*, she thought, *he was here in the study sipping her brandy*. She just hoped that when her father said he was a very dangerous man, he meant if you got on the wrong side of him.

She stood glued to the spot. 'My father said... '

He nodded. 'Yes, I can only imagine.'

'You said I could trust you, but you never said you were the Machine.'

He sniffed the air and sighed. Suddenly, he appeared ten years younger, and his previously slouched shoulders were raised and his jowls were taut.

'You can trust me, Zara. I never lied. The only thing I wasn't upfront about was the fact that I saw you go into the back of the shop. So, I parked up across the street, and when you appeared, hailing a taxi, I pulled over. I had a gut feeling you were Zara. I knew about you. Your father often talked about his daughter with such fondness. And, of course, if I was wrong, then I wanted to know who you were to have a set of keys to the great man's office.'

Zara suddenly found her tongue. 'And your wife, and the gang? Was that all true?'

His eyes clouded over. 'Yes, I'm afraid so.'

Her mind went over her father's words. This guy was supposed to be one of the most dangerous men in the country.

'Why haven't you dragged the culprits off the streets, then? Because from what my father said... '

Victor smiled and raised his hand for her to stop. 'Wait, Zara. I like to work alone. I don't work with a firm, although your father paid me a good wage. I worked in the background. Even Izzy's men never met me, and that's how I liked it. But now we've met, and you've put your trust in me, I feel I can do the same.' He placed his drink on the table and rubbed his hands together.

'I was in the SAS. I left with fuck all to my name. If your

father wanted someone taken away, removed from society, but didn't want a big deal made of it, then he would call me. He probably told you I was dangerous because the one thing I won't tolerate is not being paid. I did work for a man who fucked me off without a penny. First, I killed his brother, then I went for his cousin, and finally I went for him.'

Sitting back down, Zara grinned. 'So, you mean, play by the rules or die by them?'

Victor gave her a firm nod. 'Yes, and that saying, my dear girl, your father got from me.'

'So, I can confidently assume that the man who killed your wife is dead?'

He grinned. 'Yes, but I'm not a detective. This Hadlow gang isn't run by a load of punks. There's someone behind it all, and that's where I'm baffled. So, if you still want me on the firm, I'm all yours.'

The nervous tremble left her body and a new-found confidence took its place.

Promptly at nine o'clock, the hard knock at the door had Victor on his feet.

'It's okay. It's my men.'

Davey was first through the door, followed by Shamus and some other Irish men, who Zara had yet to meet. The sheer size of them was enough to make Zara feel she had serious backing. The manner in which they greeted her and with such respect shot her confidence through the roof.

Noticing their expressions change when they saw her guest, Zara introduced Victor before the atmosphere became edgy.

Davey gave a firm handshake and felt the power of Victor's large hand.

'Victor was a close and trusted friend of my father's. He's now on my payroll, so we can speak freely in his company.'

Davey raised his bushy brow. 'Um, no disrespect, Zara.' He then looked at Victor. 'I know you trusted your father's opinion but… '

Victor coughed delicately. 'I understand, Mr Lanigan. I have a few errands to run, so please excuse me.'

Zara didn't make a fuss and escorted Victor to the door, giving herself time to think about her impulsive decision. 'I think I was getting carried away. It was great to listen to you talking about my father. The offer of being on the payroll still stands but maybe in a different capacity. Perhaps your ear-to-the-ground skills would suit us both?'

Victor allowed a generous grin to adorn his face. 'Of course. I'll get off to Margate and do some digging, and, yes, the CCTV. I can have that fixed up for ya, if ya like?'

Zara returned the smile. 'Oh yes, please, if you wouldn't mind. That will be one thing less to worry about.'

He gave a salute and left.

The meeting went on until the early hours of the morning, every man having their input, yet each of them looking to Zara for a nod of assurance. By the time they'd left, a plan was in place. Zara was exhilarated. However, there was still the thorny issue of Eric, who preyed heavily on her mind. As she climbed the stairs to her old bedroom, she felt her body suddenly become so overcome with exhaustion that she only just made it to her bed. She flopped down and went straight into a deep sleep.

CHAPTER EIGHT

Mike arose for the first time in twelve years from his own bed. But it had been a restless night; Zara constantly appeared in and out of his dreams.

He had to put a smile on his face for Ricky's sake. Coming back to the home that his son had lived in for the first six years of his life was like stepping into a toy shop with a kid again. Ricky's beaming smile and excitement couldn't be contained. He'd run from room to room, recalling every last detail, and his enthusiasm went through the roof.

Mike could hear him downstairs, making coffee and singing along to 'Story of My Life' by One Direction. He sighed and thought about Zara for the umpteenth time.

Forcing a smile, he arrived in the kitchen and ruffled his son's hair. 'How did ya sleep in ya old room?'

Ricky turned to face him, with an egg slice in his hand. 'Better than I've ever slept before. It's hard to explain, but I feel like me again.'

Mike sat at the breakfast bar. 'So, you like ya new car, then?'

Ricky was laughing and his whole face was alive. 'Oh my God, Dad, it's like a dream. All I gotta do now is learn to drive. You should see it, Dad. It's bright red and goes like shit off a shovel. Er… not that I'd drive like a lunatic.' He handed Mike a coffee. 'I'll be careful, Dad, I promise.'

Mike nodded. 'Son, you were taken away from me twelve years ago. For eleven of those years, I believed you were dead. I couldn't lose you to a fucking car crash, so you promise me you'll be sensible?'

'I will. So, what's happening now with this police business?'

Mike ran his hands through his hair. 'Yeah about that. I've a job to do, and although we said you can join the firm, I think we need to do this on our own. You just enjoy your freedom and the new car. I wanna see that smile on your face and the spring in your step. This work could get messy. Right now, I need to have a clear head. If I'm worried about you, then I won't get the job done.'

Mike lowered his head, wondering if he felt comfortable about what he was about to do. His father popped into his mind, and for a moment, he cringed. *No way would Dad have collaborated with the police,* he thought. He breathed deeply and visited his conscience.

The Commissioner had given him the name of the pub that they suspected was a dealer's den. It so happened that the pub called the Daylight Inn was on his turf, and regardless of where that information had come from, he would have made it his business to pay the place a visit and lay down his rules anyway.

Ricky watched the concerned look on his father's face and decided he wouldn't push the issue. The last thing he wanted to do was to have him worrying.

'Okay, I get it, Dad.'

Mike snapped out of his thoughts. 'You're a good boy.'

'Dad, do you think I could go to the Daylight Inn? There's

a top DJ playing there Saturday night. Liam and Arty are going.'

Unexpectedly, Mike got up from his stool with a face like thunder.

'Dad? What's the matter? Did I say something wrong?'

Mike softened his look and sighed. 'No, Son, it's just that we have business at the Daylight. Jesus! Staffie and Willie should have run it past me first.'

'It's okay, Dad. I can stay at home. It's not a problem.'

Suddenly, Mike burst out laughing. 'It sounds so funny, you, a big lad of eighteen, who served time, asking me if you can go to a party.'

Ricky looked down at his hands covered in soap suds, then at his apron, and chuckled. 'Well, I guess if you view me like that, then this looks pretty silly too.'

Mike laughed again. 'Oh, ya know what? 'Course you can go. But you just party. Me and the lads have some business to take care of.'

Ricky saluted. 'Yes, Boss. No worries. Hopefully, I'll be tonguing some pretty chick.'

With an exaggerated raised eyebrow, Mike replied, 'Like a bird, then, do ya?'

Ricky blushed. 'Yeah, I ain't had a girlfriend, but I have a new life, and Nan reckons I'm a good catch. So I'm gonna try me luck… Dad, are these gang members gonna be at the pub?'

Mike shrugged his shoulders. 'I dunno, Ricky. All I know is we've been given a few dates and places, and the rest is up to us.'

'You won't get hurt, will ya?' asked Ricky, now very concerned that his father was entering into something more serious than they were used to. After all, if the police couldn't get a grip on these gangs, what made them think his father could?

'Nah, 'course not. All we have to do is rough up a few dealers and find out who's behind it all. I think I can handle that.' He gave Ricky a cheeky grin, hoping to put his mind at rest.

The truth was, he could easily handle a few scallywags; he'd never had a problem with getting info before, so why should this be any different? Ricky did have a point, though, and if he found out the Commissioner was holding anything back, he would take him down and think nothing of it.

He also had to put Zara to the back of his mind and take his mother's advice. 'She'll come back, once she's got herself together,' she'd said.

***

By the time Saturday night arrived, Ricky was almost hyper. This was the first time he'd actually been to a pub, and, more importantly, with his father. All those years of living with Jackie, he wasn't invited anywhere unless Tatum was going to use him to earn money, and that was generally in the form of housebreaking.

He entered the lounge, smelling of expensive aftershave and wearing his new Levi's and a white designer T-shirt. His floppy fringe was gelled back, and his tanned skin made his teeth look whiter than ever.

Mike gawped at the transformation. 'Well, look at you, matey. You're a right handsome fucker.' He laughed. 'Like your ol' man in fact.'

Ricky blushed. 'Do I look all right, Dad?'

Mike pretended to size him up. 'There's something missing.'

Ricky looked down and checked his new trainers and his jeans and then lifted his head with a quizzical expression. He thought he looked pretty good. 'What? Dad, I don't need a coat. It's still warm.'

Mike pulled a box from his jacket pocket. ''Ere, Son, I've got you a present. I can't make up for all those missed birthdays in one go, but this is a start.'

Ricky looked at the name on the box and gasped. 'What? No way!'

Mike could feel his emotions rising and coughed to clear the lump in his throat; just seeing the joy on his son's face melted his heart.

Ricky was shaking with excitement as he removed the lid to find a stunning gold-faced Rolex watch. As he gently removed it from the box and turned it over, a sudden tear fell down his cheek. Engraved were the words 'RICKY MY BOY', in the same style as the tattoo on his father's arm.

'Dad, oh my God. I love it. It's so classy.' He quickly strapped it on his wrist and moved his arm to see the diamonds catch the light.

Mike felt his heart lift; he had the money and the means to make his lad feel like someone. As his son walked towards the front door, he noticed how his shoulders were pulled back, his head was high, and his awkward gait was replaced with a confident swagger. *And so he should be confident*, thought Mike. *Ricky is a Regan, and we have a history of holding our own.*

***

Mike drove to the Daylight Inn pub; it was one of the largest in the area and was surrounded by shops and a train station. It had been years since Mike had had a few drinks in there. He was somewhat surprised to find a bouncer on each of the three exits. He inwardly laughed at the state of them and wondered if with their black stab-proof vests and walkie-talkies they could actually have a half-decent ruck. Willie and Staffie came bounding up behind him, all ready for the action.

'Lou's on his way. Liam, that great oaf, is still trying to park that oversized Beemer.' Willie looked over at his son trying a parallel park. 'I swear me boy's a tent short of a fucking circus. The little fucker only nearly filled the beast with petrol instead of diesel and had a row with the pump attendant over it.'

'Cor, Willie, the apple ain't fallen far from the tree, then, eh?' laughed Staffie.

Willie had to laugh; it was true. Liam had inherited his temper and infinite recklessness, and, like himself, he had a reputation, even at the tender age of nineteen. He was certainly a fucker.

Mike and Ricky laughed together; Liam looked so much like Willie it was untrue. Apart from the scar down Willie's face, he was his double; he was tall and lanky with a face that only his grandmother could love, yet he had a heart of gold.

Ricky watched Liam step out of the car. They had known each other as youngsters, and the homecoming party had them instantly reacquainted.

Finally, Lou turned up dressed as usual in a three-piece suit, as if he might be going into a business meeting. He was about to ruffle Ricky's hair but noticed the gel holding it in place and patted his arm instead. 'Where's Arty? I thought he was coming?'

Staffie pulled on a cigarette and griped. 'I left him in the bathroom. I swear to God, his mother has tried to bring him up looking like a fucking tart. I nearly choked on the fucking spray of smelly shit, and what's with all this fucking face balm and tanning crap? I don't know if I've got a son or a fucking daughter.'

Willie was laughing. It was so good to have the firm together on the outside and now their own sons with them. It was undoubtedly history repeating itself, from his own father, along with Lou's and Staffie's, all in the Regan firm, and now their own boys, vowing to look out for each other.

''Ere he is!' said Staffie.

They turned to see Arty, a more handsome version of his father, crossing the road. For years, Staffie was teased because his oversized biceps made him look like Popeye. Now his son, who was a good foot taller, had similar bulging muscles, but his height took the dairy off the huge arms and legs.

Mike nodded at the boys. 'Right, listen.' He pointed to Willie, Staffie, and Lou. 'We're gonna drink at one end of the bar and sort out a bit of business. Youse will stay well away, have fun, don't drink too much, and don't be pestering us. What goes down doesn't involve you guys, so, whatever happens, you've got ya wheels, so just fuck off and get away from here. Got it?'

Ricky was watching his father in action; he ran the firm, no question about that, and Ricky felt his chest puff out. His father was someone who hard men looked up to. His eyes then flicked towards Arty and Liam to see if they were happily taking direction, only to find them nodding respectfully.

'And you, Ricky. You stay with the boys, yeah?'

Ricky nodded back. 'Yeah, no worries. I won't even be looking your way, not when I'm sucking some bird's face off.'

Arty slapped his back. 'Get you, ya fucking dirty bastard.'

Liam had a high-pitched voice. 'Listen to him. Our Ricky fancies himself as some Casanova.'

Willie placed an arm around his son's shoulders. 'Well, my boy, Ricky's the looker, but, Liam, I guess, like me, you're the charmer, eh?'

Mike, for the first time, gave a hearty laugh that made his cheeks red and his eyes water. 'You, Willie? A charmer? The only thing you could charm would be a boss-eyed ferret.'

The banter between them had begun and it kicked off their good spirits and demonstrated their close bond with each other. Ricky was in his element, being treated with such affection by them all but especially by the lads. Not having a sibling and being cruelly treated by Tatum and his nasty sons, it was like a breath of fresh air.

Once they were inside, Staffie headed for the far end, followed by Willie and Mike. The younger lads sauntered over to the part of the bar closest to the DJ. Arty got the drinks in and nudged Liam. ''Ere, look at Ricky, eyeing up the barmaid.'

Liam rolled his eyes. 'Like a dog on heat, he is.'

Ricky took a swig of his drink and winked at Arty. 'And ya point is?'

They laughed and egged him on. 'The point is, Ricky, me ol' son, it's no good just staring. Get in there and chat the bird up.'

Ricky took another swig. 'I dunno. I ain't never chatted up a bird before.'

Most lads their age would have ribbed the life out of him,

yet Arty and Liam knew the history and were only too pleased to take him under their wing. They'd grown up knowing Mike and the pain he'd gone through in believing Ricky was dead, and, of course, when they all discovered otherwise, and the revelations came out about how Ricky had been so severely treated, they naturally had a soft spot for him.

'I'd chat her up meself, but I reckon she's outta my league,' said Liam, with a cheeky grin on his face. Although he wasn't the best-looking young man, the fact that he knew it gave him a confidence that was unmatchable. 'Any chubby ones, one ear missing, or a flat nose about? I ain't fussy.'

Arty nearly spat out his drink. 'Aw, leave off, Liam. You ain't that fucking bad, mate. You look kinda hard. Women like a tough geezer.'

Ricky was still thinking about how he would approach the barmaid.

Then, when she turned his way, her stubborn expression made him smile. She looked as though she really didn't want to be there. Her black hair and thick black eyebrows would have looked stupid on any other young woman, but not on her. She had green eyes, accentuated by her extra-long mascaraed lashes. The nose piercing wasn't so attractive, but her serious face was.

He raised his brows and then smiled from ear-to-ear, show-ing a small dimple. For a moment, the barmaid paused and then looked behind her, bemused that such a strikingly handsome young man was looking her way.

She faced him again and wondered whether he was really giving her the eye or if he was just pissed. Then he winked, and at that moment, she was drawn to him.

He flicked his head for her to come over, and as soon as she did, he was a little unsure of what to do next. *Come on, Ricky, get a grip*, he thought.

'What can I get ya, mate?' she said, with a confident tone.

'A smile would be nice,' he replied.

The barmaid suddenly felt her face blush. That was a first: she never blushed. In fact, she never looked at the male species as anything other than a pain in the arse.

'Give me something to smile about and I might just do that.'

Ricky chuckled at her feisty attitude. 'You have really pretty eyes, and I bet they light up when you smile.'

Arty and Liam were open-mouthed as they watched Ricky charm the knickers off the young woman.

'Look and learn, Liam, look and fucking learn,' said Arty.

'Who'd have thought little Ricky would be chatting up the first bit o' skirt? She's like putty in his fucking hands,' replied Liam, bemused.

Ricky was enjoying the challenge. 'So, what's your name?'

'Kendall. And yours?' she asked, as she collected some empties from the bar top.

'It's Ricky, but you can call me whatever you see fit.'

It was Kendall's turn to laugh. 'Okay. What about Chancer?'

'That'll do for me, babe.'

Arty was fascinated by Ricky's confidence and couldn't take his eyes off him. However, as much as Liam and Arty were looking on, so were two much older men, who also had their eye on Kendall. She was new and ready for the picking. Claydon Cable and his brother Clive had already bought her a drink the day before, so as far as they were concerned, she was their meat, not some young, flash-looking fucker, as Clive referred to him.

Claydon had already drunk six pints and snorted a line of Flakka, courtesy of the toilet attendant. His aggression was balancing on a sharp stick, and one cross word would have him seeing red and ripping someone's head off. Clive, who hadn't touched the gear, was winding his brother up because he too had six pints inside him. Totally oblivious of the fact that Ricky was not alone, they bowled over to the bar, pushing past first Arty and then Liam, as they stood right up next to Ricky. Claydon leaned on the bar and was five inches away from Ricky's face. He looked Ricky up and down with his downturned eyes and oversized cheeks and then turned to Kendall. 'Is this prick giving you grief, doll?'

Startled by this rough-looking ape, Kendall looked from Claydon to Ricky and then back at the chunky belly-wobbling man and shook her head. 'Nah, mate.'

Finding the situation amusing, Ricky laughed in Claydon's face. 'You've been right mugged off, mate, so, now, run along.'

There was no aggression or angst written on Ricky's face – just a cheeky grin and a sparkle in his eyes.

Arty and Liam were ready quickly to intervene. They knew who the Cables were: they had a reputation for throwing their heavy weight around. For men in their thirties, they really should have stuck to women their own age, instead of thinking they stood a chance with a youngster like Kendall.

Arty took a deep breath and pulled his shoulders back, which made him look so much more significant. Liam pulled his disturbing-looking expression; like his father, he, too, could accomplish the demon look and scare the shit out of most men.

However, Claydon and Clive still hadn't noticed that Ricky was with Arty Stafford and Liam Ritz.

Ricky was still grinning, almost getting a kick out of watching Claydon's expression fill up with frustration.

Claydon's face was so contorted with rage; his eyes glazed over, and his jaw tightened. 'Who the fuck d'ya think you are? Telling me to fucking run along? My arse. The only one 'ere who's gonna get mugged off is you, ya prick. Now, outside. Me and you are gonna have a straightener!'

Ricky's eyebrows were nearly raised to the roof as he deliberately sighed. 'Are you kidding me? I've only just got 'ere. I ain't even finished me pint or got this gorgeous young lady's phone number. I'll tell ya what, though, and it's my best offer. Come back at the end of the night, and if ya still want a straightener, then you can have one. I can't say fairer than that, now can I?'

Claydon couldn't believe the words coming out of the kid's mouth. In fact, he was so utterly gobsmacked, he looked to his brother for some support. But Clive was just as surprised.

'You silly little prick! Do you know who we are?' came a slightly slurred growl from Clive.

Ricky curled his top lip and shook his head. 'Nah, I can't say I do. But, anyway, like I said, come back at the end, and we'll have a straightener.'

With that, he turned to face Arty and Liam. Claydon's and Clive's eyes followed, and as violent as they themselves were, they were also aware that the likes of Stafford and Ritz were dangerous fuckers, who would pull a tool out and know precisely how to use it.

Claydon nudged his brother and both were about to leave, but Arty stood in their way. 'Not so fast. I think you owe our mate an apology. I don't like it when anyone in my company gets called a "prick".'

Claydon was now fuelled by the drugs in his system; he wasn't going to be mugged off. 'Fuck off, Stafford, or me and you will take this outside.'

Liam let out a deep laugh. 'Cor, you've got ya brave hat on, Claydon.'

With that, the Cables pushed past Arty and Liam and left.

Arty then shot Ricky a frown. 'You wanna be careful, mate. They can have a serious ruck.'

Ricky grinned again. 'Yep, Art, me too. But I just didn't wanna have one right now.'

Kendall watched the handsome young man, admiring his confidence. Yet it was his adorable grey eyes that drew her in. And there was so much else about him that was really impressive. He had gorgeous dimples and broad shoulders. She wondered if he was just a time-waster and hoped he wasn't. If she could have, she would have played hard to get, but then she clocked a small group of girls all made-up and looking Ricky's way, so she thought it was a good idea to get in first.

'So, you wanted my number, then?' She tried to keep her tone even, without sounding too eager to please.

'Well, babe, that was the idea. That was until I was rudely interrupted.'

The party was now in full swing. Arty had the pick of two girls fighting for his attention, and Liam was left with the quieter one, with the wide hips and big breasts, which he certainly wasn't going to complain about. Ricky was stealing a bit of conversation with Kendall, in between her serving the customers.

So caught up in the flirting and banter, the young lads were too distracted even to look their fathers' way.

Mike and the firm watched the comings and goings. Mike had his eyes firmly on the men's toilets, trying to suss out who the drug dealer was. Yet no one seemed to be passing anything. However, a few men were going into the gents' and coming out wiping their noses.

'Lou, 'ave ya seen anyone handing out anything?'

Lou was nursing his second pint. 'Not a fucking thing, but some of those lads look fired up, and they've only been sitting on one pint.'

Staffie was still scanning the bar. 'Nothing, Mike. I can't see anyone who's holding any gear.'

'That bloke and his mate over there by the door. Look! They've been in the gents' three fucking times. And I'll tell ya this for nuffin, whatever they're on, it ain't cocaine. But they're on something that is causing a nasty fucking comedown. Look at that fella. He's got the shakes and he's sweating like a pig.'

Mike looked in Willie's direction, and, sure enough, a young man, roughly twenty-five, was leaning against a wall. His hands were really shaking, and his grey T-shirt had serious sweat marks.

'I've been watching him. He went into the loo with his mate ages ago. He was fine when he went in, but now look at the fucking mess he's in.'

Lou looked over at him. 'Might be on heroin.'

Willie shook his head. 'Lou, I've taken every drug under the sun. That kid ain't no heroin addict. He came in looking smart, but now look at him.'

The men surveyed the young customers around them. Some looked energized and some seemed entirely fucked.

Mike got up from his stool. 'There ain't a dealer in 'ere. The fucking suppliers are in the men's toilets.'

Staffie frowned. 'Nah, Mike. The only bloke in there is that skinny black fella who sprays ya with perfume for a fucking fiver.'

'Yeah, that's right. The unsuspecting toilet attendant is the fucker supplying the shit.'

'Are you sure?'

Mike laughed. 'Well, there's one way to find out. I'll hang the bastard upside down and see if any drugs land on me feet.'

Staffie tugged at Mike's arm. 'Wait up. Mike, what if the dealer is a straight-up geezer, someone we know? Are you sure we're doing the right thing? I mean I ain't totally comfortable working for, well, you know who.'

'Staff, mate, this is my turf, and I've every right to know who's dealing, if the info comes from the Filth *or* Joe Bloggs. Now, who's gonna hang that fella up by his boots?'

Staffie nodded, now satisfied. 'Why don't we just ask him for some, then?'

Mike laughed. 'All right. Play it your way first, but if that fails, then it's my way.'

Willie shook his head. 'I prefer Mike's idea.'

'You would!' spat Staffie.

Lou, a man of few words, piped up, 'Willie, you look the typical junkie. Why don't you go in and ask?'

A crooked smile formed across Willie's face. 'Good thinking, Batman.'

Mike rolled his eyes. 'Well, go on then, but no bashing him up if he refuses. You come back out and let me have a word.'

Willie didn't answer; instead, he strolled over to the gents'. Once inside, he noticed the skinny attendant in his brown overalls mopping the floor.

The attendant looked up at Willie, who was glaring his way. A shiver ran up his spine. The man looked wild, his eyes wide and menacing with that cruel-looking scar down his face. Then the attendant held his breath as the guy pulled out a score and shoved it under his nose. He froze. This ugly monster wasn't one of his punters, and for a moment he thought he was from the police, but then, the man seemed too much of a fruit loop to be Ol' Bill.

He almost jumped when the monster spoke.

'What's up? My money ain't good enough?'

The attendant thought it best to play dumb. 'What after-shave would you like? I got—'

'You know what I want and it ain't fucking fairy lotion.'

The attendant shrugged. 'Sorry, I don't know what you mean.'

'Oh dear, never mind, play it your way.' With that, Willie left, leaving the attendant trembling.

Just as he was about to pull the toilet cistern lid off to hide the drugs, the door flew open. A young lad, dying for a piss, was grabbed by the collar and flung out by another huge man with a face like thunder.

Gasping like a girl, the attendant was glued to the spot. There in front of him was the ugly man but two others, just as large and menacing, were with him.

Another young lad tried to push his way in, but Mike forced him out. 'The toilets are full. Now, fuck off.' The kid didn't argue; he spun on his heel.

The thick, intimidating voice had the attendant needing the toilet himself.

'Your shift, mate, is over. Me and you are gonna take a walk outside, and you ain't gonna cause a scene, make a fuss, or even twitch, yeah? You're gonna walk in front of me through the exit door and then we're gonna talk.'

'Er… are you the police?'

Willie let out his high-pitched demonic giggle that made the attendant jump.

'No, we ain't the Filth, but, more to the point, we can be your worst nightmare if you so much as backchat. Got it?'

The attendant's eyes were now on stalks, and he felt his stomach churn. The knife tucked down his back pocket wouldn't be a match for these great monsters.

Willie held the door open as the attendant walked through. Anyone watching would have thought the skinny man dressed in his brown overalls was off to the electric chair as a dead man walking. Mike followed and was joined by Lou and Staffie.

Once they were outside, the attendant turned, his face now a sickly grey colour. 'What's going on?' he mumbled. His tongue had stuck to the roof of his mouth.

'Who's your lookout?' demanded Staffie.

Shaking his head, the attendant replied, 'No one. I mean, look, I just sell a few grams of cocaine to make my wages up, that's all.'

Unexpectedly, Staffie gripped him around the throat. 'I *said*, who's the fucking lookout?'

While Lou and Willie shot off to cover the other two exits to look for anyone who might try to escape, Mike and Staffie stayed with the attendant.

'I don't take too kindly to liars, so if we find your lookout, trust me, you'll wish you'd told the fucking truth.'

The attendant was now expecting a good hiding; he'd spotted Leon, and yet Leon hadn't seen him being marched out of the pub. He wasn't sure who he was more afraid of – Leon, or the guy in front of him.

Deciding to remain quiet, the attendant looked at the pavement, hoping they'd just take the remainder of the drugs and leave him alone.

A couple of young women almost fell out of the door laughing and chatting, which gave the attendant hope that the men weren't going to give him a good hiding in front of other people. However, he didn't know Mike or Staffie at all.

Staffie grabbed him by the collar and marched him down the small dark walkway to the rear of the pub, out of view of the punters.

'Aw, come on. Please, you can have the gear and the money.'

Mike's deep voice had the attendant silenced.

'I don't want your stinking drugs or your fucking money. I wanna know who *gave* you the drugs to flog in the first place. I want names, times, and places, and if you think you can mug me off, I'll rip your head off your scrawny shoulders. Got me?'

All the attendant could do was nod; he could see there was no way he was getting out of this place in one piece.

'So, first, tell me ya name, and then I wanna know who your lookout is for starters.'

The long pause was a mistake. Staffie gave him a punch to the side of the ribs. The blow winded the man badly, and he coughed and spluttered, trying desperately to get his breath.

'Cor, a bit dramatic for a little dig, wasn't it? How about

I give you a real fucking thump, this time to your head? Maybe, then, you'll think quicker.'

'Okay, okay, please. I'm Saeed. The other man's name is Leon Khouri. He's inside, wearing a white top, dark hair, black trousers. Maybe Italian or an Arab.'

Staffie hurried away to the main exit door where Willie was watching. 'He's inside. Black trousers, white shirt. Foreign-looking, dark hair.'

Willie shook his head. 'How many lads fit that description?'

Staffie shrugged his shoulders. 'Let's go and get Lou and fucking find out.'

Shortly, all three men were inside the pub, searching for the Leon Khouri fella. Willie soon spotted someone who appeared to be on edge, hovering by the toilets.

A few strides later, Willie was in front of the man. 'Leon?'

The guy instantly looked in Willie's direction, giving himself away. His eyes darted around the pub, looking for an escape route. However, two other men approached him, so he'd no way out.

He assumed they were the police and sighed, thinking he was nicked; yet, once the tall ugly man roughly snatched his collar, he panicked. These weren't the police; in fact, they were something far worse. Before he'd even had a chance to struggle, he was marched out through the side exit and dragged into the walkway where Saeed Antar, his best salesman, was standing and looking as though he would either pass out with terror or shit himself on the spot.

'You cunt!' he spat at Saeed. 'Fucking grass.'

Saeed couldn't look at his boss; he was between a rock and a hard place.

Then Leon stared at the big man. For a second, he thought he knew the guy, but while he couldn't picture where he'd seen him, the man's stature and his eyes were so familiar.

'Who does this prick Leon work for?' demanded Mike, not acknowledging him, as he placed his hands around Saeed's throat.

Saeed felt the strength of the man's grip, and he knew that any further pressure would have him gasping for breath. But even if he could say *something*, he didn't have the answer to that question because he only knew Leon Khouri.

So, in a whisper, he replied, 'I swear I don't know. Leon gives me the goods and I sell them to make my money up. That's all I know.'

It was a start, Mike reckoned. So he released his gripped on Saeed's throat.

Willie spotted the man's brick-red eyes and dilated pupils, his sunken cheeks, and the thinning, wiry hair.

'You mean you need the money to fund ya fucking habit, you skanky cunt.'

Saeed nodded. 'He—'

'Shut ya mouth,' hollered Leon.

As recklessly as Willie only knew how to be, he backhanded Leon so hard that the man's legs buckled, and he fell to his knees.

Mike rolled his eyes and sighed. 'Willie, for fuck's sake. Let me ask a few questions first, before you go wading in.'

Willie laughed again. 'Oops.' Then, suddenly, he frisked Saeed, digging his hands inside the man's side pockets and retrieving a packet of white powder. He held it close to his face and frowned. Then he opened the packet and dabbed his finger into the powdery drug and tasted it. He frowned again.

'What the fuck is this shit?'

Saeed tried to swallow against the hand that was now around his throat. 'Cocaine.'

'Fucking liar! This ain't cocaine. I should know. So, what the fuck is it?'

Saeed repeated himself. 'Cocaine.'

With that, Willie did a more thorough search and pulled out a load of packets. Everyone watched as he poured the contents into the palm of his hand.

'Mike, open this cunt's mouth. I wanna see if this shit is cocaine or not, and this fucker is gonna be my hamster.'

Staffie laughed aloud. 'You mean guinea pig.'

'Whatever.'

Mike pulled Saeed's head back and forced his jaws apart. Struggling for all he was worth, Saeed knew full well that if he swallowed that amount, he would be dead by the morning. 'No, stop!' he managed to say through gasps and splutters.

Mike let go and allowed the man to straighten up and get his breath.

'All right, it's not cocaine, it's called Flakka.'

Leon was coming around from the backhander and wasn't so cocky now.

He stayed silent as Saeed gave the men a chemistry lesson on the drug. 'It's like cocaine but much more addictive. It either sends you into a coma for a few hours or makes you aggressive.' He hoped that by giving the details of the drug, it would save his life.

Leon was shrinking into himself. With a zillion questions running through his mind, he wondered how the hell he was going to get out of this shitstorm, and, more worryingly, how he was going to escape with his life. He hoped that under these mean-looking men's clothes there was a police badge, or he was completely buggered.

Mike continued to ignore Leon, his eyes boring into Saeed's. 'How the fuck did you meet Leon?'

'I bought the drugs from him, and he gave me a job to pay for what I owed.'

'Where did you meet him?'

Leon was now crumbling; his dealer was singing like a fucking canary, and he knew that if these men sussed out who his own supplier was, he was a dead man.

Saeed's eyes flicked over in Leon's direction; he concluded that his boss was the lesser of two evils and that he would do worse if he didn't grass. 'The Pomodorra in Peckham.'

A cold feeling swept through Mike. 'The Italian restaurant? And what would a scummy toerag like you be doing dining in a classy place like that, eh?'

Saeed felt sweat dripping down his back. 'No, not the restaurant. The ice-cream van outside it. It's a known place to get gear if you have the password.' As soon as he said it, he realized he'd said far too much.

'And the password is?'

Saeed didn't reply right away; he faltered. It was to prove a big mistake. 'Er… ' He looked across the road and spotted the sign "Tudor Way" on the wall of a side street. 'Er, Tudor.'

Mike looked at Staffie. 'Ya know me, Staff. I've always been able to smell a lie a mile away, and this silly little knobsucker has just tried to take me for a fool. And you know what I do to fools that try to mug me off, eh?'

Staffie grinned. 'Do you want your monkey wrench or your blowtorch? What's ya flavour?'

Saeed gasped. *Jesus, they're gonna torture me*, he thought. He wasn't ready for such premeditated violence, and, instantly, the shock made him piss himself. 'No, look, sorry, it's not Tudor. Fuck, it's Governor.'

Mike's eyes widened. 'You what?'

Saeed's head was shaking as if he was about to have a fit. 'Yeah, it's Governor. I promise, I'm not lying.'

Mike suddenly let Saeed go and turned so fast towards Leon that the man jumped back.

'Who supplies you?'

'I don't know his name. They just call him the Governor. I swear to ya, he just calls me and meets up, drops off the drugs, and takes the money, or he tells me where to drop off the money. That's all I know.' He was now crying and pleading like a real wimp.

'Give me ya phone... I said, give me your fucking phone!' yelled Mike, directly into Leon's ear, almost deafening him.

Fumbling inside his pocket, Leon pulled out his mobile and handed it to Mike.

He gave Leon's face a sharp tap and grinned. 'Now, you listen to me very fucking carefully. I'll be coming for you if I hear or see any of that shit being peddled anywhere this side of South-East London. Got it? And if you see this bloke called the Governor, tell him from me, *I'm* the Governor in this fucking manor, and if he wants to argue the point, then he needs to see me.'

Leon wondered who the hell would win in a fight between the Governor and this giant. 'Who shall I say is looking for him?'

A fully fledged grin adorned Mike's face. 'The Big Fucking Bad Wolf. So, you run along, Little Red Riding Hood, and you tell him from me, I'll take him out if I hear of any of this shit being sold anywhere in my manor!'

He let Leon and Saeed go. 'Now, fuck off!'

As soon as they were out of sight, running for their lives, Mike looked at the phone and tried to fathom if there were any stored numbers or text messages – nothing. Had the fucking little shit lied or had he just mentally stored the Governor's number in his head? It was too late to find out now though.

In a black BMW 7 Series, with heavily tinted windows and parked in full view of the back of the pub, sat the so-called man himself: The Governor. He watched and clocked every move, every flinch, and lip-read every word that was spoken. He smiled to himself: he knew he was already one step ahead.

CHAPTER NINE

The next morning, Ricky awoke with a banging headache and walked unsteadily into the kitchen to find his dad as fresh as a daisy. He was sitting at the breakfast bar reading *The Sun* and sipping a black coffee.

'Where did you go, Dad? We turned around and you lot had gone.'

Mike laughed. 'I'm surprised you could even see straight. You were as pissed as a fart.'

Ricky laughed. 'I was just having a good time. It was such a laugh, Dad. The lads were blinding, and I did get to have a snog an' all. The barmaid, Kendall, she gave me her number. I said I would take her out tomorrow night. She's got the night off.'

'You make sure you have protection with ya.'

Ricky's eyes widened. 'What? Ya mean a gun?'

'No, ya daft sod. Ya need condoms. Ya don't wanna go getting some tart pregnant.'

Their conversation was suddenly interrupted by Mike's phone ringing. It was a withheld number. He guessed right away it was the Police Commissioner. 'Hello.' He knew his voice sounded abrupt.

'Mr Regan, we need to talk. I think you may have taken things a little too far. We want the scum taken off the streets but leaving them dead in an alleyway shows the media we have a more serious problem on our hands. The whole point of having you to help us is to stop the media scrutinizing how we are handling the situation. Leaving two dead dealers for all to see will have the papers crawling all over it.'

'Hang on a minute. I haven't killed anyone. I did shake up two deadbeat dealers and put out a warning, but we never fucking killed anyone. What did they look like?'

'One was a Somalian. The other was a white guy – black trousers and a white shirt. Well, not so much white now. Once we removed the hessian sacks over their heads, we found their faces were left completely annihilated. Look, Mr Regan, we gave you the lead, but now they're dead.'

'Right, hold on a fucking minute. You asked me to do a job. If ya are gonna start with accusations, you can forget the whole damn idea. 'Cos the truth is, even talking with you – a cozzer – turns my stomach. So this whole thing ain't doing my digestive system much good.'

Stoneham felt the full force of Regan's voice. The intimidating growl made him sit up and be very careful in future over his choice of words. Two months before Mike was released, they'd discovered two dead drug dealers with sacks over their faces, so he wasn't too surprised to hear Mike deny the murders. 'Please, Mr Regan, accept my apologies. I jumped to the wrong conclusion. I should not have accused you without establishing the facts. But your threat to their set-up has undoubtedly shaken someone's tree.'

Once Mike calmed down, his anger diminished, he finished

the call and sat there in contemplation. The Pomodorra was Zara's restaurant, run by Italians, but it was used to sell cocaine to the toffs. It was concerning that this Flakka drug was being sold from a van across the road. Something was definitely not adding up. He wondered about the Lanigans. Were they taking over right under Zara's nose and supplying her punters? As he understood the situation from Zara, years before the Segals tried to take over, she persuaded the Lanigans to go in and take back her business under their name. She was being paid fifty per cent, and as far as he was aware, the money was piling up in her offshore bank account. However, now she was back, taking control of her business. *Perhaps they didn't like the idea?* he thought.

'Damn!' he said out loud, to the surprise of Ricky, who jumped and spilled his coffee.

'What's up, Dad?'

Mike tutted. 'Nothing, Son, but I need to go and pay Zara a visit.'

'Something troubling you, Dad?'

Mike nodded. 'Yeah, there is, Son, but it don't need to concern you.'

'But—'

Mike raised his hand. 'No, Ricky. Leave it to me, Son. You just nurse that hangover. I'll be back later.'

***

By the time Mike had arrived outside Zara's house, he had conjured up a serious assumption. It was one that wouldn't bode well for her.

In his mind, the Lanigans had taken over her business and were selling this highly addictive drug to any kid and toff who wanted to get high. Of course, they would pay Zara just to keep her nose out of it. Neil Lanigan getting stabbed may have happened because one of the druggies had become high and aggressive, resulting in the Irish fella coming off worse. Immersed in his own thoughts, he didn't plan on how he would confront Zara over it. Instead, he banged hard at her door.

Zara was in the process of having the house redesigned and was flicking through some swatches. She heard the loud knock at the door and then turned to her newly installed security monitor that showed the whole perimeter of the house, just as her father had once had it set up. She stared for a moment at Mike, who was running his hands through his hair in an agitated state. Her heart beat fast as she watched him. In her mind, she assumed that by keeping herself to herself, she would rid him from her thoughts and eventually turn her feelings off. But there he was on the screen, like a thousand trombones ringing in her ears. No one could send her emotions through the roof as much as Mike.

She took a deep breath and opened the door.

Mike seemed almost surprised to see her standing there, as if he half expected her either not to answer the door or to be out of the house.

He looked her up and down. 'Are you okay?' His reason for talking business went out of the window, the minute he clapped eyes on her. 'You look good, babe.'

She stepped aside and nodded for him to come in.

'Are you looking after yourself all right?'

Zara so wanted to laugh. This wasn't her tough-talking

Mike. He was acting more like a naughty schoolkid sucking up to get out of detention.

'I'm fine, Mike, as you can see. So, what did you want?' Really, she wanted to fall into his arms and kiss his face, but he was the one sucking up, and so she would milk it for all its worth.

Her coldness annoyed him; he wanted his kind, soft-spoken Zara back. 'Well, it's about business. Are you on your own?' His tone soured.

Zara felt a little choked up; she was hoping he would get on his hands and knees and beg for forgiveness. She remained silent and waited.

'The Pomodorra, do you still own it?'

Unimpressed by his tone, she walked into her office, ignoring him, but hoping he would follow so that she could sit on her office chair that was higher than the one opposite and take up her position as head of her business and conduct it in a way her father would have done.

Mike followed and sat down, just as she planned. It worked a treat. She definitely had the height advantage. She leaned back and raised her eyebrow. 'Why do you want to know, Mike?'

He realized she was playing the tough cow and rolled his eyes. 'For fuck's sake, Zara. Stop being so bloody stubborn, will you? Look, I know what you saw after the party, but it wasn't like that. I was drunk, I fell asleep, and that little tart did likewise on the other sofa, end of. She had nothing to do with me!'

Zara stared at him silently, with those copper, catlike eyes peering impassively. She knew she'd got right up Mike's nose.

'Come on, Zara. You know me better than that. Look, I've

left you to have time to yaself, but, seriously, do you think I would be with some tart when I'm engaged to you?'

'Mike, you said you were here on business, so what do you want?'

Mike jutted out his jaw, and, like Zara, he leaned back on his chair. 'All right, Zara, fine. I think the Lanigans are taking you for a right mug. They are peddling drugs right under your nose.'

A sudden laugh left her mouth. It made Mike flare his nostrils. 'And what's so fucking funny about that?'

'Mike, my restaurants have been used to supply cocaine for years, but surely you knew that? I know while you were inside you had a lot on ya mind, but you knew about the Italians.'

Mike shook his head. 'Of course, I fucking knew. I ain't deaf or blind. I'm not talking about *cocaine*, I'm talking about this new drug called Flakka. It's being flogged from an ice-cream van opposite the Pomodorra.'

Zara's eyes narrowed. 'Well, my restaurants are all closing down. The managers have been terrorized by some gang, so they've fucked off back to Italy.'

Mike frowned. 'You never said. Christ, what the fuck's been going on?'

'A lot, Mike, a bloody lot. So, if you don't mind, I have much to sort out.'

Just as Mike was about to quiz her, there was another loud knock at the door. She looked across at the security monitor. 'Sorry, Mike. Would you excuse me? I have a meeting.'

'What? Who with?'

'Look, a lot has happened. You were away for twelve years, I was locked up for five, and then we probably fell into each other's arms because it was meant to be at the time, if you know what I mean. The party – you didn't need me, and the truth is, you probably never did. I guess, like me, you had thoughts of us being in a bubble of romantic bliss, and they kept us going during those cold, lonely nights, but reality has a way of slapping you in the face. I have a business to take care of, and you have yours, and, Mike, the only thing we have much in common is the arms business. Other than that, we owe each other nothing.'

Totally gobsmacked, Mike was stunned into silence.

'Sorry, Mike. Like I said, I've a business meeting. Would you excuse me?'

Mike's face suddenly dropped, and his shoulders slouched. It was over, and he could see in her cold, dark eyes that the former passion had gone. It was dead.

As she opened the door to Victor, Mike didn't even acknowledge him. He hurried past, marching to his car. Zara stared at the only man she really loved as he walked away. She could feel her ears tingling as the lump in her throat made it almost impossible to swallow. The hot tears pricked her eyes, and she quickly shied away, not wanting Victor to see her heartbroken expression.

But Victor was sharp. He noticed right away the chemistry between the two of them. It was perfectly apparent that the big guy was the one she gave her heart to.

'I take it that was Eric's brother? Jesus, two peas in a pod.'

'Yeah, they are. Come in. We'll talk in my office.'

Victor followed her.

After they had settled themselves, Zara asked, 'Any news to report?'

'Not really. My pal down at Margate said that these gangs

183

of Yardies made horrendous threats, and when he didn't take them seriously, he found a dead cat in his living room. The bastards actually broke into his house and left a death threat, and so he gave in, sold up, and moved. I followed Eric, but he was just going about his normal business. He was at home most of the time, and then he made a few visits to the pub, a visit to his mother's, and had a few bets in the bookies. He didn't go anywhere else, so I reckon he must have overheard your conversation with Neil or Davey and decided to take a look for himself.'

'Okay, so our next move is to reopen Antonio's on Saturday night. Davey's men will be dining, and Shamus, believe it or not, is a dab hand at pasta, so everything's in place to wipe out this fucking gang.'

Victor suddenly looked drained. 'Zara, this isn't about a few kids running around acting like hard men who can be easily beaten. This drug is evil. It makes the gangs reckless and ruthless. You do know if you take one lot out, there'll be another one taking over, and what they did to Neil, they'll do to the others, one by one?'

Zara sat back on her chair and tilted her head to the side. 'My father said you were a dangerous man. Tell me, Victor, you said you like to work alone, but after all that this gang did to your wife, how come you haven't gone all out yourself to take 'em down?'

Sitting opposite, Victor's face suddenly changed back to that evil grin. 'What makes you think I haven't already been doing that?'

Zara's eyes bulged wide. 'What?'

'Before Lennon, there was another bloke called Terian. He

was the man running the manor. He was a vile creature who gang-raped a kiddie, two doors up from me. A real little darling she was, only fifteen an' all. She was too shit-scared to call the police, but she mentioned his name, and that was all I needed.'

Zara leaned forward on her chair, listening to every word. 'Go on. Did you kill him?'

With a devious smirk, he nodded. 'Not only him. I sorted out the two other sick bastards as well.'

'Was it on the news? I never heard anything?'

He shook his head. 'These gang members, whether they rape, murder, or rob, it's all kept hush-hush, and so if they go missing, that's kept quiet too. The police don't want to be seen to be lacking in effort, if ya know what I mean, babe. It would be a public relations disaster. So Lennon won't get a mention in the newspapers either. They won't even follow it up.'

'So, when I take out these greedy fuckers who've done over my business, their disappearance won't be slapped all over the papers?'

Slowly, he shook his head. 'Nope.'

'Good, because when I meet these gang members, I want them to know who I am. They need to know that the woman with one hand is real and not some made-up story. I want them all to fear my firm and me and to think twice about ever setting foot in my premises or even attempting to peddle their fucking wares on my ground.'

'You are so like your father, but, listen, don't do that. Let your Irish guys be the front men. Don't put yourself at risk. I don't mean to hurt your feelings, but a woman with one hand will be like a challenge to them. They'll all think they can take you out and will want to try it,' said Victor, with a soft fatherly voice.

Surprised, yet pleased by his input, she smiled inwardly. He really didn't know her at all. 'Oh, and by the way, thank you for organizing the cameras for me. I really want this house back to how Izzy had it, but I want it more up to date.'

He nodded and winked. 'You need to look out for yaself, babe. You be careful, eh?'

Zara nodded, accepting his advice.

***

Eric arrived at Mike's with an Indian takeaway. The boxing was on, and the lads were all coming around to have a few beers and a bite to eat. It had been a regular thing every Thursday. Either they played poker or watched a match. Mike had decided to drop the issue with Eric over the party incident and just let sleeping dogs lie.

With the exception of Eric, they all cheered Ricky on as he got himself spruced up for his date.

Ricky was dressed to impress. Since he'd taken Kendall's phone number, they'd been continuously texting, and tonight he was going to take her out. The cab driver beeped his horn while Ricky took one last look in the mirror.

Willie called out, 'Home before midnight, Cinderella.'

Ricky, in a real bubbly mood, shouted back, 'Yes, Wicked Stepmother.'

Staffie laughed. 'More like a fucking ugly stepsister.'

Eric didn't join in the banter; he glared at Ricky's wide smile and glowing cheeks and left them all to it.

***

The cab pulled up directly outside the Daylight Inn, and Ricky jumped out and handed the driver a score. 'Keep the change, mate.'

As the cabbie drove away, Ricky straightened his jacket and walked past the bouncers, giving them a wink, and wandered over to the bar. He looked at his Rolex and smiled. He was bang on time. He ordered a pint and waited. He didn't actually know what Kendall liked to drink although he knew pretty much everything else, since they'd been glued to their phones, texting.

The pub was not as busy as at the DJ party, and it appeared so different; without the flashing disco lights and people dancing, it seemed somewhat sedate. He watched the door, eagerly awaiting her arrival, and then, as the door opened, his heart beat faster. There she was. She looked different: her hair was smoothed down and her make-up was subtle. She wore a black dress, a jeans jacket, and high shoes. Ricky looked her up and down and then whistled, which made Kendall blush. The scene was a far cry from the other night, when she seemed stubborn and played hard to get.

He leaned with one arm on the bar and gave her his trademark wink with a cheeky smile. 'What would you like to drink, babe? How about some champagne?'

For the first time in her life, Kendall could honestly say she felt like a woman; her ever-angry mood and stubborn streak dissipated the minute he'd given her that wink. She could easily have fallen right into those pools of pearl grey. 'Sounds good to me.'

Ricky ordered a bottle and took it over to a small table by the window. She sat on a low stool opposite and watched as he poured their drinks. 'Cheers,' he said, as he passed her a tall glass.

As they sipped the cold drink, the bubbles shot up Kendall's nose, which made her giggle. Even the laugh was new; she wasn't used to laughing. Her life had been centred around a sombre, gloomy, and stifling atmosphere. This was so invigorating, she really felt that at long last she had moved on from her previous life in the Mullins household. And the figure-hugging dress and high heels were giving her added confidence, enhancing her self-worth as a sexy woman.

Ricky was looking at her with admiration, and she wondered why he'd taken such a liking to her; after all, there were far prettier women in the pub on that particular night. Still, she wasn't here to question him about *that*! No, she was going to lap it up and find out what this mysterious young man was really like.

'So, would you like to have an Indian or a Chinese? There's one of each across the road,' asked Ricky, still gazing into Kendall's eyes.

The offer on the surface was a good one, but she wanted to have him all to herself. Not for one second did she want to be distracted, even by a waiter. So she made a counter offer. 'Why don't we get a takeaway and eat it in my flat?' she suggested.

It was Ricky's turn to blush. 'Um, what? You have your own place?'

She nodded and seductively placed the glass to her lips and sipped the champagne, the hint of a smile forming on her face.

Ricky's eyes widened; he couldn't believe his luck. He was dying to be alone with Kendall. 'Why not? I'll order another bottle of this stuff, and we can enjoy a little romantic meal at yours.' He winked again. 'No one to disturb us.'

'Disturb us from what, Ricky?' she teased, in her slow, alluring voice.

'From anything we wanna do. 'Cos I for one ain't too keen on a public show of affection, and those rosebud lips of yours are too tempting not to plant a kiss on 'em.'

She pretended to act coy and raised her eyebrows. 'Well, what are we waiting for?'

Ricky jumped up and headed to the bar while Kendall smoothed down her dress, her mind tingling with excitement. She wasn't into one-night stands; in fact, she really wasn't into sex, but Ricky was different. He was so sexy that she just wanted to get her hands on him. She hoped he felt the same way about her.

Holding two bottles of champagne, he asked if he should call a cab.

'No need. I live just over there.' She pointed out of the window to the flat above the hairdresser's.

Just as they stepped outside, the heavens opened, and the sudden downpour had them both taking a step back. Ricky, ever the gentleman, removed his jacket and placed it around her shoulders. 'There ya go, sweetheart.'

The darkness was creeping in, and the torrential rain made their surroundings seem a blur, but they hurried across the road towards the back of the flat, laughing as they ran. Once they were inside the building, and shaking off the excess water, Ricky followed Kendall as she rushed up the stairs. The landing light wasn't working, so she struggled in the darkness to put her key in the lock. Finally, they were inside. Ricky turned to close the door behind him, but something was stopping him. As he looked down, he saw a large trainer. With no time to react, the door was smashed open, knocking Ricky off balance. Before Ricky or Kendall could even focus on who was barging their way in, a bag was shoved over Ricky's head, and he was forced to the floor. Kendall was on the point of running, but, before she'd taken a step, she was aggressively grabbed by another man behind the one who attacked Ricky. He had a hold of her hair and pulled it so tightly she winced. He held her face away from his, so she couldn't see who he was.

With such violent force, she was dragged across the sitting room and her face pushed hard into a cushion on the sofa. 'Shut the fuck up!' he yelled at her.

The ringing in her ears, and the throbbing in her ankle from being dragged across the floor, had Kendall terrified. So many frightening thoughts ran through her mind: *were they going to rape her, or kill her*? The strong smell of a masculine body odour and the deep, gruff voice told her that her aggressor was a man – a robust and powerful man. Then she heard Ricky shouting. 'Get off me, you bastard!'

The next sound was a hard thump, followed by more. She could only imagine Ricky's head being punched against the wall. Her stomach was in knots, and she felt herself bringing up bile. With her eyes bulging in terror, all she could see was the cold leather of the sofa. The heart-wrenching screams coming from Ricky were now mere groans as the pounding sounds were relentless. Each one felt like it was an attack on her. The continual beating from his attacker, clearly out of breath, terrified Kendall. They were killing Ricky. *God, how the fuck had all this happened in less than sixty seconds*? Now motionless, she could only feel the man's grip and the thump of her own heartbeat. Not one for praying, she closed her eyes and begged God to help her. But clearly God wasn't listening. As Ricky's moans died off, it was at that point she went limp. Poor Ricky, the dear sweetheart, with eyes so full of life and a smile that would light up a dark room, was gone like the dousing of flickering flames. If Ricky couldn't fight them off, then there was not a cat in hell's chance that she could. She would have to try to talk her way out of it.

'Please, tell me. What do you want?'

'Shut the fuck up!' came the same growl.

Her mind couldn't think quickly enough; all she could do was wait quietly and hope they would leave soon. Suddenly, the tight grip loosened, but Kendall didn't move; heavy footsteps approached, and she could sense another man close by.

The man with the deep voice spoke. 'Leave off, man. What are ya doing?'

Kendall could hear the sound of a zipper being opened, and then reality hit her. In a panic, she tried to turn around, but a heavy hand pushed her head forward, into the sofa. 'Noooo!' she screamed, but her face was now forced even further into one of the cushions. She couldn't get her breath, and the more she struggled, the harder he pushed, until she couldn't breathe at all. Then, like being pulled from a deep pool, the man allowed her to take a breath, but as she gasped for air, something was shoved in her mouth. She gasped again, but, this time, the contents hit her lungs. Desperate to breathe, she coughed, choked, and gagged. But more powder was being shoved into her mouth, the taste of which was vile. Crying and pleading, she tried to grip the sofa with her nails, as the burning sensation ripped at her lungs.

The intense fear unexpectedly drifted away; incredibly,

her body was numb, and she found herself floating. She imagined herself drifting up into the clouds, feeling no pain, and, amazingly, no terror whatsoever. Her body relaxed as her muscles turned to mush. All she could hear were muffled sounds somewhere in the distance. The large hands that ran up inside her thighs felt like butterflies, and her brain couldn't comprehend what was really taking place. Then the sharp thrust of something large shot up inside her, but she was too numb to feel the pain. She was too weak even to cry out. The rhythmic movement as her body moved back and forth, like a ride on a swing, sent her dizzy. Then it all stopped. Silence and stillness pervaded the room. Unaware of the time – the minutes could have been hours – she lay there until suddenly she felt another object being pushed inside her. This time she did feel the pain; it was like a coiled spring inside her, tearing at her insides, burning and aching, as she was pushed up the sofa with such surging force, and yet she still felt too weak to fight back. The dim light from the side lamp was now just a pinprick of gold until everything went completely black. She was out cold – in the land of the clouds.

***

Mike had crashed out in the lounge. Hearing the sound of a door slamming, his eyes opened to see Eric enter the room. He was surprised to see his brother as he'd assumed it would be Ricky returning from his night out by now. 'Where did you go, Eric?'

'You were asleep, so I popped out to get some fags.'

Mike looked up at the clock. ''Ere, it's one o'clock. Fuck! Ricky was supposed to be home by now.'

'He's all right. He's probably banging his new bird.'

Mike initially ignored his comment. He went into the kitchen and started to load the dishwasher.

'Eric, I don't think my Ricky is like that, ya know. The boy's a decent lad, bless him, and he treats people with respect, especially women.'

Eric gave a dramatic sigh. 'Don't put him on a pedestal just yet, Mike, because in all honesty, you don't even know the boy.'

That comment was like a red rag to a bull. Mike had had enough and was ready to lay into Eric.

'Don't you fucking dare tell me I don't know my own son. My boy *is* a decent fella. He's a fucking good kid. If you had kids of your own then you would know the fucking difference, so shut ya mouth!'

'All I'm saying, Mike, is that you think the sun shines out of Ricky's arse, as if he's some god or something.'

'You need to be more careful what ya say about my son.'

'He's only been in your life for a few weeks, so you don't know him at all really, do ya?'

Gripping his fists, Mike used all his might to hold down his temper.

'Actually, the sun *does* shine outta his arse, and if I say me boy has a fucking halo around his head, then he has a fucking halo. I know my son. He's the same kid as he was the last day I saw him all those years ago, and I won't let anyone, brother or not, tell me a fucking thing about me own boy. I suggest you leave before I give you another hiding like the last one I gave you when you overstepped the mark regarding my son. Message received?'

Eric grabbed his phone and marched towards the door. But

before he left, he turned, and with a spiteful expression, he spat, 'I was different back then, Mike, living in your fucking shadow, but I shouldn't think you'd be able to put me on my arse again. I ain't the same. I've lived a life on the outside while you were locked up. Let's hope it never comes to a war between us because I really wouldn't wanna hurt you.'

Mike's temper was rising. 'A war? A war? You think you could handle *me*? Yeah, is that right, Eric? Do you seriously think you could have it out with me?' With each word, his voice became steadily louder.

'Don't push your luck, Mike. You've underestimated me for far too fucking long. You may think you have it all – the birds, the respect – but let me tell you something, shall I? Your name went down the toilet while you were away. You were only a Face years ago, and a lot has changed. It ain't all about fighting anymore. It's a different world out there, and I'll tell you something else while I'm here. You need to get real. The game has moved on, and you, dear brother, have been left behind along with Willie Ritz, Ted Stafford, and that smart arse, Lou Baker.'

Hearing those words was tipping Mike over the edge. So fucked up in his head, listening to his brother pouring out all that shit about him and Ricky – it felt like what it was, a personal attack on them both – Mike couldn't stop himself. 'If that's the case, then why do the fucking Filth want the men and me to fucking clean up the streets if I'm such an 'as been, eh?'

The second the words left his mouth, he knew he couldn't take them back: he'd let the cat out of the bag. He and the boys had made a pledge not to tell Eric because he needed to earn their trust before they'd let him back in the firm. Eric had bailed out when the shit hit the fan, and he'd stayed away when Mike needed him the most. So it was decided Eric could only rejoin the firm once they'd rebuilt that relationship.

Surprisingly, Eric didn't look shocked or annoyed; he just gave Mike a final look up and down, smirked, and slammed the door behind him.

Still seething, Mike searched for his phone; he needed at least to be sure that Ricky was safe.

The phone rang repeatedly. Mike sighed and paced the floor. He called once more, but there was still no answer.

His mind now in a panic, he called Arty. The phone rang three times before a sleepy voice answered. 'Mike? What's up?'

'Art, this bird that Ricky's gone out with. Where does she live? Only, Ricky ain't come home.'

Arty sat up straight, cleared his voice, and blinked a few times. 'Er, I dunno where she lives but she works in the Daylight. She's the barmaid there. Kendall, her name is. Mike, I wouldn't worry too much. I'm sure he's fine.'

'Nah, Ricky said he would be home at twelve. It's well past one, now.'

Arty sensed the urgency in Mike's voice; he knew he had to take it seriously. 'Look, I tell ya what. I'll meet you at the Daylight Inn. The pub may be closed, but they'll have the cleaners in, and the landlord's probably doing his paperwork as we speak.'

'Nice one, Arty. I appreciate that, son.'

Just as Arty climbed into his jeans, his dad came through the door. 'Dad, Mike's just been on the phone. Ricky ain't come home. I'm meeting him at the Daylight. Ricky went there to meet this Kendall, the barmaid. We need to find out where she lives.'

Staffie stood there with a look of concern. 'Fuck, that's all we need. Mike will be ripping his hair out. I'll come with ya because Mike won't be rational, I can guarantee ya that.'

***

Petts Wood Square was dead, with not a person in sight. Mike looked over at the pub, hoping to see a light on, but it was in total darkness, and his heart was in his mouth. Twenty times he'd tried his son's number, with no answer. Ahead, bright headlights were coming from a car tearing along the road. It stopped just in front of him and out jumped Arty and Staffie.

'The pub's shut up. Jesus, Staffie, Ricky ain't answering his phone, and he knows I'd be bleedin' worried. He wouldn't do that to me. Something's fucking wrong.'

Staffie patted his back. 'Listen, Mike, he's still only eighteen, just a lad. He's likely to be with a bird. You know how it is.'

'Nah, something ain't right. I can feel it.'

Arty rushed over to the pub and banged hard on the main door, but no one answered. Mike hurried around to the side of the pub and banged on that door. Suddenly, a light came on, and the door opened. Two men appeared – the landlord and one of the bouncers.

'Kendall, the barmaid, where does she live?' demanded Mike.

With a cocky leer, the bouncer, still in his stab-proof vest, stepped forward. 'We don't give out addresses, mate. Sorry.'

Staffie appeared just in time to stop Mike throwing a deadly punch. 'No, Mike, wait, mate.'

The bouncer realized he'd cocked up; the man asking the

questions looked as though he would burst a vein in his temple. 'Look. Sorry, but we have to keep information like that private. I mean, I don't know who you are... '

Mike was losing his patience; in one quick movement, he grabbed the bouncer with a hand around his throat. 'I *said*, what's her fucking address?'

The landlord's face turned white; afraid, he reached for the phone on the wall, but Arty managed to pull him back. 'And what the fuck d'ya think *you're* doing?'

Shaken up, the landlord nervously replied, 'I'm calling the police.'

Staffie gave a loud mocking laugh. 'Yeah, mate, you do that, and we'll tell them how you've let dealers in here to peddle this shit Flakka gear. Now, me mate wants Kendall's address, so I suggest unless you wanna have this place shut down, you do as you're fucking told.'

As Mike looked away from the bouncer and glanced at Staffie, the guy tried to throw a punch. But that was a big mistake. Mike flicked his head to the side to miss the contact, and with one almighty crack, he headbutted the bouncer and watched him hit the deck. Then, with a kick to the stomach, Mike stepped back. 'Cunt!' he spat.

Arty had heard how hard Mike was, but he'd never actually seen him in action. Arty was a Face and could ruck, just like his father, but Mike was on another scale. Arty would have needed a metal cosh to do the damage Mike managed with no tools whatsoever.

The landlord froze, staring at his toughest bouncer squirming around on the floor, with his head split open and his eyes bloodshot. 'Shit! Look, just go, yeah? That Kendall bird lives over there, above the hairdresser's. But you ain't gonna hurt her, are ya? She's a good kid.'

Mike growled. 'Don't be fucking stupid. I don't hurt kids or women. I only want to find my son. He was with her.'

The landlord nodded. 'Well, she lives up there.'

Wasting no time, Mike sprinted over to the back entrance of the flats. He jumped the stairs two at a time, and then he was faced with two doors opposite each other. He could see that the door to the right was smashed in. His mouth suddenly became dry as his nerves tingled all over his body. Slowly, he pushed the door open, and the sight before him made him fall to his knees. Staffie and Arty were behind, looking over Mike's shoulders. At first, all they could see was Ricky's lifeless body. Then they saw his white T-shirt covered in blood, and, more shockingly, a hessian sack tied over his head, which was stained in dark claret.

Mike let out a blood-curdling scream like a dying wolf, while he pawed at the sack to get it off Ricky's head. 'Noooo, please God, no, not my boy, please, not my boy!' With his body shaking uncontrollably, he tried to remove the strangling cord that was knotted around Ricky's neck.

Arty pushed past, shocked at the scene in front of him. On his knees next to Mike, he watched his dad cautiously remove Mike's hands and make headway as he untied the cord.

'Mikey, Mikey, he's breathing. Look, he ain't dead,' yelled Arty.

Finally, they managed to pull the sack off. To their horror, Ricky's face was unrecognizable – it was swollen like a medicine ball. His eyes were mere slits, his lips were like fat sausages, and his nose was smashed to pieces.

Gently, Mike cradled his battered son's head and cried like a child. 'Dear God, why? Why the fuck did they attack my boy?' The tears plummeted down his face as he rocked his son. 'Please, don't die. Please, don't leave me!'

Arty got to his feet and called an ambulance while Staffie's attention turned to a prone shape partly obscured by the sofa. 'Fuck! Is that Kendall?'

Arty was giving the emergency service operator details, but as he turned to see his dad leaning over Kendall's lifeless body on the floor, he said, 'Er, you'd better send two ambulances. There's a girl here who looks like she's been attacked too. Please, please, hurry.'

Staffie stared at the girl in horror and disgust. Arty slid past him and kneeled by her side, feeling for a pulse. Then he looked up. 'She's fucking dead. Oh my God, she's dead.'

Staffie looked around for a sheet to cover the girl's naked and bruised body. Unexpectedly, a tear trickled down his face. 'What animals would do this?'

On the back of the sofa was a throw. Gently, he covered her body but left her face on show as if she were asleep. Arty peered closer and noticed the white powder all over her face and up her nose. His attention was taken away when he heard Mike's haunting, desperate pleas.

'Come on, Ricky, talk to me, Son. Please say something. It's ya dad. I'm here.' The sobs that left Mike's throat would have had any grown man in tears. He just couldn't face losing him – not now, not when he'd just got him back. All those years of pain believing Ricky had been dead was hard, but if his boy died now, it would rip his heart right out, and he wouldn't want to live himself. 'Please, God, please help him!'

Arty kneeled down with Mike and held Ricky's wrist, feeling for a pulse; it was there, but it was very faint. He locked eyes with Mike. It was the first time in his life he'd witnessed the most powerful man he knew reduced to a soulless, vulnerable wreck; he looked a withered old man, expressing the essence of absolute grief. The sad sight of Mike seemingly alone in his desolation had Arty unable to speak. Tears tumbled down his cheeks. This bleakest moment of his life seemed to play out in slow motion.

Relief came when they heard the sirens. Arty got his act together and hurried downstairs to show the paramedics the way up to the flat. Then the police arrived – four carloads of them.

As the paramedics got to work, taking Ricky's vitals and preparing him to be stretchered off, Staffie pulled Mike away. 'Let them do what they've got to do, mate. Step back.'

Mike was as weak as a kitten, so consumed by torment. He looked to be in a trance. 'His name's Ricky. Please help him. Don't let him die!'

The female paramedic with a kind face rubbed Mike's arm. 'He's your son, then?'

Mike nodded with sad tears rolling down his face. 'Tell me, he's gonna be okay?'

She could feel his pain and nodded. 'We'll do what we can. We need to get him to the hospital. Do you want to come with us?'

Before he even had a chance to answer, two policemen bowled into the room. 'Hold it. Sorry, sir, you need to come with us. We'll need to ask a few questions.'

Staffie knew right away that Mike would rip their heads off

without thinking through the consequences, so he decided to intervene. 'Yes, of course, no worries. Look, officer, why don't you let the boy's father go to the hospital? My son and I will answer anything you want to know. We were all together, so we all saw the same thing as soon as we walked in.' He tried to remain outwardly calm, but inside, he knew he would also have ripped the copper's head off if he'd said no.

The police officer chewed his lip. He didn't look at all happy. 'I think we need to take all of you.'

Arty felt the need to get involved; he was sharper than his father. 'Officer, we'll help as much as we can. But I can guarantee you won't get a sensible word out of Mr Regan all the while he's worried about his son. Please let him go in the ambulance, and I promise you, we'll be completely cooperative and then you can question him later.'

The officer nodded agreeably. 'We'll want to question you, sir, afterwards,' said the officer to Mike. Mike wasn't listening; he was watching his son being strapped onto the stretcher and seeing him have oxygen shoved up his nose. Suddenly, there was a glimmer of hope – Ricky's eyes flickered.

The female paramedic leaned closer to his face. 'Can you hear me, Ricky?'

A slow nod gave Mike the reassurance he needed. 'Ricky, it's me. It's ya dad. You're gonna be all right, Son. The paramedics are here. I'm right by your side.'

Within a few minutes, the police escorted Staffie and Arty out of the flat and watched as Mike went off in the ambulance with Ricky.

CHAPTER TEN

Staffie sat staring at the blank wall of the interview room, praying that Ricky would live. His injuries looked so bad, there was a risk he wouldn't survive. He brushed away his wet cheeks as soon as he heard the door opening.

Detective Lowry, looking the worse for wear, stepped inside and closed the door behind him. With a clipboard in his hand, he sat down and leaned back on his chair. 'What a fucking mess.'

Staffie was still reeling over the incident. 'Any news on Ricky?'

Lowry shook his head. 'No. Let me just take a quick statement and then we'll call the hospital.'

Staffie felt more relaxed knowing that the detective wasn't going to act like a jobsworth's prick.

'Mr Stafford, I'm working with the Commissioner. I know the set-up. I visited Mike Regan in the nick with Stoneham. So, you can speak freely. No tapes.'

Staffie nodded. 'So, Detective… '

'No, call me Simon. Detective Inspector Lowry is too much of a mouthful.'

'Yeah, all right, and you can call me Staffie. Everyone calls me that. So, do you know who's responsible for beating the living shit out of Ricky and killing that girl?'

Lowry could see the hardness in the man's eyes. He was told how the Regan crew were a force to be reckoned with, but he'd only met Mike Regan, and he was enough to shove anyone out of their comfort zone. He could guess that whatever he'd been told about the Regans had been watered down. Staffie appeared to have much the same attributes. Underneath that rubbery-looking face was a built-in temperament likened to a Rottweiler.

'No,' he sighed, forcefully, expelling a mouthful of air. 'This is a fucking mess. I told Stoneham that it was a bad idea getting you lot involved.'

Straightening his shoulders, Staffie's expression turned to ice. 'I'll tell ya this. If you've held anything back that could've stopped Mike's son being hurt, then God fucking 'elp ya. Mike will hit this shit-hole like a tornado, smashing everything in its path. So you'd better make it clear right now why you told your chief it was a bad idea.'

Lowry didn't flinch; he expected no less from Staffie, since his reputation preceded him.

'This gang or gangs don't play by the same rules. Firstly, no fucker knows who they are. Their general, boss, or whoever he is, has these runners. They're streetwise little shitbags who have no morals. They think they're hard because they're blatantly taking out businesses from known hard-core villains. No one seems to be able to get a grip on them. We nick one, and within a day, there's another taking their place. It's like the film *Mad Max*. I ain't seen anything like it in all my time in the force. Never have the streets been so out of control. My view, which

I will share with you, is the powers that be should have taken on more detectives – a special squad – to track down the fucking head honchos who are importing or making this evil drug. Instead, they're just locking up the runners. The streets will be run alive soon, with every kid hooked and willing to do anything for the shit... even kill. If I could print off every street crime in the last month, the fucking printer would run out of ink.'

Staffie was taking it all in, yet his focus was on Ricky's attacker. 'What I need to know is this. Do you think our involvement led to Ricky and that girl... ?'

Lowry nodded, and then he frowned. 'Staffie, do you know who that girl was?'

'Well, no, not exactly. She was a barmaid at the Daylight Inn. Our Ricky took her out on a date. Why?'

Lowry took a deep breath. 'Jesus, that is one hell of a coincidence because Kendall, God rest her soul, is Stoneham's niece. She's Kendall Mullins, the MP's daughter, no less.'

Staffie gasped. 'What the fuck!'

'So, my friend, Stoneham, as much as he's the bigwig, feels he's made a wrong move. I can only guess right now, as he comforts his grieving sister, that he's feeling as guilty as hell.'

'Christ, that poor kid. What the fuck those animals did to her, only she will know.'

There was a pause and a sigh before Lowry went on. 'I guess the rules have changed now. I can only assume you lot won't just be smacking a few heads together? And I know it was probably a bit of a game to you guys, a few rucks for your liberty, but I can bet my bottom dollar you'll want blood now.'

Staffie stared into the man's eyes, sussing him out. 'And

I assume you'll turn a blind eye to a war that may well take place?'

Lowry nodded. 'Your DNA and fingerprint records have been destroyed, so the world's your oyster, therefore no worries on that score. I've been in the force for most of my life and never have the crimes been so disturbing. We don't have the powers through the courts or the manpower needed to take all these scumbags off the streets for good. So, the cycle of nick and release continues while innocent people get hurt. I really don't care anymore how these thugs end up, just as long as they aren't in a position to fuck people over or sell that evil shit and build up a small army creating druggies willing to commit murder for their next fix.'

'Simon, when we got released early, the truth was we were gonna threaten a few scallies like you asked us to and try and put a stop to the drug sellers' pitches like the Daylight Inn's gents'. But, honestly, and you were right, we weren't taking it too seriously. Working with the law, it sort of goes against the grain. But now, it's personal. We are in a whole different ballgame. So, I will promise you this. We won't stop until we find out who the fuck is responsible for our Ricky's injuries and that poor girl's death. However, you have to be upfront with us and give us everything you have, and I mean everything. We may not be detectives, but we *can* get blood out of a stone.'

Lowry gave a snort of contempt, tempered with a wry grin. 'No doubt, Staffie, you will. I know what you and the others got away with, even your fathers. They had a name back in the day, but you never broke the rules to the extent these druggies are doing, so do what you have to. If you or the others get stuck, take my number, and I will intervene. Now, let me fill out this statement. Just the facts will do.'

Staffie smiled. 'Er, thank you, Simon.' He never thought the day would come when he would be thanking a copper. Still, he never thought the day would come when the streets would be crowded with murdering druggies either.

**

Mike sat with his head resting on Ricky's bed, holding his son's hand. He had made a deal with God and even the Devil. Anyone, in fact, who would make his son better. Wired up to machines and with tubes coming from every part of Ricky's body, all Mike could do was wait.

The surgeon had operated to stop a life-threatening brain bleed and hoped the swelling would go down soon. It was now just a waiting game. But all the while that machine was bleeping, Mike believed his son would recover.

The family room just outside the intensive care unit was full. Arthur was holding Gloria in his arms as she sobbed her heart out. Arty and Liam sat together whispering how they were going to smash the life out of whoever had hurt their mate. Willie couldn't sit still; he paced the floor, and every ten minutes, he went outside for a smoke, to the frustration of Lou. 'Willie, mate, sit ya arse down. You're irritating me when you keep moving about.'

Willie didn't argue or engage in banter; he sank into the chair next to Lou and placed his hands over his face.

Staffie arrived, looking totally drained. 'How's he doing?'

Arthur looked up and gave him a sympathetic smile. His face was racked with pain and sorrow. 'We're just waiting, mate. They'll have a better idea, once the swelling goes down.'

'Christ, he's just a boy, a fucking kiddie. Who would do this?' cried Gloria.

'Well, whoever did won't get away with it, I can promise you that,' said Staffie, in a menacing voice.

An hour passed, and the side door opened. Everyone looked up, hoping to hear good news from the doctor. Instead, it was Eric. 'I just saw the message. What the hell happened?' he asked, in an overexaggerated, exasperated tone.

Arthur glared, with his nostrils flared. 'Where the hell have you been? I've called your phone a hundred times. Ya brother needs your support, and I'd have thought you'd have been the first one here!'

The room fell silent as everyone turned to see the expression on Eric's face. They all had the same thoughts as Arthur.

'I left my phone in the car. I'd no idea. As soon as I saw the messages, I got here as fast as I could.'

Gloria lifted her head from Arthur's shoulder, all her anger now centred on Eric. 'You never let that bloody phone out of your sight. It's like history repeating itself. Our Mikey needs you, and once again, you're on the missing list. You expect us to treat you the same as Mikey, but you don't act the bloody same. Ya never have. You've no idea of the meaning "family stick together", have you?'

With a face like an angry bulldog, Eric retorted, 'Christ, if it was Mike who arrived late, neither of you would bat an eyelid. You'd just assume he'd had more important things to do!'

Like a coiled spring, Gloria was up on her feet, pointing her finger in Eric's face. 'Now you listen to me. If it was your son lying there fighting for his… ' she said, as she choked on her words and cleared her throat, 'nothing on this earth would've stopped Mikey from being right by your side.'

Childishly, Eric snapped back. 'Well, I don't have a son, and like I said, I left my phone in the car.'

Gloria was in floods of tears again, and Arthur pulled her away and sat her down, patting her shoulder. 'Settle down, my love.' Then he turned to face Eric. His slow, confident words made everyone sit up.

'Eric, I'm no fool, and the excuses you pull out of your arse really don't wash with me.' He straightened his shoulders and raised his eyebrow. For a man in his late sixties, he bore a look of an army general and was treated as such. 'Your phone may well have been in your car, but I also called your landline, which certainly was working, since it diverted to your answerphone.'

Eric felt hot under the collar. 'I'm sorry but I didn't hear it. I must've been asleep or in the shower.'

Arthur gave him a slow, disapproving shake of his head.

Before another excuse could leave Eric's mouth, the door opened, and there, looking exhausted and deflated, stood Mike.

Gloria jumped up from her chair and hurried over to him, flinging her arms around him. 'Come and sit down, Son. How's our boy doing?'

Mike almost collapsed on the chair. 'He's still in a coma. I guess he's in the lap of the gods now.'

He rubbed his face to wake himself up and then looked up at his father, who was still standing.

'Dad, I think you'd better find Jackie—'

'What!' screeched Gloria. 'That good-for-nuffin tramp!'

Mike didn't have the energy to argue. 'She's still his muvver, when all's said and done, and I don't know what's going to happen to Ricky.' His voice cracked, and he coughed away the emotion trapped in his throat. 'She should know, anyway.'

'Yes, Son, of course. Do you have her address?'

'Yeah, Ricky gave it to me. I was going to see her meself with the divorce papers.'

'Shall I go now, or shall I wait to see… ?'

Mike shook his head. 'No. Please can you go now?'

Staffie's eyes filled up. Never had he seen his mate so weak with worry. 'Arthur, I'll come with ya.'

***

It was seven o'clock in the morning by the time they reached the site. It was nestled in a quiet place deep in Essex. Arthur was almost asleep at the wheel, and Staffie was sipping a can of Red Bull to keep himself awake.

'It's a fucking shit-hole!' said Arthur, as he looked around. 'To think our boy grew up in places like this one.'

Staffie had to agree. Most of the caravans seemed clean enough, yet around the perimeter were piles of rubbish, a burned-out car, two old washing machines, and half-dressed toddlers playing in the dirt.

Arthur took a deep breath before he stepped out of the car. No sooner had Staffie joined him than two scruffy-looking men wandered over. 'Yer got lost, mate?' called the taller of the two men.

Arthur didn't answer; he strode towards the caravans.

''Ere, I said, 'ave yer got lost?' the man called out again.

This time Arthur turned to face them. 'Jackie Menaces. Which one's her caravan?'

The taller gypsy, with his front teeth missing, eyed Arthur up and down. Right away, he registered the smart clothes, the gold watch, and the confident look on the huge man's face.

'Who wants to know?'

Arthur, now extremely tired, sighed. 'Me! Fucking knob-head.'

'And who's me?'

Staffie sensed that Arthur was about to let rip, but this just wasn't the time or the place. Also, he himself was too exhausted to fight. 'Her boy's seriously injured and in hospital. We just came to tell her, that's all.'

The shorter gypsy sized them up. 'What's it worth?'

At first, Staffie didn't grasp what he meant, until it dawned on him what the man was asking. He curled his lip and frowned. 'You what?'

'What yer gonna pay me, to tell you where she lives?'

Arthur stopped dead in his tracks. 'You fucking what? Ya dirty no-good scummy pikey.'

With that, he lunged forward and grabbed the man around the throat and squeezed hard. 'Now, where is she?'

The taller gypsy suddenly backed off. 'All right, mate, we don't want no trouble. There, in that caravan.'

He pointed to the filthy caravan with a mouldy roof and ingrained dirt along the sides.

Arthur dropped the smaller man to the ground and walked ahead, leaving him gasping and clutching his throat.

Arthur didn't even bother to knock. He ripped the door open and barged inside. Staffie was behind him, silently looking around, ensuring they weren't about to be jumped.

He'd never ever expected to set his eyes on the bitch again, but there, sprawled out on the disgusting sofa, was a woman in a see-through lace minidress that just about covered her body. For a moment, Arthur couldn't tell if it was definitely Mike's wife, Jackie, though. Her dyed black hair was grey at the roots, her skin was yellow, and her cheeks were sallow. What had clearly been a posh caravan at one time now stank of piss, puke, and fags.

Staffie eased inside, squeezing past Arthur to see why his friend was glued to the spot.

'Fuck me!' he said slowly. 'Is that really her?'

Arthur sighed again. 'No idea.'

As they both gawped at the state of her, she suddenly blinked, and through slurred words, she said, 'A blow job's fifty quid. No fucking less.'

The sharp tone in her ugly voice confirmed right away it was her.

Staffie went over to the sink, filled the bowl with water, and literally threw it all over her, making her gasp for air. She sat up, bolt upright, but then swayed, as if she was pissed. 'What the hell?' she screamed, trying to focus.

'Get fucking dressed. You're coming with me!' demanded Arthur, now totally repulsed.

'Are you sure, Arthur? Mike wouldn't want that thing anywhere near Ricky.'

Arthur's shoulders slumped at the thought. 'Well, it's up to him. We can take her to his place and then let him decide, but right now, with everything on our minds, I don't wanna push the issue. Let's just do as Mike asked.'

Jackie was trying to wipe her face and get a clear view of who it was who had just had the audacity to practically drown her. The moment her eyes focused, she felt her heart kicking into overdrive. Arthur Regan, her father-in-law, hadn't changed a bit and neither had Ted Stafford for that matter. Her past had come back to haunt her. At a stroke, she had a sobering moment: what if they were going to kill her? The shakes that were clearly visible weren't from a comedown but from pure fear. She tried to cover her body while shrinking back into the sofa.

'What the fuck do you two want?'

Arthur looked away. He couldn't bear to see the woman half-naked with such an ugly, pathetic, and cowardly expression on her face. 'Ricky's in hospital, and Mike thinks you ought to know.'

Absorbing those words boosted her confidence – they weren't going to do away with her then. She was about to put her brave face on and tell them to fuck off, when, suddenly, the prospect of a load of wonga weaved through her fuzzy mind like gold fairy dust.

'Oh, Jesus! What's happened? Is he all right?'

Staffie shook his head. 'Don't pretend you care, you evil bitch. I couldn't give a shit about your feelings. Just get yaself presentable and come with us.'

As Arthur's eyes fell to the floor, he noticed in among the mess was a T-shirt. It was a small lad's top, obviously used now as a floor cloth. It was ripped and faded, but he still recognized it as the one Gloria had bought Ricky on his sixth birthday. It was part of a Crystal Palace football strip. He gagged and felt the urge to turn and give her a good kicking; instead, and reluctantly, he swallowed and took a deep breath.

Once they were outside the caravan, leaving Jackie to get

herself cleaned up, Arthur turned to Staffie. 'You know what? I've never hated a woman so much. What she put our family through, it's unforgivable. I would've left her there, but I can't get Mike's terrified face out of my head. And, he must have his reasons for having that cunt up the hospital.'

As they walked towards the car, Jackie called after them. 'Wait up! I'm coming.'

''Course you are, ya gold-digging bitch,' mumbled Staffie, under his breath.

Still unsteady from an all-night drinking spree, Jackie hobbled over to them. She'd managed to find an old tracksuit to put on and to grab her bag with enough Flakka concealed in it to see her all right for a few days. She'd paid Leon by selling herself but now he wasn't answering his phone. Over the last few weeks, she'd successfully managed to control her intake. Just a small snort a few times a day had her sober enough to function but drugged enough not to give a shit. Once the Flakka had run out, though, she would need to source more or end up going cold turkey. The latter option had her petrified.

Arthur got into the driver's seat while Staffie sat beside him. Under normal circumstances, they would have held the door open for the woman, but Jackie hardly deserved the status of a lady – she was a whore of the lowest kind.

As he pulled away from the site, he almost heaved. Staffie glanced over at Arthur and knew from his expression that he could smell the obnoxious odour permeating from the back of the car. Quickly, he found an air freshener from the glove compartment; with no warning, he sprayed Jackie. 'Ya fucking stink, woman.'

Jackie held her tongue. She decided to take whatever was

thrown at her, as long as she could get her hands on some of their wealth, or even worm her way back into Mike's affections, although that would take some seriously hard work. The thought of living in that lovely big house of his with the pool and money to do whatever she wanted was becoming more appealing by the second. Why she'd left him in the first place, she was hard-pressed to remember exactly. But one thing she knew: she was Ricky's mother, and that was something none of his bits of fluff could say.

Jackie leaned forward. 'So how bad is he? I mean, what's happened?'

Staffie twisted around to face her. 'Christ, girl, have you eaten shit for breakfast? Your breath stinks.'

Jackie shrank back in her seat. 'Is Ricky okay? I thought he was in prison.'

'Shut it. I don't wanna hear your fucking voice. Mike can talk to ya, 'cos I won't,' said Arthur.

She decided to keep her mouth shut. If the truth be known, she was more afraid of Mike's father than her husband. Although physically he wasn't quite as big as Mike, he had this knack of giving someone the silent treatment when he felt like it. Today was obviously one of those moments. She knew if she wasn't careful, he would pull over and eject her physically from the car and drive off. 'Play it low-key, girl,' she said, under her breath.

As they reached Kent, a call came through. It was Gloria. 'Arthur, the doctors have decided to put Ricky in some kind of chemical coma. They said it's the best thing to do. Mike's going home. The doctor said he's no good to anyone without a wink of sleep. Where are ya? Did ya find that bitch?'

Jackie felt her jaw tighten with rage. *What?* There was only so much slander she could take. Her frustration at keeping quiet was now going through the roof.

'Yep, so I guess I'll take her over to Mike's then. She needs a good fucking bath, anyway.'

'What?'

'Never mind, Glor. I'll see you back at home. You probably need some rest too.'

***

Several hours later, Arthur arrived at Mike's place. He used the remote device that he always had in his car to enter the property and drove up the long sweeping drive. When Arthur set foot inside the Georgian mansion, he could see that Mike was crashed out on the sofa with Gloria's knock-out pills by his side. He smiled. His wife thought of everything and carried as much in her large bag.

Arthur turned to face Jackie and said quietly, 'Don't you fucking dare wake him up. Got it?'

She nodded, but her eyes were gazing around the room like one of those estate agents. Nothing had changed except for the updated décor, which no doubt his parents had been fussing over while he was away in stir. She'd actually forgotten how big and beautiful this house really was.

Staffie was appraising Jackie. He could even read her thoughts. He knew her brain was in money calculator mode. Staffie glared at her. 'If you so much as pop a fucking fork in your bag, I will promise you this. I'll cut your cold heart right out of your chest. You're only here to see Ricky at Mike's request, so don't go getting ideas above your station.'

He might as well have been talking to someone in the next room; Jackie wasn't listening. She was back home, where she should be – in her eyes anyway.

'Do you think it'll be all right if I take a shower and get cleaned up ready for Ricky?' She tried to put on a sweet, demure voice but it wasn't washing with Staffie.

'Don't put on an act, Jackie. I know you and what you're all about, girl. Go and have ya shower, but if you touch anything, there'll be hell to pay.'

'I'm not going to, I promise.'

Arthur huffed. 'Liar! As if you would ever keep a fucking promise. Just go and get yaself sorted. I'll be back later.'

No sooner were they out of the door than Jackie went mooching around the house. The first stop was obviously Mike's bedroom. She opened the drawers to see if he'd any money stashed away. Nada. There wasn't even a single gold watch lying about either. Then she heard a sound downstairs and so she hurried into the shower; she thought perhaps Arthur had returned.

***

Unbeknown to anyone, not least Jackie, Gloria had called Zara and filled her in about Ricky. She was so concerned about him that she forgot to tell Zara that Arthur had gone to find Jackie. Gloria did, however, inform Zara that Mike was on his way home for a nap.

Aware of how badly Mike would take it, Zara hurried straight over to be by his side to show her support. Their squabble was nothing compared to this situation, and so she put her grievances aside and used the spare key Mike had given her to let herself in.

She didn't know exactly how she felt as she entered the house. She was nervous, certainly, after the frosty encounter a few days ago, but the overriding emotion was disbelief and horror at the news about Ricky. It was wicked what had been done to him.

She stopped at the entrance to the lounge, and her heart went out to Mike. His face was drenched in anguish even though he was sound asleep. She crept over and kissed his forehead and moved away before a tear landed on him. Quietly, she tiptoed to the kitchen where she placed her bag on the worktop and prepared some filter coffee. While she waited, she pondered over the last few weeks and felt so sad. Perhaps she was wrong to have doubted Mike's fidelity. Why hadn't she given him the benefit of the doubt? After all, would he really cheat on her? Surely not. She'd been over that scene of seeing this younger woman half-naked – it must have been a thousand times in her head – and she knew she wouldn't be human if she didn't deduce from that that Mike was two-timing her. But now she wasn't so sure. Their last meeting had cast doubt in her mind that she was right to accuse him of playing away, and, in any case, what did it matter now? His son was at death's door, and he wouldn't want all that other stuff being thrown in his face again, when, quite rightly, he had greater concerns – namely, his son's life at stake. She would put her personal issues aside and be there for him. She loved him with all her being, and, right now, it was breaking her heart to see him like that.

Just as she poured the coffee, she heard someone walking down the stairs. She froze and waited; perhaps one of the lads was here? She had become too twitchy lately. But then, like a bolt out of the blue, a leggy woman appeared, dressed only in one of Mike's shirts and with her hair wrapped in a towel. The sight of her completely threw Zara.

Although Jackie was just as shocked to see Zara, she knew exactly who she was because she'd seen a photo. She was the only woman Jackie could never live up to – Mike's ex, or was she?

Leaning against the doorframe, Jackie raised her eyebrow, in pretence. 'And who are you?'

Zara was similarly stunned for a moment, but without the benefit of knowing who this woman was. She just stood gawking, taking the sight in. 'Um, who are you?'

Jackie took her time to respond. Then, with a cold, hard smirk and a raised brow, Jackie slowly looked Zara up and down. When her eyes landed on the prosthetic hand, she glared for a while, before displaying a malevolent, satisfied smile. 'Mike's wife, that's who.'

'What the hell are you doing here?' asked Zara, totally stunned.

Jackie was in her element; she could see the anger and jealousy pulse through Zara's eyes.

'Mike asked me to come back, start again, put everything behind us, for our son's sake. So now it's your turn to tell me what you're doing here and who you are. What the fuck are you doing letting yourself into *my* home?'

What? Zara was now fuming. 'Mike's wife? Don't make me laugh. Mike wouldn't piss on you if you were on fire, so cut the crap.'

Jackie laughed. 'Aw, no?' She looked down at her bare legs.

'He didn't say that earlier when he was all over me, love! He was in seventh heaven, having my *two* hands ripping at his back, when he was fucking the life out of me. But I guess *you* can't give him that feeling, can ya?'

Jackie had assumed too much. Zara wasn't a woman to stand there and have a slanging match – far from it. Without taking her eyes off Jackie, Zara slid her hand into the pocket of her jacket and extracted a black glove.

Jackie laughed again. 'You think that covers your ugly truth, do ya?'

As Jackie revelled in winding Zara up, she never expected it to be anything more than a verbal catfight.

Totally unprepared, Jackie watched the sorrowful expression on Zara's face cruise to a half-smile; it was almost a smirk. Without any warning and like the swift movement of a bird's wing, the gloved prosthetic hand came from nowhere, striking Jackie clean across the cheek and up under her nose. The clout instantly knocked Jackie off her feet and onto the floor. Yet this wasn't a normal backhander; a very odd sensation caused Jackie to touch her face. To her horror, she could feel her cheek almost hanging off her face and the warm, wet, and sticky liquid trickling through her hands and down her wrists. It took a second before she realized that Zara had sliced her face wide open. Her eyes bulged in fear as she stared up at the woman's ice-cold expression. Slipping and sliding on the marble floor, trying to get away from the demonic woman holding her hand up in a threatening stance, Jackie couldn't breathe from disbelief. Cowering in fear, she begged Zara not to hurt her again.

'Don't fuck with me, Jackie, because there are things that

I can do that would put the Devil to shame. Next time, I won't be so forgiving. It'll be your neck I'll slice!'

Jackie was now gripping her loose cheek with both hands, trembling in complete horror. She daren't look up, too afraid to lock eyes with the woman who she'd completely under-estimated.

Jackie was no stranger to a fight, but what Zara had done to her was out of her league. That slap alone was as harsh as any grown man's, yet it wasn't the violence, but the cold assured look in Zara's eyes that scared the living shit out of her.

Zara stared down at the state of Jackie huddled in a ball. 'I just hope Mike knows what he's doing, letting a cunt like you back into Ricky's life. You really don't deserve that boy.'

The reality of what had just happened kicked in as soon as she heard Zara leave the room; Jackie let out an almighty scream and then scrambled to her feet to make her way to Mike. The second she got to the doorway of the lounge, he was up on his feet, trying to focus. The high-pitched, blood-curdling sound had dragged him from his slumbers and made him jump up and stagger from side to side.

He blinked furiously at the sight before him, trying to reason in his mind what he was seeing. At first, he didn't recognize Jackie because the last time he'd laid eyes on her, she was younger, blonde, and not dripping with blood.

'Help me, Mike, please!' she cried.

He rushed forward and removed her hand to see two folds of skin shrivelling away from her cheek.

'What the fuck have you *done*?'

Her face was now swelling up, and her teeth began to chatter in shock. 'It was Zara. She attacked me.'

'What! She was *here*?' he exclaimed.

'She fucking attacked me. Mike, please, get me to a hospital!'

But his mind was now on Zara. 'Christ, what did she say?'

'She wanted to kill me. She said she would slit my throat. Please, Mike. Help me.'

Gripping both her shoulders, he backed her out of the lounge and into the hallway where the blood could easily be cleaned up from the marble floor so as not to ruin the cream carpet. 'Wait there. I'll call an ambulance.'

Jackie was now tasting the blood in her mouth. Once the shock began to wear off, her mind went into survival mode. 'Hurry, Mike. Please, I'm bleeding to death. That evil bitch will get five years for this.'

Having just finished calling for an ambulance, Mike heard the last of her mutterings. 'What the fuck did you just say?'

Through swollen eyes, she glared back. 'I said she'll get at least a five-stretch for what she's done to my fucking face.'

'*You* won't tell the Ol' Bill it was her. You're gonna tell 'em you slipped with a Stanley knife and cut ya own face. Got it?'

'And why would I do that?' she snivelled.

'Because, Jackie, you're lucky *I* ain't already fucking murdered you. But if you so much as ever mention that woman's name, I'll kill ya, and I won't care if I get a life sentence for it. You're an evil bitch, and I only wanted you here for Ricky's sake, but you've hardly been here five minutes and have already caused mayhem.'

Even the pain and anxiety of having her face scarred for life didn't stop the pound signs flashing up. She cried again. 'Okay, Mike, whatever you want, but please help me.' She held out the palms of her bloodied hands and revealed the gruesome sight of her gaping cheek.

For a brief moment, Mike actually felt sorry for her; she did look a right mess, and he knew no matter how well they stitched her up, she would still be horrifically scarred.

The ambulance arrived, and Mike helped her into the back before he stepped away, to the surprise of the paramedic. 'Sir, don't you want to come with us?'

He shook his head. 'I would, but my son is critically ill, and I need to go to another hospital.'

The paramedic gave Mike a questioning stare. With a sigh of dismay and a shrug of his shoulders, the paramedic entered the ambulance, leaving Mike to watch the vehicle as it headed down his drive.

***

Zara was waiting for a cab at the entrance to Mike's property. She watched the ambulance depart and shuddered. This wasn't really what she was all about – hideously scarring a woman's face through jealousy. Yet why should she feel guilty? After all the heartache Jackie had put them through, she'd had the nerve to stand there in nothing but Mike's shirt. Just by ridiculing her and deliberately reminding her that she was less than a full woman amounted to provocation. Well, Jackie, you wanted a fight so now you've had one – stitch that bitch!

Deep in contemplation, she hadn't noticed a car pull up alongside her, until a low voice called out, 'Hey, sweetheart, are you okay?' It was Eric.

Zara looked over and was met with a beaming smile.

'Have you seen Mikey?' he asked, as he turned off the engine and stepped out of the car.

She shook her head. 'He was asleep when I left.'

'Are you going home?'

She nodded. 'Yeah. There's nothing here for me now.'

Eric sensed the sad tone. 'Jump in. I'll give you a lift.'

Zara slid into the plush interior and quickly removed her glove, slipping it into her bag.

Eric clocked the prosthetic hand right away. 'When did you have that fitted?'

Now embarrassed, she slid her false hand out of view. 'Oh, that? Yeah, well, er, a few days ago. It's just a temporary one until my doctor has the real thing made up for me. I just thought it would stop people staring.'

'Zara, you're probably imagining that because I should think anyone looking at you would be drawn in by your eyes alone.'

There was an awkward silence as she stared ahead. She didn't want to be sucked in by Eric's affections, not now. So she changed the subject. 'I didn't know Mike was back with Jackie.'

Eric felt a sudden rush of excitement. He had to think carefully before he spoke. 'Well, stranger things can happen. Anyway, how did ya know?'

'I stupidly let myself in to see if I could help Mike in any way. What with Ricky being in hospital, I dunno, I thought that I should put behind us what happened after the party and go and give my support, but, well... I guess, I left it a bit too long and... ' Her voice cracked.

Good. This was his chance to put the boot in. 'Well, I'm not surprised. He took up with Jackie right after you left the first time, all those years ago. Our Mikey ain't one for hanging about, ya know. Anyway, what happened? Did ya just leave?'

A sudden concern gripped her throat. 'Oh, fuck no. Jackie was taking the piss, so I gave her a swipe and cut her face. Maybe it was a bit OTT, but it made me feel a lot better! Anyway, Mike was still asleep, so I just left. I bet the bitch grasses me up, though.'

Eric gasped. 'Shit! Yeah, she fucking will. Listen, you can't go back home. Ya need to keep low for a while until I get a chance to talk to her. She'll listen to me. She always has. How badly did you swipe her?'

'I think I've taken half her face off.'

A short chuckle left Eric's mouth. 'That'll teach her for being two-faced.'

Zara smiled. 'Really, Eric, that ain't funny.'

'Yeah, it is. She's a right horrible woman. She deserved that, but, anyway, I'll take you to mine, and we can figure it out from there.'

Zara needed time to think things over and decided his place was probably the safest for the moment. However, she had to know what Eric was up to. He seemed to know more about her business than he really should. And there was one burning question to which she needed an answer. 'Eric, the other day, when I left you on the Old Kent Road, I need to know something, and I trust you will be upfront with me.'

In a panic, his mind went back to what he may have inadvertently let slip. 'Yeah, go on,' he said, determined to keep his tone as even as possible.

'Well, that night, why did you go to Antonio's, my restaurant?' She remained silent, waiting for a feasible explanation.

'What? I don't know what you're talking about.'

'Come on, Eric. Tell me the truth, please.'

He turned into a side road, stopped the car, and turned to face her. His expression was deadly serious. 'Zara, I swear to God, I've never been to your restaurant. I've no idea what you're on about.'

Her heart suddenly beat faster. She was alone in the car with a man nearly the size of Mike, and she was confronting him without even really knowing how the hell he would react. She also shocked herself with such a stupid, dangerous idea, yet she wanted confirmation she was right. Eric had just lied to her.

'You were seen going there. You got out of your car and read the notice on the door.'

The cogs were turning as Eric thought of who would have told her. He had to play it cool and not come across as aggressively defensive. 'Oh, sorry, yes, of course. You mean the restaurant in Peckham?'

She nodded. 'Yes, Eric. What were you doing there?'

'I overheard you talking to that Davey fella at the hospital. I know it was none of my business, but I just wanted to make sure you were okay. The fact of the matter is, I don't trust the Lanigans. I don't really trust anyone. I only had good intentions, though, I promise. And I heard you say something about a note on the door and I thought I would just check. I'm sorry. I know you can handle your own affairs. I just care, that's all.'

She looked into his eyes to see if there was even a flicker of a lie. 'But why, Eric? What the hell am I to you? And, more to the point, what does Mike think about your actions?'

He lowered his gaze. 'He doesn't know. I'm not sure he would even care. The man has his own mission that he needs to accomplish, whatever that is. I understand why he didn't want me back on the firm right away. I guess we drifted apart when I didn't visit him, but, anyway, that's just how it is. Mike was locked up for a long time, and now he's out, he's acting reckless, running after bits of skirt that put it out there for him, when he could have a decent woman like you.' He drifted off the subject.

Zara felt her eyes were about to fill up again, so she took a deep breath. 'So, if Mike's not interested, why are you looking out for me?'

A gentle smile spread across his face. 'Isn't it obvious?'

The thought of Eric fancying her was strange. He looked a lot like Mike. He was the same big build and hair colour. Eric had larger eyes, and from the point of view of many women, he would probably have been classed as the better looking. Yet he didn't have Mike's qualities, his manner, or his self-control that people either feared or respected. However, Eric's face seemed to light up when she looked his way. What was she thinking? He was Mike's brother. She shouldn't be looking into his eyes that way or studying his physique. It was Mike she loved.

'Look, I'm sorry, Zara. Just forget everything I've said. You can stay at mine for a while. I can stay at Mum's.'

She suddenly took a deep breath. 'No, it's fine, Eric. You have a spare room, I take it?'

With a glow on his cheeks, he laughed. 'Yep. Four, actually!'

'Blimey, you're doing all right for yourself. Four, eh?' She tried to make light of the serious mood.

He wasn't sure if she was joking and instantly retorted, 'Why would you say that? Mike has a bigger drum than me.'

'Oh no, sorry. I was just making light of it, that's all.'

They continued the journey, with Eric feeling awkward and Zara wondering more and more if she'd made the right decision.

She was surprised how close Eric's house was to Mike's. What shocked her even more though was that inside, the décor was almost identical. The cream carpets, the marble hallway, even the sofas were an exact match. She blinked and told herself she was overthinking things.

'This is lovely, Eric.'

He smiled as a wave of tenderness washed over him. She looked at home here in his large lounge. He could see her sitting on the sofa sipping herbal tea and sharing sweet conversation.

His perfect picture fizzled out when she said, 'You don't mind me using a spare room… ? It will only be for a day or so, until the dust settles. I just need to know that Jackie hasn't put me in the frame.'

'Oh yeah, sure, of course. I'll show you upstairs.'

She followed him up the luxurious deep pile-carpeted stairs and into the last room on the left. It was a spacious room with sumptuous bed covers set on a large ornate bedframe. Taken aback by the sheer design, she turned and grinned. 'This is lovely, Eric. You must give me the number of your designer.'

'Designer? Oh no, this was all my idea. I like to keep a nice home and have my guests feeling comfortable.'

She smiled again and moseyed around the room, admiring the furniture and curtains. As she turned, with her back to the window, he was still standing there. The moment was awkward, sending a shiver up Zara's spine.

Eric sensed she was ill at ease and instantly responded. 'I'm glad you like it. Right, I must go. I've some stuff to do, so make yourself at home. There's food in the fridge and stacks of coffee and brandy, so just help yourself. Through there' – he pointed to a side door – 'is an en suite shower room, but if you prefer a bath, it's just across the landing.'

She smiled out of relief. 'Thank you so much, Eric. I really appreciate your kindness.'

'No worries, love. There you are.' He put a small bunch of keys on the bed. 'You can come and go as you please. Treat this as your own home.'

He gave her another beaming smile and left. Zara waited until she heard the front door close before she relaxed her shoulders. She didn't really have much of a choice as to where she should stay, so this had to do for the moment. The idea of a long soak in the bath was appealing; the mere thought of specks of Jackie's blood left on any strands of her hair repulsed her. She made her way across the bright and well-lit landing and went into the bathroom. Again, she admired the décor and the size of it. She grinned when she spotted all the men's products and counted at least six bottles of Joop! aftershave. He always smelled sweet. Yet so did Mike.

She thought her life was getting crazier by the minute.

CHAPTER ELEVEN

Davey Lanigan received the news that Ricky was in hospital and discovered from Zara that she was now staying at Eric's until she knew either way if she was to be arrested for slashing Mike's wife's face. He wondered if Zara was actually the brutally jealous type; nevertheless, she was still the woman in charge of half of his business, and he would have to show her respect.

They arranged to meet at Antonio's before the opening. Zara arrived ahead of time and let herself in. It was a strange feeling because she'd only ever been there when the restaurant was either closing for the night or just opening up to prepare for their customers. She'd never gone alone and so this time it seemed eerie. There was no gentle humming of fridges or any other white noise. She could hear a pin drop. The décor had been updated since she'd last seen it. Antonio had ensured the place was kept up to a high standard. It seemed an excellent way to keep any nosey busybodies from suspecting anything other than a good pasta dish being served.

She looked at the small bar area and on the far wall she saw photos of Antonio and his sons, the youngest just a toddler. Antonio appeared to have aged well, judging by the pictures.

The restaurants were her idea and one that had impressed her father the most. Supplying the upper-class cocaine addicts with their weekly fix, all under the guise of a restaurant, it was a win-win for all concerned. She had taken the initiative to buy the businesses and allow the Italians to run it rent-free as long as they kept up the sales of the cocaine. It had suited Izzy and the tenants. She ground her teeth when she thought about some threatening gang taking over. So far, they hadn't actually managed to force their way in. They'd only had success in frightening the managers to close the operation down. Yet she wasn't going to stand for it, not while her name was on the deeds, and if whoever was running this bunch of thugs wanted to argue the point, then she was all up for a war. In fact, when she and Davey were discussing the matter a while ago, she'd said to him, 'Bring it on!'

The outside sensor light suddenly came on, and she looked out of the kitchen window to see Davey and Shamus helping Neil out of the car. Behind their vehicle was another and Zara recognized the three other men who had been present at the meeting in her father's house. She felt safe now she had her firm with her.

Neil was the first through the door; he still looked a little weak, but his wide smile offset that. Instantly, he put his arms out to hug Zara. He was fond of her, and the years they had worked closely together had bonded them.

As he hugged her tight, he whispered, 'You look good, Zara. I missed you so much.'

Davey watched his son kiss her cheek and grinned to himself. She would have made the perfect daughter-in-law. He always knew his son had a soft spot for Zara, and if she hadn't promised to wait for Mike while he served his time, then she may well have ended up with Neil.

'Right, now I'm back on my feet and have my sidekick with me' – he put his arm around her shoulders – 'we can get down to business.'

Shamus coughed. 'Neil, while you were making out with all those nurses, we already got down to business.'

Neil sighed. 'Yeah, I know, but I've been thinking. First, let me summarize what we agreed about this plan of yours, Zara. You want us to reopen, pretend nothing is wrong, and then wait for the bastards to show up. Once they arrive, we agreed we'd nab them and take them out of the picture and hope that things will go back to normal.' He stopped and shook his head. 'But, realistically, guys, that ain't ever going to happen, is it?' His voice turned from upbeat and jovial to severe and stern.

For a moment, Zara was perplexed. It was a side to Neil that she'd never witnessed. Neil had been so full of vitality years ago, a bit of a risk-taker, like herself. But she was a pragmatist by default, and she accepted that the serious injury Neil had sustained was a warning shot across the bows to all of them that they needed to lance the Hadlow boil once and for all – and fast – if they were to re-establish their reputation as serious Faces in the manor.

'I don't want anyone looking in,' said Davey, as he closed the curtains at the front of the restaurant.

The others then took a seat and faced Neil, ready to discuss the plan and likely consequences again.

'So, do you have a better plan than mine?' she asked, with an air of antagonism.

Neil didn't answer right away; he pulled out a chair and sat dead opposite her. 'It's always going to be your call, Zara, but why don't we cash in on their business, let them think they've taken over and then—'

A sudden screeching of tyres and car doors slamming made the men jump from their seats. Like a well-planned defence army defending their position, they unexpectedly darted in different directions. Shamus ran to the side of the window and pulled a gun from the back of his jeans. Davey did the same but went to the other window. Minty, the tallest man, built like a gorilla, charged towards the side door. Zara shook all over; she wasn't prepared for this. Trapped inside her own restaurant with God knows who surrounding them, a pre-emptive strike on their business hadn't been predicted at all.

Neil pulled her over towards the toilets and pushed her through the door. 'Wait inside. Leave this to us,' he demanded.

With so much happening at once, there was no time to think, so she allowed him to take control.

The ladies' toilets had only two cubicles and a frosted side window. She kept the light off, but luckily she knew her way around in the dark. Listening outside, she could hear men's voices, but she couldn't make out what they were saying. Slowly, she lifted the window latch, and carefully, she pushed the window open just enough to be able to hear. Next, she heard footsteps moving away from the window. She slid her hand down inside her boot and pulled out her gun. With a quick shove this time, she pushed the window fully open, so it was wide enough for her to climb out and land safely on the ground. She guessed the potential intruders had made their way to the side door, the only entrance that led straight into the kitchen; the other door led into the restaurant itself.

Spotting two cars that were parked in the alleyway, she hurried over and felt the bonnets; they were warm. She guessed there were two carloads, maybe a maximum of eight to ten men in all. She only had six – seven, including herself. She had to think quickly.

Aiming her gun at the dashboard of the first car, she fired one round. The bullet went through the glass and hit the steering wheel, setting off the alarm. She then did the same to the second car. Now both alarms were going off.

Quickly, she climbed back through the window and closed it behind her. Her heart was beating fast, and her mouth felt as though it was filled with chalk sticks. She could hear banging, crashing, and two guns being fired. However, she couldn't make out who was shouting and who was shooting. As soon as she heard heavy footsteps run past towards the cars, she reopened the window and aimed her gun.

There, dressed in dark, heavy coats were two lean but muscular men. One wore a scruffy bandanna, holding his long light brown dreadlocks in place. He reminded her of an actor in the film *Pirates of the Caribbean*. The other guy was younger, possibly eighteen years old, and darker skinned, wearing a beanie.

Their bodies rotated around, anxious and desperate to see who had shot at their cars, while Zara quietly climbed out of the window again. As soon as her feet were planted on the ground, she called out, 'Move, and I'll fucking blast you away.'

Both Jamaicans heard a woman's voice, and so instead of freezing to the spot, their instant reaction was to turn around and face the person behind the threat.

'I said move and I'll fucking shoot you.'

The man with the bandanna was the livelier of the two; his feet danced around although his hands were in the air.

'Hey, sister, seriously! You wanna watch you don't hurt yaself with that thing,' he called out to her mockingly.

Her copper eyes snapped with fury.

The man with the beanie didn't move. Standing to attention, he was taking her threat seriously. After all, even if she couldn't aim straight, there was still a possibility someone could get shot.

'Please, don't underestimate me, or you'll be sorry. You see, cunt, this is *my* restaurant, *my* dealers, and *my* punters. And you've really pissed me off.' She took a step closer. 'Get on your knees. Now! Place your hands in front of you, flat on the ground. And you, Captain Jack Sparrow, I hate people like you, so trust me when I say it won't take a lot to make me pull this trigger.'

Defiantly, she managed to hold the gun perfectly still.

'You know you're gonna get murdered, don't you, lady?' said the guy with the bandanna. 'There are six men inside, and when they're done with your little crew, they're gonna come gunning for you.'

She remained silent and stared, with pure loathing in her eyes.

'Didn't you fucking hear me, ya silly little tart? Holding a gun means you can only shoot one of us at once.'

Her top lip curled as her eyes narrowed. 'And I bet you hope it ain't you I shoot first, eh?'

The cocky one of the two sucked his teeth. 'Go fuck yaself!'

'So, six inside, yeah, and two out here? Well, I should by rights even things up a bit!'

The younger guy drew a startled breath. 'Please, lady.'

'Shut up, Gage!' spat the bandanna man.

'Peto, I'm sorry, but look. That gun ain't a toy. She'll shoot ya.'

'Tell me who's your boss because with a cocky, foolish mouth like yours, I know it ain't you.'

Gage was now breathing heavily; beads of sweat on his forehead glistened in the moonlight, and his eyes remained transfixed on the gun.

She waited for an answer, but there was none. 'Too afraid of him, are you? Well, he seems to me to be a right coward. I mean, using pathetic foot soldiers to do his dirty work because he's too fucking chicken to meet me face-to-face. What's that all about?'

In a high-pitched, animated tone, Peto lifted his chin. 'Youse have no clue. Ya think you're hard with a weapon, but you watch. He ain't chicken. No way! He'll run you out of town, hunt you down, and bury you! All of you!'

Zara stepped forward and pointed the gun directly at Gage, who was sweating profusely.

'You, Gage, stand up against that wall and don't fucking even think of running because I won't threaten you, I'll fucking blow your head off!'

He didn't need to be told twice; he was flat against the wall in a second.

She paused and listened. Two shots, both fired from inside. She went another step closer. 'You, Peto, have ten seconds to give me the name of your boss. One, two, three… ' She cocked the gun. 'Four, five… '

'Wait! All right, I don't know his real name. They call him the Governor. I've never met him.'

'Oh, yeah? So, how the fucking hell do you get paid, then?'

'Jaguar pays me,' he replied, now shitting a brick.

'Where's this Jaguar?'

Peto flicked his head, indicating that the gang leader called Jaguar was inside the restaurant.

'Right, fucking move!' She pointed to the side door of the restaurant. 'You're gonna point him out to me.'

She watched as he nervously walked. She could sense his legs had turned to jelly, but that was just how she wanted him – a nervous, dithering wreck. As he reached the side door, it flew open and out came Shamus, his face bloodied down one side and holding a gun. He wiped off the blood with the back of his hand and took a deep lungful of air. As soon as he saw Zara with a firearm pressed against the small of Peto's back, he stepped aside. 'All yours, Gov. Neil's just cleaning up.'

'Good. There's one up against the wall. His name's Gage. He's no trouble, but just make sure he doesn't run.'

Zara pushed Peto inside the restaurant.

To his horror, his so-called heavy crew were a mess. He thought they were invincible, six-strong and tooled up. The biggest of them all, a six-foot-seven giant of a man, was now totally fucked up. One of Neil's men, an older guy, was breathing heavily and still holding a fire extinguisher that he'd used to smash the giant's face in.

Peto's eyes scanned the kitchen in horror. His own brother lay in a pool of blood, barely conscious; even with a gun in his hand, he was out of action, now severely wounded.

Neil was seated and rubbing his sore knuckles, and two of the other men were covering the front entrance, wielding their guns, ready for a further ambush.

Zara prodded Peto in the back. 'Well, which is the one called Jaguar?'

Peto's hands trembled with shock. He had to find a way out of this mess or no doubt he would end up like the battered men.

She gave him another dig with her gun. 'Hurry up! Which one is he?'

He looked around, and there, unconscious, lay a new recruit. 'That man there!' He slyly pointed.

Zara removed the gun from his back and handed it to Davey. With her new hand, she gave Peto a quick backhanded swipe and cut his face. 'Fucking liar! Who is he?'

Peto screamed in pain and stumbled back, clutching his face.

Even Davey was shocked at the fierceness behind the clump, yet he shouldn't really have been surprised. *Nothing fazed this woman*, he thought.

Neil looked at each of the attackers and then clocked the one in the corner, his eyes wide as he turned to hide his face. Launching himself from his seat, Neil bent down and gripped the man's collar, lifting him up. 'You're this Jaguar guy, aren't yer?' he yelled, before pain shot through his chest, causing him to double over.

Davey caught him before he hit the deck. 'Easy, Son,' he said, as he supported him back to the chair.

The guy weighed up his chances of escape; he really didn't want to be left with a bunch of lunatics and this feisty mare who thought she was Catwoman. 'No, not me, mate,' he responded boldly, poker-faced.

'Frisk him!' demanded Zara.

Davey stepped forward and trained his gun on the man's head. 'Empty yer pockets.'

Still as bold as brass, Jaguar flipped his jean pockets inside out. They were empty. Then, as he felt inside his jacket pocket, the hard plastic of the phone case brushed across his hand. His heart in his mouth, he tried to recall what was on that phone. It was like grabbing at smoke rings. He should have left the damn thing behind.

A tingling sensation ripped through him. The numbers he had to keep secret would be exposed. If the Governor got wind that he was responsible for leaking any information, then his house would be burned to the ground with his wife and kids inside. Without thinking things through, he pulled out the phone and threw it hard onto the floor in the hope that it would smash to smithereens, so no one would be able to retrieve any information. It turned out to be a bad move.

As soon as the phone made contact with the stone floor, the screen cracked, but otherwise, it remained intact.

Davey shook his head. 'Nice try, so this means… ' he said, as he bent down and retrieved the phone, 'there is information on this piece of equipment that you really don't want us to see. Oh dear, dear me. Too bad.'

Suddenly, the man's cocky persona changed, and he dropped to his knees. 'Please, I'm begging you. He'll kill my family… ' The man's face was ashen and his pupils like pins. 'He's so fucking dangerous. Please… ' He was now blubbering like a baby.

Zara stared at the man now on his knees. Apart from Jaguar whining, the room was quiet as they all watched her.

'If you think he's dangerous, you haven't seen dangerous. The Governor, eh? What's his real name?'

'Please, love, I don't know. I swear on my baby's life, I don't know.'

'Well, you'd better tell me everything you do know about this man because otherwise I'll go through every one of those phone numbers until I find his, and then I'll tell him his fucking panther soldier gave me his number.'

Jaguar's eyes grew wide, and his face shrank to the bones, like a skeleton. 'Jesus, he'll kill my family!'

'I know, so you'd better start talking then.'

Before he'd a chance to say another word, Shamus pushed the man with the short dreadlocks through the door and into the middle of the room. Gage's whole body was shaking, the whites of his eyes prominent.

'You!' Zara pointed in Gage's direction. 'Who is the Governor?'

He shook his head. 'I dunno. I just work for him.' He looked across at Jaguar.

'You won't get away with this!' hollered Peto.

'If you're not happy with a scar down ya face, you can have a bullet to match?'

Gripping his face, Peto looked to the floor, completely defeated.

'Right, let's start from the beginning. This Governor. Where does he come from? What colour is he?'

Jaguar knew he'd been outsmarted. 'He's white, a big man. I've no idea where he comes from, though.'

'So how did he recruit you lot of inbreds?'

Jaguar got up from his knees, holding his hands up in abject defeat. 'He runs South-East London. He has a huge firm. He pays well, and he's ruthless. Once you're on the firm, you have to do whatever he says because he knows everything about you. I've known him to do some bad shit.' His eyes filled with water and his face crumpled.

'Like what?' she demanded.

'He'll send in men to rape ya sister or ya mother, and he's

burned down a house with someone's granny in it before. He doesn't give a fuck.' His voice changed as if he might be having a regular conversation. 'He supplies Flakka to everyone, only it's not really even Flakka. He's mixed it with some other shit that makes people angry but also addicted. Once you're hooked you're fucked, because there's only one source and that's him.'

He looked around the room at the carnage. 'These are my men. I had me firm only supplying weed. I'd a good little business going, as my boys supplied Peckham, Lewisham, and Bromley. Then he got wind of it and offered me a deal to supply this new drug. He said it was like ecstasy but better. I had my punters in the clubs and so I took it on. Of course, I tried the gear meself and so did my crew. Fucking hell… ' He sighed heavily. 'I wish now I'd never agreed to it. I got addicted right away, and the more I had from the man, the more he wanted from me until I ended up in his firm.'

Zara was taking it all in. 'How did you know we were gonna be here tonight?'

'He told us you would be. He told us to go in eight-men-handed and take you lot out. He said there was twenty grand apiece in it for us, but it wasn't about the money. He said if we refused or fucked up, then he would see to it that our families were hurt.'

'Set up a meeting with him!'

Jaguar shook his head. 'It doesn't work like that. He came and found us. The man has people everywhere. He knows everything that goes down. His junkies are his spies.' He paused and breathed in deeply, before his frightened eyes glared back at Zara. 'He's like the Devil.'

'There's only one man who can claim to have had the real Devil on speed-dial and that was my father. This Governor geezer is a nobody in my eyes. So, he wants me fucked up, does he?' She clenched her jaw in a temper.

Jaguar looked at her in despair. 'No. Actually, his very words were, "Take out the Irish mob but don't harm the woman."'

Zara stopped herself from gasping. She questioningly inclined her head. 'Why not me?'

Jaguar shrugged his shoulders. 'He's not the type of man you challenge. He gives the orders and that's it.'

'How do we know he's telling the truth?' asked Neil, who was now sitting up straight.

'You don't, but what he says is more feasible than not.'

Zara turned back to face Jaguar. 'How will this Governor know that you have taken my men out?'

He shuffled uncomfortably. 'He wants photos.'

Zara laughed. 'Fucking photos?' She took the phone from Davey and scrolled down. 'What's his number?'

Unsure whether to tell her, yet reluctant to argue, Jaguar replied, 'It ends in 666!'

'Ha, very apt.'

She pointed the phone at the young guy lying in a pool of blood and took the first photo.

'No, please. When he sees that he'll know we didn't finish the job and he'll kill my family.'

'No, he won't because there'll be no point. You lie on the floor too.'

Within a few minutes, even with a few tuts and curses from Peto, she managed to stage the restaurant to look like a mass killing – to the utter amazement of her own men.

'I want to meet the Governor, so I'm gonna draw the fucker in.'

CHAPTER TWELVE

Jackie returned from the hospital after spending just one night there, only to find that Mike had rifled through her bag and removed her secret stash of drugs. After throwing a hissy fit, screaming obscenities, Mike dragged her upstairs, threw her into the spare room, and locked the door. No matter how much she begged and pleaded, he ignored her.

She'd heard how people coming down from drugs had experienced cold turkey, but she'd never imagined it to be so hard. Her face throbbed continuously, and yet all Mike would give her were paracetamol and ibuprofen, along with the antibiotics. The second night was by far the worst of the beginning of a painful nightmare. Her mind was not her own; nothing that filled her brain was of her own doing. Nightmares swanned in and out, and yet she was wide awake and literally climbing the walls. Feeling ants nesting in her bones and centipedes gnawing at her brain, they drove her mad. She cried and screamed, panicked, and then collapsed. It was overwhelming and frightening. And yet there was nothing she could do to stop it. Her arms didn't have the strength to smash down the door. Her body was wet with sweat, and her stomach steadily heaved and retched.

Curled in a ball against the wall, she stared at the piss pot, and for a moment, she wondered if she drank it, it would kill her, but her brain was too befuddled to work that one out. The windows were locked shut so she couldn't even jump out; also, the glazing was made from toughened glass, so the panes were too hard to smash, but she wasn't surprised because Mike had the best of everything.

She couldn't even see what her face looked like because he had removed all the mirrors, so she was unable to use the glass to do damage to him or herself. Suddenly, she heard the front door slam shut. He was off again to visit their precious son; she knew he wouldn't be back for hours. Nothing had changed much; he still fussed over the boy. She would have sat down and made a plan to escape or rob Mike blind; however, try as she might, her mind just drifted off to another topic or revisited dark places from the past. She closed her eyes and wished for sleep, prayed even that her brain would switch off and leave her in peace, if only for a few minutes.

***

As soon as Mike arrived on the ward, he saw the back of a suited man hovering outside Ricky's room. He hurried along the corridor to see who it was. A nurse bade him good morning, but he was not in a talkative mood. In fact, Mike had hardly said two words to anyone except the doctor to find out how his son was doing. It was breaking his heart to see Ricky wired up to everything except the kitchen sink. No sooner had he reached the private room than the suited man turned around.

Mike sighed. 'I wondered who you were.'

'I need to talk with you, Mr Regan.'

Mike could see he was washed out; the bristly facial growth and dishevelled hair spoke volumes about the man's state of mind.

'I'm sorry, Mr Stoneham, about your niece.' His words sounded compassionate and genuine.

Stoneham nodded. 'She was just a kid really, a little bit of a rebel, but a good kid, nonetheless. I am still in a state of shock.' He was clearly exasperated as he looked up at Mike. 'I remember that meeting we had in the prison and you said to me, "I'm not like you." Do you remember?'

Mike looked at his son's fragile body, the machines rhythmically forcing his chest up and down. 'Yeah, I do remember. I told you, ya wouldn't believe in an eye for an eye.'

Stoneham nodded. 'Yes, that's exactly what you said, but you, Mr Regan, are wrong. I loved my niece very much, and I want whoever… ' He choked on his words, cleared his throat, before he tried again. 'I want whoever did this to suffer, and I mean to be tortured and murdered. If I were man enough, I would do it myself, but, as you know, I am not cut out for it.'

Mike leaned against the doorframe and gazed at his son. 'We both want the same thing, and I *am* cut out for it. No one hurts my boy and lives to tell the tale. Oh… ' He turned to face Stoneham. 'I'll torture them, every fucking day, until they die of starvation.'

'How is he doing? Do the doctors think he will make a full recovery?'

'Only time will tell. At least I have hope, eh? I'm so sorry about Kendall. It must be bloody hard for the family. I know, because this is killing me.' He pointed to his son.

'Lowry told me your son had only just started dating Kendall. Is that correct?'

'Yeah, she was his first one ever. He must have liked her a lot. He texted her all the time until they met up again.'

Stoneham swallowed hard to hold back the lump in his throat. 'She had only just moved into that flat. She and her mother never really got on although my sister will have you believe otherwise. Still, the poor woman no doubt will be heartbroken and full of guilt. She will blame herself for Kendall's death.'

'I can understand how she feels. I'm also consumed by that ugly emotion. I believe whoever did this had something to do with that gang we're after. Christ, I wished I'd never taken you up on your offer.'

Stoneham found himself patting Mike's back. 'I know, and that's why I'm here. I've made a terrible mistake, one that will live with me forever. I thought the idea was good at the time. A villain with a reputation who could in some way put the fear of God into these gangs and get the streets under control. I saw it in a film once.'

Mike's eyes were still focused on his son. 'If it's any consolation, I thought the job would be easy, coming down on a few suppliers and dealers to get a message to the Faces behind this drugs racket. Blimey, this has to be a first, me agreeing with the law. You're right, though. This gang *is* out of control. They don't play by the rules. The Devil's rules maybe, but there ain't any well-known Faces this side of the Thames that have done anything close to the crimes this lot are committing. Jesus. Raping a young woman and bashing a kid with a fucking bag over his head, what's that all about? They're cowardly in that sense. Do you have any CCTV footage at all?'

Stoneham sighed. 'Yes, we do actually, but all it tells us is there was a black BMW in the vicinity. The number plates were fake and the windows were tinted. The last camera in the Square only caught the back of the men.'

'And what do they look like?'

Stoneham felt vomit rise to the back of his throat. His ears tingled every time he thought of the two men cruelly abusing his niece. 'Roughly six foot three to four tall… ' He paused. 'Approaching your size.'

Mike pushed himself away from the doorframe. 'My size? Well, that narrows things down. I don't meet many men similar in size to me.'

'No, I pulled out the best photo analysis team to examine the evidence, but all they could see was the footwear. One had the latest Nike trainers only sold in Footlocker, and the other guy had Timberlands, a size eleven. One had a black hat, which covered his ears, but we only had a side profile. He wore a long Crombie-type coat. The other man had a hoodie on, but we don't know the make. The other issue we had was the photos were obscured by the rain. It was torrential. We tried to identify any markings on the car, but the CCTV footage was blurry with a fast-moving object. I tried my best, and I'm not giving up. And you, Mr Regan?'

'Me… I will find these men, and well, you know what I'm gonna do.' He gave a false laugh. 'It was a bit of a game to start with, but things have changed. I'm going to do things my way from now on. Not rely on your leads but concentrate on me own. And, trust me, you'd better ensure every one of your men looks the other way 'cos what I will do won't be pretty.'

'Between you and me, I'm hell-bent on seeing them dead.

I don't want them arrested and tried. I want them… well, you can imagine what I want. But, if it's okay with you, I will find out as much as I can and give you every last bit of information we have. I only ask one thing in return.'

Mike stared ahead. 'And what would that be?'

Stoneham was in awe of the man's calm and yet intimidating demeanour. 'Tell me how you killed them. I want to know how they suffered.'

'I understand fully. You have my word because I've been in your shoes many moons ago, and I wanted those details too. In fact, I wanted every last gory one of them.'

Mike's sharp words sent a chill up Stoneham's spine.

'You never mentioned that the MP is your sister.'

Stoneham suddenly felt a little hot under the collar. 'No. We tend to keep our relationship private. It causes problems in our line of work otherwise.'

Mike scoffed. 'You mean you don't want the public to know that you'll line each other's pockets. Who better to have than the Police Commissioner backing her every decision regarding the streets?'

Stoneham was about to deny that statement but thought better of it. He'd learned now that the Mike Regans of this world weren't easily fobbed off with bullshit.

'Yes, that's right. Does that give you a different impression of me?'

Mike didn't answer right away. He shook his head and sighed. 'I really don't give a shit if you're the Prime Minister's brother. We all have a job to do, whether we're on the same side or not. It's about the rules – moral rules and respect. Today you've come to see my son, out of respect, regardless of the fact that we're on opposite sides in everything else in our lives. And here we are united, because when it comes down to it, we're all still human, and that, my friend, is where animal instinct takes over. The world of rights and wrongs merges into one, when our loved ones get fucking hurt.'

Stoneham looked down at the floor. 'My father was spot-on about you. You *are* a law unto yourself, but a just law in my eyes.'

'Life gives us lemons. We can make lemonade or use it to burn the eyes of our enemy. It's our choice.'

'I have to go, but when Ricky is well enough to speak, would you ask him if my niece was alive when they… ?' His words trailed off.

Mike suddenly took his eyes away from Ricky and turned to see the pain on the Commissioner's face. He grabbed his arm. 'I will, and, trust me, I'll spend my life hunting those bastards down.'

Once Stoneham had left, Mike sat by his son's side, looking at every bruise and cut and imagining him being beaten by two men the same size as himself. The doctor's voice made him jump, which was so unlike him.

'I'm sorry, Mr Regan, I didn't mean to startle you.'

It was Doctor Redwood, the neurological surgeon who had operated on Ricky. He was a middle-aged, fit-looking man with friendly eyes. 'We have run more tests. It seems the swelling is slowly going down, but I have to be fair and warn you that he may have sustained some brain damage. Until he is fully conscious, we won't know exactly. Tomorrow, we will look to take him off the drugs that are keeping him asleep. This will be a critical time. Would you like to be here?'

Mike felt his throat swelling and his mouth seemingly clamming up. He nodded and brushed away a tear.

Redwood patted his shoulder. 'We are doing our best and Ricky is a fighter.'

As soon as the doctor left the room, Mike flopped his head on the mattress beside Ricky's hand and sobbed his heart out. The tears wouldn't stop until he felt a pair of soft, warm hands wrap around his neck. 'Come on, Son. You're exhausted. I can take over for a while. Please go home and get some rest.'

Mike dragged his head away and looked up at his mother. 'He may be brain-damaged, Mum.'

Gloria was dressed in her elegant Chanel suit. She was a short woman with a big heart, unless, of course, you crossed her the wrong way. 'Now, you listen to me, Mikey Regan. Our boy's a strong lad. He'll recover just fine, you wait and see.'

She pulled him up from the seat. 'Now then, you get off home. Besides, if you leave that rotten bitch for too long, she may just start wrecking your home. Christ, as if you ain't got enough to worry about. I knew it was a bad idea, your father taking her to yours. He should have let her die in her own shit pit.'

'Mum, it's done. She's at mine, getting cleaned up. Ricky may want to see her when he comes round. I would want to see my mum.'

'Yeah, well, she ain't no proper mother, that one. She's lower than a worm's tit and shouldn't even have the steam of that boy's piss, if you ask me. And as for our Zara, Gawd love her, I'd have done the same. The bitch deserved a bashing. Mark my words, Mike, she's one shit-stirring cow. And, by the way, I know Zara. I bet you, Jackie did or said something to cause that backhander. Zara wouldn't go around acting like that for no reason.'

Mike stood and accepted the lecture. Far be it for him to stop his mother when she was in full flow. Little in stature she may be, but a pushover she definitely wasn't.

'Mum, I don't blame Zara. I just wish she'd answer my calls. I can only imagine what she thought, walking into my house with Jackie half-naked in one of my shirts. And that's the second time in just a few weeks that this has happened to me, as far as Zara is concerned. What must she bleedin' think, eh?'

Gloria gasped. 'Surely, she wouldn't think you would've... well, you know, with her, the bitch?'

'I dunno, Mum. I ain't sure of much these days except staying positive that my boy will get better.'

* * *

By the time Mike reached home, Jackie was shaking violently and relentlessly. He stared at her huddled form in the corner, like a deranged mouse, and wondered what he should do. Yet as much as she looked in a right state, with her face still puffy and the deep gash still raw, his mind kept wandering back to Ricky, so he closed the door, locked it, and left. Jackie's injuries were nothing in comparison to his son's. She would heal and would probably be as mouthy as before, but what if Ricky was left mentally damaged?

With his mind all over the place, he didn't hear someone let themselves in, but as soon as he reached the kitchen, he jumped for the second time that day. It was Eric. He looked his brother over and noticed he was bigger than ever, obviously spending time at the gym, and he seemed so at ease. That's what bothered him. He didn't look tired and anxious like his family or his mates in the firm. Everyone else was worried sick about Ricky and yet Eric didn't appear concerned. The hairs on the back of his neck went up. It seemed that every time he laid eyes on Eric, his brother wound him up. Perhaps he was expecting too much.

'So, what brings you here?' he asked, in a flat tone.

'I thought you might need some company. How are you doing, bro? You look worn out, mate.'

Even Eric's jocular tone pissed him off. 'Tell me, Eric, why is it that you just pop up when it suits you, eh? You're like some kind of god. As if I'm gonna be grateful that you've decided to grace me with your presence. We're all taking shifts to be with Ricky. I've got the lads running around the streets all desperate to find out who's responsible for beating the life outta my boy. Then, there's you, just swanning around, doing your own thing. No one can call you. No one even knows where you are—'

'Hold on a minute, Mike. I do have me own business to run, you know. You didn't have me back on your firm, did you, so what am I supposed to do?'

Mike studied his brother's clean-shaven face. For a second, he wanted to thump him, but he paused and took stock. 'So, what exactly is your business, Eric, eh?'

Eric frowned. 'Just bits and pieces. I have my fingers in many pies.'

'You know what, Eric? I hardly know you anymore. I thought you were an upfront man, but you're not. Ya sneak around and turn up when it suits you.'

'Well, Mike, I guess I learned that from you. But, anyway,

as I said, I ain't part of the firm. You and the lads are on some kind of mission and haven't included me, so why does my business interest you? I thought when we spoke on that prison visit and you said I was still part of the firm, you actually meant it. Did you?'

Mike was chewing his lip and flaring his nostrils. As much as Eric was his brother, and once upon a time they'd been very close, deep down he really hadn't forgiven him for failing to visit him for twelve years while he was in prison, when he'd needed him most.

'I did want you back on the firm, but it's not just me that needs to trust you, it's the lads too. Staffie and Willie feel a little unsure of you. Lou hasn't said much at all, but I know he doesn't feel you're kosher. So, if you were man enough, you would prove to us you were on our side. Yet, for some reason, you strut around as if ya shit don't stink. Even at that party, I could see you looking down your nose at me. Anyway, I don't give a fuck right now.'

As his eyes drifted to the floor, he noticed the footwear on Eric's feet – new Nike trainers. His heart suddenly beat faster as the adrenaline surged around his body. Then he looked up and noticed the hooded tracksuit top. Surely not? Not his brother. Holding in his temper, he had to think before he asked the damning question. 'What time did you leave the other night after the boxing?'

Eric screwed his face up. 'What?' His frown deepened as he watched Mike's face tighten. He didn't like that look; in fact, it frightened him. The death glare, he called it. 'Um, about the same time as the others. Why? What's this all about?'

'Nah, you never. You went out and came back.'

Eric shuffled, nervously. 'Yeah, I did, but I only went out to get some fags. Why? What are you insinuating?'

'When did you start wearing fucking Nike trainers and fucking hoodies?' grilled Mike, as he pointed an accusing finger.

'Mike, what the fuck are ya on about? What's going on inside that warped mind of yours?'

With a sinister glare still plastered across Mike's face, he stepped forward. 'You don't like my boy, do ya?'

Eric flinched and stepped back.

'I said, do ya?' yelled Mike, now an inch away from Eric's face.

'Mike, seriously, ya don't for a minute think... Oh my God, you can't believe I would hurt Ricky? Christ, I love the boy. Why would I do that? That ain't me. What's got into you?'

With a sudden jolt back to reality, Mike dropped his shoulders and shook his head. 'Oh fuck, I dunno,' he sighed.

The sudden tension in the room subsided as Mike walked away. 'Listen, Eric, I think you'd better leave. I'm very tired and I wanna be left alone.'

Eric now felt he had the upper hand. He could immediately tell Mike was feeling guilty for accusing him. 'Hold on a minute. Don't you fucking dare accuse me and then walk away. Who the fuck do you think you are, eh?'

That voice of Eric's was really doing his head in. So much so that Mike spun around and shot his brother an evil look. 'Don't you fucking push it, Eric. If you're gonna go around like a cagey cunt, then take the consequences. Your secrets will be irrelevant one day, but the fact that you have them won't stop me from wondering if you're really on me and our family's side.'

'I don't have secrets. I'm just a private person.'

Mike rubbed his forehead and took a deep breath to stop his fist from clenching through frustration. 'We don't even know you anymore. You're like a bleedin' stranger that pops up and pretends you're in the fold, when, in reality, to me, you smell like the enemy. Now, fuck off!'

Knowing how reckless Mike could be, Eric decided it was best that he left – intact – while he still could.

Mike slammed the door and clutched his head in exasperation. He had to calm down and think straight or he would never find out who'd hurt his son. Just as he was about to pour himself a stiff drink, his phone rang. It was Zara.

His pulse raced; of all the people, she was the one he wanted to speak to. 'Hello, love. Look, can we meet? I really do need to speak to you.'

There was a pause. 'Mike, I just need to know if your skanky wife grassed me to the Ol' Bill?'

His heart dropped to his stomach. There was still no change in her voice. Her tone was so cold, he could sense it. 'No, babe, 'course not. I made sure she wouldn't. Look, this has all got so messy. I don't care why you cut her face, I just want you to know, she's here 'cos of Ricky, nothing else.'

'Not my business, Mike, but getting nicked certainly is. That's why I called. I'm really sorry about Ricky. I mean it. I hope to God he makes a full recovery. I genuinely mean that. I wouldn't wish any harm on any of you, but I think it's better that I stay away from your family for the moment and focus on my own business.'

He felt his throat tighten with hurt. He really needed her, but she was turning her back on him. 'Zara… I, um, I care so much about you, ya know.'

'Well, you just concentrate on Ricky. Don't worry about me. I'm fine.'

'It's all my fault, Zara. I think I've fucked up, and now he's lying in that sick bed, fighting for his life.'

'Mike, don't blame yourself. How the hell could what happened to him and that girl have anything to do with you?'

He sighed and had a sudden urge to tell her why he was released early and what his mission was really all about; however, his pause was too long.

'Mike, I have to go.' With that, the phone went dead. As he stared at the blank screen, he felt his world caving in. His dreams of having Zara by his side as his wife, the two firms united, had now vanished into the stratosphere. And it was all because of that fucking party and her stubbornness to see things at face value and not listen to him. As for Jackie's little cameo appearance, dressed in his shirt, what a balls-up that was! He couldn't have made it up. It would be laughable if it wasn't so bloody serious. He'd only made matters worse. He poured himself a second drink and knocked it back. A sudden wailing from upstairs just irritated him even more. The lunatic bitch was the cause of all his troubles, and, for a moment, he thought about ending her life. After yet another drink, he felt his shoulders relax, and his head began to take control over his heart.

***

Jackie had finally stopped shaking. The sickness was still plaguing her, but her mind was now more her own. She stepped out of her soaking wet clothes and crawled under the covers.

255

The feeling of ants inside her had gradually receded and was now nothing but a niggly annoyance. As she pulled the soft duvet over her sore body and lay the uncut side of her face onto the pillow, she sighed with relief. Closing her eyes was heavenly as the nightmare visions were now gone. Sleep was calling; at last, she could rest.

***

Mike lay on the couch, unburdening his tired limbs; however, no sooner had he drifted off than the phone startled him. This time it was a withheld number. 'Hello!' He knew he sounded only half-awake.

'Mr Regan, could you come up to the hospital? Ricky is coming round. We didn't top up the medication, but he seems to be making headway.'

'Yes, of course,' he replied, hearing the positive tone in the doctor's voice. 'I'm on my way… Is he…?'

'We don't know just yet, but I think that when he sees you, it will make him less anxious and this, as you know, is a critical time for him. We don't want anything to happen that might cause him to fall back into a coma. I'm sure your presence will help him immensely.'

'I'll see you soon.'

With scarcely concealed excitement, Mike reached the hospital, now in an upbeat mood. So many negative vibes had been running through him recently, but the doctor's phone call had lifted his spirits.

But his improved frame of mind didn't last. The car park was full, so he parked in the side street for permit holders only. As he stepped out of his Porsche Cayenne, a traffic warden was onto him like a rash.

'You can't park there. You haven't got a permit.'

Mike looked the scrawny, prune-faced warden up and down. 'My son's in the hospital. I ain't got time to scour the streets, and the car park's full.'

The warden looked at his notebook, shaking his head. 'Not my problem, sir. You can't park there.'

'Didn't you just hear me, mate? There's nowhere else to park, and the doctors want me there, like fucking now!'

His sudden loud and aggressive tone made the warden look up with grave concern. 'I'll call the police, if necessary!'

'Oh, yeah, you little jumped-up prick? And you'll need a fucking ambulance an' all, if ya do. Best ya shut ya fucking cakehole and get out of my way. And if you so much as touch my motor, I'll come back and find you and stick that pen of yours right through your eyeball!'

The warden shrank into his oversized uniform and stepped aside.

Mike sprinted along the path and into the main entrance of the hospital. The queue for the lift was long enough for him to jump the stairs two at a time. Once he reached the ward, he was out of breath and took a full gasp before he straightened himself and made his way to his son's private room. The vision of four nurses and two doctors took him aback; they all seemed to be rushing about changing tubes and fiddling with the machines.

Doctor Redwood spun around and hurried over to the doorway to face Mike. The look on his face had Mike fearful. Again, he felt the world on his shoulders.

'He's struggling. His blood pressure's gone up, and I'm afraid it's serious. Look, wait outside for a minute or so, please.'

Mike could hardly breathe, he was so fearful for his son. Ignoring the doctor, he pushed the nurses aside to find Ricky almost having a fit. His eyes were rolling around and his muscles were twitching.

'Ricky, it's Dad. I'm here, Son. I'm right here. It's gonna be all right. You're safe, I promise.'

Constance, the nurse, was studying the cardiac monitor and she called out, 'He's stabilizing.'

The doctor pulled Mike back. 'Let me see.'

He watched as Ricky's body slowly stopped shaking and contorting; his eyes began to blink, and his breathing slowed down.

Mike was still holding his breath, willing his son to live. 'That's it, Ricky, my boy. You're okay, Son.'

The doctor's concern for his patient changed; he allowed Mike to get closer to him because whatever he was doing or saying, it seemed to be working.

Mike leaned over the bed and stroked Ricky's head. He kissed his cheeks and continued to whisper. 'You're all right. Dad's here, and I ain't going anywhere. Come back to me, Son.'

'Please, carry on talking to him. He may be reliving the incident, which, at this stage, is very critical. We can't have his heart rate or his blood pressure going through the roof.'

In all the commotion, they didn't see Gloria standing in the doorway with her hands over her mouth, until Constance looked over.

'Please, come in. You're his grandmother, aren't you?'

With tears flowing down her cheeks, Gloria just nodded. She

slowly stepped forward, afraid of what she might witness. As she peered down, she saw the gentle flicker of her grandson's eyelashes. Gently pushing Mike aside, she held Ricky's hand. 'You are my sunshine, my only sunshine… ' she sang through her tears.

She had always sung that song, ever since he was a newborn baby. It was the only thing he remembered when he was reunited with his family.

The combined efforts of the Regans had brought about a change in the room; the tension had palpably lifted.

The nurse smiled. 'He's definitely stabilized. We have him back.'

Mike looked up and saw a dark-haired woman in her late thirties with tears in her eyes. For a moment, she reminded him of Zara. It was her narrow nose, the copper-coloured eyes, and that serene classy look about her. He smiled back.

'Look! He's opening his eyes,' cried Gloria.

Ricky blinked a few more times, and then he looked straight at his father and grandmother. Gloria felt him grip her hand.

The doctor had hurried around to the other side of the bed, not wanting to intervene as the family's presence was working wonders. He pulled out a pen light and shone it in Ricky's eyes.

'Ricky, I am Doctor Redwood. Can you hear me?'

Ricky gently nodded.

'Good. Can you see how many fingers I'm holding up?'

Ricky whispered, 'Two.'

Redwood looked over at Mike and winked. 'We'll need to do further tests, but, so far, so good. Please try to keep him calm.'

Mike nodded, and an unexpected tear fell down his cheek. 'You get some rest, Ricky. You need to get better, so we can have you back home.'

'I'm okay, Dad,' said Ricky, with a dry, muffled voice.

***

Alastair tried to put his arms around his wife but was swiftly rebuffed. 'Get off me,' she yelled.

'I'm only trying to help, Rebecca.'

'Help? And how do you think you can help me, eh? My daughter's dead. Nothing will ever take this pain away. She hated you, she left because of you, and now I will never see her again.'

Alastair flared his nostrils in a raging temper. He was sick to death of the same words spewing from her mouth.

'Now, look. I never did this to her. Stop blaming me. She never hated me.'

'Yes, she did!' she screamed. 'She couldn't stand you.' With her face now bright red and a vein prominently pulsating in her temple, she went on, 'I know how she felt. I am... I mean, I was her mother. I knew how she really felt, not you. You knew nothing about her!'

'Stop it will you, just stop it!' screamed Poppy, who had dashed downstairs to see what all the fuss was about. 'I can't stand this anymore,' she yelled, her face red and blotchy. 'My sister is dead and all you do, Mother, is place the blame on everyone else. It's Dad, me, or Brooke. Well, you need to be told the truth!'

Rebecca was stunned that her quiet, studious daughter was spitting out words with so much venom.

'Poppy!'

'Oh, shut up, Mother. Don't act so bloody self-righteous.

We've all had a bloody skinful of your high-and-mighty ways. If I'd had the same father as Kendall, I'd have gone too.'

'Poppy, stop it!' shouted Rebecca.

'No, I won't, Mother. I'm sick of you. You've blamed everyone, even your own brother for not doing his job, but the fact of the matter is, she left because of *you*. I'm surprised she even lasted as long as she did. You have no idea about any of us, have you? And I'd also be surprised if you even know yourself. All you are is the fucking MP.'

Rebecca was open-mouthed and shocked to the core. Never had she heard her daughter raise her voice, let alone swear. Once again, she said the wrong thing. 'Don't you use language like that in front of me, young lady!'

'See, there you go again. It's all about fucking appearances with you, isn't it?'

Rebecca spun around to face Alastair. 'Will you bloody say something? Tell her, will you!'

Alastair sighed. 'Leave it, Poppy, yeah?'

She shot him a hostile glance. 'Why the hell should I stop? We all know that Kendall hated her... and with good reason.'

Suddenly, Rebecca threw her coffee mug into the sink, smashing it into a thousand pieces. 'What good reason, eh? Tell me why you think my daughter hated me?'

Poppy's eyes flicked towards her father to find a shift in his composure. A wry smile lifted the corners of his mouth, and she knew he was about to use his sarcasm mixed with empathetic words in such a passive-aggressive way, it made her feel sick.

'Oh, come on, Rebecca, love. Let's not kid ourselves. It's probably time to face the truth, if we're going to be honest with ourselves. Kendall never wanted to leave her father's home. It's not your fault. You probably thought you were doing what was right, but we have to face the truth, darling. She wasn't happy here, she never really was. Can't you remember, sweetheart, how she begged night after night to go back? I know it must be hard for you because you expected her to fall into your arms and be the doting daughter. Perhaps Kendall believed you only took her back because it would look good for the press.'

Totally stunned by this somewhat cryptic self-analysis, it took Rebecca several moments to absorb the waspish words coming out of her husband's mouth. *So much for husband and wife loyalty*, she thought. She gawped at Alastair and then at her daughter. 'So, what's this all about, then? Are you all blaming *me*?'

'No!' sighed Alastair, now wishing he'd stayed at work.

Poppy let out an explosive sigh and shook her head in exasperation.

'Well, I am! You're so superficial that all you wanted was the area clean and pretty. Spending money on fucking new street signs, roundabouts with flowers on them, street cleaners by the dozen, updating a poxy shopping centre... the list is endless. There you are in your Givenchy suit, cutting a poxy ribbon with a false, sickly grin on your face, fussing over the fucking voters. I've watched the oohs and aahs, as you make your pathetic speeches, preaching to the uneducated, when, really, Mother, you ignored the violence and the drugs and took your eye off the ball. So, it's not surprising, is it, that the crime rate is increasing? You should have been a cheap, talentless celebrity, making your money from a stint on *Big Brother* instead of being in part responsible for people's lives!'

The room fell silent as both Alastair and Rebecca stared at

their child, who, from nowhere, had suddenly found her voice, and, it seemed, was wasting no time in using it, much to the shock of her parents.

'Huh. Don't look so surprised. The truth hurts, Mother. How the hell you got into politics is beyond me. The only bench you should be sitting on is the fucking garden bench. Have you even listened to Brooke? Because if I were you, I would start now. If you don't, mark my words: I will make sure that sister of mine is educated about your ways. Her attack has been brushed under the carpet. You want to keep it all hush-hush because it will look bad on you. We aren't babies, Mother. We have minds of our own, and she needs counselling. And I know why she hasn't had it because God forbid if that bit of news ever went viral.' Her voice suddenly became sarcastic. 'The local MP's daughter raped by three druggies!'

Without warning, Rebecca stepped forward and slapped Poppy hard across the face.

Like Kendall would have done, Poppy didn't move but stared daringly back at her mother. 'That, Mother, just about sums you up. The truth is shocking, and you just can't bear to hear it. Well, slapping me won't stop it coming out sooner or later.'

Suddenly, the atmosphere became toxic, the three entities in the room each paralysed by their own thoughts.

To make matters worse, had they but known it, their nightmares were only just beginning.

Hell called with a loud knock at the front door. The sound was just enough for them all to stare at each other for a moment. Rebecca shot a questioning glance at Alastair, who, in turn, shrugged his shoulders.

Poppy marched from the room and along the hallway to confront the source of the heavy bang at the door. Just through the frosted glass, she could make out a towering figure with a mop of dark hair. She guessed who it was. *This will be fun,* she thought. Pulling the door wide open, she stepped back to invite him in.

He stared for a moment at the pretty blonde-haired young woman, with an unusual blueness in her eyes that probably never gave anything away. She looked nothing like Kendall except for the cold expression. But when the light caught her face, something suddenly stirred inside him.

Lance Ryder took a deep breath and stomped his way through the hallway and straight into the kitchen. It was apparent an argument had ensued, judging by Rebecca's flushed cheeks and red eyes. He turned his head to face Alastair. Through exhaustion, grief, and fatigue, Lance seethed at the man who appeared to be unmoved by the death of his daughter. His big frame stood there defiantly with a veil of conceit cloaking his expression. Then he looked over at his former wife. Lance clenched his fists and squared his jaw. The sharp edge of rage poked him, as she stood there brooding and looking sorry for herself. The atmosphere was thick with poisonous fumes.

Still reeling, Rebecca directed her anger towards Lance. 'Who the hell do you think you are, just walking in here?'

Standing six foot six with broad shoulders and a thick chest, Kendall's father studied them like an interested bystander would a road rage incident. He didn't answer right away, merely absorbing his surroundings, and drinking in Alastair's smug demeanour.

'Well?' spat Rebecca.

Lance turned to face her. He was quite surprised to see that the woman who was once so attractive and unbelievably feminine had now become decidedly ugly and manly. Her solid waist and dowdy clothes, along with her shorter hair, did her no favours at all. She had gone from being a gentle and slim girl who, had she been older, could easily have been a product of the flower power movement, with not a care in the world, to some tyrant with a massive chip on her shoulder. She so reminded him of his old schoolmistress.

'I believe I've every right to walk into this house. Remember, I still bloody well own half of it.'

'That will change pretty soon,' she mumbled under her breath. 'What do you want?'

Relaxing his shoulders, he massaged the back of his neck. 'I want to know if you've made arrangements for Kendall's funeral?'

Her sudden fury subsided as quickly as it had begun; she'd been so caught up with everything that she'd failed to contact Lance and discuss the details. 'Yes, of course I have. It's next week on Thursday.'

Lance lifted his chin. 'Nice of you to inform me!'

'Well, I would have told you, but—'

'Told me? What do you mean *told* me? I'm not a long-lost relation, Rebecca, I was her bloody *father*!'

His cold and controlling tone had her riled up again and she instantly started shouting without allowing her brain to engage first gear. '*Father*? If it weren't for you, she'd still be alive now, you bastard. *You* talked her into moving out of here into one of your flea-ridden flats. If you had just stayed away… My God, she would still be here.'

Lance's characteristic smirk followed by the false laugh had Rebecca spitting feathers. 'Get out, Lance. Just get out and stay the fuck away!'

'I really thought you were just a puppet, you know that? I thought Alastair had his claws into you, pulling a few of your strings, and your father and that twat of a brother of yours were pulling the other ones.' He stepped back and looked her up and down. 'I guess I was wrong, though. You are a complete Punch and Judy act all of your own making. Before I leave, I want you to know that unless you pay me half of my assets, which I've only allowed you to hang onto because it was the roof over *my daughter's* head, I'll take you to court. I want the house either on the market or the money transferred to my account, PDQ. The cottage in Wales I also want sold. I'll be at the funeral, so best you be upstanding in front of the press, because if any snide remarks come my way, I'll let the whole media circus create a full-length feature film all about *you*!' he spat.

He turned to walk away, but as he reached the kitchen door, he spun back. 'Oh, and for your information, Kendall *asked* me for a place to stay. I didn't want her to leave here, but she was insistent, and you know why, don't you? It's because she couldn't stand *you* anymore.' His eyes flicked across to Alastair. 'Or you!'

With that, he marched ahead to the front door, followed by Poppy. As he pulled the door open, she caught his arm. 'Um, can I ask you something?'

He stopped dead and faced her, his anger clearly shown by those hooded eyes. 'What?'

'Kendall? Was she happy in that flat before she… ?' Her eyes brimmed with tears.

Lance immediately felt the girl's sorrow. She was Kendall's younger sister; he didn't know if they were close, but she was still a sibling. 'Yeah, she was. She got a job in the pub across the road. The landlord said she was a really good girl. All the customers loved her.' He suddenly cupped her cheek, noticing for the first time that it was badly inflamed. *So words had been said before my arrival*, he thought. 'She didn't leave because of you or your twin sister, you know. She really cared about you two.'

A fat tear followed the contours of her nose and her eyes widened, like a young child's. Just for a moment, the anger left him, and Lance felt himself soften.

'Can I ask another question?'

Lance nodded. 'Of course. Go on.'

'Why did my mother break up with you?'

Lance raised an eyebrow and stared at the inquisitive eyes. She was a perceptive little thing. 'I was away on tour a lot of the time, so I guess she got lonely.'

'What? Were you a performer, then, in a band or something?'

The idea lightened his mood. A soft chuckle left his lips. 'No, no. I was on duty in Afghanistan.'

'Oh, sorry to ask, and I'm also sorry Mother didn't keep you informed about the funeral. I'll make sure she does from now on.'

Touched by her refreshing honesty, he smiled again at her and left. Poppy leaned against the front door, thinking about the big man who she'd only ever seen in photos. She realized that her mother was a liar, an adulterer, and a selfish woman. She had known that in part all along, but now Lance had just confirmed it.

CHAPTER THIRTEEN

Eric knocked hard at Zara's front door. She noticed from the camera he was vexed. She swore under her breath and turned her computer screen off. He was like a bloody dog with a bone: he just wouldn't let go. She would have to tell him once and for all that she was more than happy to be back at home. It had been very kind of him to allow her to stay at his house for a couple of days, but, really, she didn't like how familiar he had become; he acted as though there was more between them than there was. Then there was Mike, and if in the future there was to be any chance of a reconciliation, then it wouldn't look good if Eric exaggerated the point that her stay was anything more than friendship.

She opened the door and gave him her most sickly, sweet smile. 'Hello, Eric. So, what can I do for you?'

He looked past her and down the hallway before his eyes met hers. 'Look, have I upset you in any way? You just upped and left the minute I was out of the house, and I haven't seen you since. I've called a few times, but obviously there was no answer. What's going on?' He looked over her shoulder again.

She made no effort to step aside and invite him in; instead, she just smiled again. 'Oh, nothing's going on. It was good of you to let me stay at your house, but it was just a temporary arrangement, wasn't it? I just needed to be sure that I wouldn't have to face a load of awkward questions from the police. It looks, though, as it turns out, Jackie hasn't pressed any charges.'

Looking flustered and agitated, Eric said, 'How d'ya know that?'

'Mike told me.'

'When did you speak with Mike? I thought you two were… ' He knew he sounded too eager. 'I just assumed you weren't talking.'

'Yes, well. Look, I'm pretty busy at the moment, so do you mind if we talk later? I've a lot to do.'

Eric fidgeted on the spot. 'Why don't you let me help?'

She inclined her head and frowned. 'I'm not doing house-work, Eric. I'm sorting out business.' Her tone was firm and cold.

Not taking the hint, Eric went on to say, 'Yes, but I can help, Zara. I ain't a stranger to business. Christ, I run my own well enough.'

'Yes, but I don't need your help. And, Eric, I don't mix business with pleasure. I'm sure you mean well, but I like to handle stuff my own way. It's not as if I've asked for your help, is it?'

Eric leaned against the wall with one arm and shook his head. 'Well, you certainly needed it in the past. Anyway, what's so special about the Lanigans?'

Now annoyed at his mocking attitude, Zara gave a false laugh. 'You're partly right. Obviously, I'm grateful for every-thing you did to secure my release. Without your help and your family's, I don't know what my future would have been. But the Lanigans are my business partners and still are... Look, I'm sorry, but now I've made myself clear enough regarding the Lanigans, I would prefer it from now on if you just kept out of my affairs entirely. Sorry if that sounds ungrateful for your concern earlier, but I need to get my life back on track.'

The thought of Neil Lanigan sucking up to Zara made Eric seethe with anger.

It was the age-old problem with Eric, and if his mum had been a fly on the wall at this point, she would have predicted what would happen next. In fact, she would have been spot-on.

Without carefully considering what he was about to say, the words were fired faster than an AK47 on full auto, and his fist bashed the doorframe, as he shouted, 'What the fuck is it with you and him, eh?'

Zara's face went almost white with shock at this outburst. Unlike Eric's family, she'd never been on the receiving end of one of Eric's raging fits. Nevertheless, although stunned by what he'd said and the manner in which he'd said it, she had no intention of backing off.

She viciously retorted, 'Mind your own fucking business, Eric. For Christ's sake, stop acting like a jealous kid. I owe you fuck all. You're Mike's little brother and that's it. It's nothing fucking more than that. So back off, will ya?'

Those words 'Mike's little brother' were like a knife being twisted in his gut. His eyes widened, and the whites turned dark with anger. Unexpectedly, he grabbed her shoulder to pull her close. 'What about *me*? You know I like you, Zara, so don't play the dumb bitch!'

'Get off me, Eric!'

He leaned closer and grabbed her, this time with both hands.

'Look at me, Zara, just look at me! I'm more man than that fucking Neil Lanigan and especially my own two-timing brother. What is it with you, eh? You only want what you can't have!' he told her bitterly.

'I said, let go of me!'

'No, Zara, I won't, not until you tell me you care about me too, that I mean something to you.'

She looked at his face, an inch away from her own and was staggered to see that although there were obvious differences between him and his brother, they were more than enough for her to find him gross. The look in Mike's eyes was so different: they were open and caring. And Mike's rugged skin and that controlled expression of his were all the things she loved about him. Eric wasn't blessed with any of Mike's physical attributes or his personal qualities. In fact, when she really looked at the man standing before her, she wondered how it could be that Eric had ever been born a Regan. Arthur, Gloria, and Mike were the epitome of a caring family. The problem was that Eric had none of their special qualities and probably never would.

Without warning, he forcibly kissed her, ignoring the fact that she was desperately trying to pull away.

'For the last fucking time, Eric, get off me!' She tried to move her face away, repulsed by his advances.

He didn't listen but attempted to kiss her neck, leaning closer.

An instant wave of fear pushed Zara to lift her arms in defence; however, she was wearing her black glove. As her hand came up to drive him away, the blades caught his wrist and instantly sliced through the skin and into the bone.

Blood shot out in a spray, covering her cheek. At once, Eric let her go, jumping back in shock. He looked up from his wrist in horror at seeing the blood on her motionless face. 'What the fuck? Oh my God! Why did you do *that*?'

She just stared at him, a glacial expression transforming her normally lovely facial features.

'You shouldn't have put your hands on me. You, Eric Regan, are no one to me. *Never* touch me again, or I'll kill you.'

The words were said slowly but with so much venom that for a moment Eric just looked perplexed. But his response was shockingly cruel.

'You fucking psychopath! You no-good ugly whore! Go on, then. Go and fuck your Irish wankers. I hope you get raped and shot next time,' he yelled, as he clutched tightly the wound that was pissing claret.

Like a bolt through the head, she realized what he'd just said.

'Hey! What do you mean by "next time"?'

But Eric was now out of earshot, making his way back to the car; he needed to get the deep cut stitched up or he would pass out. He couldn't stop the blood. He couldn't even think straight, and he wasn't into listening anymore. He had to get away and get fixed up.

As soon as she slammed her front door shut, she slumped to the floor and cried and cried. Her world was going mad. Nothing seemed to make sense. When it came down to it, who did she have on her side? She'd lost Izzy, her much-loved dad. Her mum had passed away years ago; the death was questionable, and although she was never told the facts, she did believe her mother was murdered Russian-style. And her fiancé… well, where was that relationship going, if anywhere?

She was alone, when it came down to it, except for Neil and Davey, who, by rights, were just her business partners. As the tears streamed down her face, she looked at the blood on the glove, which she tried to pull off. She'd certainly never meant to hurt Eric; she would never have done it, no way, but she'd forgotten the glove was on her prosthetic. Suddenly, she felt sick. What if she'd missed his arm and caught his neck? *Christ*, she thought, *I could have killed him.*

Finally, she pulled the glove off and threw it down the hallway. The blade in the glove replaced some of the strength she felt was missing with only having one hand. As she looked at her prosthetic, she sighed. Really, this should be enough. Why she'd needed to add blades to the glove was ridiculous. However, her perceived weakness had made her vulnerable. She blinked back the tears, wiped her wet cheeks, and picked up the glove. Just then, there was a knock at the door.

'Zara, it's me, Victor. Are you okay, love?' he called out.

Wiping the tears that had flooded her face, she opened the door. The sheer size of the man, taking up the entire doorframe, blocked out the sun's rays.

'Come in.'

'Are you okay, love? Only I saw that mate of yours, Eric, flying down the drive like a looney-tunes. He almost hit my cab.'

Zara saw the expression of concern on Victor's face and gave an almighty sigh. 'Yes. I slit his wrist for him.'

Victor tugged her shoulder before she walked off. 'You did *what*?'

She sighed once more. 'I slit his wrist open. He's probably gone to get it stitched up.'

'He didn't hurt you, though, did he?' His eyes scanned her body before they settled on her face. 'That's not your blood, babe, is it?'

She touched her cheek and felt the sickly remnants of Eric's claret. 'No, it's his.' She shook her head. 'No, he didn't hurt me. It was an accident, I suppose. Anyway, come through, Victor. I was hoping you would arrive soon. I need to tell you about an earlier incident at the restaurant. We got ambushed. The Lanigans and I were having a meeting at Antonio's, but before it had even got underway, two carloads of men turned up, ready for a serious fight.'

Victor's expression was one of shock. 'What? What happened? You didn't get hurt, did you?'

'No, not at all. Neil popped his internal stitches, but that's about it. As for the thugs who came to take us on, though, they were pretty well fucked up. The stupid bastards. As if a bunch of hooligans could even think they could take on the Lanigans? Anyway, they won't fuck with my business. And Antonio is going to open as usual.'

'So what happened to this gang? Did you have them killed?'

'I couldn't say what happened to them, but they took a serious bashing. Anyway—'

Before she could change the subject, Victor was onto her again. 'If you let them go, they'll come back, ya know. I tell ya, Zara, if it's this gang, they ain't goin' to give up, love. They've too much to lose.'

Of course, he was right, she thought. Accordingly, she dropped her guard. 'No, Victor, they ain't coming back. However, under extreme duress, they did say they were working for a guy called the Governor, a right evil bastard, it seems.'

Victor stepped back and rubbed his chin in deep thought. 'I've heard about this bloke, and by all accounts, he's one dangerous man. No one knows his real name, but I've been told some of the toerags call him the Devil. Did you get any more information outta those fellas?'

But Zara's mind was back on Eric. She felt so guilty and hoped that he was okay. A thought entered her head that perhaps she should call Mike.

'Er, sorry. What did you say?'

'Those fellas. Did you find out anything else about this Governor bloke?'

'No, I didn't, I'm afraid. All I know is that he's the main man who heads this gang or rather rules them with an iron rod, using threats that include their families. And I feel a touch insulted by him calling himself the Governor and people referring to him as the Devil. After all, it was my father who ran that manor and he was called the Devil. If I ever get to meet the bastard, I'll take that fucking title from him. If he thinks he'll live by that name, then he'd better be prepared to die by it.'

Victor gave her a knowing smile. 'Just be careful, little lady. He does sound like a nutcase.'

She turned to face him and looked him squarely in the eyes. 'And, Victor, what makes you think that I'm not?'

Unperturbed by that question, he teased, 'And how do you propose to find this guy?'

She didn't rise to the bait; instead, she replied, 'I'll do what my dad would've done. I'll play him at his own game. No doubt there'll be someone special in his life, his Achilles' heel. All I need to do is to find out who it is. So, if he uses intimidation by means of holding a knife to an innocent child or by burning down a family home, then he'll just learn what it's like to have the same thing happen to him. I play fair, but trust me, Victor, I'll stoop to his level – lower even – if I have to. So, what I want you to do, if you can, is to find out who this bloke is and if he has a family or someone close to his heart.'

Victor stared at her in complete shock. 'You what? You're bleedin' serious about this, ain't ya?'

Her eyes narrowed and darkness swept over them. She looked up at him, her catlike eyes unblinking, as she replied, 'Deadly serious, Victor. Fucking deadly serious. That man has written his own book of rules, and I intend to make sure I break every one of 'em!'

'So, what's in place? What can I do?'

She took a deep breath. 'Start by doing some digging. Be the unsuspecting taxi driver and find out what you can. I have other plans in place, so don't worry about me.'

A cruel smirk crept across his face; it was matched by an evil grin of her own.

***

Two days later

Ricky was helped from his hospital bed, the swelling on his face now going down, and his eyes were no longer slits.

'Here, boy, take my arm!' said Mike.

Ricky gave him as much of a smile as he could, considering his cheeks were still sore on the inside.

'I've got to do it by myself, Dad.'

Mike sat back down, carefully watching to make sure that his son wouldn't lose his balance.

Constance was assigned to Ricky to help him fully recover. She handed him a Zimmer frame, which made him chuckle. 'No way. I'm not old. Let me, please, try walking by myself.'

Mike looked at the nurse and shrugged.

'Okay then, Ricky. Walk towards me,' she replied.

Much to their amazement, Ricky stood completely upright and shuffled one foot in front of the other. 'Excuse me, I want to use the loo. I ain't pissing in that cardboard potty thing again.'

The nurse stepped aside and allowed Ricky through; however, she was close on his heels as he made his way along the corridor. After a few shuffles, he actually lifted his feet, and although his movements were slow and somewhat uncoordinated, he did manage to walk properly. Mike was right behind and clapped him, just as he'd done the day Ricky took his very first steps.

Constance turned to face him, her eyes glowing from the beaming smile across her face. 'That's it! He needs encouragement, Mr Regan.'

Mike nodded, pleased with the way the young nurse was dealing with her patient. 'Hey, please call me Mike, love.'

She blushed. 'Okay, Mike. He's doing well and so much better than we anticipated. I think the doctor will discharge him soon, but he'll have to take it slowly.' No sooner had she said those words than she saw Ricky quickening his pace. Ever the vigilant, caring nurse she was, she called out after him. 'Slowly, Ricky!'

'I need a piss!' he called back.

Mike laughed and was joined by Constance, as he jokingly said, 'Why not say it as it is!'

While Ricky was in the toilet, Constance faced Mike.

'I admire you, Mike. You've been by his side, and when you were talking to him as he was coming out of the coma, there was a connection right away, as if you were his lifeline, not the machines.'

Out of character, Mike blushed; he wasn't used to being complimented in such a serious way by a beautiful, bright young nurse. It was very different from his world.

'Well, actually, I wanted to thank *you*. I may have been worried to death over Ricky, but I saw how you looked after him. You are a real angel.'

Now it was her turn to blush. She had been in Ricky's room more than perhaps she needed to because, if she was being honest with herself, she was intrigued by Mike and enormously attracted to him. Her ex had been too feminine and sensitive for her liking; she wanted a real man's man, a big, straight-talking, and no bullshit kind of guy.

'May I ask, where's Ricky's mother?'

Mike laughed. 'Mother? Well, he does have one, but she's in her own world. Let's just say she has a few issues, if you get my drift.'

Immediately, Constance got the impression the wife wasn't part of the picture. 'Aah, that's a shame. I think at a time like this you need support.'

He knew she was fishing, but, still, he didn't mind. 'Well, we're separated, going through a divorce. She's... not on the same page as Ricky and me. In fact, she doesn't live with us.'

Her eyes twinkled as she blushed again. *How embarrassing*, she thought. She'd found out what she wanted to know but hadn't expected some of Mike's personal life to be handed to her on a plate. An awkward laugh followed, emphasizing the fact that they were both looking at each other for far longer than they should.

'Look, Mike, Ricky will be going back to sleep in a few minutes, once the tablets kick in. Would you like to have lunch? The canteen upstairs isn't so bad.'

'Why not.' He needed a break, and he hadn't eaten for a while. Perhaps the change of company would clear his head. He could use the opportunity to talk about all the issues falling heavily on his shoulders regarding the care that Ricky would need.

Constance was beaming; this would be her fantasy come true – a date with this handsome hunk of a man, albeit in her lunch hour. Her mind was moving faster than Mo Farah's legs, and she actually began to imagine a future together. First up would be working out how she could invite him out for dinner, once they'd got to know each other. And what better chance than to start a romance on the basis of each having a single goal – namely, the well-being of Mike's son and her patient? It would be the best way to a man's heart – well, in this case Mike Regan's.

That was the theory, anyway.

***

Zara was delighted with the arrival of her new cars that morning. It wasn't the fact that she now had two brand-new vehicles – a sporty Mercedes-Benz C-Class AMG and a Range Rover Vogue SE – but the independence she was now afforded after five years of confinement in her father's basement suite. She had freedom, and boy, was she going to use it. She had to remember she was an autonomous, liberated woman, and she was determined to make the most of who she was.

Both cars came by transporter and were accompanied by the dealer principal himself, who had decided to make a personal appearance. Zara Ezra was a cut above even the most well-heeled of his customers at his West London showroom, specializing in the high-end market.

All the paperwork had been completed, but if he were honest, he fancied the knickers off this hot woman and thought he might be in with a chance if he impressed her by supervising the final handover himself.

But he was soon to have his nose pushed out of joint! Not only was her body language all wrong, she hardly gave him the time of day. Having received the keys, she went over to the Mercedes and was off down the drive in a jiffy, leaving both the dealer principal and the transporter driver aghast as they watched her zoom away while they were still standing on her driveway.

As she reached the main road, she stopped and wondered where she should go first. Five years was a long time not to be behind the wheel, and yet she was easing back into the driving seat seemingly with no problems. The controls made it so much easier, and she found that there was no need to rely on her stiff prosthetic hand. Ricky had been on her mind for a few days. Gloria had kept her up to date with all that had been going on. Zara made it clear she didn't want to talk about Mike, and Gloria, ever the diplomat, just stuck to conversations regarding Ricky. Now, with the news that Ricky was recovering, Zara felt the urge to pay him a brief visit to let him know she was thinking about him and not ignoring the dreadful ordeal that he'd endured.

With the aid of the on-board cameras, she reversed the Mercedes expertly into a fairly tight space in the hospital car park and made her way over to the ward. Inside her bag was a small sentimental gift, a gold signature bracelet that had the word 'BRAVE' inscribed on it.

The ward was quiet as it was too early for visitors, yet Zara knew Ricky had a private room and hoped the nurses wouldn't mind her just popping in. The staff were too busy to notice, though, so she made her way along a well-lit corridor, carefully checking the names on the last two private rooms located at the end of the hospital wing.

Ricky was propped up, looking through his phone. The tablets hadn't kicked in, and he was busy on the internet trying to find out how to speed up his recovery.

'Hello,' she whispered from the doorway.

Ricky's face lit up. 'Come in, Zara.'

He put the phone away and gestured for her to take a seat. Looking her up and down, he was surprised to find her wearing a pink soft woollen tracksuit and trainers. It was a very different look from her normal dark fitted clothes that always gave her an edge. Today, she looked more mumsy. It actually suited her to a T.

'Oh no, I won't stay. I just wanted to see how you were doing, and I've brought you something.'

'It's good to see you, Zara. You can't guess how much I've missed you.'

Zara felt a lump in her throat. She hadn't really had a chance to get to know Ricky, even though she'd spent years trying to track him down. Unbeknown to her, he'd been carted off by that bitch of a mother. But, in a way, the experience had made the connection between them all the more special.

'Here, I thought you might like… well, it's just a little thing. Maybe it's a bit old-fashioned, really, but anyway, I wanted you to have something from me.'

Ricky was still smiling, and as soon as he opened the box, his eyes widened as he read the engraving. 'Oh, wow! How cool is that! Brave, eh? I love it, Zara. I will wear it with pride.'

'I wanted you to have it for a very special reason, though. My father gave it to me when I was your age.'

'Oh, then I can't possibly take it. I know how close you and your dad were. Dad has told me so much about you and Izzy. There's no way I'm accepting such a special gi—'

She held up her hand to stop him giving it back. 'No, I want you to have it. I would've given it to my little boy, but… anyway, I want you to have it. Always remember you are very brave.'

Leaning forward she kissed his forehead; it seemed so natural. There was a bond between them that was unexplainable, but it was there, nevertheless.

Ricky felt it too. His dad had told him how she'd tried to find him, how she'd also lost a child, who, if he'd lived, would have been Ricky's elder brother.

'Ricky, listen. I've done something that I'm really not very proud of, and I just want to say, I know you won't forgive me, but I'm sorry.'

With an understanding grin, Ricky replied, 'Hey, Zara, if it's what you did to Jackie, then she bloody well deserved it. She's a nasty piece of work. I should know more than anyone. But she didn't hurt you, did she?'

Zara gave Ricky a cheeky grin in reply. 'Not physically, no, but she really hurt my feelings.'

Ricky's face dropped. 'No! Well, she has a habit of doing that. She hurt mine on a daily basis. I think she used to get a real kick out of it. The fact is, you know, I don't regard her as my mother… ' He paused, and his eyes opened as wide as they could. 'I'm too old to have a mother, but if I could've chosen one, you know it would've been you, don't you?'

Hearing those words was so magical, they made her heart melt. 'And, Ricky, 100 per cent, you would've been my choice too.' She swallowed the lump and changed the subject before it became a full-blown blubber affair.

'So, when will you be allowed home? Have they told you yet?'

'It won't be long now. Maybe in a few days' time, but I bet Dad won't let me out again.'

Zara smiled. 'No, you must've given him such a fright. My God, Ricky, what you must've gone through yourself, though?'

She looked down.

'I don't remember much of it. One minute, I was walking into Kendall's flat, and the next, I had a bag forced over my head. That's all I remember.'

Zara's natural curiosity got the better of her. 'Did they say anything that you can recall?'

He shook his head. 'Nothing at all. Maybe, when I'm fully better, something might come back to me. Dad keeps asking all the time. He's desperate to track 'em down. I'm worried though, Zara. I really don't want him to get hurt. You know what he's like. It's an eye for an eye – or worse – with him. I can see the anger in his eyes. He won't rest until he knows who did it.' Suddenly, his face looked pale and full of sorrow.

'What's up, Ricky? Do you feel unwell?' She panicked.

'No, it's just I feel so guilty.'

'Why?'

'Because I'm alive, and Kendall… well, she was adorable, ya know. I liked her such a lot. She didn't deserve that.'

Zara leaned forward and hugged him. 'I know, darling, I know. But you need to get better, and then you may think of something that'll help the police capture the men who did it. So, you just concentrate on your recovery.'

'The police?' Ricky shook his head. 'Dad's working with them. He's going to pin down this gang anyway—' Suddenly, he stopped.

He thought he'd said too much. Dad had told him about the mission when they were in prison, but it was on the understanding that he was never to disclose what they'd discussed outside the firm. And he'd made it very clear that Zara wasn't to know either because he didn't want her to worry.

'What?' Her tone became more serious.

'Nothing, Zara. Sorry, I get confused.'

She knew then she shouldn't press him and have him worrying unnecessarily.

'Well, listen, babe, you just get better, and once you're up, perhaps we'll go for a nice meal somewhere special.'

'Yeah, I'd like that.'

She kissed him once more and left. Her mind was on what Ricky had let slip. That was until she saw Mike with his arm around a nurse. She was giggling and obviously flirting. Mike didn't see Zara right away. He was still talking earnestly and laughing. Then the nurse stopped and faced him. She was twiddling a strand of hair that had come loose from her ponytail. Gazing into Mike's eyes, she was oblivious to any potential bystander. In fact, she was giving it all she had in the flirting department. But Mike, it appeared to Zara, wasn't so shy himself; he was nodding and intently listening to the nurse. As she watched the scene play out in front of her, Zara's heart was in her mouth.

Then, as if Mike sensed the presence of someone, he turned and froze, his eyes wide in utter disbelief. *Zara! Oh shit!*

Zara didn't hang about. Her expression inscrutable, and her eyes focused on something far down the corridor, she blanked both Mike and the nurse and marched on ahead.

'Zara! Wait a minute.'

Near to tears, Zara hurried her stride to the lift, hoping to slip inside before it closed, so she could avoid having to face her fiancé. But then he was there in full view, looking ashen-faced with shock and powerless to do or say anything as the doors closed on what in reality was a chapter of her life.

So he didn't hang about. First Jennifer, then back to Jackie, and now a nurse. She wondered if their own relationship hadn't been so much a mistake but an actual out-and-out lie. Or had she foolishly believed it was more than it really was?

Mike walked back along the corridor with his head down, feeling utterly miserable. Constance, unsure of what had just happened, chose to be thick-skinned and continued with her play for Mike. She offered a generous smile and gained back his attention.

'Er, sorry about that. I wanted to talk to, um… Oh, never mind. Sorry, Constance, what were you saying?'

Constance spotted the auxiliary room ajar, and in a blink of an eye, she'd grabbed Mike's arm and led him inside.

'Hey, what's going on?' asked Mike, now nervously laughing.

'I just thought we could have a more private conversation,' replied Constance, in a slow, seductive voice.

Mike didn't know how to react. He wasn't in the right frame of mind, and it had been a long time since he'd had the eye from another woman.

Constance wasn't going to hang about. She stepped nearer and placed both her arms around his neck and tried to pull him closer. At first, he was rigid, but then his muscles relaxed as her come-to-bed eyes lured him in.

'Why don't you come over to mine for dinner tonight?'

Flushing slightly with embarrassment and feeling a little warm, Mike gently removed her hands. 'Why not? Listen, babe, I need to see to Ricky before I shoot off.' He pulled his phone from his pocket and handed it to her. ''Ere, stick your number in there, and I'll call you later.'

Constance added her number, winked, and said, 'See you tonight then, handsome.'

***

Zara's eyes were firmly on the road ahead, but her mind was faraway. The excitement of the new cars meant nothing now; driving home, feeling so flat, she wasn't aware of a black BMW 7 Series following her at a discreet distance all the way to her home.

***

A sound outside alerted Poppy. She looked at her bedside clock. 3 a.m. She listened to footsteps on the drive and someone entering the house. *Sod it,* she thought, *I need a drink now.*

Creeping downstairs, she expected to encounter at least one of her parents, but something made her stop on the last tread of the staircase. Mother was on her mobile in the kitchen.

At once, Poppy's brain kicked into gear as she silently crept along the hallway and listened. The conversation seemed to be dominated by her mother, so Poppy heard pretty much everything.

And her mother's words sent a shiver down her spine. Thoughts of entering the kitchen went out of the window. Quietly, she retreated upstairs to the bathroom, where she drank from the bathroom tap, before she headed back to bed. But it turned out to be a long night. Sleep was the furthest thing from her mind.

***

In the morning, the house was quiet. Rebecca had gone out and Alastair had headed off to the gym. Poppy rose from her bed and padded down to the kitchen to make a cheese toastie for herself and Brooke. There was so much to think about. She decided to keep what she'd heard to herself for the time being. But her sister's plight was very much a concern. So, taking the bull by the horns, she made a decision to help Brooke herself.

Calling through the slightly ajar bedroom door, Poppy balanced the plates and cups of hot chocolate. 'Can I talk to you?'

'No, you can't. Go away,' came the voice inside the bedroom.

'Brooke, please. I have one sister now, and as much as you are hurting, I am too. Please, let me in.'

The door slowly opened wider, and there in her pyjamas, and with her hair almost a matted mess, stood her sister.

Poppy walked in and placed the plates and cups on the chest of drawers. Then she looked around Brooke's room and saw the chaos. Clothes were strewn across the floor, her make-up and curling tongs had been knocked off the dresser, and there was a conspicuously large soiled patch on the carpet, which looked like a red wine stain. *Was Brooke into serious drinking?* The whole room was filthy and stank to high heaven. *Her sister needed to get a grip on her life.* As Brooke clambered back into bed, Poppy opened the sash windows.

'Right, sit up,' ordered Poppy firmly. 'We need to talk… ' There was no response.

Poppy could see that it was going to be a lot harder than she thought to bring Brooke back into the land of the living.

'Brooke, I really need you now. The family is one fucked-up mess, and I'm wandering around like a tit in a trance. Just like you, I can't get Kendall off my mind. But it's you I'm seriously worried about now. Me and you need to find out who did this, and I can't do it alone, Brooke. I really do need your help.' There was a prolonged silence, and Poppy looked at her sister and wondered how it was possible for families to grow apart so easily, with each member living their own agenda in life.

The quilt suddenly peeled back, and Brooke blinked furiously. 'I can't, Poppy. I can't bear to even leave this room. I'm so terrified. All I keep seeing is those *men*. It was awful, Poppy, and I bet it was the same ones who did it to Kendall. But she didn't escape, she's dead… But what I want to know is *why*? Why is this happening? I feel like they're out there preying on us. You mustn't go out alone, or you'll be next!'

Poppy stared at an almost virtual mirror image of herself.

They weren't identical, but anyone could see they were twins. They didn't look like either Alastair or Rebecca, though.

'No, I won't. But listen. It was purely coincidental.'

She wasn't sure who she was trying to convince, yet she couldn't be like Brooke, shutting herself away from the world.

'We can beat them!'

Those words should have been well intended and a comfort to her sister, but whatever it was that Poppy was selling, Brooke wasn't at all interested. Instead, Brooke just slouched her shoulders and scowled at her sister. 'We can't, Poppy. They were… Oh my God, I just can't bear to think about it.'

Poppy decided to change tack. 'Brooke, I know what happened to you was bad, really bad, but you're alive. Kendall's not. I need you to remember that, okay? All the time you stay in your room, those bastards are still out there. The police are doing nothing. Don't you find that fucking strange?'

Brooke didn't find anything strange about it at all. She was still so brutally traumatized and gave her sister short shrift. 'I don't know anything anymore, Poppy. I really don't know what to think. And worse, I don't even know who I *am*.'

Like a grown woman, Poppy rose from the edge of the bed. 'Well, I do, Brooke. *I* know who you are. You're a brave person who's been seriously let down by our fucking parents. Now, drink this hot chocolate and eat some food. We're going to make a pact… just you and me.'

Brooke felt her eyes filling up again. 'Did you remember to put sprinkles on the top?'

Poppy chuckled. 'Yeah, kiddo, just how you like it.'

Before Poppy picked up the drinks, she put her arms around her sister and hugged her tight. That was the first time ever that they'd embraced. They'd never been a tactile family. It was just how they were, and it stemmed from having a mother and father who were cold in outlook. Poppy couldn't remember a single hug from her mother, for God's sake. It wasn't normal, was it? Both of her parents were cold and stiff; there were no kisses on the cheeks, even.

Brooke broke down in Poppy's arms. Holding on tight, she didn't want to let go, which completely shocked Poppy.

'Hey, come on. I'm here for you. Let's give being sisters a go, shall we?'

Brooke sniffed and then laughed as she wiped her wet face. 'Well, that will be a first.'

'Brooke, have you never wondered why the police haven't been to the house to follow up your dreadful attack or why Mother hasn't organized some professional help for you?'

Brooke frowned. Her white, thin, and sunken face looked so fragile. 'No.'

Poppy shook her head and sighed. 'I've been doing some research on the internet. By rights, you should've had *some* counselling at the very least.'

'I don't think it will help me, Poppy. I just keep seeing those men. I'm so afraid all the time; I can't even bear to take my clothes off. It's like they'll suddenly appear from nowhere.'

Poppy could feel a lump in her throat. She just couldn't imagine being that scared of anything. 'Hey, listen. Why don't I run you a bath and sit beside you? You'll feel safer then, I promise.'

Brooke lowered her head and looked up through her eyelashes. 'Maybe.'

'You stink!'

Brooke laughed. 'I know. Okay, but please, stay with me?'

Grabbing Brooke's hands, Poppy nodded. 'Always, sis. And always remember we are together in this. Fuck Mother and fuck sodding Father. It's you and me now, yeah?'

Brooke nodded, and her cheeks showed just a little more colour, and those blue eyes gradually revealed a spark of life, as she gave Poppy a gentle smile. 'Yeah, all right, then. Go for it.'

***

By the time Rebecca had returned home, Brooke was downstairs. Her hair was no longer a dishevelled mess. Now, having been thoroughly washed and blow-dried, it glistened as it hung well below her shoulders, almost down to her waist. She was very thin, but the food that Poppy had made her had restored some colour in her cheeks.

Rebecca was stunned to see her two daughters on the sofa side by side, looking through a magazine. However, what she didn't expect to see was the cold, dirty look she received from both of them. In her usual matter-of-fact manner, she said, 'Well, it's good to see you finally up, Brooke. How are you feeling today?'

The high-pitched sugary tone caused both girls to return an ugly grimace.

Brooke's eyes narrowed. 'Why didn't you arrange counselling for me, Mother?'

What? Rebecca wasn't the least bit prepared for that question and appeared visibly awkward, her eyes darting around the room. Stunned by that searching question, she bit her lip and retreated speedily to the kitchen.

In just three hours, the strength Poppy had given Brooke was immeasurable. It was a pivotal moment in her life. Brooke leaped to her feet and was immediately followed by Poppy. They marched into the kitchen and stood there blocking the doorway, so that their mother couldn't run off again and bury her head in the sand.

'I said, why didn't you get me the help I needed?'

Rebecca turned her back on her daughters to fill the kettle.

'Mother!' bellowed Brooke.

In a fit of rage, Rebecca spun around. 'For goodness' sake, do you not think I have enough to deal with? Kendall's dead, in case you two have forgotten. Can't I even grieve in peace?'

It was Poppy's opportunity to take the initiative, and her debating skills, which had won her awards at school, gave her the confidence to answer her mother back with logical and rational argument. 'Yes, we know Kendall is dead. We're all well aware of that, Mother. But where is your duty of care to *us* as a parent?'

Rebecca's face was a picture as she just stared goggle-eyed at her daughter's use of words.

But Poppy wasn't finished, not by a long chalk. She continued. 'And in case you're ignorant of the fact, you should know we're also grieving, but, if I remember rightly... ' her voice now the height of sarcasm, 'Brooke was attacked *weeks* ago. So, your excuse for her not receiving help is... ?'

Rebecca's eyes looked cold, dark, and spiteful. 'Because, you stupid, stupid girl, we are in the public eye, and if anyone had an inkling, the press would have Brooke's face plastered all over every bloody newspaper in the country. So, it would only make matters worse.'

Poppy was about to launch into another argument when Brooke put her hand up to stop her. 'But at what point, Mother, did you feel *you* should be making decisions like that on my behalf? Did it not ever occur to you that it may be an idea to discuss this with *me*? I mean, if having my face on the front of the newspapers would in some way help to find those animals and prevent it happening again, then why would I mind?'

'It's your future, Brooke, I'm trying to protect. It would destroy you, having reporters hounding you in the streets for photos. Your life would be horrific. I just wanted the best for you, that's all.'

Brooke really laughed at that last remark. 'The best for me, yeah? Stuck in my stinking bed, away from the world, with no studies, no friends, all alone, with just the smell of BO and the visions of those awful men. And you actually think that's *better*?'

Now Rebecca felt trapped. Her two daughters – who'd hardly ever spoken two words to each other in God knows how many years – were now behaving like a pack of wolves, daring her to leave the kitchen. In her annoyance, she bit back. 'Well, you look just fine to me!'

That crass comment, and the tone in which it was made, was enough to send Poppy into an almost apoplectic rage. 'You evil *bitch*!' she screamed, as she tried to push past Brooke to reach her mother.

But Brooke, even though she was weak, managed to pull Poppy back. 'No, Poppy. I think our mother has just confirmed to me just how cold she really is. Well, I'm not a child, so I will go to the press and give an interview, and, hopefully, it may help to find those animals and bring them to justice, and you, Mother, will have nothing to do with it.'

Rebecca's eyes were on stalks. 'What? No, you certainly can't do that!'

'And who's going to stop me? You?'

'Yes, Brooke, I will. You have no idea what you're doing, and I won't stand by and—'

'Let your career go down the drain?' replied Poppy, finishing her mother's sentence for her.

'No, it's not like that at all. Right, you listen to me and listen well. I had a call from your Uncle Conrad. That was where I was this morning. They have found the men who they believe attacked you.'

'Mother, can't you actually say the *word*. They raped me, Mother. They fucking *raped* me!'

Rebecca held her hands up. 'Yes, I know they did. I am sorry. But listen, they have found the men.'

Poppy was stunned into silence, but Brooke clearly wasn't. 'I haven't even given the police a proper statement, just a few details that I could remember at the time. Christ, Mother, they didn't even examine me, let alone take a DNA sample, and I guess once again that was your doing. So, how the fuck do they know they've got the right men?'

Rebecca looked down at the Italian marble floor tiles and visibly sighed. 'Because one of the men was found with your bank card and another had your watch.'

'So, what now? Do I go and identify them in a line-up or what?'

'No, you can't. They are dead.'

'What!' screeched Brooke.

Poppy laughed out loud. 'Oh, come on. Is this another ploy to shut her up so you can put an end to this?'

'No, Poppy, it's not. They were found dead early this morning. That is where I was… with your uncle.'

Brooke's forehead crinkled in bewilderment as she glared at her mother, looking for any sign that she was telling the truth. 'Can I go and see them and identify if it was them or not?'

Rebecca shook her head. 'You won't be able to because not even their next of kin would. Each of them had their head covered in a hessian sack and they were beaten to a pulp.'

'So why should I believe it's them just because they had my belongings? What you've told me doesn't amount to much really. Those men could have obtained them from anywhere. And here's another thought for you and your friends in the police. Have any of you considered that the evidence might have been planted?'

Poppy was now fuming. It was her opening to turn detective. 'You see, Mother, if the police had taken a swab from Brooke instead of just giving her the fucking morning-after pill, they could've done a DNA match, and we would've known for fucking sure.'

Rebecca knew her daughter was right, but she decided to brazen it out. 'It is them, Brooke. Your uncle is absolutely convinced it's them.'

'And was he fucking there then when I was gang-raped? How the hell can he be so sure, eh? Do fucking enlighten me.'

Rebecca threw her an irritated look. 'I am not going to discuss this anymore. They have found the men who raped you, so that's an end to it. Stop looking for an argument, both of you. You should just trust me. I am your mother.' With that, she stomped past the two girls and headed upstairs.

But if Rebecca thought she'd got away with her final rejoinder, she was wrong.

Poppy wasn't done. She stood at the bottom of the stairs and screamed up, 'Trust you, Mother? You obviously don't know the meaning of the word "trust". Fuck you, Mother. The only word you know the meaning of is "fuck", don't you?'

She took a few deep breaths and returned to the kitchen to find Brooke making coffee, now immersed in thought. The jigsaw puzzle was complete.

'Poppy, maybe we went over the top just now. The chances are they do have the right men, especially if they had my stuff.'

Poppy tutted and sat on the breakfast bar stool. 'You and me, in fact, all of this family, aren't at all close, are we? Kendall hated it here. In fact, she hated every day of it because she wanted to be with her dad. He was here the other day. He's a really nice man. I'll tell you this, though. He had grief stamped on his forehead, unlike Mother and Father. It's all a facade really, but things will change. From now on, it's you and me against the world.'

Brooke took the two cups of coffee over to the breakfast bar. 'Sounds good, Poppy, that does. I've always felt alone, you know. Mad as it sounds, growing up in this dysfunctional family with two sisters and two parents, I felt like I was on my own.'

Poppy nodded. 'Yes, me too. It's Mother's fault entirely. She's always fussed over everything other than what's really important. As for our father, he's a right slippery bastard. I'm not sure I even know him. And our mother is in her own little world. I think she regrets having us. All she wants is Dad. It's so embarrassing to see her running after him all the time.' She sipped her coffee and looked at her sister's delicate face. 'I think we're not close because Mother wanted it that way. I know there are different views on how to bring up twins while still ensuring they have separate identities. But I think she probably read too many books on the subject and went too far. I can't remember playing a single board game with you. She even sent us to different after-school activities and demanded we were in separate classes.'

Brooke screwed up her face. 'How do you know that?'

'Because I heard her once on the phone to the school. Kendall always called me "Secret Squirrel". I'm going to miss her smart remarks and rebellious ways.'

Brooke stared off into oblivion. 'Why did she always call you that?'

'Because, Brooke, that's what I am. I want to be a detective one day. I listen to everything, even their phone calls, because the truth is, I've never trusted either of them. It's as if there's something very secret going on, especially when Mother can put on this stupid act of being fucking Miss Perfect... ' She paused. 'There's also something else you should know.'

Brooke looked at her sister and inclined her head. 'Go on.'

'You know Mother said those men had hessian sacks over their heads? Well, when Kendall was murdered, she wasn't alone. She was with someone called Ricky Regan. He was beaten in the same way, with a sack over his head.'

Brooke gasped. 'What? Tell me you're joking?'

Poppy shook her head. 'No, straight up. You know me, Brooke. When have you ever seen this face crack a smile?'

With her furrowed frown, Brooke glared at her sister. 'This makes no sense. So now we have to assume that whoever attacked those men, they were also responsible for killing Kendall then?'

Poppy nodded. 'Yeah, I know. It makes no sense at all.'

'But how do you know all this?' asked Brooke.

'I overheard Mother talking to Conrad in the kitchen when she arrived home in the early hours.'

'Christ, how the hell can Kendall and I end up in the middle of two warring gangs? Nothing adds up.'

CHAPTER FOURTEEN

Absolutely fuming, Mike returned home from the hospital. It was now three times that Zara had misunderstood a situation, and two of them he could have explained, given time, but not the third.

He slammed the door shut and growled to himself. What Zara had witnessed didn't look good at all, yet he wasn't interested in the nurse in that way. Of course, he found her pretty, but it was only because she reminded him of Zara. Retrieving his phone, he looked up Constance's number and decided to text her. The initial attraction was nothing more than that. He couldn't lead the sweet nurse on. He was worlds apart – the villain and the nurse, it sounded like a porn movie. Besides, he loved Zara, whether she loved him now or not. He had values.

> **Hi Constance. I need to be fair and honest. We are two very different people. I am very sorry. I think it is for the best that we remain as friends. I hope you understand. Mike Regan.**

He hesitated whether to leave a kiss but thought better of it.

The noise upstairs brought him back to the darker side of reality. He'd left Jackie locked in one of the spare bedrooms all day. He realized that there was no point in keeping her here forever; if she wanted to be a junkie, then so be it. Ricky was on the mend, and, really, he didn't want to see his mother, so all she was good for now was signing the divorce papers.

He wasted no time and hurried up the stairs. As soon as he unlocked the door, he was quite amazed to see Jackie looking a more fresh-faced thirty-eight-year-old; she was sitting upright at the end of the bed.

'Right, Jackie, I'm taking you back home. First, though, I want you to sign some papers I have downstairs. I'll call my dad's solicitor to witness it.'

Jackie stared up at her husband, her mind now clear. The drugs were out of her system, and, for the first time in fifteen years, she was completely sober. 'Do you mind if I have a shower and get dressed first?'

Mike was surprised by how more softly spoken she was. Her animalistic expressions and disgusting foul mouth had disappeared. He nodded. 'Yes, a good idea. You do that, and I'll make you some coffee.'

She smiled sweetly. 'Actually, I would prefer tea.'

Without replying, he left the room.

Jackie couldn't wait to get cleaned up. The sweat that had coated her body a hundred times left her smelling like a dirty fox. Her hair, hard and gritty, needed a damn good wash. She wondered if all of her clothes had been dumped years ago when she'd left.

The last room on the right was a spare room-cum-storeroom no one ever used. She stood in the doorway and looked.

Nothing seemed to have changed at all, unlike the rest of the house, which had been updated. She remembered storing her old clothes in there but now wondered if any would fit.

She hurriedly pulled plastic boxes from under the bed, popped the lids, and looked down. The top outfit was a plain white shirt, with some designer logo on the pocket. Underneath it was a pair of black jeans. She smiled. She remembered why she'd thrown them into the box; it was because they were too big. Rummaging through, she found more clothes that would do for now, along with underwear and even old jewellery that for the moment looked lovely compared to the crap she had back at the caravan.

After a long hot bath, she got herself dressed and made her way downstairs. Mike handed her a cup of tea, and she followed him into the dining room.

'How's your face?'

Jackie was actually surprised at how little the scarring stood out. Initially, she thought she'd look like a victim of a Glasgow kiss, but, surprisingly, the swelling had gone down, the actual pink scar having thinned out. And given time, she thought it would fade into insignificance.

'Yeah, not so bad.'

Mike was amused by how different Jackie was. She seemed resigned, almost ashamed.

'So, you want me to sign the divorce papers?'

Mike laughed. 'Of course I do, Jackie. I want you out of my life completely.'

She nodded calmly. 'I don't blame you. Okay, then, I'll sign them.'

Mike wasn't convinced that she was genuine, simply because

she'd never been so in the past. *Does a leopard really change its spots*, he thought?

'And I assume there's a settlement? I mean, you don't expect me to walk away with nothing, do you?'

He knew it – she was after money. But he'd already made provisions long before he had her brought to his house. 'Yeah, you do walk away with something, although it's meaningless really. You get to have your life.'

She didn't expect any other answer. 'Ha, that was predictable, Mike. So, I'm not entitled to anything then?'

Mike gulped back his drink. 'Jackie, you bought your own house from the money you syphoned from me. You took away my son, and he'll vouch for how you treated him. So, Jackie, be thankful, love, that, seriously, you're still alive. So, when the solicitor arrives, just keep your mouth fucking shut and sign on the dotted line.'

She grinned then. 'And what if I don't?'

'I'm not going to spell it out because I don't have the fucking time or the crayons to explain it to you.'

'Okay, fair enough. It was worth a try, I suppose.'

Mike shook his head in annoyance. 'And, by the way. Those bags of cocaine you had, I flushed them down the toilet.'

Jackie smiled sweetly. 'Good. I needed to get off that shit. Oh, and it's not cocaine, it's called Flakka. It's bleedin' vile, evil stuff. Anyway, I guess you did me a right favour locking me up or I would still be selling my arse to buy the next hit.'

Her words came out of left field. Mike suddenly turned cold. 'Flakka, you said?'

'Yeah, why? What do you really care, Mike?'

'Who supplied you with that shit?'

Jackie sensed the urgency in his voice. 'Why? What's it to you?'

He glared with his nostrils flared. Jackie read the signs – she'd always been able to read him like a book. Still, there was an upside for her, if she played her cards right. If he wanted this information, he could sodding well pay for it. *Softly, softly, catchee monkey*, she thought. She would play it cool.

'Because, Jackie, I wanna know, and you're gonna fucking tell me. Now!'

She sipped her tea slowly, knowing every second was ramping up his anger. 'I don't wanna say, Mike. I don't want to think about it again. I'm clean now, and that's the way it's going to stay.'

In a flash, he gripped her arm. 'Oh no, it fucking ain't. Who supplied you?'

She tried to shake him off. Now she had the measure of him, she thought she would box clever.

'Mike, I know that after I sign those papers, you'll have everything, and I'll end up back in that shit-hole of a caravan. You'll live in this beautiful home with our son, and I'll have fuck all. So, if you want something from me, then be decent. Give me something in return.'

Mike let go of her wrist and leaned back in his chair. He had to hand it to her. She played the game well. *But then*, he thought, *she'd learned from a great mentor*. 'Fair enough.' He smiled. 'I'll pay you for information. How about that? Five grand for starters, then?'

She thought she had him – hook, line, and sinker. 'Make it ten grand, and we have a deal.'

He nodded. 'Fine by me. Now, who the hell supplied you?'

'He's called Leon Khouri.'

Mike held back any expression on his face; he knew who Leon Khouri was, and he also knew the man was dead. 'And how do you know about him?'

'I want twelve grand now for that bit of info.'

He nodded. 'Yeah, okay. Go on.'

'Wait up! Let's see the wonga, Mike.'

Mike sighed deeply, but the expression wasn't so severe as before. He looked at Jackie with a measure of respect. He opened the concealed lid of a footstool and grabbed a wad of notes, much to her surprise. She'd never known about that hiding place and could've kicked herself.

'Tatum asked me to visit Leon to pick up some drugs for him. It was for someone called Dez Weller. He's a seriously dangerous bloke, by the way. Anyway, I was supposed to pass it on, during a prison visit... ' She realized she'd just let her mouth run away with her, and if she mentioned that it was their son who was supposed to take the drugs from her, then Mike would go spare.

Mike was taking it all in. Dez, his arch-enemy, dealing that shit inside, wound him right up, but he kept a deadpan face.

'Do you have this Leon's address or pick-up place?'

'Fifteen grand, Mike.'

He nodded. 'Yeah, yeah, sure.' While he moved over the next tranche, he asked, 'What's the man's address?'

'It's in my bag, on the back of one of my court summonses, I think.'

Mike shot up from his seat and pulled her bag out from behind the bar area. He didn't behave like a gentleman and hand it to her, so she could rummage through it. He merely tipped the contents out. There on the floor was the court summons. 'Right, thank you. Now, who was this Leon working for or with? And before you say twenty grand, I agree. I'll give ya twenty grand for that information.'

Jackie studied him like a gamekeeper would a poacher. With narrowed eyes, she folded her arms before replying. 'Twenty-five grand!'

Mike gritted his teeth. He had to admire Jackie, but this was a piss-take of Olympic proportions. 'Fuck off, Jackie. Twenty grand and no more.' He had to be believable.

She looked at him with an imperious stare, until he broke away from her gaze and added more to her increasing pile. *Not a bad day's work*, she thought.

'Right, all I know is the man that Leon is scared of is a guy called the Governor. I didn't see his face, but I did get a glimpse of him when I was spaced out. Leon gave me the shit to try, and not being used to drugs… '

Mike rolled his eyes.

'No, seriously, Mike, I drink and I've smoked weed but nothing hard-core. Anyway, I was as high as a kite, and the next minute, I sort of came out of a trancelike thing, and I could hear this man's voice. It was deep and gruff – a bit like yours. Anyway, I opened me eyes and saw the back of him. He's a big fella, like you, with cropped hair, like yours… ' She paused and frowned. ''Ere, it wasn't you, was it?'

Mike took a deep breath. 'Watch it, Jackie. Don't be a div.'

The knock at the door killed their conversation stone-dead. It was Brandon Miles, his father's solicitor. A tall and immaculately dressed man in his late sixties, he'd been the family's lawyer for decades. Armed with a briefcase and a broad smile, he shook Mike's hand. 'Good to see you, Mike. How are you? How's Ricky?'

'Yeah, he's on the mend, Brandon. He should be home very soon. The whole incident has had us in bits. I'll be glad when he's home and giving me cheek.'

Miles followed Mike through into the dining room, where he locked eyes with Jackie. He'd met her once before at a family gathering and had never thought much of her then. He nodded without a smile and sat opposite her.

He pulled a pen from his top pocket and looked up at Mike. 'So, do you have the papers?'

Mike smiled. 'Oh yes, ready and waiting.'

He turned to the side cabinet and retrieved the envelope. Then he slid out the documents and placed them in front of Jackie. 'Sign there and there.'

She took the pen proffered by Miles and paused, just for effect.

Miles's eyes bored into hers, but he didn't say a word. Then he gave Mike a sly wink.

Jackie scribbled her name in all the relevant places.

Miles pulled out another form for her to sign. 'And this one too, please,' he said.

She snatched it from him and signed where the crosses were shown, without reading it. Miles took all the papers and signed as the witness. As soon as he popped them in his briefcase, he then smiled and chuckled, still staring at the woman.

''Ere, what's so funny?' she spat.

Miles shook his head, still grinning. 'I love it when I feel like I have taken a small part in revenge. You hurt this family so much, and we all stood back, unable to help, but at least I can walk out of this house knowing that there is nothing you can ever do now to hurt them. You have signed the divorce papers and any claim you have to anything Mike has. You didn't even read what was in the divorce petition that you signed your name to. Lying, kidnapping your son, stealing, coercion, and fraud. So, Miss Menaces, if you ever try to make a complaint to the police or any authority about Mike, I will show them all the papers and statements that you've just signed.'

Jackie's eyes widened in shock. 'But you're a solicitor. You can't do that.'

'Yes, I am a solicitor, which means I can do exactly that, and I just have.'

Mike had his hand over his mouth to stop himself from laughing.

'Mike, you didn't need to do that. I wasn't gonna con you out of money.'

Jackie's face was a picture. Both men couldn't stop grinning as they high-fived each other. For her part, Jackie realized she'd just been played. Although she'd had a good pay day, the thought of blackmailing Mike would have been so much sweeter.

Mike's expression changed and with a scowl he said, 'No, Jackie, you're right, there. You won't ever con me again.' He forced a fake laugh. 'Jesus, twenty-five grand, Jackie? As if I would ever give you a penny! In fact, I wouldn't give you the shit off my shoe. Now, get out!'

Her face was a picture of pure shock. She made a stupid attempt to grab the money but was forcefully pushed away by Mike. 'Get out of 'ere, Jackie, while you can still walk.'

As she steadied herself, her eyes took on the dark, evil glare that had always cast a dark shadow. 'You bastard, Mike. You fucking bastard. I will—'

She stopped in mid flow when she saw his jaw tighten and his chest inflate. He was so big, one clump from him would knock her into next door, and the look on the solicitor's face told her he wouldn't prevent the situation either. She was hated, and if she was honest with herself, she wasn't surprised. She snatched her bag from the floor, scooped up the contents that were scattered, and made her way to the front door.

Mike was on her heels, making sure she didn't nick anything on the way out.

'Mike, I don't have money for the cab fare.'

Mike opened the door and glared. He didn't even bother to answer her.

Once he'd slammed the door behind her, he turned to Miles. 'Thanks for that. I don't trust her.'

Miles nodded. 'No, neither do I, and your gut telling you she wouldn't read the details in the documents proved spot-on. Now you can wash your hands of her. It was good to see you, Mike. I'm so pleased Ricky's out of the woods. Keep in touch.'

As Mike opened the front door again to see Miles out, he noticed Jackie hanging around by the gate. He pulled a twenty-pound note from his pocket. 'Brandon, do me a favour and give this to her, will ya? She's making my property look untidy.'

Miles got into his sports car and drove towards the gate where he lowered the window and dropped the twenty-pound note on the ground.

Mike laughed as Jackie chased after it, the wind blowing it further and further away from her.

Two hours later, Mike, Willie, and Staffie pulled into a dusty drive that led up to Leon Khouri's cottage.

'This doesn't look much like a druggie's den, more like a fucking quaint farmhouse,' said Willie, as he gazed around the area.

'Looks can be deceptive,' remarked Staffie.

'Yeah, you're right there. Look at me. I might be ugly on the outside, but I'm proper handsome on the inside.'

Staffie laughed. 'Shame you can't turn yaself inside out, then.'

'Cor, after that curry last night, I reckon I fucking did.'

Mike remained quiet, not listening to the men's bantering tones; he was planning his next move, now hell-bent on finding the men who'd hurt his son.

What they couldn't see, of course, were the two off-road bikes behind the cottage.

Willie got out first and lit up a cigarette as he leaned against the car. Staffie hopped out next and stared at the face of the building; no lights were on, no smoke was visible, and there was no noise evident.

'I think it may be empty!'

Mike closed his car door. 'Well, lads, let's find out, shall we?'

Willie pushed himself away from the Porsche and stubbed out his cigarette. 'Remember, looks can be deceptive.' He pulled a gun from the back of his belt and giggled like a madman.

Staffie shook his head. 'Seriously, Willie, you need to look in the mirror, mate. You resemble that bloke out of *The Shining*.'

Willie nodded and laughed. 'Thank you. I'll take that as a compliment.'

Mike was silent as he approached the front door. He leaned sideways against it and listened.

From the corner of Staffie's eye, he saw a curtain twitch and suddenly shouted. 'Duck!'

Mike was the first to lower his head. Willie, however, didn't. Instead, he went into reckless mode and was about to charge at the front door with his full body weight.

In a flash, Mike pulled him back. 'What the fuck are you doing?'

'What did ya think I was goin' to do?'

'On my say-so, dickhead. You're too flaming reckless!'

Willie felt himself blush. 'Sorry, Mikey.'

Mike rolled his eyes and then winked, feeling somewhat guilty he'd been so harsh. 'All right. After three, you and me.' He turned to Staffie, who was crouching down by the car, and flicked his head to join them.

After the count of three, Mike lifted his foot, and with one almighty bang, the door came off its hinges and crashed down into an open-plan room. They piled in, wielding guns, with Staffie behind them. Inside, it was almost completely dark, due to the heavy curtains across the window.

Their eyes were instantly drawn to two scruffy figures, standing near a sofa. As they became more accustomed to the gloom, they saw each of them raise their hands above their heads.

Willie, wide-eyed, looked at Mike and pulled a face that said, 'Fuck. How did we get this so wrong?' He looked at the staircase, and, without a plan, he tore up the stairs and ran into each of the three bedrooms and the bathroom. To his amazement, there were so many beds crammed into each room that not even a fifty-pence piece would fit between them. More shocking, however, was the bloodied bathroom. Deciding not to hang about, he hurtled back down the stairs.

Mike and Staffie stood motionless, pointing their guns. They only let out a breath when they heard Willie come charging down the stairs.

'Well?' demanded Mike.

'It looks like Snow White and the Seven Dwarfs 'ave moved in, but there's no sign of Snow White and the only dwarfs are Itchy and Scratchy.' He pointed to the two tatty-looking men.

'Anything else, Walt Disney?' asked Staffie, with a quizzical expression.

'Yeah. It looks like the Brothers Grimm have been here too. The bathroom's covered in claret.'

'Who are you?' bellowed Mike, as he turned to the men.

'Please, we don't want no trouble,' one of them replied, in a strong Polish accent.

It was time to throw some light into the room. Just as Staffie edged his way past Mike and Willie, he suddenly gasped. 'Jesus, what the fuck's going on?'

Once the curtains were opened, Mike and his friends stood still in shock at the sight before them.

A dead woman, her white, waxy, and naked body drenched in blood, was lying on the floor. She had been gutted like a fish.

'Well, there's Snow White, then,' said Willie.

It took a moment for the three men to take in the devastation. The woman was young, probably in her mid-twenties. Her eyes were still open, and she looked absolutely terrified. Her mouth was black and gaping as if she had gasped for air. But what was worse was the butchered remains of her torso.

The deep cut went from her chest all the way down. Spilling out onto the floor were the intestines and other internal organs. Mike glared at the mess; it reminded him of strings of sausages on a butcher's shelf. Beside the entrails, there were wrappers, condoms, and clingfilm. More shockingly, next to the girl's head, was a small bloodstained hessian sack.

The disturbing scene hit Mike like a ton of bricks. All he could imagine was his boy lying there. The blood left his face, and, instantly, he gagged. Staffie and Willie glanced over at their boss and were stunned by what they saw. They'd never seen Mike act so physically distressed. He was always the cold-faced one who was never affected by any gruesome scene, and he'd witnessed enough of them.

'Please, please help us!' cried one of the men by the sofa. He was shaking with fear. His face was grey and his eyes had sunk. He looked what he was: a physical wreck who had lost all his dignity.

Suddenly, they heard the sounds of motorbikes starting up. Willie instinctively ran to the back door to see two men on scrambler bikes, who were tearing across the field, away from the cottage.

He shot back to Mike, who was still staring at the grim remains of the woman.

Mike snapped out of his trance. 'Staffie, frisk these men, will ya?'

Staffie dragged one of them away from the sofa and patted him down. 'He's clean.' He then did the same to the other man, who also didn't put up a struggle.

'Who are ya?' asked Mike once again.

The paler of the two replied, 'I'm Serco and my friend is

Fabian. We need help. She… ' – he pointed to the dead woman – 'has already died, and I am sick. Are you the police?'

'No, we ain't. Who gutted her and why?'

Serco looked down in shame. 'A man called the Governor. We were all supposed to be paid but not until the men had our drugs. They are still inside us. She's dead because her parcels exploded. She died before she could even see dis country.'

Staffie felt his stomach churn so much, he had to go outside to get some fresh air.

'Please help us. One of the parcels is leaking inside me. I feel it. I am unwell, and I know I will die soon like Cillag did.'

'So the men who've just left were waiting for you to discharge your drugs, then?'

'Yes, they would not let us leave. They said we had to produce the parcels first, but I cannot pass them. The flight has made me not able to shit.'

Mike looked at Fabian. 'And you?'

Fabian shook his head. 'Same as him, but the men were impatient. They said if we do not give them the goods, then we will be cut open, like her.'

'Staffie, do us a favour, will ya? Take 'em to the hospital. Me and Willie will stay here. I wanna see who turns up. Serco, my mate here, will get you help. But, tell me, what does this Governor look like?'

Serco replied, 'Like you, he's a big man, with short hair, but maybe he's older.'

'And how did you get here?'

'We came by aeroplane.'

'Did this Governor geezer meet you at the airport?'

Serco shook his head. 'No, another man, a younger man did. He came and brought us here.'

'How the fuck did they let you on a plane?'

Fabian stepped forward. 'We have passports, money, everything we need. All we have to do is take the parcels, and we will be set up with a job, a home, and money, but it has not happened, and I think if we do not get help, Serco and I will… ' He nodded to the dead girl.

'What else do you know about this Governor?'

Fabian shrugged. 'He is the boss, a powerful man… an evil man.'

Mike drew in a deep breath and clenched his jaw. 'A fucking powerful man, yeah? He'll be a dead man when I find the fucker.'

'Well, the police can get the CCTV from the airport, and we'll know then,' said Willie.

Fabian, looking exhausted, lowered his head. 'He wore a hat, moustache, and glasses. I don't think they will recognize him.'

'Staff, get them to the hospital. We'll meet you at my gaff later.' He turned to Fabian. 'The police will want to question you, so, for your own sake, tell them fucking everything.'

Fabian smiled and gave him a weak nod. 'I will.'

***

Mike and Willie stayed behind while Staffie helped the two men into the car and headed off to the hospital.

'We need to search this place before we call Stoneham,' said Mike, as he rifled through the drawers. 'Whoever did this hurt my boy!'

After an hour or so of turning the place upside down, they concluded that there was nothing that would lead them to the man everyone called the Governor.

As Mike called Stoneham, he knew in his mind that this would be a big test to see if Stoneham would have his back. To his satisfaction, the Police Commissioner told him that his officers would meet the two foreigners at the hospital. Before he ended the call, Stoneham sighed. 'I knew making this agreement with you was the right thing to do. Your efforts have produced more information regarding this gang leader than we've managed in six months.'

But Mike wasn't so friendly in his response. 'I'll tell ya this, Mr Stoneham, I might be helping you, but I need your help in return. Whatever you find out from those two fellas, I wanna know pronto.'

'You have my word, Mr Regan.'

'Thanks. By the way, I need a lift home. Staffie has taken the two foreign men to hospital in my car, so I'm without wheels.'

'Forensics will be over shortly. I'll arrange for someone to take you.'

Mike took another look at the poor dead woman and shook his head. He knew then why Stoneham wanted this gang caught and taken out. No way was this the work of some cocky little wannabe gangster outfit. In fact, he realized that he was facing an enemy who was not only evil but who also had powerful connections. It was downright demonic. As hard and calculated as he could be, this was in the realms of something far outside his own world. It crossed his mind that the man behind it was Colombian or Brazilian. Surely, the typical British gangsters wouldn't do this, would they?

CHAPTER FIFTEEN

Antonio's was open – by 7 p.m., the restaurant was full and buzzing.

Three of his usual punters, all stockbrokers, eagerly arrived. They swiftly took their seats in the corner, ordered an antipasto starter each, and shared a bottle of champagne. After thirty minutes, they asked for the bill. Antonio went to the kitchen, pulled the packets of cocaine that were wrapped in gold foil to look like after-dinner mints, placed them on the plate, and nodded to the new waitress to take them over. Dressed in fashionable tight-fitting suits, the three young men pocketed the packets and went to the bar to pay. They left a ten-pound note as a tip for the waitress, who was very quick to pocket the money. That tip alone would pay for her to have a takeaway that night with her boyfriend.

'Nice one, Antonio. Next week, we'll have the main course,' said one of the suited men. He winked and the three left.

By the time the restaurant had emptied all but the last of the customers, Antonio was a bag of nerves, and he struggled to string a coherent sentence together.

Neil was perched on a stool at the small bar and Shamus sat at one of the tables for two in a bay window. 'Antonio, come on, mate. Look, your family are safe in Italy, yeah? I'm fecking tooled up, and me cousin over there is too. If anyone so much as gives you a dirty look, we'll be on them like a couple of rabid dogs.'

Antonio was cleaning one of the glasses. The bags under his eyes were prominent from the overhead lighting. He looked old and his usual happy-go-lucky personality had been sucked out of him. He would have got on that plane and never come back, but he owed Zara and Izzy so much. They had set him up in business, and for years, he'd been running a successful restaurant. Even the police ate there; yet under everyone's nose, he was dealing cocaine first for Zara and then the Lanigans. He couldn't turn his back on her now.

'Antonio, wipe that sweat from your face, mate. You look so fecking edgy. You've still got a few customers here.'

Antonio looked across the bar at four men who were finishing their drinks. He quickly rubbed a tea towel over his face. 'What do you expect, Neil? You weren't here. But those guys who came here a while ago were reckless.'

Neil nodded. 'Well, mate, if from your description it's the same ones who stabbed me on the fecking sly, I'm ready. We're gonna be one step ahead and show this firm that we ain't backing off.'

Antonio sighed. 'I just hope you know what you're doing, that's all.'

Neil grinned and sipped his brandy. He had a liking for a Hennessy. 'Yes, that I do.'

A black BMW 7 Series drove past slowly, the tinted windows hiding the occupants of the car. Shamus got up from his seat, mooched over to the bar, and whispered in Neil's ear. 'I think we're gonna have visitors.'

'Good. It's about time. I was wondering if they'd show up tonight.'

The remaining four diners, who were finishing their meals, rose from their seats and straightened their suits. 'Compliments to the chef!' one of them called out.

Antonio waved. 'Thank you. Please call again.'

He nodded to the young waitress to give them their bill. Once the men were out of the door, she folded her pinny and asked for her wages. Antonio gave her a fifty-pound note. 'Good girl. I'll see you tomorrow.'

'Fifty?'

Antonio smiled at her and nodded. 'Yes, Tiffany, you worked hard. Now, get yourself home safely.'

Tiffany smiled in response. Quickly, she shoved the money in her bag and was on the point of hurrying over to the front door before Antonio had a chance to change his mind about her wages. But she didn't go out of the restaurant.

'Aw, I just need the toilet quickly. It's quite a long walk.'

'Er… remember the ladies' is out of order. Only the men's is working.'

There was silence as they all waited. Antonio poured both Shamus and Neil another drink and gave himself a double measure to calm his nerves.

Tiffany was now back in the dining room, waving goodbye.

Outside was pitch-black; the lamp over the restaurant hadn't come on. Suddenly, Neil spotted how dark it was. 'Wait up, love,' he called, as she stepped outside.

She was on the point of turning back to smile at him; she'd been quite taken with the handsome man. But before she'd even had a chance to give him a flirtatious look, a huge hand

318

grabbed her around the mouth, and she was lifted from the pavement and dragged towards the thugs' car.

The shock had Neil on his feet and running to the door. Shamus looked at his phone; the text was ready to send as soon as need be. He pressed the forward icon and heard the sound of the text message from inside the ladies' toilets. Minty and Jacko, their own men, who were hiding inside the restroom, came tearing into the dining area.

'Lads, go around to the side door,' shouted Shamus, as he hurried towards the front door.

Outside, Neil watched in horror as a massive man, wearing a balaclava, held a knife at Tiffany's throat. Instantly, Neil put his hands up. 'Leave off. Jesus, she's only a kid!'

From the BMW, which was idling by the kerb outside the restaurant, two more men jumped out. They were just as large and were also wearing balaclavas. But it was their practised threatening movements that would have put the shit up most bystanders if they'd been there. Wielding crowbars, they demonstrated they were up for a serious fight. Almost in tandem, again as if their movements were rehearsed, they dared Neil to take them on.

This wasn't supposed to happen, thought Neil. He stared in disbelief as the young girl's eyes bulged in abject terror. He thought his plan was fucked until he saw Jacko and Minty creeping up behind the three men. Jacko had a metal bat; in one quick movement, he struck the man holding the kid hard around the head. The resounding bang was so loud that unless he was a machine, he would have hit the deck in a jiffy. Neil and Jacko were both stunned that although he let the girl go, he didn't otherwise move. Quickly, Neil lurched forward and snatched the girl, pulling her behind him. But the man holding the knife lashed out, causing Jacko and Minty to back off.

Whoever was in the vehicle suddenly started the engine; in a second, all three of the men jumped in and tore away.

Zara had been parked in a side street, nervously smoking. Davey and two more of his men were inside the Range Rover with her. The text that came through almost made her jump out of her seat. Discarding the cigarette, she pulled away smartly and was about to turn left but another car was in the way, making a three-point turn. In frustration, she banged the steering wheel. 'Fuck! Fuck!' she screeched. As soon as the road was clear, she tore away and pulled up directly outside the restaurant to find Neil shaking his head and staring up the road at the BMW leaving an exhaust trail in the cold air. Jumping out of the car, her first priority was the distraught waitress, who looked as though she would have a panic attack at any moment.

'What the fuck just happened?'

'The cunts grabbed Tiffany and held a knife to her throat.'

Zara went over to the traumatized kid and hugged her. 'It's okay, love.' She stroked the girl's hair, trying to calm her trembling body, and hushed the sobs that were now becoming louder and louder.

'Lads!' she called out. 'I want one of you to drive her home!'

'Oh my God, I thought they were gonna kill me! Who-who are-are they? Wh-why us?' Tiffany cried out.

Zara pulled her against her own soft cashmere jumper. 'Now, listen. Those men have gone. They were probably nothing more than some opportunists who were pushing their luck. Don't worry, darling, you're safe now. I'll make sure you get home safely.'

Tiffany's make-up was running down her face in streams. 'Are we calling the police?'

'No, there's no need. They won't be able to do much, but you're safe enough now.'

Tiffany pulled away and looked Zara up and down. She was surprised that the woman looked so in control, and then she eyed the men around her, realizing that the one-handed woman was the boss.

'Er, who are you?' she asked, with a nervous tone, although the sobs had now stopped, and she felt very comforted by the tall, dark-haired lady.

Zara gave Tiffany a compassionate smile. 'This is my restaurant, sweetheart. Now then, I think you deserve a little compensation.'

Tiffany's eyes widened in astonishment. 'What d'ya mean, like? What, you want to pay me off to keep me mouth shut?'

Zara studied the youngster's face to see if she could easily be fobbed off.

'Look, you seem a bright young lady, so, darling, I won't fuck about. Yeah, I want you to keep quiet. There's no point in making a drama out of a crisis, is there? In return, I'll give you five hundred pounds. Now, how does that sound?'

Tiffany was suddenly in awe of the woman who spoke with an air of confidence that oozed sophistication. If the truth be known, she would love to model herself on her. 'How about a grand and you have a deal?'

Zara tapped the youngster's nose. 'Good girl, you played the game brilliantly. That's what I like to hear, a negotiator. Well, you've got yourself a deal. But!'

Tiffany suddenly felt very cold. She nervously swallowed

hard at seeing the posh woman almost become a different person as she stood over her, her mouth set sternly and her eyes cold and penetrating her own. Tiffany was shaking, and it wasn't because of what had happened earlier.

'But… if I pay you out, and I hear you've opened your mouth to anyone, then you'll wish you hadn't crossed me. Understood?'

Tiffany nodded so hard, it appeared as though her head might fall off at any moment.

'I won't say a dicky bird… I know I'm just a kid really compared to you, but can I ask ya something? I wouldn't mind working for ya, if you'd take me on?'

Zara raised her eyebrow. 'Oh yeah? Well, that depends on what you can bring to the table, love. Let me have a think about it. In the meantime, are you still up for working in the restaurant? I like strong people on my books who I can trust.'

Tiffany blushed. 'Well, yeah, sure. I'll be ready if those bullies turn up again.'

The men surrounding Zara relaxed their shoulders at last. The cheek of the young waitress had definitely released the tension, and Tiffany had given them a good laugh to boot.

'Anyway, what the fuck happened? I got the text, so we came hammering down and… '

Neil was shaking his head. 'They must have hidden behind the wall, and as soon as Tiffany went to leave, they grabbed her. I thought we were fecked for a minute. The sly bastards. Did you see the fecking size of 'em? Jesus, all three were huge. The one with the knife was a colossus.'

'Yeah, but did ya see the bandage around his wrist? He's already been in a war,' said Tiffany, joining in, acting as though she was already part of the firm.

'What? He had a bandage wrapped around his wrist?'

Tiffany enthusiastically responded. 'Yeah, and he was wearing Joop! aftershave. *And* he had a gold ring on his little finger.'

Zara grinned. 'Work for me, eh? You could get a job as a detective.'

Tiffany chuckled. What a day it had been.

***

When the house was quiet, Poppy crept into Brooke's bedroom. 'Hey, we need to talk, but I really don't want to upset you. How strong are you feeling?'

Brooke beckoned her sister in.

Poppy sat on the edge of the bed. 'Are you feeling any better?'

'Yeah, I am, thanks to you. Who'd have thought it, me and you becoming friends?'

Poppy gave Brooke a weak smile. 'You were always my friend. I just think our mother controlled us so much we didn't even have a chance to be buddies. But, listen. I want to talk about our father.'

With a frown furrowing Brooke's brow, she sat up straighter. 'What about him?'

Poppy fiddled with the edge of the bed cover. 'Do you ever get the feeling he's not part of us as a family? It's hard to explain. It's like he's not interested. I mean, I feel I don't even know him. Do you, or is it just me?'

Brooke stared off into the distance, and her face dropped in sadness. 'I thought it was just me, Poppy. I honestly thought he never loved me.'

Feeling a sense of sadness, Poppy studied her sister's face. The girl had been through so much, and there she was like a little angel, sitting up in bed, doubting her father's love.

'He never loved any of us. But while we're being honest, I think he had a thing for Kendall. It was just the way he looked at her. But I've been thinking a lot about stuff lately, and I want to move out. How about you?'

Brooke's eyes suddenly lit up. 'What? Do you mean me and you?'

Poppy nodded, pleased with the way the conversation was going. 'Why not? This house is full of secrets, and it's strangling the life out of me. Think about it. Kendall was miserable, and they made her unhappy, I just know they did. I've never felt that this is a healthy situation. It's all fake and stifling. I want to leave and begin to live like Kendall wanted to.'

'Yes, I hate it here as well. There's no love in this house. Mother only loves her job, and Dad, well, he just loves himself. And as for his job, I don't know what it actually is, do you?'

'Overseas property, I believe. Anyway, I've secured a job at the post office. I start on Monday. Fuck uni. I'm done with that. It wasn't a great course anyway, and I did some reading up on that too. The educational system is all about job statistics and providing jobs for university staff. My media course won't get me a job. There are thousands looking for work. I was thinking that maybe we could ask Kendall's father. He has property. He gave Kendall a flat.'

Brooke gasped and put her hands to her mouth. 'What? Poppy, you can't ask him, it would be... well, insensitive.'

Poppy shook her head. 'You didn't meet him, I did. He isn't

the type to get all sentimental. You should have heard him. He put Mother in her place.'

'How will you contact him?'

Poppy winked. 'I went through Kendall's stuff and found his phone number. I could call him, if you want. He can only say no.'

'Go on, then. I'm up for that. I would love to get away from here, from them.'

Both the girls began to giggle and started to make a plan. 'Let's just go and not tell them,' said Brooke.

Poppy bounded to her feet. 'Mother won't be back 'til midnight. She's got one of her meetings. I'll go down to the log cabin. I know Dad puts the suitcases there.'

Brooke pulled her quilt off. 'I'll start sorting out my stuff. This is so exciting. Where will we go tonight, though?'

'Nowhere. Let's just get packing and be ready to leave tomorrow, once we sort out a place.'

Brooke tied her hair into a ponytail and began going through her wardrobe while Poppy headed down to the garden to Alastair's man cave, as he called it. It was so dark that she couldn't see her own hands in front of her; that was until the sensor light almost blinded her. It was so long ago when she'd last been down to the cabin, which she knew was rarely used by the family, apart from Alastair storing his old files and all their suitcases.

She used her phone to light up the lock on the door and was surprised to find it was made secure with a sturdy industrial padlock. She wondered for a moment if it had always been on there. 'Damn!' she said aloud. The cold air made her shiver, so she hurried back. She tried to think where her father would keep the key, and then had a thought.

Her parents' bedroom was a real no-go area. Neither she nor her sisters had ever been allowed in their room. She made her way back up the stairs and stood for a moment outside their door. It was as if she was entering a different house. Slowly, she turned the knob and pushed the door open. She didn't really know what to expect, yet it all looked relatively normal. There was a large double bed, built-in wardrobes, and bedside cabinets. A sudden shudder shot through her like someone had walked over her grave. What did she really know about her parents? She knew the answer to that question, though – nothing.

She crept over to the nearest bedside cabinet and assumed it was her mother's because it had antidepressants, a nail file, and a chick lit book inside the drawer.

The drawer to the other cabinet was full of stuff: there were keys, old phones, batteries, a small miniature bottle of whiskey, a box of condoms, and a pen. She snatched the keys and left, remembering to close the door behind her, but forgetting to shut the drawers.

Grabbing her trendy oversized coat from the hallway, she chose to exit via the patio doors and hurried down to the end of the garden. She was in luck with the first key she tried and instantly she released the padlock. On entering the cabin, she used her phone again to search for the light switch.

Like the shrewd little madam she was, she figured there must be a reason for the curtains to be closed. She switched on the light and saw that in the corner of the room there was a computer. It was a new one at that. The set-up in here was nothing like Poppy had expected at all. In her mind – or even the last time she'd been inside the cabin – *when was that?* – it was a glorified shed, with old paperwork, photos, and the usual garden furniture. Seeing the present set-up, though, was a surprise and very troubling. And Poppy, being the inquisitive one, she *had* to take a look. She'd expected to find a collection of porno films and magazines. Why she thought that, she wasn't sure, but somewhere in the back of her mind, she had this weird notion that her father was a mysterious man. All the women always gave him a double-take because not only was he an exceptionally good-looking man, but he was built like a bodybuilder. She found the cabin odd. It was too comfortable; it was as if someone spent a lot of time in here. The office chair seemed worn, yet it wasn't dusty and neglected. It had a new cushion for extra back support. Even the black lamps showed not a speck of dust. The filing cabinets had a plant on the top that was vibrant, which told her something here wasn't quite right. The trunks on the floor she'd never seen before, but then, everywhere appeared alien. Except for the suitcases in the corner, that was.

She would just have grabbed two cases and left, but it wasn't in her nature to turn a blind eye. As she tugged at the cabinets, she soon discovered they were locked. Fumbling through the keys, she finally was able to access the drawers. Inside, she found some papers, yet when she read the details, she couldn't make head nor tail of them. It was as if everything was in code. She decided to put them in her pocket to read later. The computer sparked into life but required a password. Although she tried all of her family's names, she was out of luck. Her attention was then drawn to the trunk in the corner. She tried to find the key, but nothing fitted. Her heart was beating fast, and as she stepped back towards the suitcases, she noticed that on the side of one of the trunks was a piece of material that had been trapped outside when it was locked. She bent down and felt the brown fabric. It was hessian. Suddenly, her mind went into overdrive, and her breathing increased. She had to get out. Grabbing both suitcases, she turned to leave, ensuring she switched off the light. Once she was outside, she locked the padlock and hauled the cases up to the house and through the patio doors.

It was so strange. Why hadn't she known what was going on down there? Her bedroom faced the back garden. However, the answer to that was now blindingly obvious. The cabin was fitted with blackout curtains. And the door and window didn't face the house. She didn't know why she did it, but something made her go back and have another look around the cabin's exterior. She walked past the door and the window until she was looking at the back fence. There, tucked behind the cabin, was a gate. She'd never seen it before though.

The eerie thoughts tumbled over themselves, and she wasted no time in running back to the house.

Out of breath and shaking, she rushed into Brooke's bedroom with the suitcases to find her sister carefully placing her clothes in piles.

'Brooke!' The slight tremble in her voice made her sister spin around.

The sight of Poppy, her face paler than she'd ever seen in her life and her eyes looking nervously towards her, took her by surprise.

'What's the matter? You look strange. Are you sick?'

'No, Brooke, I'm not. But I've seen stuff I'm not supposed to know about. We need to get out of here. Like *now*!'

'What! Why? What on earth's the matter?'

Poppy sat on the bed and placed her head in her hands. Brooke could see she was in a state, which was so unlike Poppy. She was the cold, stern one, much like Kendall.

'Brooke, I think our father's up to something. There was a piece of material sticking out of a trunk. You'll never believe what it was. It was hessian.'

Brooke didn't see the connection right away. 'And?'

'*Hessian*, Brooke. What's he doing with fucking hessian? Seriously, think about it. Mother said the men were found with hessian bags over their heads. That Ricky guy, Kendall's boyfriend, was beaten, with a sack over his head too.'

Brooke laid down the pile of T-shirts she had in her hand. 'Poppy, don't get carried away. You're spooking me. Besides, hessian is used for loads of stuff, like putting inside the hanging baskets that Mother insists on.'

'It's not just that. You should see the cabin. It's being used as an office, not as a shed, and I think it's our father who is working in there. It's all warm and cosy, not just a shed. There are even blackout curtains up at the window. And, Brooke, did you know we have a rear entrance into the garden? Did you ever see the gate in the back fence because I for one never knew it was there?'

Now Brooke understood why Poppy had come into her bedroom in such a state. Brooke looked at Poppy with fear in her eyes. She was vulnerable as it was, but with all these details about their cabin and what Poppy had found, it was sending her once more into a scary, crazy place where those mental visions of being attacked came back to haunt her again. 'Oh my God! Poppy, don't tell me anything more about the place.

Let's just go. This is so strange. I need to figure this out. I tell you what. Let's go to Grandpa's place. He'll know what to do.'

'Well, just grab a change of clothes and let's go now. Mother will be home soon.'

They agreed to leave the suitcases in situ. Brooke pulled a small holdall from under her bed and threw a few bits in.

Poppy eyed up the sweatshirts. 'Throw in one for me. They're nice.' She was surprised that Brooke had so many lovely clothes. 'And that pair of jeans. You've got loads.'

Brooke did as she was told, and, within a few minutes, they were packed and ready to leave. They hurried down the stairs, but, as they reached the front door, they both stopped dead in their tracks. There, looking white-faced, stood their father. Brooke's body language urged Poppy to do something.

'Hello, girls. Where are you off to at this time of night?'

Poppy observed that their father didn't even act surprised that Brooke was out of her room. In fact, he appeared washed out with a couldn't-give-a shit attitude.

'We're just going to a friend's slumber party. See you tomorrow.'

Alastair frowned and stared at the two girls. 'It's a bit late to go to a friend's house, isn't it?' His expression changed to a knowing smirk that had Brooke shaking in her boots.

'Hello! Dad, we're not twelve years old, you know. And why would we be answering to you? Christ, when I was at uni, you never worried then.'

He slowly looked down at the holdall that was not zipped up and bulging with clothes. 'A slumber party, eh?'

Poppy barged past him. 'Yes, that's right. See you later.'

Suddenly, he gripped her arm. 'Not so fast. Where's your mother?'

'At her meeting. Let go of me, Dad. You're hurting me.'

He released his grip and stepped aside, silently watching as they tried to slide past. Out of the corner of his eye, he recognized something poking out of Poppy's back pocket that he knew she shouldn't have. Instantly, he grabbed her arm again before she got through the front door, and roughly, he pulled her back inside. Brooke was horrified.

'What the hell are you two up to?' he growled, as he pulled the paper from her pocket and waved it in front of her face.

Brooke was now outside and shaking even more. She looked at her sister, who was glued to the spot, and decided the best course of action was to get help. She dropped the bag and darted. She was the fastest runner in the family and wasn't going to stop now.

'Wait!' screamed Alastair, as he let go of Poppy and chased after Brooke.

Poppy made the most of her chance. She set off to run, which she did, but in the opposite direction.

The road was dark, and her mind was now focused on getting away. She darted between two parked cars and straight into the road, checking behind to see where her father was. So she didn't notice the car that flew around the corner.

Shit! All she saw were blinding lights. The impact was so hard that she somersaulted into the road and spun round – devastatingly – into a parked car.

Rebecca's heart was in her mouth. The rush of adrenaline, sending pins and needles over her body, left her shaken and too stunned to leave the vehicle. She had knocked someone down. Used to making spur-of-the-moment decisions, her brain went straight into action. It was about damage limitation now. Quickly, she assessed the consequences and the trouble she would be in. The meeting had gone on so long she'd needed a drink or two to keep her mind going. *But she hadn't consumed a drink or two, had she?* she thought. She'd actually had a lot more, at least four, by her reckoning. She was the MP, for fuck's sake. She would not only be done for drink driving but possibly arrested on a manslaughter charge as well, if whoever she had run down was dead. She'd not seen who the person was who was lying in the road. That was it! It was so dark, there were no cameras in her street, so she could get away with this one. Her heart was pummelling like a bongo drum, and she was breathing heavily. She put the Lexus into gear and drove away, not even looking back to see who she'd potentially killed. In her mind was the headline DRUNK DRIVER REBECCA MULLINS MP KILLS PEDESTRIAN.

***

Poppy lay motionless. However, as she opened her eyes, she could just see the car's rear lights with the distinctive number plate REB 1M illuminated as the car turned into her drive. She closed her eyes and fell into unconsciousness.

***

Rebecca was still shaken up. She was almost in complete meltdown. Unsteadily, she drove her car into the drive, clicked the remote, and waited for the garage shutters to open before she drove carefully inside. She wondered if the garage was actually clear since she hadn't parked in there for a year. It was an irritant if she needed to be somewhere else quickly. It was the shutters – they always took forever to open, so she generally parked in the drive.

As soon as she stepped out, she flicked on the light switch and looked at the damage. The front passenger wing was dented, and the headlight was cracked but still in one piece. She sighed heavily. 'Thank God,' she murmured. She felt pretty pleased with herself for using her head and not panicking. At least there wouldn't be any evidence that the incident was her fault; if there was no debris at the scene, which she thought was the case, then no one could trace the accident back to her. She would take the car to a body shop first thing in the morning and say she'd hit the lawn mower while parking the Lexus in the garage. With that inspired thought clearly in her mind, she calmed down and walked into the kitchen from the side door. For a moment, she felt her heart sink. She peered at the breakfast bar and imagined Kendall sitting there swaying to some modern music with her headphones on. She wondered if she'd even had a chance to grieve. What with arranging the funeral, being preoccupied with her work, and Brooke suffering from the attack, she'd barely had time to give Kendall much thought. She stared at the cup left on the side and decided to make herself a coffee. Then, as she tried to remember some good times with Kendall, she drew a blank. Had she ever even loved her? She must have done, surely? She'd given birth to her, she'd nursed her... well, for some of the time. A tear fell down her cheek, but she quickly brushed it away. Who was the tear for anyway? Was it for Kendall or herself?

As Poppy felt herself going in and out of consciousness, she could hear a voice asking her name. The problem was, though, she couldn't speak. The numbing feeling in her head was blocking the pains in her back and her hip. She tried to move, but it felt as though she was wrapped in a cocoon. Her eyes flickered open. It was still dark and a figure was kneeling beside her, but all she could make out was the bright light coming from the person's phone screen. Then she heard the words 'ambulance' and 'quickly' said urgently into his phone. Those words were bittersweet; she knew she was seriously injured but at least help was on its way.

Barely conscious, she heard the sirens in the distance and then more voices. However, everything was a blur; she didn't know where she was or who was there, but the one thing she did recall was her mother's number plate. How could she ever forget that?

***

Rebecca's nerves had calmed considerably with a strong coffee. It wasn't until she left the kitchen, though, that she realized the front door was open. Tutting and cursing her girls for forever leaving something open – the fridge, the milk top, and now the bloody front door – she slammed it shut before she wandered upstairs, expecting to find Alastair in bed. Curiously, he wasn't there. Yet, on closer inspection, both the bedside cabinet drawers were open. Something was afoot, but she couldn't put her finger on what it was. Brooke's room was also unoccupied. She noticed two suitcases partially packed on the bed and ran into Poppy's room only to find she wasn't there. A cold sensation ripped through her like an icy winter wind.

Her first thought was that Alastair had left and taken the girls with him. With her hands shaking, she rang him on his mobile, but it just went to voicemail. When she called Poppy's number next, she could hear her daughter's phone ringing in her bedroom. Her nerves were now seriously on edge and her trepidation wasn't lessened when she tried Brooke's number and this one too went straight to voicemail.

The bastard! He had done it. All those times he'd threatened to leave. How could he do this to her? She'd given him whatever he wanted – always – but now he'd turned his back on her and walked out. Sitting on her bed with her face in her hands, she cried like a baby.

***

The witching hour. Zara awoke to feel as though she'd slept on concrete slabs; her body ached all over. Tossing and turning, her mind tried to unravel the mess. She hadn't mentioned her concerns to Neil or anyone. It was something she would normally never do. Her father had taught her that. 'Whenever things are going arse-up,' he would say, 'keep your thoughts to yourself, until you are sure you know what to do next.' It had proved time and time again to be the right course of action. She had to be sure of her conclusion: Eric, in some way, was involved in the plot to take her down. She was pretty sure of that. Proving it, though, might be challenging.

The bandaged wrist, the strong aftershave, and the fact that the man was huge, all pointed to him. Yet why would he do this to her? Why, in fact, would he *want* to do this to her? Well, in all honesty she did have a clue! There was the small matter of her kicking his advances into touch and slicing his wrist. But was he trying to worm his way into her affections or were his overtures simply a means to discover how her business ticked so that he could gradually take it down and replace it with this evil shit drug called Flakka?

Desperate to rationalize the situation, she decided to call the only man right now she could trust – Victor. If her father had once confided in the man and shared his best brandy and his darkest secrets, then Victor was her answer.

Lighting up a cigarette, Zara was about to make herself an espresso when the doorbell rang. She stopped dead in her tracks, her heart beating fast, hoping it wasn't Eric. The security monitor showed it was Victor. 'Speak of the devil!' she said under her breath. Stubbing the cigarette out in the sink, she hurried to the front door to let him in.

'I'm so pleased to see you, Victor. Come through. I'm just making some coffee. We need to talk.'

Victor leaned against the doorframe in the kitchen, with almost no room to spare. 'So, what's this all about, Zara? Are you okay, love? Ya look peaky.'

She poured another espresso and handed him the cup. 'Last night, Antonio's was ambushed *again*. Well, some men tried to make an attack, but they didn't get far. But I think I know who one of the men was.'

Victor nodded. 'Go on.'

'Eric Regan!' she exclaimed.

Casually, he took a sip of his drink. 'I hope you don't mind me being kinda upfront with you. I mean, I know I'm on ya payroll, but ya dad always confided in me, and I guess it's a natural reaction, but let me know if I step outta line.'

'No, Victor, please. I need as much help as I can get. Do carry on.'

'If you recall, I said he was up to something. When I followed him, remember, he was outside the restaurant reading that notice. See, Zara, you need to remember hell is empty, all the devils are here, so watch ya back.'

She smiled. 'That's another one of my dad's sayings.'

'Yes, I know. It's a common saying. Shakespeare's, I think. Anyway, blood *is* thicker than water. I know you had a thing with this Mike Regan, but let me warn you, Zara. Girlfriends come and go, but brothers will always stick together.'

She looked at his face and wondered if he was being sarcastic or whether he was treating her as a silly lovesick woman, which she most certainly was not. 'Mike isn't like that. He would go mental if he knew.'

Victor stood up straight as if he was about to make a pronouncement. 'Zara, you said I could be frank, so, as an older man, I can see right through situations. I'm not clouded by emotion, and I hate to tell ya this, but you are at the moment.'

Irritated by his words, she spat back, 'I'm no idiot. Far from it!'

He gave her an exasperated look. 'No, Christ, I didn't mean it like that, love. But, Zara, I'm surprised that you seem to underestimate this Regan family. Eric is a sneaky bastard, and I know he is up to something. As for Mike, how did he get out of prison so early? And, more to the point, if you are so close, why did he not tell you? Do you even know what Mike's been up to?'

Zara felt her hand go clammy and an uneasy sensation knotted her insides. Reaching for the pack of cigarettes on the worktop, she quickly lit one and blew smoke up at the ceiling. He was telling her truths that if she were being honest with herself, she knew all along; she just hadn't wanted to confront them. It was too painful. But then her mind cast back to the conversation with Ricky recently.

'Hold on, I think I do know what Mike's been up to. Ricky told me.'

Victor frowned. 'Ricky told you what?'

'I know Ricky's not fully recovered, but he did say that Mike was working for the police. At first, I was stunned but then I thought perhaps he may be confused.'

Victor stared off into nothing before he snapped back to face Zara. 'No way. That just doesn't make sense. Mike Regan working for the Filth after serving a lump inside? No. That's a cock-and-bull story, surely?'

Zara placed her cup on the side and sighed. She realized now that Victor wasn't treating her like a kid. This firmness was probably how he used to converse with her father. She had to rein in her annoyance and listen to the man.

'I wish I could just get to the bottom of it. I hate more than anything this uneasy feeling and uncertainty. But what about Ricky? Why would the Regans hurt their own flesh and blood if it's them behind all this? No, sorry, I just can't believe it.'

Victor nodded. 'Whoa! Stop! I agree, from what you told me a while ago, what happened to Ricky was not Mike's doing. Mike obviously worships his son, so you have a point, love. But again, from what you've said, I wonder if Eric is working alone or perhaps the culprit is one of the Lanigans. I tell ya,

Zara, greed is a huge motivator. Your father would have told you that. If any of the Regans are behind this drug, then they will have enemies, won't they? An enemy who would try to bring the Regans down by hurting someone they value. Think about it, Zara.'

His reasoning stuck in her throat, yet she was unable even to consider the obvious.

'I have no idea who would have done that to Ricky, but what I do know is Mike won't let them get away with it, that's for sure... And neither would I, if I found out who did it.'

'Zara, do you trust me?' he asked confidently.

She took a deep breath, stubbed her cigarette out in the vintage bronze ashtray, and smiled up at him. 'Yes, I guess I do. If my father did, and he was no fool, then there's no reason for me not to trust you, is there?'

'Good, because I liked your father a lot, and for his sake, I want to make sure you're not being mugged off. Right now, though, I believe you are. I know what you've been through makes you a little susceptible and in a frame of mind that is eager to solidify friendships, but they have to be based on trust. You're too trusting for your own good, my love.'

Zara inclined her head and leaned with her hand on her hip. 'Excuse me?'

'When you were locked up for all those years, what did the Lanigans do to find you?'

Zara really didn't want to have this conversation because although Victor was her father's good friend, she looked to the Lanigans as family. They respected her, didn't they? But she had to consider the question that was posed to her, to be objective.

However, it seemed as if her brain now had two voices: one was doubt and the other was confusion.

'No, Victor, you have that all wrong. Neil took a knife defending my restaurant. And a week later, I was there when they ambushed the place. Neil pushed me into the ladies' toilets to protect me. They—'

Victor held his hand up to stop her continuing. 'He never fought for your business, he was stabbed outside the restaurant. You once told me yourself. No one saw or heard anything. If they'd been doing their job properly, the businesses would never have been closed down, and as for the men having to return to Ireland, don't you think that's a load of bullshit? Seriously, they aren't that stupid, and I didn't think you were either.'

'No, Victor, I don't think they would do that to me.' But she knew she didn't sound very convincing.

He stepped forward and placed his hand on her shoulder. 'Your father would have seen right through them. I know he thought you were ready to take over, but, Zara, for your father's sake, you need to listen to me, darling.'

His sympathetic words irritated her. She shrugged his hand away. Turning to pour herself another coffee, she decided to light another cigarette first. She needed time to think.

'Five years, Zara, five fucking years you were locked up. Seriously, neither the Regans nor the Lanigans sussed out that it was your own brother who'd betrayed you. Well, whether you like it or not, you need to face facts because if it was Mike Regan who had gone missing, you would have found him, wouldn't you? I mean, your own brother was pushed out of the business, but there he was, living in this mansion of a house, and no one thought to look at him. Seriously, if

I'd been searching for you, this home is the first place I would have come to, and Ismail would have been at the top of my list of suspects.'

Unexpectedly, Zara burst into tears. He had just verbalized so succinctly all those haunting thoughts she assumed she'd buried many years ago. After all that time spent locked away and hidden in the basement, she'd struggled to understand why the Lanigans hadn't properly checked out her brother. Of course, she would have. He would have been in for a fortune eventually. Izzy had passed the business over to her and virtually ignored Ismail in the will; it was common knowledge and not a decision that everyone in her Jewish community felt was fair.

'Hey, come on,' whispered Victor, as he put his arms around her and pulled her close. 'You've been through a lot, and it's okay to cry, but you have to be objective. The Lanigans have always had a reputation, and I, for the life of me, couldn't understand why they'd still put money into your accounts when you were off the scene and presumed dead.'

She stopped crying and wiped her nose with her sleeve before she pulled away from him. 'Well, that goes to show they cared and lived in hope. Surely that's not the hallmark of a traitor, is it?'

A wicked, sarcastic grin appeared on his face. 'Stop being naive, Zara. From everything you've told me lately, I can look at things as an outsider. They told you they put fifty per cent of *everything* into your account but how the hell do you know it was? You need to face facts. You're worth a lot of money. Certainly, you can buy your muscle, you even own enough businesses to run the manor. *But* there are other firms out there ready to wipe you out. And another thought. Do you seriously think the Lanigans, who, I admit, are a strong firm, will have you running their operations? Ask yourself why they would? And if you think it's because you're friends, then think how your father would respond to that statement. There are no friends in business, and that goes for the Regans too. Things are not adding up, and the question is, are the Regans involved with this new drug?'

She looked through him with a fierce, cold stare. 'No way. I can't believe that.'

Victor shook his head. 'Christ, Zara, men like Eric Regan are only after earning money, and so are the Lanigans. Do you honestly think they care where or how they earn it, just as long as they do? The world has changed a lot in five years, darling. Cocaine is drying up, the dealers are trading the newer drugs, and the more ruthless firms are selling it.'

'I just can't get my head around it. It all seems so fucked up.'

'I can only give ya my views. You did say I could be open. Zara, whatever the truth is, ya have me, love. I ain't going anywhere, and, like I said before, I'll look out for ya, for your father's sake. I owe him that much. I'm just repaying him the favour.'

The confidence in the man had grown over the last few weeks, and Zara could see why her father had respected him so much. He had a good head on his shoulders and was brave enough to air his concerns, knowing how close she was to the Lanigans and the Regans. She was now beginning to question the people around her, including Mike. Whatever he was doing, he'd absolutely no intention of revealing it to her.

Victor's phone was vibrating, and he took it out of his

trouser pocket. 'Right, I have to go back. The old lady up the road from me needs a taxi to get to the shops, bless her heart. She's still too scared to walk the streets. But, listen, if Eric or Mike turn up here, make sure you don't let either of them in. I don't know what they'll do next, but it won't be pretty, will it?'

**

She held in the tears as the thud from his heavy boots on the age-old parquet flooring echoed along the entrance hall. As the door closed behind him, she slid to the floor. Pressing her fingers to her throbbing temples, she broke into uncontrollable sobs. The thought of Mike – of all people – keeping secrets from her seemed like a betrayal. It was enough for her to rip out her own heart.

That was the last thing she needed. 'Jesus, Dad, why did you leave it all to me?'

CHAPTER SIXTEEN

Ricky sat up and laughed at the jokes that Arty and Liam had sent him; the lads had been brilliant in keeping his spirits high.

The last text had said: **See you in a minute**. Ricky frowned, and then, there in the doorway, Arty stood in fits of laughter, holding a teddy, with the caption 'Get well soon', which he aimed at Ricky's head.

'Stop milking it!' he teased.

Liam came bowling in behind and sat awkwardly on the bed. ''Ere, have ya seen the bird in the dayroom? Cor, she's a right tasty little number.'

Ricky's smile drooped at that question. 'I know you're trying to cheer me up, but I feel so bad about Kendall.'

Arty looked down. 'Er... yeah, sorry, mate.'

Liam, the less conscious of the two, and ignoring the sullen mood, said, 'She might need cheering up. Poor cow. She looks like she's taken a clump around the head. Her face has a fat plaster on it, and I think she might have broken her ankle.'

'I ain't seen her yet,' Ricky said, feeling sorry for himself. 'I've been stuck in here. The doctor reckons I won't be out until the end of the week now. Something about fluid on the brain.'

Liam laughed. 'Cheer up, mate. That's good news. At least they think you have one, then!'

Ricky joined in the laughter at that quip. 'Come on, boys, help me up. Let's go and meet this bird, 'cos if I'm in here for a few days, I might have someone to talk to, eh?'

With no finesse, both Arty and Liam grabbed Ricky's arms and pulled him to his feet.

Liam joked again. 'Shall I get ya a Zimmer frame?'

Ricky punched him on the arm. 'Fuck off.' He chuckled.

Carefully, Ricky steadied his legs and began by shuffling along.

Liam still had the giggles. 'Are you sure about that Zimmer frame, Grandad?'

Arty shot him a look that said, 'Reel your neck in,' to which Liam just pursed his lips and smiled.

The dayroom was a short walk along the corridor. Although small, it was pleasant, with bright lemon walls and green blinds, and the hospital had furnished it with a few cushioned plastic chairs, a large wall-mounted TV, and a few magazines. Ricky was the first to enter and paused in the doorway. *They weren't kidding then*, he thought.

'Hi,' said Ricky, as Liam pushed him forward.

The blonde slowly turned her head away from watching *The Jeremy Kyle Show*. She tried to smile, but her cheek was still sore.

'Mind if we join ya?' asked Ricky.

She looked at the three lads and was quite taken with how handsome two of them were; she was intrigued, though, by the cheeky grin on the ugly lad's face.

'It's a free country, I suppose,' was all she could muster.

Ricky tried to walk without his shuffle and only just made it to one of the chairs, where he slid down and caught his breath.

'Ricky, ya wanna a drink? Some chocolate?' asked Arty.

A full smile lit up his face. 'Yeah. I'll have a cold beer or a Tango and a Snickers bar.' He looked at the girl. 'Fancy a cold juice and some chocolate?'

She smiled at him then and nodded. Her curiosity and interest piqued at the offer of refreshments and by seeing people of her own age.

Arty peered at Ricky and raised his brow. Ricky saw the wink and chuckled again quietly.

Liam was giggling like a kid as he pushed Arty back out of the door so Ricky could have some privacy.

'I'm Ricky, and you are?'

The girl sighed. 'I'm Poppy but... er... please, don't tell anyone, will you? They don't know my name. They think I'm still concussed. And that's what I want them to think. But why they've stuck me in front of a bloody telly, if that's the case, is beyond me.'

Now curious, Ricky leaned closer and looked around. 'Why are ya pretending you're concussed? Is someone after ya, babe? Is it ya ol' man?'

Her eyes clouded over. 'No, a lot worse. Anyway, please... '

Ricky shook his head as he studied her worried expression. 'My lips are sealed, so don't worry yaself. Are you okay, though? Was it just concussion?'

'Yeah, I believe so,' said Poppy, her eyes having a vacant look, now lost in some memory.

'How did you get hurt?'

She snapped back to reality. 'I got run over. I've broken my ankle, but apart from this bloody great lump on my cheek, I'm all right, really.'

Ricky was bemused by her posh voice and hard attitude. He loved the way she spoke, though, and even with the swelling, it didn't detract from her very pretty bluebell-blue eyes and her dinky nose. She reminded him of a pixie or a fairy.

'And you, Ricky? Why are you in here?'

He gave her a wry smile. 'I was attacked, so I don't remember much. Anyway, hey, I'm alive… ' His eyes darkened. It was hard not to reflect on how he came to have his injuries when any mention of them was made.

Suddenly, Poppy blinked in surprise and her skin began to tingle in anticipation. 'Oh my God, are you Ricky *Regan*?'

He nodded. 'Yeah, I am, but how would you know me?'

Quickly, Poppy glanced over her shoulder to check the doorway. Quietly, she whispered, 'Listen, this is really important. Please, you mustn't tell anyone, but I'm Kendall's sister.'

Ricky had heard of all kinds of coincidences, but this one beat them by a mile. He then studied the worried expression on Poppy's face. 'It's okay, I'm not going to say anything. Listen, I'm so sorry about your sister. She was lovely. I really did like her. We only just started… '

'Yeah, yeah, I know. Maybe we'll have time later to be sentimental. However, there's something far more urgent and serious that concerns me right now. I need to ask you something. The man who attacked you. Did he really put a hessian sack over your head?'

Ricky nodded eagerly, wondering where this conversation was going. 'Yeah, he did. Why do ya ask?'

Sidestepping his question, she went on, 'Do you remember anything about him, anything at all?'

'No, I don't, but why are ya asking?'

Poppy gave him a thoughtful look and lowered the excitement in her voice. 'Oh, I dunno, I'm just eager to find out who killed my sister, I guess.'

Ricky looked at the hospital gown and bathrobe. 'None of ya family know you're here, do they?'

She looked down at the paper-thin garments. 'No.' She forced a laugh.

'You don't look like Kendall.'

Poppy shook her head and then looked Ricky over; he was handsome in a boyish way. She could see why her sister had found him attractive. His eyes crinkled at the sides, and when he smiled, a dimple appeared in his cheeks.

'Kendall was my half-sister. She had a different father. We called her "the rebel", but I admired her, really. She had gumption and a mind of her own.'

Ricky tilted his head to the side and smiled gently. 'She was sweet and funny.'

Poppy frowned. 'Sweet? Funny? I don't know about that, but she was strong-willed and took no shit.'

'She never said she had a sister. Well, she never spoke about her family at all, to be honest.'

Poppy felt a tear welling up; she hadn't had time to grieve. But she held it back. 'I'm not surprised, really. She hated Mother. And she wasn't close to either me or my twin sister. I just wished she'd escaped to a better life, a longer life.'

Ricky's mind wandered off to his own recent experiences. He knew how lucky he was to be alive and effectively to start his life anew. Then something she'd just said alerted him. 'Escaped? From what?' he questioned.

Poppy shook her head and let out a long sigh, her eyes on the door. 'Look, she and my mother didn't get on. She was so unhappy. I think it's because Mother made her live with us. Kendall always assumed that my sister and I had it easy, but we never did. In fact, we've had it hard, but not in the way most people struggle. From an early age, we were controlled... Look, I think I should go back to the ward.' She averted her eyes from the door and then looked back to him, wondering if she'd said too much. After all, she didn't even know Ricky.

He smiled again. 'I'll walk you back.'

The soft glow in his silver-grey eyes made her look twice this time; he really was good-looking, although she wasn't one for handsome men. Unexpectedly, she had the urge to know more about Ricky and Kendall's relationship, perhaps as a way of understanding more about her sister before she was killed.

'Did you sleep with my sister? Oh, er, shit, sorry, it's none of my business.'

Ricky laughed, and his cheeks flushed. 'It's all right. I guess you would want to know as much as possible about her last few days. Well, no, Miss Poppy – nice name by the way – but anyway, the answer is a definite no. Kendall and I only talked and texted on the phone, and then we went for a quick drink, and we were going to order in a Chinese from her flat and...' He paused and took a deep breath. 'I'm sorry, but that was it, really. I would have loved to have got to know her a bit more, though.'

Just the openness in his eyes told her he was a genuine guy and someone she felt she could trust. 'Ricky, I know you're poorly, but I need some help.' Her face crumpled in pain. 'About your friends. Do they know of a place where I could go for a while? I need to stay away from my parents and try and get my head clear.'

He placed two hands on the side armrests and pushed himself up. Poppy was already on her feet, struggling with her own crutches.

'How can you go anywhere? Ya can't bleedin' well walk.'

She blushed and looked at him with fear in her eyes. 'You don't understand. I *have* to get away. It was my sodding mother who ran me down!'

Ricky felt the blood drain from his face. 'Jesus. But why?' he asked, as he steadied her balance.

'I don't know, and I don't know if she meant to do it, but she didn't stop. She just drove off. It was dark, I ran out into the road, and she came hurtling around the corner.'

As Ricky again steadied her, he could smell the sweet perfume from her hair. His heart went out to her as she looked so helpless. 'But what I don't understand is why you were running in the first place?'

Her eyes widened, and Ricky could tell from her expression she was probably reliving the experience. 'I was running from my dad. I think… Oh God.' Her eyes now filled with tears, she choked on her words. 'I think he may be the man behind Kendall's murder. I don't know, for sure, though. I don't know anything anymore. I'm just a mess!'

With his brows knitted together, and darkness filling his eyes, he gripped her tighter. 'What! Your own *farver*?'

She nodded and bit her bottom lip. Tears were falling down her face steadily now, as the two of them left the room.

'Right, okay. Let's think about this. Have you told the police?'

She shook her head vehemently. '*No*, absolutely not! I have no proof. It may be nothing at all, but I just get this awful feeling something isn't right. There was bloody *hessian* hanging from a trunk inside his log cabin in the garden.'

Ricky sighed and relaxed his grip. 'Poppy, that doesn't mean he was the man who attacked me. I get that you are looking for answers but finding some hessian doesn't make him the murderer.'

'No, of course it doesn't. But there's more, a lot more, but it's hard to explain… ' Suddenly, she looked up to see Arty and Liam walking along the corridor, holding cans of drink and bars of chocolate.

'You all right, mate?' asked Arty, with a very concerned look on his face.

Ricky glanced back at Poppy. 'Er, I can help, but please tell me this ain't no fantasy detective game, is it?'

She shook her head. 'No, I'm deadly serious. Please, Ricky.'

'A bit cosy, Ricky, ain't it, mate? We leave you for five minutes and you two are like ol' buddies… ' The banter stopped abruptly when Arty realized that Ricky wasn't in a joking mood.

'Art, I need your help, mate.' He turned to Poppy. 'Do ya know what the doctor said? Did ya hear him mention anything about surgery?'

'No. They're keeping me in because I wouldn't tell them my name or anything. So they suspect I've got concussion. I think I'm fine, though. It's just my ankle, but that's in plaster, so, really, I can just leave.'

Liam screwed his face up. 'What the fuck's going on here, Ricky? Who is she?'

351

Ricky pulled Poppy closer to him; her whole body was trembling. 'Liam, Arty, can you get her out of here? Take her to yours or mine but tell no one. She thinks she knows who attacked me. She's Kendall's half-sister.'

Arty jolted in shock. His eyes almost appeared to bulge out of his head. 'No fucking way?'

Ricky nodded, affirmatively. 'But listen. You have to get her away from here without anyone knowing what's going on. Her muvver's only gone and run her over, and when she saw what she'd done, she did the off. And she was running from her ol' man. She thinks he may have something to do with my attack. Take her to me dad's.' He looked at Poppy. 'Me dad's a good man. Ya can tell him everything. He'll help ya, and I promise ya this – he won't call ya muvver.'

Liam sighed. 'Come on, then. You, Art, find a wheelchair, unless… ' he giggled at Poppy, 'ya want me to sling you over me shoulder?' He tried to keep upbeat although the news was shocking.

For the first time since the hit-and-run, Poppy chuckled. Maybe it was the relief. 'I don't mind either way, as long as I get away from here before the police arrive.'

Ricky removed his own dressing gown, one his nan had brought in for him. 'Take this, Poppy. You stay safe, babe, and I'll call me dad, and tell him what's going on, like.'

She looked at Arty and then at Liam.

'Hey, trust me. You're as safe as houses with those two.'

Arty hurried along the corridor until he found a wheelchair. Liam helped her onto the seat and carried her crutches. They nodded to Ricky and were gone in a heartbeat.

In a daze of confusion, Zara wandered from room to room, her mind desperately trying to take everything in. First Mike, then Eric, and now there was a niggling doubt about the Lanigans. Knowing she should never make a rash decision when under so much stress, she sat down at her father's desk, in deep thought. What did she really want for herself? Was running a firm exactly her idea of the good life? Did she really need all the excitement? Surely she'd had enough drama to last a lifetime? She contemplated the events of the past few days, marshalling her thoughts in order. She owned the restaurants and could easily sell them and retire from the money. Did she want the headache? And as for the country now being slowly pulled to bits by unruly kids hooked on this new drug, did she even want to live here anymore?

She sighed in defeat and pulled out the title deeds that she'd only recently placed in the drawer of the desk. Previously, they'd been stored in a hiding place that not even Ismail had known about – luckily. *Not that it would do him much good now*, she thought.

The manila folder even smelled of antiques, it was so old. She stared at her father's handwriting and imagined him once more sitting at the desk and planning his next good deal. As she opened the file, there in Old English was the first set of deeds. Then her eyes glistened as soon as they fell on the black-and-white photo of her mother. The tall, slender woman, with thick chestnut-coloured curls that hung loose, framing her heart-shaped face, was beautiful. The soft, loving expression in her eyes really showed the person she had once been. Zara allowed the tears to cascade down her cheeks. Her dear, sweet, and wonderful mother was taken from her far too soon. She never got to share her daughter's teenage years and be there for her. The empty feeling brought with it a sense of loneliness. No mother, father, or brother, and now, not even Mike was in her life. *What was she really doing? Was it all worth it?* she pondered.

As she reminisced, a loose sheet of manuscript slipped from her hand. This wasn't from another set of deeds, it was a letter. But it wasn't any ordinary one; she guessed it was a letter from the grave. She took a deep breath and studied it very carefully.

Dear Zara, if you are reading this then I am no longer with you and you are considering selling the business.

She stopped for a moment to take in the detail of the beautiful handwritten note. He really was quite artistic. She read on.

Life often leaves us with impossible decisions, and this may be one of them. Hopefully, you are in your older years now and wish to retire.

You may be strong, but you are also human. I hope you use the money from the sale of the business to enjoy your life. I also hope that by now you have found happiness, no doubt with Mike Regan. He was the only man I ever truly trusted, by the way.

You are my daughter and a leader but sometimes in life we need someone to lean on. Your mother was always my crutch, until she passed away. So, my child, don't be afraid to share your worries. I wished I had done it more often.

Yours, your father, Izzy.
I love you.

She read and reread the note, kissed the paper, and allowed a tear to drop onto the folder. 'Oh, Dad, what the hell am I doing?'

She quickly closed the folder. Instead of placing it back into the drawer, she returned it to its original hiding place in the void under the floor. With her back straight and her head held high, she wiped away the tears and readied herself to make a plan – one that would show the firms who was in charge, even if it meant she might die in the process. One way or another, she intended to demonstrate to everyone how it really worked, starting with rule number one – no one should underestimate the daughter of Izzy Ezra. And then follow up that with rule number two – no one fucks with the skinny, one-handed Jewish bird and lives to tell the fucking tale.

***

Ricky tried desperately hard to get through to his father but to no avail. He assumed he hadn't charged his phone again.

He lay back on his pillow and sighed, hoping that Arty and Liam had made sure they'd got the girl to his father's house. What she'd said wasn't really a cause for concern but how she'd said it certainly was. He kept visualizing her pretty blue eyes shadowed with fear.

***

Mike sat opposite Stoneham in his office. Lowry put a bag of pastries and three mugs of coffee on the table. He edged himself onto the only vacant chair and shuffled to pull it to the table.

Stoneham looked at the spilled coffee and tutted. 'Lowry, get a napkin, will you?'

Lowry pulled a serviette from his pocket and quickly wiped the mess.

'Did the men survive or… ?' asked Mike.

'Only just. They had two hundred grand's worth of drugs inside them. Each!'

Mike shook his head and clenched his jaw. 'He's a fucking animal, this bloke they call the Governor, ain't he?'

'Yes. We believe he's the man responsible for the spread of this vile drug. Everything seems to lead back to him. But, again, we have drawn a blank. I've had forensics assigned purely to this case. They are working around the clock trying to find even a hair sample. It's like looking for a needle in a haystack. The DNA from that cottage is throwing up known criminals – not big-time ones, but petty thieves and druggies. I've had half the force questioning them but nothing of importance to this case has been discovered.'

'If there ain't one single informer among them, then you really do have a problem. The only reason they won't grass is that they fear this Governor geezer more than they do time in prison.'

Lowry entered the discussion. 'Oh yeah, for sure. I've had doors slammed in my face by grown men who were paralysed with fear and shaking in their boots. No one will give this man up.'

The Commissioner looked rough: his hair was greasy, he was wearing a five o'clock shadow, and he had bags under his eyes. 'Last week we found four men dead with hessian sacks over their heads. Three were killed in the same place at the same time. Very brutally, I might add. We couldn't tell from their faces who they were because they were so horrifically smashed in. The fourth was a known drug dealer and not any candyman either. You may know him or have heard of him. Kai Lin.'

Mike took a sharp intake of breath. 'Yeah, I do. Who don't, to be fair. Hang on. I thought this Governor guy was running or taking over the South-East? Kai ran his drugs in the North.'

'Well, he was found in a skip behind a Chinese takeaway in Lewisham. Forensics confirmed he was killed there too.'

Mike shook his head. 'Sounds to me like he was working away from his own manor. This Governor, if he thought Kai was trying to muscle in on the South-East, he probably took umbrage. Probably a turf war, I should think.'

'A month ago, we found two other dead cocaine dealers. We didn't think much of it at the time. You live by the sword and so on, but now there is a common theme: the hessian sack. This Governor character seems to be taking out the dealers so that the addicts can only go to him. There's a pattern emerging.'

Mike raised his thick brow. 'Well, if there's a pattern, then there's a clue. Surely you detectives can find him?' He curled his lip and shot Lowry a sarcastic smirk.

Lowry went bright red with disgust at this deliberate slight. 'Hold on a minute, Mr Regan. We're doing our best. I haven't slept in months, working every hour to find these bastards. I've one of the toughest of all the Yardies in that cell next door who's clammed up. He's my number-one informant.'

Mike leaned forward and glared with dark brooding eyes. 'A Yardie as an informant? I find that hard to believe, but, obviously, your line of questioning isn't working. Let me have a word.'

Lowry sat back, unsettled. 'Er… no, that's not how it works. You can't do that.'

Stoneham rubbed his temples, deep in thought. He was known for his ability to find answers to seemingly intractable problems. 'Lowry, what time will you be releasing the man?'

With a concerned look on his face, Lowry placed his mug of hot coffee on the table and uncurled his fat fingers. His eyes darted from Regan back to Stoneham. 'Gov, I'm really not sure about this.'

Stoneham flared his nostrils. 'I'm not asking your opinion, detective. I asked you when he will be released.'

'Well, now, I guess.'

Mike stood up to leave. 'I'll call you later if I have anything. I hope you'll return the favour.'

Stoneham nodded.

Mike was on his way to the door when he turned and said, 'Lowry, could you make it an hour, mate? We don't want our paths to cross, do we?'

It took a moment before Lowry realized what Mike was getting at.

'Dreadlocks, did you say?'

Lowry frowned again, until he understood the cryptic message. 'No, I didn't. He's wearing a Rasta hat and a heavy gold chain.'

***

358

As soon as Mike was outside the police station, he turned his phone on and called Staffie, Willie, and Lou to meet him. With his mind on the lads, he disregarded for now the missed calls and text messages he'd received.

He waited in his car, dead opposite the front entrance to the police station, and watched just in case Lowry decided to let the informant out early. He didn't trust the police. Not only that, he didn't have much confidence in their efforts to get around thorny issues. However, he thought the Commissioner had played a blinder at the end of the meeting. As he surveyed his surroundings, he spotted two black guys a short distance away. Blinking, he had to squint to confirm he wasn't seeing things. One had long dreadlocks, the other had shorter ones. 'Fuck me, if it ain't Dez and his brother,' he mumbled under his breath. It was obvious from the facial characteristics that this must be Randy, Dez's brother, even though he'd never met him. But he'd made it his business to know exactly who Dez's brothers were, and now he was going to kill two birds with one stone – literally.

Dez had been the one man he detested the most, all the while he was in prison. The evil bastard had burned nearly all of his photos of Ricky and held a knife to his son's throat. A sly smirk eased along his lips as he watched and waited. No doubt Dez and Randy were waiting outside for their eldest brother. He laughed to himself. Now he realized who the informant was. The so-called nasty, hard Yardie who everyone knew and feared was Woodrow. What a turn-up for the books – he was nothing more than a snitch. He looked down at the passenger's footwell – at his arsenal. The heavy chain, the metal cosh, and his torque wrench were all there. All he needed now was to get the bastard – and his brothers – to a place where he could fucking do what he did best – extract information.

Lou drove past Mike and parked in a side street. He was followed by Staffie and Willie in a separate car. They slowed up alongside Mike and lowered the window.

'Are you gonna take the grass to the lock-up?'

'Behind you, Staffie, are Dez and Randy, his brother. I want them too. Tell Lou to come with me. I want the cunts alive.'

Staffie grinned and Willie suddenly scooped a lump of cocaine from his pouch and snorted it hard.

Mike laughed. Willie hadn't changed a bit, always being ready for any action to be had. But before he did, he loved to pep himself up with his livener, as he called it. Staffie drove on ahead and turned into a side street to inform Lou what was going on.

Within a few seconds, the brothers, who up to now had just been hovering around, began to walk towards the police station, passing Mike's car. Too busy chatting, they didn't notice Mike. Quietly, he slipped out of the car and followed the unsuspecting prey.

Once Staffie and Willie had delivered the message to Lou, they returned in their car, they stopped in the middle of the road, ahead of Mike's Porsche, and stepped out, looking nothing less than daring.

It gave Dez and his younger brother a reason to look up. It took a second before Dez recognized both men and then another before his brain kicked in and told him to run. He was totally unprepared for a battle; he'd left his knife in his car, just in case the police wanted to frisk him.

Randy and Woodrow had a dangerous reputation – Dez

had lived off it for years – but Willie Ritz, Ted Stafford, and Mike Regan were well known to him from his prison days.

Willie might look like an ugly, lanky dope, but he was a reckless maniac, a downright fearless fucker. Dez certainly didn't want a fight with him in the middle of the street because he was aware that Willie wouldn't give a flying fuck that they were close to the cop shop. And as for Staffie, he was another strong bastard who would never back down. It would take more than a lead cosh around the head to bring him to his knees. He just hoped that Regan wasn't with them, having been on the end of his sledgehammer fists. Another punch like that from Regan and it would be game over.

Without even considering Randy, Dez was quick on his toes to scarper. As he turned and sprinted in the direction he'd come from, he didn't see Mike, who, with one hand, stopped Dez in his tracks. 'You no-good, spunk-faced prick. You're captured, mate.'

Dez tried to struggle, but it was like fighting with a metal vice. Suddenly, one mighty fist came down and struck him so hard on the collarbone that he instantly yelled in pain and felt the strength in his arm disappear. Mike had snapped his bone clean in half. The pain intensified, and the blood drained, leaving his face almost grey.

Mike then grabbed him by the throat and dragged him back to Staffie's car. Meanwhile, Staffie was standing up against Randy; the only sound was Willie, who was blowing his nose. Mike opened the back of Staffie's car and threw Dez inside. He nodded to Willie to make sure that Dez didn't do a runner.

As Willie opened the back door, he leaned in and smiled. 'Well, if it ain't the stinking, fucking paedophile. This is a nice surprise.' Mike pulled Willie back as Staffie gestured for Randy to climb in next to his brother. Randy's eyes were glued to the gun in Staffie's hand.

Willie got into the driver's seat and pulled out his own gun. 'Move, either of ya, and I'll shoot ya!' He was giving his best sadistic laugh, and both Randy and Dez knew then that one false move and nutty Willie could easily fire a bullet.

Staffie hopped in the front passenger seat and then took over. 'Right, you two fuckers are coming with us. We need a word.' He didn't take his eyes off his captives all the time it took for Willie to drive like a madman to the lock-up in Knatts Valley.

***

Lou and Mike sat patiently, waiting for Woodrow, the eldest brother. 'Nice suit, Lou, but it's gonna get kinda messy because I'm gonna fuck that Dez up, and I'm also assuming it's gonna take more than pulling a couple of teeth out to get information from this prick… There he is, look! Take a fucking butcher's at that swanky cunt.'

Lou peered across the road at the tall, slim Rasta, his dreadlocks piled high inside a Jamaican woollen hat. His long white shirt was open at the waist, revealing a black vest and a heavy gold chain. He walked with such a swagger, he was almost doing the moonwalk. They watched as Woodrow stopped for a moment. He pulled out his skunk from inside his hat and rolled a fat spliff while he leaned against the wall.

He looked up and down the road. Mike guessed he was waiting for his brothers. 'Right, let's make our acquaintance, then, shall we?'

362

Lou got out first and headed towards Woodrow with a smile on his face.

'Hello, mate, I'm Lou Baker, your friendly adviser.'

Woodrow stopped licking the fag paper and frowned. 'Sorry, but you got the wrong bloke.'

Mike was laughing to himself. Lou could always pull off a city slicker or a lawyer when the need arose, like now.

'No, mate, I've got the *right* bloke.'

Woodrow glowered at Lou, with his eyes twitching. 'Fuck off. I don't know you.'

Lou, the smallest of the firm, stood defiantly with his hands on his hips, shaking his head. 'No can do. You need some advice and me and me pal are gonna give ya some. End of.'

Woodrow looked over Lou's shoulder to find a massive man with a chest the size of a fridge-freezer and hands like whitewater rafting paddles. The Yardie's eyes protruded, and his heart raced. Pushing himself away from the wall, he was stopped by Lou, who suddenly whipped a blade from his pocket.

'I wouldn't, mate, if I were you.'

Woodrow looked down at the knife, and then he heard a click; it was a recognizable sound that turned him to stone. As his eyes slowly looked up, the huge man was holding a gun in his hand.

'What the fuck is this all about?'

Mike didn't answer; he flicked his gun to indicate that Woodrow should follow him. 'You're gonna shut ya fucking mouth and get in that motor over there. You even think of trying anything clever to escape, or hurt either of us, and I'll rip your lungs right out through your scrawny chest and shove 'em down your throat.'

Woodrow glared at them, but his heart rate was at full throttle and he looked what he was, a scared and defeated man. Until now, he'd never come face-to-face with somebody who would give Satan the shits.

Without a struggle, he nervously walked forward and did as he was ordered.

Mike shoved the gun in Woodrow's face and clambered in after him, while Lou hopped in the driver's seat and adjusted the positioning, since he was so much smaller than Mike. As he pulled away, he looked in the rear-view mirror and smiled.

Woodrow looked like a frightened lamb; beads of sweat covered his brow and his nostrils opened and closed as he breathed.

Mike held the gun at the man's stomach, away from any public view. There was a cruel smirk on Mike's face but also a self-satisfied one, indicating a job well done.

After about ten minutes, Woodrow managed to control his breathing. 'Who are you guys and what do you want from me?' His voice remained on an even keel, unusual for someone with a gun still aimed at his stomach.

The smirk left Mike's face, and he let his lips fall into their natural position. 'It's simple, really. You won't tell the Ol' Bill who this man they call the Governor is, but you will tell me.'

Now looking visibly shaken, Woodrow shrank further into his seat as if Mike had held a naked flame to his face. 'I don't know who—'

'Don't even attempt to tell me you don't know who the man is because this is where me and you are gonna get off to a fucking bad start. You see, you really don't wanna piss me off just when we're getting acquainted because I'm a fair man but not when I'm upset, am I, Lou?'

Lou glanced into the rear-view mirror once more and could see the blinding whites of the man's eyes. 'A little friendly advice. Don't upset him, 'cos he don't have a reset button.'

For a moment, Woodrow saw the man as Robocop, and he instantly shuddered.

'So now you can see where I'm coming from, I need answers and the right ones. You even try and give me a load of ol' bollocks and me and you are gonna fall out big time. Now, here's your starter for ten. I know that you must be fucking thinking that this Governor bloke will cause you harm, even maybe your family, but I'm gonna rip the guy apart with my bare hands after I've tortured his family in front of him. So, you decide who the fuck you should be more scared of.'

Woodrow felt his limbs weaken so much that his hands flopped down by his sides as if he'd just had a stroke. Pins and needles pricked every bit of his skull, and his skin glistened with sweat. He felt his stomach contents begin to rise, and he knew he could be sick at any moment. He told himself he needed to breathe evenly and bring his heart rate back down to a more manageable level, but he was under such intense pressure, and what was worse, he couldn't see any way out of this nightmare that had unfolded in the space of twenty minutes. There was no escaping, fighting, or even bullshitting this man because the calm but terrifying glint in his eyes spoke volumes.

'So now we've cleared that up, we're gonna have a nice chat at my premises, and you're gonna tell me everything you have on this cunt.'

Woodrow looked around out of the windows, and his hands began to shake. He wasn't blindfolded, he would know where these men worked from, he could tell the police, he could tell anyone. So, all of this amounted to just one thing: he wasn't getting out of this alive. Panic well and truly set in. His cocky manner, put on for his own crew, wasn't going to work with Regan, that was a given. The big man was obviously old school, the most dangerous kind of gangster. Those brooding eyes told him one thing: the man was fearless and angry.

'Look, bruv… '

'Shut it with the bruv, bro, or any other form of family reference. I ain't your family, got it? You wanna address me, you call me Mr Regan.'

Woodrow's eyes widened. He'd never met any of the Regans face-to-face, but he knew exactly who they were, and worse, what they were capable of. His brother Dez had stupidly pissed off Mike Regan and learned the hard way with a scar down his face to prove it.

'So are you *Mike* Regan, then?'

'Yeah, I am. So now I want some answers.'

'Er, I ain't getting out of this alive, am I? Even if I tell you all you want to know, my life's over, innit?'

The devastating realization was evident and mirrored in Woodrow's eyes.

'That all depends, really. If you're upfront and I don't smell any bull, there ain't any reason why I should top you off, is there?'

Woodrow frowned. 'But I'll still know where your place is.'

Mike laughed aloud and made Woodrow jump. 'Come on, I already know you're a police informant. I came from the cop shop. How the fuck did you think I knew where you were?'

Woodrow was confused, but as long as he could escape with his life, he really didn't give a shit. Then it occurred to him that if Regan was prepared to spare him his life, why would he do so when the location of his lock-up could be revealed?

The answer came as soon as they entered the place. Woodrow wasn't used to the countryside and wouldn't have been able to tell anyone where he was, even if he'd had the mind to do so. The location was unusual, but anything outside of London was completely alien to him. Surrounding cabins and acres of land disguised the large metal lock-up. It would appear to the unsuspecting Joe Public as a garage for the car collector enthusiast. Yet once inside the building, it was a very different picture.

Mike prodded Woodrow in the back, forcing him to walk through the doorway.

Staffie and Willie were inside, standing over Dez and Randy, who were tied to chairs. They were gagged, and yet they were still trying to run their mouths.

Woodrow slumped his shoulders. 'Jesus, man, what the fuck?' His words were slow and drawn out.

'Sit down!' demanded Mike, as he placed the gun back inside his belt. Staffie and Willie stood alongside Mike, while Lou stayed outside the lock-up, keeping watch.

'Right, now you tell me what I wanna know, and if you try and fuck me over, then your brothers here will get hurt.'

Woodrow was seated on a chair opposite his brothers. He averted his eyes from them. There was no way he could witness his siblings getting tortured, and he fervently wished Dez would remove the cocky expression from his face.

Mike towered over the man. 'Right, question number one: who's the Governor?'

'Fuck, I dunno, man,' replied Woodrow, unconvincingly.

'Wrong answer, mate.'

Mike's cold dove-grey eyes penetrated those of Woodrow's, who gulped in pitiful terror at those chilling words.

The sizeable tool racks were filled with everything from screwdrivers to nail guns, all housed in the familiar red Snap-on toolboxes. Mike pulled out a heavy-duty spanner. In one quick movement, he cracked Dez across the left kneecap. Everyone except Mike cringed at the sound of the bone splitting.

'No!' screamed Woodrow. 'Come on, man, I really don't know who he is!'

The spanner was lifted high and swung again as if Mike was playing cricket. This time, the tool connected with Dez's right kneecap and left him writhing in pain.

'Please no, please! You don't understand. I really don't fucking know who he is. I'll tell you everything I know, but, I swear, I promise on my baby's life, I don't know his real name. I know what he's doing, though. He's going to take over South-East London and then the whole of the city. He's done a deal with Tiggy Marlon from North London and Spider Day from the west side. He's swapping all their supplies of cocaine for Flakka and also giving them a good cut of the profits.'

Staffie stepped forward and looked into Woodrow's eyes. 'Are you fucking shitting me?'

Mike pulled Staffie back. 'I know who Marlon is, but who's Spider?'

Staffie licked his teeth. 'He's a fucking nightmare of a man. He runs the Hells Angels.'

'Well, the cunts have done away with Kai Lin an' all. Him and Tiggy had split North London right down the middle.'

Staffie shrugged his shoulders. 'Well, it looks like Kai Lin wasn't gonna follow suit, but I don't reckon it was Tiggy that killed him either because they were two men with respect for each other. So, I guess this Governor bloke is not only taking over but causing a shitstorm as well, yeah?'

Mike rubbed his bristles and sighed. 'Right, then, let's get this straight. This Governor geezer is trading the cocaine for Flakka with the Yardies *and* the fucking Hells Angels. Who else?' He glared at Woodrow.

'Anyone who has any power and influence, the Governor will take over. Any businesses that deal in cocaine will either be burned to the ground or taken over. He's totally ruthless. I tell ya, man, he's fucking mental.'

'Your DNA was found at the cottage. That's why you were taken down the nick for questioning. Why were you at the cottage?'

Woodrow looked shamefully at the floor. 'I'm a dealer. My supplier gave me a phone number to call if I needed gear… ' He looked at Dez. 'My supplier disappeared shortly afterwards. He was found dead with a sack over his head. The Governor is like Banksy. He can create a masterpiece, but no one sees him do it.'

Mike was listening and watching for any sign that the man was lying. His instincts told him that Woodrow was not.

'Did you ever meet this man?'

'I only saw the back of him. But he's a big lump with broad shoulders, cropped hair, and he's white.'

Mike decided on another line of questioning. 'What the fuck do you know about my son's attack?'

Woodrow's reaction was one of confusion. 'Nothing. Why would I? I don't even know who your son is!'

Mike continued to stare, and at that moment, he definitely believed the man was kosher, but out of the corner of his eye he also clocked the sly, nervous expression on Dez's face. It wasn't a look of pain from his broken kneecaps, it was the coarse edge of fear mixed with guilt.

Woodrow watched in surprise as Mike's huge bulk moved faster than Tyson Fury.

In one fluid motion, Mike ripped the tape from Dez's mouth and clenched the spanner tight, threatening to use it if Dez so much as said the wrong word. 'You knew my son because you, ya creepy little shit, wanted to fuck him. You held a blade to his jugular, so you knew I had a son. Now, you're gonna tell me who's responsible and why my boy took a fucking pasting with a sack over his head!' *Your days are numbered anyway*, he thought.

'It wasn't nothing to do with me!' he yelled.

'Liar!' screamed Mike, as the spanner came smashing down onto Dez's right wrist.

Dez reeled in pain before he let out a blood-curdling scream, and his head lolled forward. The intense pain almost made him pass out.

Randy was now sweating buckets and praying he wasn't next. He was aware of who the big man was; Dez had told him all about Mike Regan. Yet, for the moment, he felt safe. Regan was intent on getting answers from Dez and had no firm reason to beat the life out of himself; it was clear Regan hated his brother anyway.

'Who battered my boy?' he bellowed, as he swung the spanner intimidatingly. But instead of hitting Dez, yet again, he hit Randy on his right kneecap, and then, in a sick turn of events, he removed the tape from Randy's mouth, allowing him to issue a blood-curdling scream too, but it was even louder than his brother's. 'You two are close. Now, who hurt my son?'

Staffie and Willie were stunned; they hadn't expected that. Willie was high on cocaine and laughed in his usual high-pitched girl's giggle, but Staffie stared, wondering if what he was witnessing was too personal and Mike was losing the plot. He knew though that it would be pointless to intervene when Mike was in a mood like this one. For the first time in his life, Staffie questioned his own motivation for doing work of this nature. It was okay when they'd been younger, but he wondered if he even had the stomach for this kind of torture anymore.

As Mike raised the tool again, Randy yelled, 'Wait, please! Let me talk!' He cried in pain and tried to get his words together, but it was the look on Dez's face that said it all. Mike suddenly stopped and lowered the spanner. He stepped back and breathed in, allowing his chest to inflate and his chin to rise.

Randy was gasping for breath, the pain in his thigh turning from an acute ache to a burning sensation.

'Please, wait!' He tried to catch his breath, but Mike's eyes were now fixed on Dez, who abruptly shied away.

It was the moment he'd been waiting for, and, if he was honest with himself, he'd anticipated this. No one could endure this kind of treatment for long. Mike knew then that Dez and Randy had something to do with his son's attack. Which meant that they must have been involved in the death of the girl who was with Ricky. He had to think very carefully how to play this one. He knew how sly Dez was, but he knew nothing about Randy, except for the fact that the man claimed to be innocent. He hoped this was the case. In one respect, Randy appeared to be similar to his brother Woodrow – more aware of the consequences.

'So, Randy. This is how it's gonna work.' Mike remembered the name of Dez's sister, because, years ago, he'd overheard a row between Dez and another inmate concerning his beloved sister Alice. 'Me mate Willie is gonna go and get Alice… '

Immediately, Woodrow spoke up. 'No, wait, she has nothing to do with this. Please, leave her out of it.'

'I want to, but I also want assurances that Randy will tell me the truth because Dez certainly won't, will ya, you bastard?'

Sweat was now running down Randy's face. 'I swear, I'll tell you everything. Just leave her alone. She's a good girl.' His head fell back, clearly struggling to keep conscious.

Mike grinned cruelly. He could see Randy was consumed by agony. 'Right, then. Why was my son attacked and who did it?'

'It was the Governor or his men, but I honestly dunno who exactly.'

Mike nodded. 'And why?'

Randy flicked a look in Dez's direction, and Mike knew then that it was all Dez's doing. It had all the hallmarks of an underhanded weasel written all over it. 'I'm waiting, Randy,' he said, as he stared at Dez.

'A bloke called Leon Khouri, who worked from the cottage, asked us if we knew anyone on the manor who would be dealing drugs… and… ' He nervously swallowed. 'Dez said your son was.'

Mike felt the hairs on his neck stand on end, the anger curling inside his stomach. 'And you, Randy? Did you know who I was?'

Randy shook his head, sweat glistening on his forehead.

He thought he would pass out at any minute. 'No, I didn't, I swear.' He gave another sceptical look at his brother. 'I didn't even know that passing that information on would end up with your son getting attacked.'

'And the girl they murdered? Do you know anything about her?'

His face formed a frown that was etched in pain. He shook his head. 'Jesus, why, Dez, did you get me involved in this fucking shit? It's fucking yours, man! It's got nothing to do with me at all.' He looked back at Mike. 'That's the first mention of any girl being involved, I assure you. So a girl got killed as well?'

Mike nodded. 'Yeah, she was raped, and I mean *brutally* raped. Not only that but she had that Flakka drug shoved down her throat.'

'You bastard, Dez!' hollered Randy. He looked across at Woodrow. 'And you never knew?'

Woodrow shook his head in sorrow and looked down again in shame. 'I never knew, but I'm not surprised. The Governor doesn't care if you're black, white, young, or even a bird. If you get in his way, he'll kill you, no question.'

Mike was now boiling. 'And you all know that?'

Woodrow looked up at Mike, wondering what planet the man was on. 'Of course. Everyone does.'

The only sound in the room was the heavy, nervous breathing as the three brothers awaited their fate.

'Well, I wanna meet this animal, and you're gonna inform him of the fact.'

Woodrow's eyes widened. 'Jesus, if you ask me to do that, you'll be signing my own death warrant.'

Mike shook his head and tightened his jaw. 'I don't give

a fuck, and if you value the lives of your brothers and sister, you'll do exactly as I tell you. I want the man toe to fucking toe with me.'

'But I don't know how to contact him. How am I gonna get a message to him?'

Mike suddenly threw the spanner across the room, making everyone jump and Willie giggle again.

'I don't give a fuck how you do it. If you want your family to stay alive and well, you'll fucking do it! Otherwise, they'll have hessian sacks tied over their heads, and they'll be strung up from the nearest tree.'

CHAPTER SEVENTEEN

Although Brooke felt a cold chill entering the room from the open window, the paradox was that this didn't apply to her own inner state of well-being, following the assault on her. Her mind was now determined – no longer was she continually reflecting on the past. Perhaps it was because she was away from her home – her mother and even her father. She also wondered if, somehow, it had something to do with Lance.

It was strange because even though the relationship was somewhat tenuous, she felt so very much at home in what essentially to her was a stranger's house. She channel-surfed the wall-mounted widescreen TV and settled back into the soft leather sofa with her feet on the pouffe, ready to watch a romcom.

Heavy footsteps descended the stairs, and she could feel Lance's presence before he was even in the room.

'Brooke, I'm going out shortly, once I've made a phone call. I'll return later with some food. Don't go nosing around, 'cos nothing in this house is any of your business. You can watch the TV, listen to the radio, use the bathroom, and make a drink, but, other than that, you're not to move,' said Lance.

Brooke so wanted to laugh. His deep, scary voice, and his

bossy tone, along with his scowling face, actually made her feel safe and secure. In fact, she wasn't in the least intimidated by him. She could now understand why Kendall had wanted to live with him and why it must have been a real pain in the arse for her to be living at home with their mother.

'Yes, sure, and, look, thank you, Lance. I mean, I'm so grateful. Really, I am.'

'Um, yeah, well, I lost ya sister. I ain't bleedin' losing you an' all. I'm gonna go and phone your mother.'

Brooke smiled at his miserable face, or was it just an unhappy one, she wondered? Perhaps he was just a man who'd been worn down by what life had thrown at him.

Lance stared for a while at the girl's attractive blue eyes and her innocent smile. It sickened him to think of what had happened to her; she was such a sweet little thing, a waiflike china doll. Different from Kendall, perhaps, but her eyes were so familiar.

Straightaway, he chose to respond in kind. 'Chinese take-away then, is it?'

The upbeat tone in his voice gave Brooke the impression that she'd cracked the moody nut. 'Yes please,' she replied.

With the TV rattling off in the background, and Lance in the kitchen, Brooke was alone with just her thoughts. What a coincidence that Lance had happened to drive along the street at the same time she believed she was running for her life. She remembered the headlights and the car coming to a halt and then the massive man in front of her preventing her from running. Her initial thought was fear – this giant gripping her wrists, with her father on her heels. She didn't know at the time who she was more scared of – her heart had been running like crazy. That was until the giant spoke.

'Hey, calm down. Stop struggling. I'm not trying to harm you. Are you okay? Do you need the police?'

Those words – 'the police' – made her stop struggling and look up into those dark eyes. When she did, the street lamp cast a light on his face, and then she realized who he was. From that moment on, she remembered, she calmed down. She knew she was safe. Safe from Alastair, who she was now very unsure of. She respected Poppy's gut instinct. Although, in the past, she and her sister had had very little to do with each other, leading very separate lives, when all was said and done, they were still twins – maybe not identical twins, for sure, but still alike in many ways.

She had the greatest respect for Poppy's intellectual mind and even more so for her common sense. Something was up, so thank God she wasn't back in that bloody house! But she wished she knew where her sister was. Losing one sister was bad enough – losing two would feel like the end of her world.

And Kendall's photos of her father on her bedside table were the reason she'd not been terrified of him; he was so distinguishable that she'd recalled his face. Instantly, she'd said, 'Lance?'

He'd nodded, and then he'd squinted in the headlights, as he peered down at her face. 'Poppy, is it… or… ?'

'Brooke,' she'd replied. 'I'm so glad you've found me. Please help me. Please!'

She remembered he'd bundled her into the back of his car and driven away. They'd passed her father, who was still running down the street. He hadn't seen her get into the vehicle or even noticed as they'd driven past him.

So as much as Lance wore a scowl and was sharp with his

words, he was also her saviour. In some ways, he was a bit of a pussy, although she wouldn't dare to say that to his face!

Poppy was right to be worried about their father. He frightened *her*; it was that look on his face – that sudden demonic expression – that scared her, as it obviously did her sister. Her heart skipped a beat and started a string of palpitations. *Please be okay, Poppy. Please be okay.*

Lance returned to the lounge, wearing a lighter jacket and with a bunch of keys in his hand. 'I'm gonna see if Poppy's at your mother's.'

'Lance, my dad has secrets. That's why we were running away. Poppy said something about hessian material in the log cabin and—'

Lance suddenly stiffened. 'What?'

Brooke could see the concern on his face. Perhaps Poppy was onto something back in the log cabin.

'Yes, he uses the cabin as an office but something about the whole set-up had Poppy worried.'

'Listen, stay put. I'll find your sister, I promise.'

Brooke didn't have a chance even to answer before he left.

***

An hour later, Lance arrived outside Rebecca's house – half his by rights, of course. He paused before getting out of the car. Looking up at the windows, he wondered if anyone was actually in. There were no vehicles in the drive, so he assumed no one was at home unless of course a car was parked in the garage. *But who parks their motor inside a garage these days?* he thought.

After he stepped out, he slammed the door shut and marched to the front door. He rapped the brass knocker hard and waited briefly before, impatiently, he knocked again.

The door was eventually pulled open by a very distraught-looking Rebecca. Lance looked her up and down and had to blink; the woman was a complete and utter mess. Her hair was dishevelled, the bags under her eyes had aged her by ten years, and her breath reeked of stale wine. Hastily, Lance stepped back. 'Something on your mind?' he sniped viciously.

Her sore eyes narrowed. 'No... er... what are you doing here?'

He didn't answer but stepped forward. The sheer size of him automatically made her retreat slightly.

Without being invited in, he walked ahead straight into the kitchen, with Rebecca following.

'Lance, what are you doing here?' she repeated.

'Where's Alastair?' His voice demanded an answer.

'I don't know. He's probably at work. Why? What's it to you?'

Lance just stood there, staring at her unblinkingly and impassively. A chill began its way up her spine. She couldn't explain why, though. She averted her eyes and he peered out at the back garden.

'Look, what's going on here, Lance? You can't just push your way into my home like this.'

He spun around and towered over her. 'Lady, I can do whatever the fuck I like. This is still half my house, as I've told you time and time again.'

Her jaw clenched tight, and she laced her words with venom. 'That may be so, but it's not your *home*. It's mine, so get out, Lance!'

Lance leaned against the worktop and folded his arms across his broad chest. Once again, he gave her that stare and followed it up with a mocking grin.

His whole mien was winding her up. He was the last person she needed to see right now; she had enough bloody problems of her own. What with Alastair, Brooke, and Poppy all missing – she was going out of her mind with worry.

'Where's Poppy?' The question was spat out, like an Exocet missile.

The frustration and stress on her face were both replaced with confusion and fear. 'I... I... don't know.'

'And Brooke?'

She felt her stomach churning. *Did he know something she didn't?* 'I don't know about her either. Why? What's going on?'

'Rebecca, you need to tell me where Alastair is. Like *right now*!' he bellowed.

Rebecca nearly jumped out of her skin with shock. When her ex-husband – her *ex-military* husband – wanted to be, he was one scary man, and so she shouldn't have been surprised by his actions. But she wasn't in a good place herself. She wondered if he ever switched off. *Was he still living in the past?*

'Don't shout like that. You know how it scares me.'

'Well, then, tell me. Where is he?'

Rebecca let out a jaded sigh, and her shoulders slumped in resignation.

'Look... really... I honestly don't know where any of them are. I came home, and they were gone. There are two suitcases partially packed upstairs, so I think they may have left me... ' She peered at his cold expression. 'He never really wanted to be with me anyway, you know.'

Lance watched a level of serenity wash over her face. She appeared resigned, almost helpless, and it showed in her eyes. She was a lost child. For a split second, he wanted to laugh. Rebecca Mullins, the MP – with the perfect life, her nose high in the air, who could give lessons on how to patronize people – now reduced to an ugly mess. Then he remembered how easily she could manipulate people, her ability to go from powerful and measured, to giving off this pretence that she was just a sweet girl. It had worked on him many a time. But that was in the past. He'd learned from his mistakes with her. She couldn't bullshit him anymore.

'So, let's get this right. You came home, and they were gone. That's how it was. Is that correct?'

Rebecca wasn't listening; she was staring off at nothing, wishing her life had turned out differently. Why had she done it? Why had she fallen for Alastair and played away from home every time Lance was on tour? Well, it wouldn't take a psychiatrist charging her two hundred and fifty pounds an hour to tell her the answer to *that* question! She'd been lonely – very lonely. She was hungry for affection and Lance was fucking three thousand, five hundred and thirty-one miles away in Afghanistan. And it wasn't as if her present husband wasn't a good catch – Alastair was probably the biggest dish of them all. The tall, broad, handsome man with eyes that would have her knickers off in two seconds flat. He'd been what she needed – at the time.

'Tell me this, Rebecca. Where does Alastair work?'

The impromptu question dragged Rebecca completely out of her thoughts. 'Er... what?'

He smirked at that response. He knew it. She didn't have

a clue. He thought he would push her buttons a little more. 'Do you even know *what* he does?'

Angry that Lance was prying into her concerns, she was rattled and wrestled for control before she opened her mouth and regretted it. Taking a deep breath, she composed herself. 'Of course I know what he does for a living,' she said acidly. 'Please don't interfere. Now, what do you want because I'm sure it's not a pleasant chat over coffee, is it?'

She soon realized by his conceited expression that he knew something she didn't. 'Lance, I don't have time for this nonsense. If you have something to say – something actually *relevant* – then say it or kindly fuck off!'

Lance raised his eyebrows and grinned. 'Language, Rebecca.'

She ignored him and walked over to the kettle; she needed a distraction to think straight and he certainly wasn't helping.

'What I'm worried about, Rebecca, is that you don't seem the least concerned about your girls. What makes you so sure he's taken them with him?'

She slammed the kettle down and spun around. 'Oh, for God's sake, if you must know, I think the girls hate me! All right? They hate me. Kendall couldn't stand me, Alastair barely looks at me, and as for Poppy and Brooke, they won't even have a single conversation with me.' She gave a shuddery sigh and then covered her eyes as the tears filled up.

Lance watched her chest shaking as she silently sobbed.

Under normal circumstances, he would have comforted her, but actually he was getting a huge kick out of seeing her in this state. He had to admit to himself that this was probably the first time he'd ever seen real emotion emanating from her. He couldn't stand the woman. She was so fake and the most underhanded person he'd ever known. He dropped his shoulders again and stared out of the window, down the long expanse of lawn, which was only just visible due to the October morning mist. He'd loved this garden once upon a time. One of the reasons he'd bought the house was because there was so much land attached to it. In the far distance, he saw the swings and slide. He'd bought them for Kendall for when she was old enough. The sad thing was, though, she never was, as he'd moved out, taking her with him.

***

She was a year old and such a sweet baby with masses of dark hair and the roundest happy eyes that always brightened any mood he was in. Perhaps he should have made Rebecca move out or bolted the doors when she returned from her dirty weekends. He'd never forget those times.

He was back from duty and looking forward to seeing his wife and baby. He'd missed them so much. Armed with presents, he'd made his way home from the airport to surprise them. Yet once he reached the house, it was he who'd received the mother of all surprises. Their baby was asleep in a cot in the living room, but when he picked her up, he felt the sodden, filthy nappy. He didn't call for Rebecca at first. He placed the parcels of gifts on the floor and opened Kendall's nappy. He remembered feeling sick at the sight. She was red raw with blistered skin that even covered her thighs and tummy. Then, even more shocking, he saw the shit moving – it was full of maggots. As he held his baby, she opened her eyes, and without even a sound, a tear trickled down her cheek. The cot sheets were dirty, and stuck down the sides, there were empty bottles of sour milk that stank to high heaven.

The thought had crossed his mind that perhaps Rebecca was poorly herself. However, the moment he called up the stairs, he heard movement as if people were running around. In combat style, he stormed up the stairs to find Alastair grabbing his clothes and Rebecca red-faced and in a panic.

He could have killed them both, but, instead, he marched back down the stairs, wrapped Kendall in a blanket, and left with her.

For years, he carried that hurt around like an invisible veil.

**

'Perhaps, Rebecca, if you'd learned how to love your children more than yourself, you wouldn't have had this issue!'

'Don't you tell me I didn't love my children. Of course, I did. I mean, I do.'

The anger in his eyes eased, and a hint of sadness crept over them. 'I loved Kendall even after I was told at the custody case that she wasn't mine. You couldn't have got much lower than that, could you? For years, she was mine – until you pulled the DNA defence crap. That was such an evil thing you did to her and me. Using the fact that she wasn't mine to get her back, just so it looked good for you. You never loved her. She was simply the product of your infidelity. That poor girl never even had a chance to meet her real father, and I know why, because the truth is, you probably didn't even know who he was yourself. And you were controlling her life by letting her believe I was her father, even after the fucking court case. You know something else? It made no difference to me that she wasn't my biological daughter. I always loved her. And now I feel guilty for pushing her away, pushing her into your arms, all because I couldn't face being hurt again, the way you hurt me by stealing her back.'

With a loud snarl, Rebecca morphed into her stuck-up persona. 'You were a lousy father. That's why I applied for custody.'

Lance shook his head. 'That's so weak, Rebecca, and you fucking know it. I wasn't lousy. But you were delusional. Anyway, she's gone now.' He stopped before he choked on the grief.

'Yes, and it's all your fault!' she shouted.

The sudden silence conjured up dread... and guilt. She was right, of course. The last thing he remembered was when Kendall invited him in for a cup of tea, after he'd handed over the keys to the flat, and he'd cold-shouldered her.

'I know.'

Rebecca frowned. She never expected *that*.

'But I'm now going to do everything in my power to protect my other two daughters.'

Rebecca tilted her head in confusion. Then her eyes widened. *Surely, he didn't know the truth?* 'What do you mean?' Her eyes frantically searched his.

'Poppy and Brooke!'

She shook her head, but her eyes were full of worry. *So he knew then that they were his.*

'You were pregnant when I left. They were never Alastair's children, they were mine. You pretended they were born early when in actual fact they were full term. You were so desperate to hang onto that prick that you pretended they were his. You really are one conniving bitch. I won't forgive you for denying me my rights to my girls!'

'Don't be so ridiculous. The twins are not yours. You are demented. Now get out, before I call the police. This is absurd.'

'Thou doth protest too much.'

The fury took hold of her. In a flash, she threw the kettle so hard it ripped from the socket in the wall and just missed Lance, leaving a dent in the American style fridge-freezer.

'Get out!' she screamed.

Lance let out a guttural laugh at the sheer anguish on her face. 'No! I'm here for a reason, not to see you get riled up.' He pushed himself away from the worktop and headed to the back door.

'What the hell do you think you're doing?'

Blanking her, he went outside and marched towards the end of the garden.

Rebecca wrapped her dressing gown tighter around her fuller waist and slid her feet into the Wellington boots that stood by the back door.

Ignoring her calls, he reached the log cabin and tried to open the door, but it was locked. He raised his hand and felt the heat from the top wooden slats and noticed the condensation on the window. He knew then that the cabin had been heated and not so long ago. The closed curtains blocked his view.

He listened. There was silence, except for Rebecca's voice getting closer. He took three steps back, by which time Rebecca was by his side. 'What the hell are you doing? There's nothing in there that belongs to you.'

He pushed her away and lifted his leg. With one hard kick, he smashed the door in.

'Lance!' she screamed. 'What are you doing? Christ, I'm calling the police!'

He stopped and turned towards her. 'Good. Why don't you fucking do that!'

Without wasting time arguing with her, he ducked his head and made his way into the cabin, while she stomped off back to the house. *If she called the police, so what?* he thought. By police, she would of course mean her incompetent brother, and he would have fun coming face-to-face with Conrad. There was certainly no love lost between them, and if he did turn up, then there would be no holding back – this time he would definitely be telling the *Police Commissioner* a few home truths.

It was still daylight, so he pulled back the curtains. The cabin was warm, and as he touched the keyboard to the computer, the screen instantly lit up. But like Poppy before him, he couldn't access any files. A coffee cup, which lay beside the computer, didn't have the dark ring that the dregs would have left after a long period of time. His eyes shifted to the filing cabinets, and he pulled the drawers open, one at a time. Apart from a few old pens and some bills, there was nothing here. Right away, he sussed that the place had been emptied. The question, though, was why. Brooke had mentioned she'd seen a trunk, and when he turned around, he saw a well-worn Army one. The lid was open, revealing it was empty. He shook his head.

He marched back up to the house with suspicion on his mind. 'Rebecca!' he yelled.

She appeared in the kitchen, looking very different from the demonic, screaming bitch who had left the cabin and stormed back to the house. Her face was relaxed and sorrowful.

'Where is he?'

'I honestly don't know. What were you looking for, Lance? Please tell me?' Her calm manner was the real deal; there was no more pretence, no more histrionics.

'Your husband is up to something, and I intend to find out what it is, but it's apparent that he's hiding something and probably from you too. Those filing cabinets are empty. He's removed whatever he had in them.'

'How do you know he had stuff in the cabin in the first place? Not even I know what's down there. I thought it was just used as a shed.'

'Brooke told me.'

A gasp left Rebecca's mouth. 'So you *do* know where Brooke is? How… when… I mean, why would she tell you that? Where is she now?'

Lance waved his hands dismissively, brushed past her, and hurried through the hallway to the front door.

'Wait! Lance, where are Brooke and Poppy?'

He stopped and turned. 'Brooke's now in a safe place. But I was hoping you would know where Poppy is. That's why I came here… And before you deny the truth again, I know they're *my* children.'

'No!'

His anger rose again, and he clenched his fists. 'Admit it! They look nothing like you or Alastair. Come on, Rebecca, admit it. Those girls are not his, and how do I know that? Well, because they are my sister's double. She died at their age. You never got to meet her, but I'll never forget her beautiful, unusual-coloured eyes. The girls have the same soft blonde hair and round bluebell-blue eyes. So, don't you fucking ever tell me they're not mine.'

Rebecca felt her chest cave in. She knew that the minute she tried to deny it, he would have her shot down in flames. That evil glint that shone in his eyes when he was raging was there now, and she was fully conscious that if she pushed him too far, he would let rip and she would be hurt.

'All I need to know is when did you last see Poppy?'

Her throat was tight; she tried to recall the last time she'd laid eyes on her. 'It was the day before yesterday. Er... wait... Lance... ' she called after him. But it was too late. He was inside his car and starting up the engine.

Her world had come apart like a chocolate orange.

* * *

Poppy sat on the plush sofa in Ricky's home as Liam dragged the pouffe over and placed it under her feet. She watched his efforts with affection. Arty was still trying to get through on his phone to either his father or to Ricky's dad. She admired the lads and their sweet ways, but she found Liam more interesting; he was good at lifting her spirits with a joke or two.

'So, you all have a key to each other's houses then?'

Liam gave the last gentle shove so that her legs were resting comfortably, and he sat back on the carpet. 'That's right. It's always been that way. Our grandads – mine, Arty's, and Ricky's – have known each other since their school days. They became best buddies. That's how it's been with us as well. We're like one large, extended family. We're all there for each other. It's bred into us, I suppose.'

Poppy gazed around the sizeable room and soaked up the

luxury. 'I thought we lived in a posh house, but this is so beautiful. It's so big and classy.'

Liam got up from the floor and plonked himself next to her. 'Yeah, there's plenty of room to get lost in.' He looked at her bruised cheek. 'Does that hurt?'

She placed her hands on her face. 'No, not really. I think I'm hurting inside, though. Everything has been such a shock and it's playing with my mind.'

He patted her knee. 'Once Mike gets home, we'll sort out how to find your sister. Does she look like you?'

Poppy nodded. 'Yeah. We're not identical twins but we do look alike.'

Liam smiled, and his eyes lit up. 'Blimey, two lookers in the family then.'

Poppy blushed. 'Well, I don't know about that.'

Liam looked at Poppy with a sorrowful expression. He wished he could have a girlfriend like her, but he knew she was way out of his league.

Arty was still trying to call his dad. 'I can't get hold of me dad. And Mike's not answering either and neither is your ol' man. They must be busy.' He sighed as he sat in the chair opposite. 'Have you no way of contacting your sister?'

Poppy suddenly had a thought. She looked at him excitedly. 'Facebook! Are you on Facebook?'

Liam chuckled. 'Who isn't? Arty's got more mates than David Beckham.'

'Look up Brooke Mullins, then.'

Arty stopped what he was doing and looked over to Liam and Poppy. It was a great idea of Poppy's. He'd wished he'd thought of that. He was always into social media. He stared at his screen and scrolled through lists of names. There were quite a few, but one photo that made him stop was of a blonde girl who looked a lot like Poppy. He showed the screen to Poppy. 'Is that Brooke?'

Poppy peered at the screen and smiled. 'Yeah. Can you message her?'

Arty was like greased lightning with his thumbs. 'Right. I've just said, **Call me. Urgent**. Is there anything else I should add?'

Poppy gave this some thought. 'My sister's not right at the moment. She's very wary now of people she doesn't know. You'll need to get her onside, otherwise she'll ignore the message. Say to her this: **Secret Squirrel here**. She'll know it's me, then.'

'Right, that's sent.'

A few minutes later, Arty saw a message appear on his Facebook page. He stared at the screen. 'She's seen it,' he announced excitedly.

Poppy held her breath. 'Oh God, I hope she's okay.'

Liam cheekily patted her knee again. 'She'll be fine. Stay calm. We'll get to her.'

At once, his words seemed to soothe her mind like a hot drink of cocoa.

Arty was glued to his phone. 'She's typing a message.' They all held their breath and waited.

'She said she will call my number.'

Poppy leaned forward. 'Oh, come on, Brooke, please let it be you.'

She was about to find out. His phone rang, and, like a shot, he answered it and handed his mobile to Poppy.

'Brooke?'

'Oh my God, Poppy. Where are you? I've been so worried.'

'I'm safe. I'm okay. Where are you?'

'At Lance's house, would you believe it? Dad chased me, but Lance was in the street. He stopped his car and drove me to his house. He's out at the moment. He said he was going out to look for you. So I'm waiting for him to get back.'

'Are you sure you're okay? I mean, with Kendall's dad? After all, we hardly know him,' questioned Poppy.

Brooke laughed. 'It's funny you asked that because I feel safer with him than our own father right now. I'll text you Lance's address. Can you come over? By the way, who are you with? I didn't know you knew someone called Arty Stafford?'

Poppy looked across at Liam and Arty. Both could hear the conversation. Arty nodded to her and whispered that he and Liam would take her over to where Brooke was staying.

'Listen. There's too much to tell you on the phone. Brooke, *don't* try to contact Mother. She ran me over. Actually, she nearly killed me! I've been in the hospital. I've a broken ankle, but I'm fine, I promise. As for where I am, we'll catch up on all that when I see you. I can't wait, sis.'

'Fucking hell, Poppy, what were we really born into? Are you sure you're okay?'

'Yes, honestly, I am. I'll see you soon. Text me the address.'

CHAPTER EIGHTEEN

Zara was in an uncertain mood when she awoke from a sleepless night. The ramifications of her conversation with Victor were the cause of her malaise.

She looked at the missed calls and just couldn't bring herself to call anyone back. Neil had rung four times. That was an hour ago. It crossed her mind that perhaps he would turn up on the doorstep if she didn't answer him. But she knew she wouldn't have been at his door if the situation had been reversed.

Victor's words whirled around inside her head, and now she was slowly doubting her alliance with the Lanigan family. Even Mike. Why hadn't he called to see if she was okay? Surely he would have questioned Eric's injury? And if he knew she'd been responsible, wouldn't he have called to check she wasn't hurt?

Just as she was about to make her way upstairs, there was loud knocking – more like a banging sound – at the door. This time, in her resigned state of mind, she didn't check the CCTV, assuming it was the decorators. She opened the door to be hit by a bracing wind that blew the hair from her face and took her breath away.

With his hands spread out on each side of him, Eric gripped the two pillars and glared, like a brooding statue. He looked dark and foreboding, his skin covered in a layer of sweat and grease. In fact, he resembled an old wino. The brown rings under his eyes showed a lack of sleep at the very least. Either way, he emanated ugliness, sending a tingling sensation through her body.

Afraid in the knowledge that he was one underhanded, dangerous man, she knew she mustn't let him enter her house. Her first reaction was to slam the door in his face, but as she tried, he shoved his size eleven Timberland boot in the gap. His scowl and tight lips frightened her; no way was this the Eric who'd pulled her from the underground prison and saved her – this man was a stranger. His presence unnerved her so much that she really couldn't think straight. What would he do this time? Would he rape her or kill her? The silence, as they locked eyes, was terrifying; thoughts of who he really was made her tremble. Her eyes then switched to his bandaged hand and to the gold ring on his little finger. Then she breathed in the strong sweet aftershave that he always wore – Joop! It *was* him! He was the man who'd held the knife to Tiffany's throat and had planned to take her down – to ruin her business and to destroy her firm. Eric was the sly and devious bastard who'd tried to plant doubts in her mind about the Lanigans. Here was the jealous brother who'd acted like a spoiled child. She felt her tongue stick to the roof of her mouth as his grimace turned to a cruel smirk that showed his top teeth.

With her attention firmly fixed on him, she struggled to believe that someone like Eric could run a business that would eventually take over South-East London and turn innocent kids into savages. How could he and Mike be so different? Or were they?

She had to do something because once he was inside her house she would be fucked.

'As you can see, I'm not dressed, so please remove your fucking great boot!' She knew she sounded pretty feeble and was stating the obvious, but she felt especially vulnerable; she was only wearing her pyjamas and a robe, although he had seen her in those before.

'No, I wanna come in!' he growled.

His face looked charged with spite. She was helpless; there were no weapons to hand and she didn't even have her bladed glove on her. And right now, she was too weak with fear to fight. 'Go away!' was all she could say.

He pushed his way through the door and into her hallway. 'No, Zara, I'm not going away. You're gonna fucking listen to me. You nearly took my fucking hand off!'

He held up his bandaged wrist. 'I didn't deserve that.'

'You bloody well did! You should never have forced yourself on me.' She knew she had to keep the argument about them and not let on that she knew he'd held Tiffany at knifepoint.

He rubbed his sweaty forehead and took a deep breath. 'Look, Zara, you have to listen to me. I want you to come with me. Please, just come back to my house. I need to talk to you.' He grabbed her arm so tightly it made her wince, and she was no fairy.

'Get the fuck off me! Now!' She tried to break free, but with no other hand, she was defenceless. She attempted to kick him, but she missed and instead slipped on the wooden floor. Nevertheless, he held her up.

'Stop it, will you! For fuck's sake, you're coming with me. Now, stop struggling!'

She tried again to kick him hard. This time, she didn't miss; she managed to strike him on the inside of his thigh. His leg buckled, forcing him to release his grip. She kicked him again, which made him holler in such pain that he needed to lean against the wall for support.

It was enough time for her to run back along the hallway to her father's office. Her eyes searched the desk for her gun, but she suddenly panicked – it was under her pillow upstairs. All she could do was to grab her phone and call someone. But as soon as it was in her hand, he was there like a monster, trying to snatch it from her. She just managed to pull away from him, but in doing so, she dropped the phone, and now he had it.

He went to seize her again, but she sidestepped and missed his clutches. From the corner of her eye, she spotted her father's heavy glass ashtray – it was the only weapon available. She ran around the opposite side of the desk to Eric, grabbed the heavy object, and went for him, ramming it into the side of his head.

She gasped as he fell back. She knew she'd hurt him; she'd felt the impact from the ashtray making contact with his bone. He staggered and tried to focus. The clump had disorientated him. She watched as he stumbled about, but she couldn't move. Then a sudden feeling of guilt swept over her. His eyes looked so full and frightened. Yet she wasn't going to be fooled; he was a devious bastard.

Slowly, she stepped backwards, walking away from him, before he could hurt her. As if he'd taken control of his senses, he straightened up. Zara's heart beat faster; he was like the man who wouldn't die. Yet, as she gritted her back teeth to stop them from chattering, he looked harshly at her.

'You should have listened to me, but you're so fucking stubborn, and it will be the death of you, ya stupid woman!'

Zara felt her heart beating almost outside her chest and her body was alive with fear. Still gripping the glass ashtray, she remained steadfast and watched as he swayed from side to side and stumbled out of the office and back along the hallway to the front door.

Once she heard his car start up, she let out a lungful of air and relaxed her shoulders before putting the ashtray down and hurrying to the front door. With her hand trembling, she pushed the door shut.

What the fuck was that all about? she thought.

After she'd managed to calm her erratic breathing, she went back to the office where she noticed the blood on the glass ashtray and suddenly felt sick. This should never have happened. Eric was supposed to be a part of her family; he would have been her brother-in-law.

She had to call Victor; he would know what to do. He was always there giving her advice; it was as if he'd taken over from her father. *The phone! Oh my God*, Eric still had her phone. Pulling open the drawers, she looked for an old phone, and there in the bottom drawer, she found a Nokia, along with the charger. Luckily, after plugging it in, it fired up and still worked. There were, however, no numbers saved.

She retrieved the ledger from her bag and leafed through the pages until she came to the number next to the word 'Machine'. She sighed and keyed in the digits, leaving the ledger on the desk. Easing herself down on the old leather office chair, she waited as the phone rang, her eyes staring at the phone number.

Then, as the phone suddenly died, she spotted something

on the page of the ledger that made her look more closely. It had been written in there and then rubbed out. She twisted the book so that the light would catch the indented words. It was hard to see. In among the pot of old biros was a pencil, now almost blunt. Gently, she used it to trace over the letters until she could see more clearly what was written. *Oh shit!*

She dropped the notebook and gasped. Her hand felt clammy with sweat, and pins and needles pricked the back of her neck. A thousand thoughts ran through her mind. Snippets of conversations and timings flashed through her head like a computer processor, until, suddenly, she realized the truth. She'd been played big time. The anger took over her shock and fear. The saying her father rammed home to her – always – came to her in a flash: knowledge is power. She could hear him saying those words. 'Oh, Dad, you were so right, but now you watch me,' she mumbled under her breath. 'I will show them who the fuck is running this manor.' She waited for the Nokia to become fully charged because she was going to make a call that might well last a long time – she just hoped she had the right number.

***

Arty turned left into an avenue, which had large detached properties that were sitting on substantial plots. 'It's got to be on this road, in three hundred metres.'

Liam laughed. 'What, is there an echo in this car? 'Cos we can hear your sat nav, mate. We don't need an interpreter.'

Arty ignored him. He wasn't in the mood for a bit of ribbing. 'Here we are,' he said, as he entered a long drive.

Liam was the first to help Poppy out of the car. He gripped her arm and laughed. 'Oops! The neighbours are gonna talk. You're still in ya pyjamas.'

She was an inch away from Liam's face, and for a moment she felt like kissing him. He may not be Liam Hemsworth, but the Liam holding her certainly had some features she liked, not least his beautiful eyes and his sunny disposition that had her warming to him.

Arty pulled his shoulders back and smoothed down his Ralph Lauren polo-shirt collar. 'Is that your sister?' he said, as he looked up at the window.

Poppy tried to grip her crutches but was making a pig's ear of it. 'Yeah!'

Suddenly the door opened, and Brooke ran over to them. She took Poppy's other arm, while Arty removed the crutches.

'Poppy, I was so worried. Look at your face! My God! Does it hurt?'

Arty watched Brooke fussing and decided she was right up his street. The girls may look alike, but Brooke had the edge; perhaps it was her puffier lips or her fuller mane. As soon as they were all inside, Arty shut the door – it signalled an intention that they weren't leaving just yet.

Liam and Brooke helped to get Poppy comfortable while Arty felt a bit like a spare part. 'Um, shall I get us something? What about a burger, drinks?' As soon as he said it, he felt silly, yet when Brooke finally noticed him, her face looked prettily pink.

She smiled, and her neat pearls of white teeth sparkled. 'Oh, that would be lovely. What do you think, Poppy?' she asked, full of excitement.

Poppy looked at Liam. 'Will you stay for a while, then?

I mean, I don't actually know Lance. I only know that he was Kendall's father.'

Liam felt it was his responsibility to sit beside her, and so he took it one step further and put his arm around her shoulders. 'Yeah, we'll make sure you're safe, won't we, Art?'

Arty grinned. The day was getting better by the minute. Then his face dropped. 'Your father. You don't think he was behind the attack on Ricky and your sister, do ya?' He looked Brooke's way, aiming the question at her.

Her face suddenly lost its sparkle. 'Well, yeah, it's possible because something's not right. He was like a different person. He actually frightened me. Me, afraid of my own father. Anyway, I just don't want to go back there, not after the grim look on his face.'

'Okay, I'll pop up the road, grab us a bite to eat, and hopefully, me dad will have his phone back on by then, and they'll know what to do.'

Just as he opened the front door, he came face-to-face with a tall, broad, dark-haired man, with a snarl that would shit the life out of the king of the jungle. Not knowing if he was Lance or the girls' father, he stepped back but squared his shoulders as he did so. 'Who are you?'

Lance grabbed Arty's shoulders and propelled him backwards down the entrance hall. He was in two minds whether to beat the shit out of the lad but decided to give him the benefit of the doubt for the moment. His words though were frightening enough. 'Not relevant! So, who the fuck are you?' he replied, with a deep, hoarse voice.

'Lance, it's okay. It's… er, they brought Poppy back!' said Brooke, now standing in the hallway.

Lance let go of Arty's polo shirt, but the determined scowl didn't leave his face. 'Who are you?' he demanded again.

'Arty Stafford. I'm friends with Ricky Regan, er… Kendall's boyfriend.'

It took a moment before Lance could make sense of what Arty had just said. 'Did you say Stafford?'

Arty nodded, now beginning to read Lance's body language and see the change in the man's tone. 'Yeah, and me mate's Liam. We brought Poppy back from the hospital.'

Lance marched into the lounge to find Liam in the doorway and Poppy with her foot up and in plaster, her face badly bruised. 'Fucking hell! Who did that?' he demanded.

Poppy looked a little shaken, hearing Lance's deep voice. 'Well, actually, it was my mum. She ran me over.'

Lance was so shocked. He jolted back as he grasped the significance of what Poppy had just said. 'You what? You can't be serious? No way. I've just left your mother's. She never said—'

Before he'd a chance to say another word, Liam piped up, 'Well, she wouldn't say, would she? The bitch ran her over and did the off.'

Lance looked at Liam and his brows knitted together. 'Are you Willie Ritz's boy?'

Liam nodded. 'Yeah, that's me. Why? D'ya know me dad?'

'Oh yeah, I know him all right.'

Before the charged atmosphere in the room settled down, a buzzing sound came from the cabinet. Lance spun around and pulled open the drawer. It was his 'other' phone. He stared down at the flashing screen on his mobile and thought for a moment. Then the phone rang off. 'Look, guys, do me a favour, will you? Stay here with the girls. I need to do something.' His demeanour instantly changed, his shoulders dropped, and the tight, angry expression faded. No one said a word until he was out of the room.

'He's one scary fucker him, ain't he?' said Liam.

Brooke laughed at the expression on Liam's worried face. 'I think his bark's worse than his bite, though.'

Arty screwed his face up and rubbed his shoulder. 'Oh, I dunno about that. He's got a tasty grip on him.'

Brooke fluttered her eyelashes. 'Did he hurt you?'

Arty was a little bruised from the encounter, but he wasn't going to admit *that*. 'Nah, not at all. I'd have bashed him, but I didn't want to clout the wrong fella, if ya know what I mean.'

Liam could see Arty was showing off in front of Brooke, so, as a loyal mate, he helped boost Arty's ego. 'Cor, yeah, not 'alf. Arty would've had that bloke on his arse in one blow, if it went too far.'

With her peachy cheeks and shiny eyes, Brooke laughed. 'So you really are our knights in shining armour, then?'

Arty puffed out his chest and winked.

To Liam's surprise, Poppy turned to him, nudged his arm, and flicked her eyes to Arty as if to say, *Take a look at those two*. Liam pulled her closer and kissed the top of her head. 'Are you, okay, babe? You're not in any pain, are ya?'

She snuggled into his chest. 'No, Liam, I feel fine now.'

As he kissed the top of her head again, he looked up at Arty, beaming. Never in his wildest dreams would he have thought he'd pull a bird like Poppy. He'd assumed she was way out of his league, unlike Arty, who could click his fingers and have the pick of the bunch.

As Arty left the house to fetch some food and drinks, he spotted Lance on his mobile, walking up and down the drive. His face was taut and his eyes moody. The second Lance caught sight of Arty, he placed his hands over the phone and beckoned him over. 'What are you doing?'

'Getting some burgers.'

'Be quick, then. I don't want the girls left alone… and I mean it. You can handle yaself, lad, can't ya?'

Arty nodded. 'Is their father a lump then, or what?'

Lance sighed. 'I don't know what's going on. All I know right now is I want those girls looked after, and if you, Stafford, and Ritzy in there are anything like your fathers, then my girls are in safe hands!'

Arty frowned. '*Your* girls, did ya just say?'

Lance gave a slow, meaningful nod. 'Yeah, I did. They're mine!'

'Okay, Lance, no worries. We'll look after them.'

'Good. See ya later.' He turned his back on Arty and returned to his conversation on the phone. 'So, tell me, what does this geezer look like and what does he drive?'

Arty knew Lance was finished with him, and so he left with speed in his step, unsure of how dangerous this situation actually was. He wondered who Lance was talking to on the phone, who this man – the girls' father – was, and what all this had to do with Ricky. Once he was in his car, he called his father's number. The phone was still turned off.

***

Mike left Staffie and Willie guarding Randy and Dez, while he drove Woodrow back to London.

The journey had a very different feel about it. For a start, Woodrow was sitting in the front – as a free passenger – and, secondly, there was no gun aimed at his stomach.

'How the hell are you so cocksure that I won't go to the Ol' Bill?' His question wasn't meant as a threat; he was just very curious.

Mike laughed. 'Seriously, mate, don't underestimate me. I have my reasons, but you're the one who should be asking yourself *that* question.'

Woodrow was tired, the shock and horror of the last few hours having sent him into his shell. He thought he was hard; his little firm were scared of him, and they gave him respect and a name. He looked at Mike and realized that he himself was such a small fish in a big pond; his way of dealing with business was nowhere near in Mike's league. At one time, he thought that it was a myth how the old-school gangsters were cool and yet fucking dangerous. Not now, though. He felt as if he'd just stepped out of a film about the Kray twins. The vision of Mike swinging that heavy-duty spanner with so much aggression, and yet doing so with such deliberation, as if it was all planned, kept filling his mind. Of course, he wouldn't go to the police. If Regan's firm ever caught up with him, then God knows where his body parts would end up.

'Is it true that Dez was gonna rape your son?'

Mike's knuckles went white as he gripped the steering wheel.

Woodrow could see the man's anger appear from nowhere. 'Sorry, I guess that question was a bit close to the mark. I just wanted to know, that's all.'

'Yeah, he was, as a matter of fact. He also fucking burned all but one of the photos I had of my son when I thought my boy was dead. It was lucky for your brother he was in prison when he held a knife to Ricky's throat, 'cos if he'd been on the outside, I'd 'ave killed him.'

Woodrow inhaled slowly through his teeth, and his top lip quivered. 'You're gonna kill Dez, ain't ya?'

Mike nodded. 'Yeah, I am… but Randy will live, and ya sister will go about her daily business, if you do as you're told.'

Woodrow's muscles tightened in his chest. 'Me sister's a good woman. She's a nurse, so please don't hurt her. I didn't think you old-timers hurt women and kids. Some rule like that, anyway.'

'Well, you're right, but that depends on the circumstances. Someone has hurt my kid – badly – and I ain't taking that lightly. I want revenge, and if it means I tear through every fucker in South-East London to find this cunt, then your sister is expendable.'

Woodrow wouldn't argue – he knew that the Governor had met his match with Mike Regan. As they approached Peckham, Woodrow clocked a woman with a pram; she was walking with an older person. His heart was in his mouth; it was his mother, accompanying his sister and his baby niece. They looked so happy, so innocent. 'Mr Regan, can we talk? I wanna do a deal with you.'

Mike pulled off the main road, where there was a small gap among the parked cars, and he nodded. 'I wondered if you would. Ya see, I have this gift. I can tell when someone's holding something back. I would've smashed it out of you eventually, but if I'd done that, you'd be no good to me with no face to talk to.'

Woodrow gulped. 'I'll tell you who hurt your son and killed that girl, in return for my sister's life. She's kind-hearted – works at King's College Hospital – and she's got a baby of her own. She looks after me muvver as well. She does all her shopping. Ya know, just… ' He stopped when the tears tumbled down his cheeks. 'She doesn't deserve to be hurt for us. I mean, me and me brothers. It wouldn't be fair.'

Mike remained poker-faced. He wouldn't lose his temper with Woodrow. He wanted the truth, and now he felt that at long last he was going to hear it, even though he'd had a strong suspicion who'd hurt his son. 'Go on!'

Woodrow stared, looking for some compassion in Regan's eyes, but he should have known there wouldn't be any. 'If I tell you, will you leave her alone?'

Mike nodded. 'You give me their names, and not any cock-and-fucking-bull story either, and I won't touch her.'

Woodrow slowly closed his eyes as more tears plummeted down his cheeks. The words almost choked him to death. 'If you must know, it was Dez. He did it. I never knew he'd killed the girl that was with Ricky, but I do know he raped one a while ago. Well, he's raped more than one. He did it by shoving drugs down their throat, so I guess he did it to her as well. I heard what'd happened on the grapevine, and I told him to leave it. I never knew all the details, only that he'd had a beef with you and Ricky in prison.'

'And who was the other bloke with him?'

Woodrow shook his head, with regret clearly showing on his face. 'That, Mr Regan, I really don't know, but I know it wasn't Randy.'

'Why are you so sure?'

'Randy's sick. He's got something wrong with his heart. He was up the hospital the last two weeks, so he wouldn't have had the strength nor the will. He ain't like Dez. In fact, none of my brothers are like Dez. We try to help him, but for years he's lived off our reputation and bullied people. Mr Regan, I am what I am, a drug dealer, and, yeah, I've bashed up people. I've done wrong things, like all of us, but nothing like Dez.' He wiped his tears away, and gave a sad, defeated smile. 'You won't hurt me sister, will ya?' His eyes begged.

Mike blinked slowly as he shook his head. 'No, Woodrow, the war is between good and bad, really. This Governor may have hurt your sister, but me and my firm wouldn't do so, not in a fucking million years. Did you honestly think I would?'

Woodrow nodded. 'I have to say I did. That's why I told you it was Dez.'

'I'm a ruthless bastard, but hurt a woman? Never, mate. Before you get outta me car, don't get too complacent, though. I still have Randy, so you do as you're told, yeah?'

Woodrow smiled. 'Believe it or not, Mr Regan, I'm now on your side. Ya see, this Governor man *would've* hurt my sister. That's the difference between you and him. It's why I want to help. You need to find this bloke and kill him!'

'Oh, believe me, I fucking will. Now, I need to find out who this other bloke is who bashed the life outta my son.'

'And Randy, he's a kid, he's not like Dez. Please… '

'Don't worry, I'll get the boy to the hospital, but be warned. If you fuck me over, I can soon 'ave a change of heart.'

With his eyes looking directly into Mike's, Woodrow replied, 'I swear to you, I won't do that. I want the Governor dead as much as you do. I hate this drug. I hate even more how we're all held to fucking ransom, and more than that, I hate that this cunt has so much power. He's raising a fucking army.'

'No man is that invincible. President Kennedy got shot!'

Woodrow raised his brow, and a hint of a smirk adorned his face – a thought he digested as he left the car and headed to the estate.

CHAPTER NINETEEN

Dressed in a black jacket, a crisp white shirt, and dark jeans, Zara sat behind her father's desk. She looked at her prosthetic hand and then at her own hand. 'It's who I am now!' she said to herself. The days of mourning her lost limb, her fingers, and self-worth were now a thing of the past. This was who she was. She may be alone, but she wasn't *lonely* anymore. All those years, all that heartache, it had made her into the woman she was today. There was a piece of her heart broken, and nothing on earth would ever fix that issue. Mike was out of her life, so the images and dreams she'd once had of living a family life with Ricky as her stepson and Mike as her husband would always stir a heartache; however, she was strong enough now to hurl them to the back of her mind. She had a business to run and a plan to put in place.

The calls had been made, and now she waited for the reaction. Right on cue, she could see the taxi on her monitor, making its way up the drive. Getting up from her chair, she sauntered over to the drinks cabinet and selected the most expensive brandy. It was only used by her father on rare occasions. She placed it on the desk and then used her one hand to pick up two cut-glass crystal tumblers, one at a time. Only the best would do for her guest-cum-minder.

The heavy rap at the door put a smile on her face, and it was even broader when she welcomed him in. It was Victor.

'You sounded excited on the phone. What's going on?'

She nodded. 'Oh yes, I've thought about what you said, and you were right. I think the person who's trying to run me out of town is right under my nose and has been all the bloody time. A drink?'

Victor followed her into the office and grinned when he recognized the brandy label. 'Ooh, this *is* a celebration. Your father's best, no less.'

Zara poured the drink into the two glasses. 'It's such a shame because he would have loved to have shared this with you.'

'Yeah, I do miss Izzy. I loved his riddles and his philosophy on life.'

Zara gave a wry smile. 'I know what you mean. I can still hear his words as if he were next to me. Anyway, I have some news, and I want you to help me.'

Victor clasped his hands in front of him. 'Anything, sweetheart. You know, you only have to ask me.'

'Yeah, you've been such a tremendous help. I know no one can fill my father's shoes, but, I dunno, I feel you've been, like, well, perhaps an uncle to me.'

Victor blushed and looked down at the amber liquid. 'That's a kind thing to say, and, babe, it's my pleasure.'

Zara leaned back on her chair. 'Okay, so, as you know, my cocaine business has almost dried up. The supplier's disappeared, the Colombians have well and truly backed off, and the dealers are moving towards this new drug.'

Victor was nodding. 'Yeah, it's a shocking state of affairs.'

'Well, I've contacted a friend of Izzy's today. I didn't even realize I had his number. But lo and behold, I've a new supplier. He's managed to deal with a new importer, and, apparently, the cocaine is the best there's ever been in the UK. He can supply me with enough to cover the whole of the South-East and more if I need it. If I can get my restaurants back up and running with my own men, then I'm in business again, and so, hopefully, it will push the demand for that shit stuff lower down the line. You see, there has to be an alternative. No one will just go cold turkey. The toffs will always want a bit for recreational use, and I intend to be their supplier.'

Victor held his hand up to give her a high five, and, with a chuckle, she responded likewise.

'Sounds like a plan… but I can see one fly in the ointment. More than one, actually. It's the gangs behind this Flakka drug. How do you propose to tackle them?'

She sighed heavily. 'I don't know yet. I would have said involve the Lanigans, but after what you said earlier, it has got me wondering. I've been over and over these last few days, just thinking about all of this, and something just doesn't add up. You were right: I think the Lanigans are after running me out of London. When Neil pushed me into the ladies' toilets when those cars pulled up, he wasn't protecting me, he was placing me in there as a sitting duck. None of the men were killed. It was a set-up, clear and simple, and I think they intended to do away with me.'

Victor frowned. 'What? No way. I don't think they would go that far, would they?'

She nodded. 'Did you know that many moons ago, I nearly killed Davey Lanigan? I smashed him around the head with a rock.'

Victor shook his head. 'What? You? But you are so sweet and dinky.'

'Yep, I nearly knocked his head clean off his shoulders.'

Victor laughed. 'Well, I'll be buggered.'

'Then something else puzzled me. It's Eric.'

Victor leaned forward on the edge of his seat, drinking in everything she said. 'Eric as in Mike's brother?'

'Yeah. He knew stuff that he could've only known if he'd spoken with the Lanigans.'

'Right. See, I knew he was a sly ol' git. He comes across as slimy, if I'm honest. I've seen him sneaking around. I told you about when he went to Antonio's restaurant. So, what you're saying is that Eric and the Lanigans are in cahoots. But what about Mike?'

She took a sip of brandy and placed the glass down, clearly annoyed. 'Eric and Mike were close. I mean, really close. Maybe it's because I was so in love with Mike that my brain wasn't able to analyse stuff at a personal level. It was a head versus heart thing, I suppose. So I was resisting the idea that Mike had any involvement with all of this backstabbing. You see, the thing is, Mike and Eric were making a mint from supplying arms to the Lanigans before Eric fucked off to Spain or wherever he went while Mike was locked away. With Mike inside, that little bit of business dried up. Well, so I thought. I know Davey went to see Mike in prison to discuss setting up a business again. Mike gave Davey Staffie's name, but then, funnily enough, Staffie, Willie Ritz, and Lou Baker all ended up inside. That's a bit convenient, wouldn't you say?'

Victor's eyes were bulging. 'Fucking hell. So, what you're saying is that someone – perhaps Eric – took over, grassed them all up, and worked on the QT with the Lanigans, cutting everyone out of the business?'

Zara nodded slowly. 'Yeah, that's exactly what I'm saying, and not only that, remember I told you I had cut Eric's wrist?'

'Yeah, well, I don't blame you.'

'The guy who rushed to ambush the restaurant had a bandage on his wrist. My young waitress said he smelled of Joop! aftershave, and he wore a gold ring on his little finger. So, it must've been Eric.'

Victor put his hand to his mouth. 'Jesus, Zara, he could've killed you. After all, he knows where you live.'

'That's why you're the only man I can trust. You had your suspicions from the start, and you were right too. I'm just so grateful I have you because everyone else around me is a fucking snake.'

Unexpectedly, she rose, her eyes filled with tears, and she cried into her brandy. Victor jumped up from his seat and pulled her into his arms. 'It's gonna be all right, sweetheart. I'll look after you.'

'Oh, Victor, why am I so weak sometimes? One minute, I think I'm strong, and then the next, I just fall apart. It's like I've two voices in my head.'

'Babe, you've been through a hell of an ordeal, and by Christ, most men even would have turned it in and laid down and died, let alone a woman. You'll be okay. You just need a break.'

She pulled away from him and sat back down, wiping away her sodden cheeks. 'I can't, not yet. I've got this cocaine delivery, so I need to be there. Oh Christ, why did I even get involved? What was I thinking? You're right, you know. I'm all over the place at the moment. I do need a break, just to clear my head of all the crap that's been fed into it by people who I thought I could trust.'

Victor looked at the brandy bottle. 'Here, d'ya want a top-up?'

She nodded and sniffed back a tear that had run down her nose. 'Will you come with me? I don't think I should go alone, and I can't trust the Regans or the Lanigans anymore.'

Victor topped up her glass and his own. 'Of course, babe.'

She laughed through her tears. 'Look at us. There's me, a skinny bitch on the one hand, and you… '

He raised his eyebrows. 'An old man?'

'No, I was going to say a taxi driver.'

He straightened his shoulders and presented a half-grin that appeared like a cruel smirk. 'You and I both know that I'm more than that, Zara. Your father never underestimated me. I didn't have the nickname 'The Machinist' for nothing, ya know.'

Zara gulped back the brandy and gritted her back teeth; the liquid was so strong it burned the back of her throat. 'Yeah, you're right, of course. My father thought very highly of you.' She sat up straight and took a deep breath. 'So, shall we get down to business?'

Victor placed his glass back on the table. 'Okay. What's the plan?'

'Well, I don't really have time for an elaborate plan because the drop-off is tonight.'

Victor's eyes were on stalks. 'Tonight? Shit. Are you sure you know what you're doing?'

She shook her head. 'No, not really, but the advantage I have is that no one knows – only you, the dealer and me. The sole risk I face is if he turns up with a firm and takes the money without leaving the gear.'

'He'll be one foolish man if he does that on the first drop-off. In my experience, dealers, if they are inclined to, will only do that after a few exchanges. It's only once the buyer gets complacent and doesn't take precautions at every one that they get screwed.'

Zara's eyebrow raised as she grinned. 'You seem to know a lot?'

'And where do you think I learned it from? It was from your dad, of course. He had me on board for many an exchange. He said he didn't trust anyone else, so he always called me... but he paid me well.'

'Oh yes, sorry, about the payment. I was thinking ten grand... in cash?'

Victor stared at her, in contemplation. 'I take it the deal is for two hundred grand, then? So, that's five per cent?'

'That's what my father paid, wasn't it?'

Victor beamed. 'No flies on you, girl. Yes, it was, so ten grand, in cash, and you have a deal. Now then, what d'ya know about our new supplier?'

'He worked with my father in the past. I remember Izzy talking about him. He'd always come up trumps. You must have met him if you accompanied my dad on the exchanges?'

'What's his name?'

'Josh.'

Victor frowned. 'I don't remember anyone called Josh, but, then again, your father didn't disclose any names. I was just there as the backup, you know, inside the wings, just in case.'

'Well, anyway, he did a lot of business in the past, so you might recognize him.' She paused. 'I am making the right decision, aren't I?'

'I know your father never looked a gift horse in the mouth, and if you're getting a good deal and you reckon you can get rid of this nasty shit drug and turn the South-East back to how it was, it can only earn you respect.'

Zara stood up. 'Right.' She took a deep breath. 'Let's do this. I'm going to meet Josh at nine o'clock. Presumably, you know where my hangar is?'

Victor nodded. 'Of course. Your father loved to show off his light aircraft.'

'Good. Could you meet me there at say eight thirty? I need to gather up the money first.'

Victor knew she was giving him a hint that it was time to leave. 'Are you sure you'll be okay, driving around with all that dosh in your car?'

Zara nodded and walked with him towards the front door to see him out. 'Victor, I'm putting my trust in you completely. No one else will know. Once we've done the swap, I've another plan for Eric and the Lanigans, but I need that cocaine first.'

'Sounds ominous? What plan is this?'

She winked and tapped the side of her nose. 'Let's just say, they'll see me in a different light.'

'Zara, listen, if what we believe is true, then Eric is one dangerous man. You won't do anything reckless, will you?'

She grinned. 'No, because you'll be there. I'm going to arrange for Eric to turn up after the cocaine deal.'

Victor sighed. 'Have you really thought this through, babe? I mean, what if he turns up with the Lanigans or Mike?'

She shook her head. 'No, he won't because the one thing that Eric wants, apart from my business, is me. Leave it to me, Victor. I'll reel him in.'

'I dunno, sweetheart, what if... ?'

Zara waved her hand. 'Look, I thought you said you could handle shit like this? My father trusted you, so what's the big deal?'

He stiffened. 'No, honestly, you can count on me. I just don't want anything to go wrong and you to get hurt.'

'Well, do you have any mates who you trust to come along? My father usually had a couple of men during a swap. Would you know who they are?'

Victor gave a resigned nod.

'Good. Well, that's settled, then. Meet me at the hangar at eight thirty.'

Victor kissed her cheek and left.

As soon as he was out of the door, she returned to her father's office and picked up the phone. She looked at the framed photograph of Izzy set above the mantelpiece and smiled wickedly.

***

Eric leaned back on his sofa with a bag of frozen peas pressed to his head. His eyes watered, the blow having been very hard. Zara's eyes had looked at him so fiercely he wouldn't forget that moment, not ever. It was not just the anger, there was so much disgust shown towards him.

Why couldn't she look at him the way she looked at Mike? The sound of a ringtone made him snap out of his thoughts.

It wasn't one he recognized. He removed the phone from his pocket and saw instantly that it wasn't his phone. Zara! He remembered now. He'd grabbed hers off the floor at her place. He thought about ignoring the call. But then something told him to answer it.

Perhaps it was her.

'Hello,' he answered eventually and somewhat dubiously.

Her voice was calm as she spoke. His heart was beating so fast, he wondered if she could hear it down the phone. He held his breath and listened. Although his head was still thumping from the clout, she'd given him, his shoulders finally relaxed. Just hearing those words that she'd forgiven him meant the world to him right now.

***

As Mike approached Kent, he called Staffie and gave him the low-down on Randy but was irritated by the bleeping sound until he realized it was another caller trying to get through. He ended the call and answered the unidentified caller. He quickly recognized the voice and before he'd a chance to talk he was told just to listen and listen very carefully. He didn't argue. Unexpectedly, his phone died. Damn! He wanted to check up on Ricky one more time. He had a full battery when he'd left the lock-up. He wondered if there was a problem with his Bluetooth connection. But then, what did he know about phones?

Once he reached the A20, he put his foot down, hoping that Randy was still okay after what Woodrow had told him. It was a wonder the lad's heart was even ticking. Staffie had mentioned that the boy was sweaty. He flew up West Kingsdown, along School Lane, and down into Knatts Valley. As soon as he entered the narrow lane and leaped from the car, the cold air hit him. The night was drawing in, and he hoped that Randy was fit enough for a trip to the hospital.

The moment Mike pushed the door open, Staffie clicked his gun. 'It's all right, Staff, it's me.' He scanned the large room and spied Dez out cold in the chair, still tied up. Randy was also laid out cold on an old leather sofa, which was against the far wall by the kitchenette.

'How's he doing?'

Willie jumped up. 'He'll live, the poor fucker. I've given him a spliff.'

Mike rolled his eyes. 'For fuck's sake, Willie, he's got something wrong with his heart.'

Willie screwed his face up. 'Yeah, so ya said. Look, I never gave him any cocaine. I just thought a joint might calm him down, sort of ease the pain a bit.'

Mike studied the lad. 'Ease the fucking pain? You've knocked him right out! Jesus... well, anyway, you and Staff, get him in the car and run him down to Darent Valley Hospital. Stick him in a wheelchair and leave him at A&E.' He looked back at Randy. 'I guess, if he comes to again, give him another spliff, knock him out, and then get back here. We've a little matter to take care of. 'Cos, see that cunt there?' He pointed to Dez. 'He was the spunky rat that hurt Ricky.'

'How the fuck d'ya know *that*?' asked Staffie.

''Cos his own brother told me. And another thing, lads. I've just had a big tip-off. I think we're gonna be rubbing our hands together tonight. So, let's get our arses into gear. We've some serious fucking work to do and not much time either. Staffie, give us ya phone. My poxy thing's died. I need to make a call.'

Staffie rolled his eyes and threw his phone over to Mike.

Willie grinned from one ugly ear to the other; he loved that cheeky look on Mike's face. It only meant one thing – they were back in business.

***

Neil leaned across the bar. 'Antonio, you can relax, mate. The lunchtime punters are all gone. See, no trouble. Now, pour yourself a stiff drink and also me one, while you're at it.'

Antonio sighed wearily. 'This is all getting too much for me.'

As he poured two tumblers of Irish whiskey, Shamus strolled over. 'One for me?'

With another sigh, Antonio took another glass off the shelf and poured a generous measure.

From across the room came Tiffany's upbeat voice. 'What are ya celebrating?'

Neil winked. 'Aah nothing much, yer know. But we've had a great day's work, so why don't yer come and join us?'

Just as Tiffany was about to fold her pinny, Neil's phone rang. He frowned at the number and found a more private spot away from the bar to take the call.

Both Shamus and Tiffany watched the change in expression on Neil's face. They waited for him to return.

'Everything all right, mate?' asked Shamus.

Neil shook his head and looked at Tiffany. 'Right, Antonio, lock up and get off home. Tiff, I'm gonna drive you home. Shamus, are yer loaded?'

Shamus nodded and tapped the butt of his gun, which was held secure at the back of his trousers. 'Aye, that I am.'

'Er, what's going on?' questioned Tiffany, her eyes wide and curious.

Neil smiled. 'Nothing, sweetheart, for yer to concern yerself with. It's just safer if I drop yer home.'

'I can walk, you know. I'm okay.'

Neil shook his head. 'Nah, babe, I'd feel so much better knowing you're all right, that I would.' He brushed her cheek with his hand, making her blush. 'Look, I'll tell yer what. You get in the car with us, and I'll explain everything on the way.'

Tiffany's eyes sparkled. 'Well, if you're sure?'

Neil gave her a wide grin. 'Yes, I'm sure, darlin', that I am.'

CHAPTER TWENTY

Zara drank two strong cups of coffee, having drunk too much brandy earlier. She wasn't used to it, and tonight she had to be clear-headed. As much as she thought she was in control, she still trembled. She looked around her father's bedroom and smiled to herself. He loved his hideaways, and he should have been an architect. The tall cabinet, which stood alongside his wardrobes, had a false front on it. For a moment, she wondered if Ismail had known about that hiding place too. As she pressed the far-right corner of the top panel, it unleashed the lock and popped open sufficiently for her to reveal another secret storage place. She sighed. There on a hanger was her father's bulletproof vest and behind it there was a smaller one. Just once, she recalled, she wore it when she was a teenager. He'd had it made specially for her. A pang of sadness crept over her when she thought back to the day she'd worn it. He was at war with someone, and she was unsafe. He was terrified that the firm who had tried to take him down would hurt her. That was the day he sent her away. She begged and pleaded, but she remembered his words to her: 'Zara, you will get me killed, if I'm worrying about you. I will take my eye off the ball, and that will be the end of me.' So, of course, she acquiesced. Her father was the love of her life.

Her heart was broken that day because she couldn't even tell Mike where she was going; in fact, she couldn't even tell him she was leaving the country.

She pulled the jacket from the hanger and held it to her face. The smell reminded her of Mike, the pain, and the empty feeling she'd felt that day – from the fear of her father being killed and the dread of her unborn child being hurt. She'd planned to tell Mike that evening. She'd been so excited, so full of dreams of hope and happiness. They'd hidden their relationship from Izzy, or at least had tried to. As it turned out, it hadn't done much good. Later, much later in her life, Izzy admitted he'd known about their affair all along.

A sudden hot tear pricked her eyelids. Her little boy, her precious baby, had never even met Mike. He'd died of a heart condition. She felt the chain around her neck on which hung the tiny ring and the cross. She was Jewish, and, really, wearing the cross was forbidden, yet it was the nurse who had given it to her the day little Michael had passed away, and she couldn't bear to take it off. Instead, she had slipped her son's ring on the same chain.

The bulletproof vest still fitted perfectly snug under her top. With a thick coat, no one would even guess she was wearing it. Not that it would stop her from getting killed by a bullet through the head, though. She looked down at the wooden cases below and pulled out two handguns. She shoved one into her waistband under her jacket and tucked one in her boot. She tried to walk but it felt awkward, and the boot looked bulky. Deciding to swap the second gun for a knife, she replaced the false front and closed the cabinet door. She then looked in the mirror. The vest didn't show, and her right boot hid the knife sufficiently.

She took one last look around her father's bedroom. 'Oh, Dad, if you can hear me, send me good luck. I think I just might need it.'

As she opened the front door, she felt the cold air hit her face. Winter was definitely on its way. The sky was dark, and yet she felt so alive; perhaps it was fear or excitement, but either way, she was charged up on adrenaline and ready for the fray.

Her Range Rover was kept out of view beyond the four-car garage. She marched across the gravel drive before she took one last look around and then she hurried behind the garage and opened the car door. It was freezing inside, so she turned on the heaters and waited for the windows to clear. With her new leather gloves covering her hand and the prosthetic, she gripped the wheel and pulled away. There was only one road to her house, so she was safe in the knowledge that no one was following her. She paused at the end of the long drive and looked right carefully, studying the passing points along the narrow lane. It was clear there were no cars waiting, except for an old banger that had been dumped at the side of the road. No one was inside, so she knew she wasn't being watched. She had her hair in a ponytail, her hair now being long enough to do so, and with a pair of night driving glasses on, she thought that it was very unlikely anyone would recognize her. To ease her nerves, she put the radio on, and to her delight, Alicia Keys was singing 'Girl on Fire'. *How apt*, she thought, as she sang along to the words. The beat and the lyrics boosted her conviction that she was in the right frame of mind for what lay ahead. That was until the song came to an end, and a sudden icy feeling crept over her body. The lane was pitch-black, but her powerful headlights guided the way.

As a young woman, she would have been tingling with excitement at this point. Sat next to her father and off to their special place, the hangar still held so many beautiful memories and secrets. It was an extraordinary piece of architecture, a cleverly designed building, built by a genius – Izzy Ezra. Still, it was hers, with all its secrets.

She could see the entrance to the hangar up ahead. The most important night of her life was about to begin – there was no going back now.

When she'd visited the building a few days before, she discovered that her brother had sold her father's favourite plane. However, Ismail hadn't known about a very important piece of engineering inside the building itself. Only a select few knew, including Staffie, Willie, Lou, and her cousin.

As she approached the private lane that ran past the hangar, she turned her headlights off. Zara could drive along that lane with her eyes shut, she knew it so well. As soon as she was halfway, she stopped the car, pulled out her binoculars, and watched, but there was no sign of any activity, not even a light from a phone screen or a cigarette. Good. She would just wait awhile and monitor the situation.

***

After the disturbing phone call, Conrad rushed into his car and headed straight to his sister's place. The last few weeks had been exhausting, and now that phone call; he just hoped it wasn't the straw that broke the camel's back. He frowned when he arrived. Rebecca's car wasn't in the drive. 'What's she bloody well playing at?' he mumbled under his breath. Still, he parked in the street, walked up the drive, and was about to knock when the door opened.

She didn't welcome him in but turned on her heel and headed for the kitchen.

Conrad followed. 'Right, what's going on?'

'Coffee, Conrad, or something stronger?'

'Coffee's fine, so do you want to tell me what all this is about, or do I have to play guessing games?'

She handed him a coffee and gestured for him to take a seat at the breakfast bar. 'Oh, Conrad, where do I start? There is something very strange going on. Alastair... '

Conrad's phone rang. It was Lowry. 'Sorry, Rebecca, it's work.'

She tutted. 'For God's sake, can't you listen to me for five minutes? This is much more important than bloody work.'

The harsh and firm pitch to her voice made Conrad look up. 'Sorry, you're right, of course.' He cancelled the connection, feeling rather guilty.

'Yes, it's Alastair. I think... '

Conrad's phone rang again.

'Turn the bloody thing off for a minute, will you?'

His finger hovered over the Off key, undecided, but as he looked at the fraught expression on his sister's face, he decided to do as she asked. They'd all been through a lot, and now she wanted his attention, he would be all ears.

'Sorry, Rebecca, what were you saying? Something about Alastair, wasn't it?'

'Alastair's gone missing. He won't answer his phone, and Lance was here—'

'Lance? What the hell for?'

Rebecca knew that her brother had every reason for being sceptical of Lance, but he'd never divulged his concerns to her. She knew it was to do with work.

'He wanted to know where Alastair and Poppy were.'

Conrad's eyes narrowed. 'What the blazes has Alastair or Poppy got to do with him?'

'Well… he—'

She was on the point of replying when the sound of car doors slamming and a loud bang at the door interrupted her.

'What the hell's going on?' asked Conrad, as he stepped down from the bar stool.

'Police! Open up!' came a deep voice.

Conrad and Rebecca both gazed at each other, totally dumbfounded.

As Conrad headed for the door, Rebecca was hard on his heels. However, on opening it, he gasped in utter shock. Two policemen, one with paperwork in his hand, looked grimly at Rebecca and Conrad. But that wasn't the issue. It was the sea of reporters, microphones, and TV cameras behind them, ready to make the most of this heaven-sent opportunity to claim the scalp of the local MP.

'Sorry, sir. Would you step aside? We've a warrant to enter these premises and to arrest Mrs Rebecca Mullins for failing to stop and report an accident.'

'What? Don't be so ridiculous.'

'Sir, her neighbour across the road has presented us with his camera footage of Mrs Mullins knocking down a young woman in this road a few days ago and driving away without stopping.'

Conrad turned to face his sister. 'What the hell are they talking about?'

She didn't have a chance to answer before a reporter started snapping away. 'Is it true, Mrs Mullins, you drove away from the scene of an accident? Were you drinking that evening? Do you know who you knocked down?'

The barrage of questions left Rebecca speechless.

The officer held up his warrant. 'We need to look at your car, madam.'

'Rebecca, is this true?'

His sister's face was whiter than white, and the look in her eyes said it all.

'Jesus, what the hell have you bloody *done*?'

Before Rebecca could answer, a car came tearing along the road and stopped next to the police vehicles. It was Lowry. He was out of breath and flapping. 'Sir, I've been trying to call you.'

Conrad's expression of disgust at his sister's incompetence was written all over his face, and he shook his head. 'You stupid, stupid woman.' He looked at the officer. 'Was the woman killed?'

The officer shook his head. 'No, sir. Details, however, are sketchy. The woman in question absconded from the hospital. All we know is she is roughly in her late teens, with blonde hair and blue eyes. And the nurse removed a gold necklace with a squirrel on it from the injured woman. Other than that, sir, we don't know who she is.'

Conrad felt as though a cold spear of ice had hit him in the chest. It was obvious who the injured woman was. Assuming it was true, then it was unforgivable.

'Commissioner, did you know about this? And do you intend to cover this up?' asked one of the reporters.

Conrad sighed. 'No. I do not intend to cover this up at all.

If Mrs Mullins is guilty of a hit-and-run, then she will have to pay the consequences, like anyone else.'

A police officer stepped out of the garage and nodded to the arresting officer, confirming that there was evidence of damage to the front passenger wing of Rebecca's car, suggesting she had been involved in an accident.

Rebecca watched as her brother walked away. He didn't even look back to see her being read her rights.

CHAPTER TWENTY-ONE

Satisfied with what she'd seen, Zara started the engine again and slowly crept along with her lights off. As soon as she arrived in front of the hangar, she smiled. The floodlights were deactivated; no one had turned them back on. The shutters were open. It was another bright idea thought up by her father. No one would ever suspect that this vast building would have steel shutters that could instantaneously reach the floor by using a remote device. She'd only seen it happen once when she was younger; the loud bang as the shutters hit the concrete base had almost made her jump out of her skin. She fingered the remote control hidden under her gloved prosthetic hand, her body trembling with nervous excitement.

As soon as she stepped out of the car, she felt the cold, damp air hit the back of her throat. She shivered and zipped up her padded jacket. She liked how it looked on her, although it was just an illusion. It was fitted but had an even padding all over it, making her appear two sizes bigger, and yet sufficient for hiding the bulletproof vest. She just prayed that if she did get shot, it would be in the chest. She knew it would hurt because although the vest should prevent her from being killed, the impact alone would probably knock her clean off her feet.

The small room to the side door of the building contained the toilets. As Zara's eyes were adjusting to the darkness, she managed to find the handle and squeezed inside. Then she pulled her phone from her pocket. She had to hide any light just for the moment in case she was being watched. She looked at the time – it was now eight o'clock. Her hand shook, and her heart was punching her in the chest. *Get a grip*, *Zara*, she told herself. Victor should be here in thirty minutes. She wouldn't be alone.

As her body moved rhythmically, with each forceful pump of her blood pulsing around her body, she went over and over in her mind every move she would make. Yet she couldn't be 100 per cent sure that the man she believed to be the Governor would turn up. The two voices in her head were at it again: one was cautioning her by saying *What if?*, the other was saying *Greed is a prime motivator*. Suddenly, the text came through; it was the one message she was hoping for. Joshua was on his way, so the deal was going ahead. She waited silently, listening with her ears pricked, but there was not a sound.

For half an hour, she waited patiently, praying that Victor would get here soon. She'd remembered telling him that Joshua would arrive at nine o'clock, so she needed Victor here by eight thirty. He had to be here before Joshua, or she would be on her own. She looked at the phone again; it was now ten to nine. 'Come on, Victor. Hurry up, please,' she whispered.

Then she heard a car.

She crept out from the toilet and hid behind a steel pillar and looked to see who it was. Christ, it was Joshua. He'd arrived early. Damn! 'Now, Victor, where are you?' she whispered again.

She watched as the silver BMW reversed into her hangar and stopped. She thought he'd clocked her before she'd taken up a position behind the girder. Shaking now from head to toe, she took a deep breath. She needed to pull herself together; this was ridiculous, and yet the stories she'd heard about this evil, sadistic bastard that everyone called the Governor plagued her mind.

Worst of all, he was expected to be in her company – right under her nose.

She looked on as the tall, solidly built man stepped out of the car. Even in the dark, she could see he was striking, in his long black coat and with his dark hair combed back. She studied him as he pulled on a pair of black leather gloves, straightened his coat, and walked with long strides to the back of his car.

'I can see you, Zara!'

She stepped out from behind the girder and looked him over. His upright and thickset frame was new, but because she hadn't seen him for so long, she guessed he would have changed over the years. She smiled to herself at how solid and confident he was now.

'You're early, Josh.'

'It doesn't matter. I have everything in place.'

She looked across the field, praying that Victor would arrive soon.

Then her shoulders relaxed; for there, across the field, were headlights. But then she frowned at the speed of the vehicle and wondered what was going on. Victor drove a taxi. Black taxis couldn't reach the speed of that car. As it got closer, she realized her instincts were right. It wasn't a taxi but a black BMW 7 Series, although it was hard to see who was inside.

Joshua stepped from behind his car when he heard the sound of the approaching vehicle. 'Who the fuck is *that*?'

Sliding his hand into his coat pocket, he gripped his gun. 'Zara?'

She shot a look his way. 'I don't *fucking* know.'

Zara was straining to see who was in that car, praying it was Victor. The vehicle came to a halt, right in front of the hangar, and, to her relief, the first man out of the BMW was indeed Victor.

Unlike the gentle taxi driver she'd met on the Old Kent Road, Victor looked so different; he appeared so much younger, fitter, and ready for business. 'Hello, Zara. Sorry I'm late.' He looked towards Joshua and blinked. All he could see was a dark figure, as his eyes hadn't adjusted to the darkness.

'I take it, then, you're Victor, and you're here to ensure the exchange of merchandise takes place properly, as agreed by Zara?'

Victor squinted at the man, still trying to see his face. 'Yeah, that's right.'

At that moment, the rear passenger doors of Victor's car opened and out climbed two other men. Zara felt her body quiver; they were big guys with broad shoulders and short hair. At first, she frowned at Victor, before remembering that she'd asked him to bring along some heavies.

'They're my lads. You said you wanted some muscle.' He looked at Joshua. 'Just a precaution, you understand?'

Joshua nodded. 'It won't be necessary, but, Zara, if it gives you piece of mind, the more the merrier. You see, I'm hoping to continue our business. Let's hope for a long and fruitful relationship.'

Zara loved the way he spoke; it was soft and warming. 'Right. Let's get on with it!'

As if someone had waved a magic wand, she felt her heart rate slow down and her muscles relax. She was now in charge. Let the fun begin!

The bang as the shutters hit the floor made everyone jump – but not her. Now they were all in total darkness.

Victor shouted, 'Zara, what's going on? What's fucking happened?'

A sudden whirring sound could be heard as the back wall, which was her father's genius of an idea, began to move across and open up part of the room to the rear of the building. The secret hidden room. No one could imagine what the hell was going on except Zara; she knew every footstep, every move, because she was the co-mastermind behind it. Instantly, the lights came on, almost blinding everyone with their brightness. She stood behind the steel girder, hoping her plan of having her men hidden behind the secret wall would fall into place with no one getting hurt. Sure enough, after scuffles and the sound of guns being cocked, there was silence. She stepped away from the pillar, content that the Governor was secured.

All eyes were on her as she stood there confidently as the woman behind the firms. There was an uneasy quietness in the building as her captives – now in shock – tried to take it all in. Mike, Staffie, and Willie stood like stone statues, their guns aimed at their adversaries. Tonight was all about closure – the so-called Governor was to be terminated, once and for all.

Mike looked across at Zara for direction. He tried not to be distracted by her presence. It was as if she had stepped off the cover of *Vogue* magazine. With her hair pulled back from her face, her long, sleek neck holding her head high, and her lips coated in a subtle shade of pink lipstick, she grinned wickedly.

She was really enjoying this, the earlier nerves now a thing of the past. Her lips turned into a self-assured smirk, as she said, 'Let me introduce myself. *I* am the fucking Governor.'

Mike couldn't take his eyes off her. She was everything he'd ever wanted in a woman, and now there she was putting them all to shame – a feisty, clever lady, who no one should ever have underestimated. His mother's words went through his head: 'She is stronger than you think.' She was right, although he would never have believed it. Standing there with her feet apart, facing them like the Devil's daughter, there was not even a flicker of fear in her eyes. He watched as Joshua moved by her side, sliding his hand around her shoulders. He planted a gentle kiss on her cheek. Mike would have given anything to swap places with that man, just to smell her skin, but it was too late. He knew he'd fucked up. It was over.

She looked over at Mike's men and wanted to laugh. They hadn't changed at all, really. Despite their age, they still looked as tough as any youngster. Then her eyes went to Victor. She stared, hugely enjoying the fury on his face and studying the angry red eyes that seemed to bulge from his head. Sweat had gathered on his brow. His determination to break free and tear into her was like watching a caged tiger, frustrated and going out of its mind with pent-up rage.

She smiled mockingly, and then she looked at the two men held captive by his side. The one with a tattoo on his neck and across his chunky knuckles, to the right of Victor, seemed fearful. His round blue eyes were identical to Victor's, yet they held a look of terror not anger. The man to Victor's left was different. There was no show of emotion, no anger, no fear, no frustration but just a level-headed poker-faced soul. As she locked eyes with him, she could almost taste the evil he possessed. He was no doubt a psychopath. She remembered the saying about the Devil – that he always posed as someone beautiful on the outside. How strange then because this man was indeed very handsome, his tanned skin and soft eyes giving one the impression that he could easily disarm you with his good looks. Behind those pursed lips, she could only guess he had a set of pure white teeth to go with his carefully groomed face. Not even an eyebrow was dishevelled.

Her eyes flicked back to Victor as he tried to struggle, but Willie held his diver's knife against the man's throat.

'Don't kill him, Willie!' demanded Zara. 'Staffie, please would you have my guests seated?'

Staffie nodded and pushed himself away from the wall and walked to the back room. Everyone remained quiet, not moving. The atmosphere was so heavily and bizarrely charged, they could have created an electric storm of their own making.

Staffie brought over chairs, placing them behind Victor and his two sidekicks, while Joshua casually walked over and collected the three guns that the captives had been forced to drop. Then Mike, Staffie, and Willie tied the men to their seats.

Victor and his men were bound so securely they could hardly breathe, and to their obvious annoyance, gags were stuffed into their mouths. Zara couldn't resist giving them a wink as they sat there in complete and utter humiliation.

Willie bent down and whispered into Victor's ear, 'Nice to meet ya, Hannibal Lecter.'

Once their captives were secured and entirely defenceless,

Mike, Staffie, and Willie stepped away. Willie took the opportunity to snort a line of cocaine, while Staffie lit up a cigarette and Mike went over to the kitchenette area and put the kettle on.

Along with the other two men, Victor watched with frightened intrigue. He likened it to a film set. Zara, the director, clearly knew the script, but he and his men were sitting there effectively blind.

Victor's eyes followed Mike Regan around the room. He was the dangerous one. Victor speculated on his form of torture – he knew it would end like this. A concoction of boiling water and sugar, for example, was excruciatingly painful. He should know; he had used that method on more than one occasion. Staffie nonchalantly approached one of the tall metal toolboxes and opened the bottom drawer, the largest of them all. The clanking of metal as the man moved heavy tools around had Victor's stomach turning over. He fidgeted in terror.

Joshua returned to his position next to Zara. That was when Victor glared in recognition. Joshua wasn't a dealer, a stranger – this was Joshua Ezra, Izzy's beloved nephew.

Zara noticed how Victor was unravelling the events in his mind. 'Is that the so-called Governor, Joshua?'

'Yes, that's him, Zara.'

She smiled and then instantly wiped the smile from her face and pulled from her pocket the little ledger and threw it on the floor. It slid across the concrete and stopped directly at Victor's feet.

'I must say, that little stunt was ingenious. I am impressed, *Torvic*!'

Torvic's eyes widened. It was over; she knew who he really was.

437

'You may have thought you would get away with it, and I'm sure if this drugs deal was real, you would've taken the drugs and the money and probably killed me. I suppose in your sick, warped mind you were just marinating me ready for the oven. Slowly, but surely, you thought you would gain my utmost trust and turn me against my men, against the Regans, and anyone who really cared about me.'

The look on his face told her she was right.

'You hoped to brainwash me into believing that you had my back, that I couldn't survive without you, while you picked and clawed away at my business and my money, but, most of all, my name and that of my father.' She sighed aloud. 'You tried it once before, but you were younger then and yet so was my father. However, I will admit he was stronger than me, he knew what you were up to, and he knew how low you would stoop, so he sent me away.' She laughed. 'I bet you never thought I would ever come back and take over, though, did you? That must have been one hell of a shock for you, huh?'

Torvic's brain was desperately trying to work out how she'd managed to find out so much, but he didn't fight the gag to speak. He'd no choice but to remain motionless and let her continue, since she was on a roll.

'My father told me how smart you were. Only one other person ever got to see your face and that was my cousin Joshua. I guess you assumed he was too young to remember, but a kid doesn't forget a face like yours when he witnesses the violent act you committed. You poisoned my mother, you evil cunt. It was Josh who saw you doing it.'

She looked down at the ledger and shook her head. 'Yeah, you nearly had me fooled. But ya know what? I think someone was watching over me the other day. You see, my book opened to a particular page, and there, as the light streamed in, I could see your phone number, but I could also see another number rubbed out. You knew about my father's office, his secret box, the ledger, and you watched me.'

Mike felt his chest swell at the thought that this evil bastard, who was the reason she was sent away, had been secretly watching her. He wanted to rip Torvic's head off his shoulders there and then, but she had warned him to stay back and just do as she said. After all they had gone through, he would do exactly as she asked; he owed her that much at least.

'But, Torvic, I had my suspicions about you when your accent changed. You're a master of language, I'm guessing. You see, you started off by talking like a real old East End taxi driver, but once you were comfortable in my presence, your accent changed a little. I didn't hear the Russian, but your cockney banter disappeared. I found it hard to imagine that you were once a sniper in the army, a dangerous ninja, as my father described you. In fact, you fucked up when you said this morning that you were the Machinist because the real sniper is called the Machine. In fact, he is just how I imagined him to be, which, Torvic, is the complete fucking opposite of you. Oh, and by the way, he wants to meet you, to tick you off his bucket list.'

Torvic squirmed. The realization hit him hard like a rabbit punch to the stomach; he was going to die – probably a horrific death too. He turned his head to his eldest son who was paralysed like a deer caught in the headlights. Eyes glued to the woman, he looked traumatized. Annoyance pricked him. His son should be harder, not sitting there looking afraid. He'd instilled into them his mantra: 'Show no fear, Son, until the very end. In that way, you show people what you are made of.' He turned his head to his youngest son, the apple of his eye. The sleek, clever, and perilous one. The son he was most proud of. The one who would have taken over his business once he'd taken control of all the manors. There was no expression on his face; he still appeared cool and calm like a praying mantis, just there watching and listening, with no sweat on his brow, no trembling of his hands, but just a dead soul – exactly how Torvic liked him.

The sound of heavy footsteps approaching pulled Torvic's gaze away from his son to face the man who owned those boots. He looked up to find a colossus with deep brooding eyes and a heavy brow that knotted together in anger. If there was such a thing as the Devil, Torvic was now coldly staring at his face.

'Meet the Machine, the real McCoy!' said Zara.

For the first time, Torvic's youngest son showed a reaction. Torvic could sense his son's breathing increase; he turned his head to see his nostrils flaring, his face redden, and his eyes protrude.

Torvic wasn't surprised or even shocked as to who the real holder of this name was; he knew all along and so did his sons.

'The day of reckoning has finally arrived, Alastair,' said Lance, with a deep, gruff voice. 'There is only one thing I can thank you for, and that is fucking my ex-wife. You suited each other perfectly. You're a cunt and she's a bitch. But there's only one fucking cunting thing I want to know!' His breathing was noisy as his anger increased. 'Which one of you killed my daughter?'

'Willie, would you remove their gags, please!' ordered Zara.

Lance stood towering over them like a bear ready to bite their heads off, but he stepped back when he saw Willie Ritz, the nutcase, appear, wielding his diver's knife. The man was too reckless to get in his way when he had that tool in his hand.

'With pleasure, Zara!' Willie laughed, with his madman's high-pitched chuckle.

Alastair was the first to have his gag cut loose, but the blade didn't just slice the fabric, it sliced a deep line down Alastair's cheek. He didn't scream – he merely flinched slightly.

Zara raised her brow; the man was harder than she'd given him credit for.

'Who killed Kendall?' bellowed Lance.

Without even blinking, Alastair curled his lip and glared in silence.

'I *said*, who killed her?'

Alastair wasn't going to back down; he remained stony-faced as if he was getting a kick out of winding Lance up. But he knew it would be Lance who would have the last laugh. Alastair wasn't stupid. He knew there was no way he was getting out of this alive. But he was adamant he would go down with a smile on his face.

'You cunt. It was *you*! You raped my daughter, 'cos you wanted her for yourself. I knew she wanted out of that house for no other reason than she couldn't stand you. Kendall could handle Rebecca, but you ogling my daughter was just a step away from you touching her. I fucking knew it was you, all along.'

A small laugh escaped Alastair's lips. 'But she wasn't your daughter, Lance.'

Lance was on the point of laying into him, but Willie grabbed Lance first. 'Easy, mate. He'll talk. Trust my girl here. When she gets started on him, he'll sing like Susan Boyle on crack.'

Lance received an arrogant smirk from Alastair, but instead of going for him again, Lance turned his head away. He needed to be bigger than the other man – to stay in control and not kill him stone-dead.

'Willie, cut Torvic's gag and try not to fuck his face up. I think I would like to do that myself.'

Willie, now in his element, couldn't contain himself. 'It's not ladylike, babe.'

She nodded in a cold, controlled fashion. 'Oh, I know, Willie, but shit happens!'

Willie chuckled again and removed the gag, leaving just a minor graze. Torvic couldn't get the words out quickly enough.

'You fucking stupid fool. You think you could ever step into that prick Izzy's shoes? Dream on, lady! He may have run me out of the country once, but that was a big mistake. The manor wasn't his to run, it was mine. And whether you like it or not, you'll never take control.' He looked around the room. 'The Regans are history. You'll all fall flat on your faces. You should've listened to me. I would've helped you to build a fucking empire,' screamed Torvic.

'I would never have worked with the likes of you. I may never be able to walk in my father's shoes, but the one thing I will always do is to follow in his footsteps and play by the rules.'

Torvic let out a deep, harsh, and forceful laugh. 'Rules? Are you delusional or what? There *are* no rules, you silly bitch.

There is *no* honour among thieves. And there is no such thing as live by the sword or die by the sword. We write our own rules, lady, and that's where you've fallen down. You're weak, feeble, and sentimental. You said to me once that if you ever came face-to-face with the Governor, you would stoop to his level.' He laughed again. 'You haven't got it in you, have you? You said the Governor had written his own rule book, and you, ya stupid cunt, said you would break every one of them. Play me! Me! At my own game? The only game you could fucking play is snakes and ladders.'

Zara stayed motionless, not even flinching, as he ranted.

'Oh, I don't say things lightly, I meant every word of them. Beside you are your two precious sons, and you, Torvic, will kill them. You see, you might think that by terrorizing innocent families and killing innocent people they were expendable, a necessary means to an end. And you might believe that I couldn't stoop any lower. You are probably thinking that I haven't the guts to match your game, but ya see, old-timer, I can stoop just that one unbearable step lower.'

Torvic suddenly went quiet. His face paled over, and his eyes filled up. No way. There was only one move she could make that would be lower than what he'd ever done. He held his breath, praying he was wrong.

'Mike, you wanted answers. Do you want to take over for a bit? I need a coffee.'

Mike watched her in admiration. She was ruthless, the Devil's daughter, but he loved her with every bone in his body. 'Yes, Boss.'

The tables had been turned; never in his wildest dreams would he have ever thought he'd call the love of his life 'Boss'.

Over the years, they'd grappled over power in an affectionate way. It had been a real tug of war; but tonight, she'd shown her worth, and he had to respect the woman.

He stormed into the backroom and practically dragged the almost dead weight and threw him on the floor in front of Alastair.

Torvic sighed with relief. His worst fears were misplaced if Dez was the best they could do. He wanted to laugh. He had no affection for the man; he was just another foot soldier hooked on Flakka and eager to please. His eldest son, Stephan, suddenly came out of his shock and looked down at the bloodied mess in front of him as Dez writhed around the floor in agony. The blood-soaked jeans and anguish on his face made Stephan almost faint with nerves.

Mike kicked Dez in the back. 'Look up, you piece of shit!'

Dez gasped for air as the kick had severely winded him.

'Which one of these cunts helped you to batter my son?'

Dez didn't even attempt to lie or argue. Straightaway, he pointed to Alastair. 'Him. He did!' he cried.

'Are you fucking sure?'

Dez curled in a ball. 'Yes, yes, it was him. I didn't want to hurt the girl. I only wanted to give your son a beating. I never thought it would go that far. Please, I'm begging you. No more.'

Lance was balling his fists, trying desperately hard to hold his temper. The anger was at boiling point. With flared nostrils, he turned to Zara, who'd just reappeared with a cup of coffee in her hand. 'Are you done now?'

She shook her head. 'Wait, Lance. I'm a woman who stays true to her word. I promised Torvic that I would stoop lower than him. That's going to happen. Now!'

Torvic closed his eyes, afraid to hear another word. The thought of what she'd planned ripped the heart right out of him. He knew what was coming, and he knew he would rather die a thousand horrific deaths than face her wrath.

'Neil!' she called out. 'Bring her in!'

That was it. Torvic felt a pain that only death could stop.

He had to open his eyes, he had to see, although he knew it would totally break his heart.

From behind the door, Neil and Shamus appeared, holding a woman between them. Tiffany, his treasured granddaughter, she was the only person alive who he would die for. His sweet little angel, who he used to tuck up in bed, who he watched grow into a beautiful woman. She was the child who was tougher than both his two sons together. His eyes met hers, and he trembled as he witnessed the fear on her little face. A face that was pleading for help. Her eyes, soaked in tears, had turned down at the silent pleading. Her round white face and her pretty heart-shaped purple lips were bursting through the gag. The cloth shoved in her mouth may have stopped the words, but he knew she was begging him to help her. He had always supported her. She called him her guardian angel. Yet she wanted to be like him and run the firm. She loved the excitement, the exhilaration, and for a woman, she was strong. He pushed her time and time again to see how far she would go and how much she could handle. He was proud. He once watched her plunge a knife into his runner who disobeyed him. She didn't flinch when she threw the acid and watched the skin peel from the woman's face. In fact, she threw another load on her just to hear the blood-curdling screams. His Mighty Mouse, he called her. She listened, and she learned, and she did as she was told.

Stephan, her father, wasn't as strong as Tiffany; he may have been her flesh and blood, but he was pathetic in comparison.

'Oh God, no. Please! Don't hurt her. You can kill us but spare her. She never hurt you or anyone!'

Zara began pacing the floor. 'I must admit you have a clever little granddaughter… but she's not intelligent enough to out-smart me. You see, Torvic, something disturbed me immensely when she was held at knifepoint. Oh yes, the attack was defi-nitely the actions of this so-called Governor, and, for a moment, I thought it really was Eric. The thing is, though, while you made out a strong case for me to believe Eric was involved in all this shit, I could never believe in my heart that he'd really hurt a woman. And he certainly wouldn't hold a knife to a young girl's throat.'

Mike watched and was saddened to think that it had ever crossed Zara's mind that his brother would do something as callous as that. As much as he was fed up with his brother's antics, he still knew the man's level, and hurting girls wasn't in his blood. He was just relieved that Zara had come to her senses before it was too late – she could have cut more than Eric's wrist.

Zara took another sip of coffee before she continued. 'So, I was puzzled by Tiffany's detailed knowledge of the person she described. It was a bit like the TV programme *Through The Keyhole*. The clues were painstakingly obvious. It was almost as if she was handing me the evidence on a plate. But then I thought about things. If a man suddenly grabbed me in the street in the dark, with a knife at my throat, I wouldn't be taking much notice of his aftershave, or the bandage on his wrist, or the gold ring on his little finger, would I? You see,

Tiffany fucked up. She was so eager to give me such a detailed description, it was just too rehearsed. Imagine a young woman having a blade under her chin. Now would she even be able to look at the perpetrator's wrist and their little finger? And would she *honestly* be able to tell you what type of aftershave the villain was using? You can't kid a kidder as they say, and I'm afraid the girl chose the wrong person to try that stunt.'

'Yeah, look, please, I did put her up to it. It was me, it was all me. She never hurt anyone. Please let her go. Kill me, but just let her go!' Torvic begged.

Zara took one last sip of her coffee and placed the empty cup on the draining board.

'Are you sure about that, Torvic? Your sweet, innocent little granddaughter, a law-abiding citizen who wouldn't hurt a fly? 'Cos, I know different. She threw acid on a woman. She destroyed her pretty face.'

Torvic gasped. 'No. That wasn't her, that was me. She didn't do it!'

Zara laughed. 'Oh, fuck off, Torvic. Mike told me about the police report, a woman fitting your granddaughter's description, who poured acid over that innocent woman's face.' She sneered. 'Accept it – you taught her everything she knows.'

'No, I swear. She's not like that. She's a kid. Look at her, for Christ's sake.'

Zara turned and faced the young woman. 'Hmm, she looks over twenty-one to me, which, to my eye, makes her a woman, doesn't it? Like me, eh?'

Torvic shook his head. 'No, she's not like you. Please, she's… '

Zara laughed. 'Yeah, I know, she's how my father saw *me*,

his precious child. But, hey-ho, life's a fucking bitch, and then you die.'

'What do you want from me?'

Lance was now growling under his breath like a vicious dog. 'Enough, Zara. I'm gonna kill 'em!'

Mike pulled him back. 'Hang on, Lance. I have as much right as you.'

Lance turned and faced Mike dead on. He poked his finger in Mike's chest. 'Don't you fucking tell me you have as much right as me. Remember this: your son survived, but my daughter didn't, did she?'

Torvic was watching, praying that a fight ensued between the two most prominent men in the room. It was his only chance of fucking up Zara's plans.

Mike stepped back and hung his head. 'Ya know what? You're right, mate. I'm sorry, buddy, really sorry.'

Mike's altered stance, the change in his body language, and especially his soft, compassionate words produced the desired effect. Lance backed off.

Alastair, as cold and emotionless as he was, was unnerved by seeing his niece in fear for her life and by the mess Mike had made of Dez. It was a salutary moment; it was time to take stock of his situation – his life. For once, he didn't feel invincible. Life had been good to him. He knew his exceptional looks, smart clothes, and the way he spoke, set him miles apart from the double life he'd led. Now he realized that things looked decidedly ugly for him.

Sleeping with Lance's wife, he'd enjoyed outwitting one of the country's most valued assets in the SAS. Yet once Lance had fucked off out of the army and out of Rebecca's life, he was able to plan for the future – his future. He realized that Rebecca was good for business – an MP he could manipulate to reduce the police budget and to enable him to run a drugs business more efficiently. All he had to do was bite the bullet and shag the ugly bitch every so often. He had to hand it to Lance, though. He was a perceptive bastard.

Although he suspected Kendall had never voiced to Lance his own carnal desires for her, she knew he liked her, and she was very aware that her scornful looks and piss-taking smirks had riled him up. His obsession for her was probably why she'd wanted to leave home, but he couldn't bear it. After all, he was used to getting what he wanted.

Alastair looked over at Lance, who appeared to have expanded like one of those building foams in a matter of minutes. The man's shoulders seemed huge, and his chest was like a gorilla's. Maybe a sudden whoosh of fear was making himself see things out of perspective. This was new; he'd never felt fear in his whole life. Everything was always on an even keel; a rush of adrenaline was alien to him. He looked at his father, who was showing every emotion under the sun. Again, it was unnatural to him. His father had once told him that he was the epitome of a psychopath, and somewhere in the same sentence, he'd said he was proud. Yet looking at Dez reeling in such agony did something to him. He thought maybe it was because of the fact that he hadn't inflicted the pain. For when he watched his victims writhing around, he got such a kick out of it.

Stephan's head bobbed up and down as he shook all over. What disturbed him the most was this whole set-up. The partition wall half-opened, with men making an appearance as if

Zara was a host on *This Is Your Life*, was scary to say the least. His eyes looked to his left, to see if there was anyone else about to turn up. Had she rounded up all their enemies to put on some display to make it clear that she was the boss – that she was the bitch from hell, who won every turf war?

As if Zara could read his mind, she called out, 'Eric, can you bring me the acid, please?' She turned to Torvic. 'A nice try, old man. It was lucky I came to my senses before I actually killed Eric. You failed, Torvic. Your silly idea of turning our firms against each other might have worked if you'd only known me well enough, but you underestimated me. Izzy never did, though. He put me in charge because he knew I was smarter than the likes of you.' She turned to see Eric entering the room and holding two decanters of acid.

She gave him a generous smile. Their long phone conversation had been a salutary lesson in how to put all their grievances aside and look at each another anew. 'Thank you,' she said, as she took one of the glass bottles. 'How's your head?'

He smiled back. 'I'll live.'

Lance stepped forward and put his arm around Eric's shoulder. 'Ya did well, mate, but I think the Boss, here, was just a tad smarter.'

Eric gave Lance a smile. He looked up at the man with whom he'd been only too willing to join forces. Lance had left the SAS ostensibly to retire from the Services, but, actually, he'd been invited to become part of the chain of specialists in the field of covert intelligence. Lance's brief, sanctioned by COBRA, the cross-departmental committee that comes together to respond to national emergencies, was to act as a conduit – a middle man – and he hired Eric to infiltrate a group led by the Governor.

Although Eric had made a few mistakes and followed wrong leads, he knew that the Governor, whoever he was, would hone in on Zara or his family. The one thing Eric would die for was his family. He'd hoped that by proving his worth, he could get back in Mike's good books, although he couldn't help but still feel jealous. He prayed that one day he would overcome his inferiority complex and become his own person.

Torvic glared, his mind now awash with confusion. How did Lance know Eric? What was the acid for? What were they going to do next? And the biggest question: would they let his precious Tiffany live?

'Willie, would you cut loose Torvic's ties? The man is going to need his hands.'

Instantly, Torvic saw a way out. If he could get a grip of Willie and that knife, he could have a hostage and a bargaining tool. Yet, as if the men in the room were telepathic, they all pulled out their guns and released the safety catches. The simultaneous *click, click* from their guns was so loud in the charged silence. His eyes widened as he watched Zara hold a decanter of acid above Tiffany's head.

What the fuck were they about to do? Panic set in and his body became rigid with terror; Sonya Richard's plight was now at the forefront of his mind.

In one fluid movement, Willie cut the rope that held Torvic's upper body to the chair. The diver's knife was as sharp as a surgeon's scalpel. The slice ripped into him but not deep enough to cause his innards to spew out. He winced at first and then felt the blood returning to parts of his body that had gone numb from the tight rope. Pins and needles fizzed around his chest and along his arms. He was in no state to take on any of these men and neither would he risk his granddaughter's life to go for Willie; besides, he would only have a ten per cent chance anyway.

'You really believed I wouldn't be cold-hearted enough to take revenge in the same way that you do business, but you were wrong. Now then, this is what you're going to do. But, before I tell you, you need to know why. You see, in the last few hours, I've managed to gather so much information about you. Turning all of you in to the police would be just and fair, but they're not bothered if we finish you off ourselves.'

Torvic's quick breathing was now noisy, yet he wouldn't interrupt her in any way, in case Zara let that acid drop on his granddaughter's head.

'You see the reason that the Regan firm was released early was to clean up the streets, to find you and your gang, and to take you all out. Eric, who wanted to run his own firm to reclaim his brother's respect, was given a tip-off as to who the Machine was. Eric and Lance then made a pact. Their aim was to discover who was behind the drug called Flakka.'

She looked over at Lance. 'It's just so sad that Kendall Mullins was murdered by the evil drug at your son's hands. You see the Police Commissioner, Alastair's brother-in-law, wasn't fit for purpose, really. The army seconded Lance, at the government's request, to find out who you were. Even the government want you dead and buried. They see little upside in bringing you to justice. In fact, they've removed your rights as British citizens. I just thought you should know.' She paused and looked at Eric. 'Hand Torvic the acid, would you?'

Eric looked rough; his wrist was still bandaged, and his head was badly bruised. Zara felt a twinge of guilt. If only he'd said.

She could have forgiven him for trying to make a pass at her; she guessed he couldn't help who he loved. The same could be said for her, in that she couldn't just turn off her feelings for Mike.

Torvic watched Eric approach with the decanter in his hand, and, for a moment, he stupidly thought of throwing the contents in Zara's face. However, firstly, the liquid would in all probability not even reach, and secondly, would she instead pour it over Tiffany's face? The thought wasn't worth thinking about. He took the decanter with both hands and shook all over. Flashes of scary images shot through his mind as to how devastating this evil liquid would be once it touched and devoured a person's skin.

If he'd been handed a knife, he would have ended his own life, but he was too frightened to pour acid on his own face; not only would it hurt like nothing on earth, but he'd still be alive to see the consequences.

He turned to look at his handsome and favourite son, and he knew what she was about to ask him to do. Although he detested Zara and everything she stood for, he had to admire her. The innate cold expression and the demonic glint in her eyes were unique. She had all the characteristics of a ruthless leader.

'You know what I want, Torvic, because if the shoe were on the other foot, you would do the same!'

Everyone watched in anticipation. Willie chuckled in excitement, Staffie's stomach churned over, Mike and Joshua just stood there in amazement, but Zara – she didn't move a muscle.

Neil and Shamus stood with their backs against the wall, their eyes glued to Zara. It was shocking how calm and deliberate she was when conducting an act that would have grown men turning their eyes away.

'Aw, come on. Please. This is sick. I can't do it. He's my son,' he begged.

Torvic was resigned. The fire had gone from his eyes, and the anger and the frustration had dissipated, leaving a sad, trembling, and pathetic wretch.

She stared motionlessly.

'Please, I can't. I just can't do it.'

With one hand, she flipped the lid and tilted it slowly until the acid reached the neck of the bottle. One millimetre more and the acid would burn a hole in his granddaughter's head.

Terrified she would hurt her, Torvic gave in. 'Okay, I'll do it.'

Flipping the lid from the container in his hands, he turned to face Alastair. 'I'm so sorry, Son.'

Alastair's eyes were now huge, as the realization had just caught up with him. 'No! No! No!' he screamed in a high-pitched, petrified, and blood-curdling voice. With his body jolting, as if he were in the electric chair, he cried like a girl.

Lance watched on in pleasure. This was a better form of retribution than he could ever have devised.

'I'm sorry,' repeated Torvic, shaking his head in submission.

The fight had left his body like a demon during an exorcism. He closed his eyes, lifted the bottle above his son's head, and poured the contents. The screams were so horrific that only Lance and Zara kept their cold stares focused on the scene of destruction. The others had to look away. Stephan lost consciousness, and his head flopped down to his chest. Torvic just closed his eyes; the sight and sounds were too much to bear.

Zara continued to stare, her eyes fixed and her expression emotionless, as she watched Alastair shaking his head and screaming as the acid ate into his skin. It ripped into his bones.

It devoured his eyes, leaving them as sunken sinkholes. The screams subsided as Alastair's face melted away.

Torvic couldn't look; all he could smell was the distinctive odour of burning skin. The decanter fell onto the concrete floor, and he instantly vomited over the glass fragments.

The macabre scene witnessed by everyone stunned them into silence, until Zara spoke. 'Willie, would you sort out Stephan for me, please?'

Willie, already high from the exhilaration, instantly hurried over to the man slumped in the chair. Before anyone had time to grasp what he was about to do, he pulled Stephan's head back and cut his throat with his knife.

'Fuck! Willie! I meant, I wanted you to wake him up!' shouted Zara, as she rolled her eyes.

'Oops, sorry. Shall I give him the kiss of life instead?'

It might have been laughable if they'd been together watching a scene like this from a make-believe show in the comfort of Zara's home. However, like the acid 'show' before it, this was death at its rawest. It wasn't pleasant – and it wasn't funny.

'Oh dear, Willie!' she sighed.

Torvic was numb. He looked at Stephan, who died instantly, and then he locked eyes with his granddaughter's. Never in his life had he wanted to see her die, and he couldn't bear it if they did the same to her. She looked so traumatized that he wondered, if she ever managed to leave this place alive, whether she would be normal again.

'Right, Torvic. It's time for us to get down to business.'

Torvic felt vomit rising again, but he nodded to show he was listening.

'I take it you don't want your granddaughter screaming like

your son did, do you? So, I'll let her go. But there are conditions. I want names and places. I want the name and details of your supplier. I want the codes you use. In fact, I want everything you know that will have me face-to-face with the man who makes this shit you call Flakka. And if you tell one little porky, your granddaughter will be put into an acid bath alive!'

Torvic assumed he'd nothing else to lose with the one exception: his granddaughter. He expected to die anyway, and yet he could save Tiffany. 'I swear, I'll tell you everything, in return for her life.'

'Good. At last, we're on the same page. So, then, start talking… Willie, would you remove the remains of Alastair and Stephan? You know where the acid pit is, don't you?'

'Yes, Boss!'

She then looked at the floor where Dez was curled in a ball, convulsing. 'Oh, yes, and you see that cunt?' She turned to Mike. 'Do you want to use the tools or give him a slow death? I mean, Willie loves using his knife. I think a few slices and a dip in a cesspit will leave him rotting for a day or two.'

Mike grinned coldly. 'Sounds like a plan.'

For a moment, Zara wondered if Mike was looking at her with admiration or love; for the most part that evening, the impassive expression had given nothing away.

Staffie and Willie dragged away the three men, leaving Torvic alone in the middle of the room with just his fear for company.

'Right, let's begin. Who's your supplier?'

'Barak!' he replied, without any hesitation.

Zara frowned and straightened up. A tingling covered her entire skin. 'Barak who?'

'Segal!' he spat, as his eyes darkened, and his lip curled.

It was Joshua who intervened. He had stood back and watched his cousin in action, but the name Segal had him raging. 'Barak Segal? You liar. He's dead!'

Slowly, Torvic shook his head. 'No, he's not. He's coming for you, Zara, mark my words, and you'll be sorry. You thought that you were the hunted, you and the Regans, by Guy Segal, but, you silly woman, you were hunted by Barak. Oh, and yes, the man is clever— silently devious. Although Guy and Benjamin are in prison, Barak is alive, and he's coming for you!'

It was the first time that Zara lost her calm expression. Her eyes widened, and her mouth fell open.

But Joshua stepped forward. 'Oh, he'll be the one who's hunted, and you, Torvic, you'll be the man who leads us to him, or all you'll have left are the bones of your granddaughter to hold.'

Those caustic words ousted Torvic from his mocking pulpit. Zara composed herself. 'Where will I find him?'

'He's in Poland.'

'You know I'm going to keep you alive until he's captured, don't you? And you wanna hope it's soon because your darling Tiffany will be begging to die by the time I'm done.' She turned and grinned at his granddaughter who looked traumatized. 'So, every day that it takes me to find Barak, Tiffany will lose a finger and no doubt her sanity.' She peered down at her own false hand.

Torvic nodded. 'You have my word, Zara, that I'll tell you everything you need to know to catch him, but... ' he sighed, 'like me, he has no scruples.'

'And like my father, he'll feel my wrath!'

CHAPTER TWENTY- TWO

The sun was just peeping through the clouds, and for the first time, Lance felt alive, as if he'd stepped out of a big black hole. *Did all that really just happen?* he asked himself. The feeling was surreal. He'd just been through an unbelievable experience, akin to his days in the SAS. The hangar – the woman – the violence.

Now he had one final job to do. Pulling into the Police Commissioner's drive, Lance smiled. It had been a long time since they'd butted heads and this morning's meeting would be a sweet taste of revenge for all the heartache and misery the Stoneham family had put him through when they helped Rebecca take back custody of Kendall. The first knock at the impressive double oak doors was ignored. The second one resulted in Stoneham hollering, 'Go away. I have nothing to say.'

Lance grinned. He guessed that Conrad was assuming he was just another reporter, since he'd heard the news of Rebecca's arrest on the radio. 'Open up, Conrad. It's Lance. We need to talk!'

Conrad was nursing a brandy, staring at the photo of Kendall. Still wearing yesterday's clothes and with his hair unbrushed, he rose from his chair and slowly walked along the hallway. After he opened the door, he walked back to the lounge and sat down. There was not even an acknowledgement of Lance's presence.

Lance looked around the room, a picture of perfection, but that couldn't be said for the tired-looking commissioner.

'What do you want, Lance, because I am sure it's not to gloat, is it?'

'Gloat?'

'Oh, you must have heard about Rebecca? I should think the whole country has by now.'

Lance stared at the resigned expression on Conrad's face. 'Oh, *that*! Not relevant. I came with a message from Regan.'

Conrad frowned and looked up. 'What? How do you know Regan?'

Uninvited, Lance took a seat opposite. 'Where do I start?' He sighed. 'I'm not who you think I am, Conrad. I left the armed forces and worked for various people – whoever paid me the most, I guess. Then I was called into the special operations team.' He paused and waited for a reaction.

Conrad's eyes widened, and he sat up straight. 'You? I mean… the special operations team?'

Lance slowly nodded. 'Yep, the project set up to oversee your work, your *sloppy* work. Please don't tell me you assumed that your method of dealing with the shit on the street was to hide it from the press, hire the likes of Mike Regan, and thereby hope that your little scheme wouldn't go unnoticed by those in government?'

Lowering his head in shame, Conrad stared into his glass, swirling around the dregs. 'Yes, well, I made a mistake. I thought perhaps Mike Regan would… Anyway, what does it matter now? I'm resigning.'

'You thought Mike Regan would find the man they call the Governor, didn't you? Tell me, what did you have on him to make sure he carried out the job?'

'Well, his mother, for one. We're pretty sure she killed Tracey Harman. Proving it, of course, would have been a stretch, although he wasn't to know that. But Regan saw the deal was a win-win for him and his firm: being let out of prison, going about his business as usual, and having our backing in doing so. The only leverage we had was his fiancée, Zara Ezra, who played into our hands. We had her on CCTV at a BP garage close by to where a druggie called Lennon was murdered. A witness saw this one-handed woman. There are not too many around who can kill with their bare hands, or, in this case, one hand. He never knew I had that over him, though. But none of that matters now. Anyway, what's Regan's message?'

Lance could have wound him up and taken great pleasure in digging the knife in, but something in Conrad's face said the man's spirit was completely broken.

'We've found the Governor and his two accomplices, Alastair being one of them.'

In total shock, Conrad jumped to his feet. 'What? Who? Are you serious?'

Lance nodded. 'Deadly. He raped and killed Kendall.'

The blood vessels almost popped out of Conrad's neck as the anger surged around his body. 'Where is he now? I will fucking… '

'Oh, he's dead.'

Conrad suddenly realized who he was talking to and shrank his shoulders. 'Did you make him beg for his life or hear his screams?'

Lance smiled. 'Oh, more than that. I watched his skin peel from his body before he died.'

There was silence for a moment as Conrad took it all in. Then his expression changed. He appeared older, more sorrowful. 'You will never forgive me, Lance, will you, for allowing Rebecca to take Kendall away from you?'

So much had happened in the last few hours that had changed Lance's stance on life. 'It wasn't you, though, who was pulling her strings, was it?'

'No, she was her own woman. So much like Father, it's untrue. Me, I am nothing like them. As for Alastair, I think he and my sister were well suited. I often wondered if she was mentally unhinged, like my father. Sadly, now I know she is. I just hope Brooke and Poppy—'

Lance instantly interrupted. 'They weren't Alastair's, they're mine.'

Unexpectedly, a huge smile, filled with relief, spread across Conrad's face. 'Thank God. Are you *sure*?'

'Definitely.'

'Er, by the way, Lance, this Governor fellow. Who was he?'

'His name's Torvic, but he's not dead. He's helping us with our enquiries the Regans' way.'

Conrad nodded. 'So I *was* right to release Mike Regan, then?' He was looking for some credit.

'Yes, you certainly were. The funny coincidence is that while I was on the same mission, I employed the help of his brother... A strange world, really.'

Conrad held out his hand to Lance. 'Maybe not so strange. It seems we found the best men for the job.'

Lance shook his hand. 'No, not men. It was Zara Ezra. She was the mastermind.'

As Conrad saw Lance to the door, he chuckled. 'I wanted to be a train driver, really. I never wanted or expected to become the Police Commissioner. I was trying to impress my father. I won't again, though. I'm done.'

The two men went outside and stood on the porch overlooking a copper beech tree. Lance thought he could find it in him to proffer some advice.

'Conrad, the special unit are not so interested in how you get the job done, as long as it is, and with the Governor out of the way, the drug will be off the streets and no one will be looking at what you're doing. I wouldn't resign if I were you. You've done a good job – in fact you chose the best: Regan. That must count for good judgement.'

***

It was seven o'clock in the morning by the time Lance arrived home. He soaked up the comfort and looked at his warm, inviting hallway, with the soft woollen carpet, and then heard the sound of his girls' gentle snoring coming from the lounge. *His* girls.

He tiptoed into the room to find the snoring wasn't from his daughters but from Arty and Liam. He stared for a while, and a smile lit up his face. There was Liam, a dead ringer for his mad father, sleeping like a baby; but that being the case, how did Willie manage to end up with a boy whose personality was so different? Then he looked at Arty; even curled up under the fur throw, his legs could still be seen, on account of his tall stature. There was a resemblance to Staffie although Arty was far more handsome. He slipped away quietly so as not to wake them and tiptoed up the stairs. He reached his own bedroom and leaned against the doorframe, soaking in the cherub-like sight. His two girls were asleep in his bed. Brooke had her arm around Poppy. A lump formed in his throat; out of all the carnage in the world, there was still such innocence, and he vowed there and then that he would work hard to help keep it that way. He looked at Poppy's bruised face, her glasses skewwhiff on her nose. Carefully, he reached down to remove them and laid them on the bedside table.

He was so proud to have them in his home away from that bastard Alastair and Rebecca. He wondered for a moment what his daughters' reaction would be when they discovered she would be convicted and locked up. He hoped they could get over it, given time, and learn to accept him as their father. He did have one thing over Alastair though – he loved his girls with all his heart.

***

Neil and Shamus drove back to their rented flat in London. Shamus was quiet in contemplation. Neil was bursting with pride and was so satisfied that after all the years of searching for Zara, not only had she been discovered alive, but she'd overcome her adversity so forthrightly, despite the loss of a limb. Business partners they may be, but it was so much more than that – it came down to trust and faith. The day they'd first met and vowed to trust each other was the day he knew in his heart that come what may he would always have her back.

'What a woman, eh, Shamus? What a fecking woman!'

Shamus nodded; he was exhausted, but the last few hours had built up his adrenaline, and he was now wired as if he'd been on cocaine all night. 'One fecking classy woman, that she is!'

Neil chuckled. 'And there was me thinking I would shut her in the ladies', so she wouldn't get hurt. Ha, I should've known she'd climb out of that window and let rip. See, Shamus, I think that's where people go wrong with Zara. They assume she's just this refined woman who's playing at being a gangster, when, really, she's the fecking teacher on how things should be done... and, as you say, she does it with class.'

Shamus was suddenly quiet.

'What's up, mate?' asked Neil.

'I dunno. That Torvic and his granddaughter may be locked up behind the hangar, but what if... ?'

Neil waited for him to continue, but Shamus only laughed. 'Oh, no matter. I just think after tonight, I need to sleep. My mind's running away with me.'

'Tell me, what's bothering you?'

'Okay, what if Zara has underestimated Torvic? What if this Barak fella isn't in Poland and is here now and watching us? Yer know, like being one step ahead of the game?'

Neil sighed. 'Yeah, Shamus, you're right. You do need to get some sleep.'

**

Zara waited until nearly everyone had left and the hostages were secured. She sat in the small kitchenette area on a stool while the men cleaned up.

Lou had been the lookout from the far lane where the cars were all parked up, and once he'd received the text that it was over, he'd driven through the small opening in the bushes, along the unmade road, and stopped outside the hangar. His mind went back to the previous time he was here – the fight Zara had had with Paris Harman, and his lips turned into a smile. The shutters were opened, and he could see her in the corner of the small kitchen with a drink beside her. She looked worn out, but the tiredness had not detracted from her stunning looks.

Then he saw Mike appear from the backroom. He mentally urged Mike to talk to Zara to make things right. Everyone knew he loved her, and she loved him. That wasn't the issue. The problem was that they were both stubborn – and in that respect, they were very well suited to one another. But, although this was the case, like anyone with an alpha personality, one of them had to give a little to make the relationship work. He watched as Mike just stood there like a lost lamb and Zara had her head tilted as she stared at the floor. 'Go on, Mike,' he mumbled under his breath, 'pull ya fucking finger out. Tell the woman how you feel.' He had the urge to get out of the car and demand that they both listen to each other.

Lou felt his heart sink as soon as he spotted Eric. *Now there was a fly in the ointment, if ever there was one*, he thought. What a mess: two brothers, both loving one woman. 'Oh, Eric, you idiot,' he grumbled.

He hoped that this day would not end in a fight between the Regan brothers; there had been enough battles lately. He watched as Eric walked over to Zara and placed his hands on her shoulders.

She looked up, her face full of sorrow. He kissed her forehead, and he then turned to face Mike, holding his hands up. Lou knew what that meant: it was over.

Surprisingly, Mike grabbed his brother's hand, pulled him close, and hugged him. 'Yes, that's it,' said Lou, quietly. 'Brotherly love. Fuck the past!'

Lou's eyes followed Eric as he marched towards him. He'd never seen Eric cry, but tears were streaming down his face. He walked around to the front passenger door and stepped inside. Lou noticed how his whole being was different; Eric didn't even hide the tears.

'I can't believe they both forgave me. What was I thinking, Lou, eh?'

'You, me ol' son, must have been so proud of your brother. You wanted to fit in his boots in every way, and I know you always liked Zara, but you need to know, mate, Mike was seeing her long before you said you liked her. She was his first. She always was and always will be... if he ever fucking gets his act together and makes a move... Christ, this is frustrating. Look at him, Eric. He's like a wet weekend. Aw, I wanna kick him up the fucking arse.'

Eric sniffed back the tears and laughed. 'Me mother always said, "Love will find a way."'

Lou turned to Eric and frowned. 'A bit philosophical, ain't ya, mate?'

With emotion radiating from his face, Eric said, 'Maybe it's where I've been going wrong all these fucking years. Wanting what I can't have. Trying to be someone I could never be.

Anyway, another saying me mother has is "Honesty is the best policy." So I told Zara the truth about that tart at the party, and how I sort of set Mike up. Let's hope those two obstinate sods let go of their pride.'

Lou smiled, hearing that revelation. 'Well, you did good. I'm proud of ya, mate. Er, where's Staffie and Willie?'

'Just finishing off. See, they're over there.'

Lou looked over to find Staffie trudging towards the car; his face was drawn with tiredness.

'What's Willie doing now?'

Eric began to chuckle. 'Willie is being Willie. He's got no social skills whatsoever, the daft bastard.'

'He's like a kid in a playground.'

Staffie looked over his shoulder and shook his head before he climbed into the back. 'All right, Lou? Look at Willie. He thinks he's fucking Cupid now. Jesus, someone needs to tell him he's got a diver's knife in his hand, not a fucking arrow.'

They all watched as Willie dragged Mike over to Zara. He put his arms around both Zara's and Mike's shoulders as if he was attempting to bash their heads together. Then he left them alone with a chuffed smile on his face.

'Gawd help us!' said Staffie.

Willie ran to the car and jumped in the back to face three pairs of eyes glaring at him. 'What? Well, someone needed to bash their fucking heads together. There ain't no point in pussyfooting around, is there?'

They all laughed as Lou pulled away. 'Let's give them their privacy.'

***

'You showed them, babe,' said Mike.

Zara looked into his eyes. She saw the real Mike, the man who held her heart in his hand. 'It's not over, Mike.'

'No, I know, babe, I know.' He took a deep breath. 'I got so much wrong, didn't I?'

Zara shrugged. 'Maybe, maybe not. Who knows?'

He moved closer and took her hand, cupping it gently. 'Your father knew, though. He said I would work for you. But not in my wildest dreams, did I ever believe I would answer to you. It was for no other reason than I wanted to be the one you looked up to, that you felt protected by. I wanted to be the man that would wrap you in my arms to keep you safe.'

She looked up through her thick eyelashes and longed for his arms to hold her close and protect her. Because at that moment, she knew that as much as she had a tough exterior, she had a fragile heart. But she was safe now – safe in the knowledge that she would be loved unconditionally and secure in the fact that he was her man. It was inconceivable that he could ever destroy her by breaking her heart. He was the one man who had the potential to crush her. He never would though.

'I'm so sorry, Zara…'

'Shush.' She smiled. 'Let's just take this one step at a time.'

'No, we won't. There are only a few steps we'll take and those will be up that fucking aisle. Now then, woman, you're coming home with me to our house, and that's the end of the subject.'

Her face suddenly shone with laughter. 'So you think you're the boss, huh?'

'Sometimes, babe, I'll dish the orders out, starting with now. Kiss me!'

Just as she was about to lean into him, his phone rang. She pulled away.

Mike looked down at the number. 'It's Ricky.'

She nodded. 'Well, answer it, then.'

'Hey, Son, is everything okay?'

'Dad, they said I can come home tomorrow, around lunch-time. Can you pick me up?'

'Yes, my boy. We'll be there, don't you worry.'

'We?'

'Yes, Son. Zara and me.'

'Dad, don't fuck up this time. She's... '

'I know, Son, I won't, not ever again. I'm gonna hang on tight to my family. See you soon.'

He turned to Zara. 'Now, where's my kiss?'

Acknowledgements

I would like to thank my editor Robert Wood for his hard work and dedication. His generous input and advice has been invaluable.

Deryl Easton and the members of the Notrights book club who have given me so much support.

Annie Aldington, the voice behind the audio who has done a fantastic job.

Lee, my hubby, for all his patience.

ONE PLACE. MANY STORIES

Bold, innovative and
empowering publishing.

FOLLOW US ON:

@HQStories